BROWSING COLLECTION
14-DAY CHECKOUT
No Holds • *No Renewals*

D0965769

the lost cause

also by cory doctorow

novels

*Down and Out
in the Magic Kingdom*

Eastern Standard Tribe

*Someone Comes to Town,
Someone Leaves Town*

Little Brother

Makers

For the Win

Pirate Cinema

The Rapture of the Nerds
(with Charles Stross)

Homeland

Walkaway

Attack Surface

Red Team Blues

short fiction

*A Place So Foreign
and Eight More*

*Overclocked: Stories of the
Future Present*

With a Little Help

*The Great Big Beautiful
Tomorrow*

Radicalized

graphic novel

In Real Life (with
Jen Wang)

children's picture book

Poesy the Monster Slayer (with
Matt Rockefeller)

nonfiction

*The Complete Idiot's Guide to
Publishing Science Fiction* (with
Karl Schroeder)

Essential Blogging (with
Rael Dornfest, J. Scott Johnson,
Shelley Powers, Benjamin Trott,
and Mena G. Trott)

*Content: Selected Essays on
Technology, Creativity, Copyright,
and the Future of the Future*

*Context: Further Selected Essays on
Productivity, Creativity, Parenting,
and Politics in the 21st Century*

*Information Doesn't Want to
Be Free: Laws for the Internet Age*

*How to Destroy Surveillance
Capitalism*

*Chokepoint Capitalism: How
Big Tech and Big Content Captured
Creative Labor Markets and
How We'll Win Them Back* (with
Rebecca Giblin)

cory
doctorow

the
lost cause

tor publishing group
new york

This is a work of fiction. All of the characters, organizations, and events portrayed in this novel are either products of the author's imagination or are used fictitiously.

THE LOST CAUSE

A Tor Book
Published by Tom Doherty Associates / Tor Publishing Group
120 Broadway
New York, NY 10271

www.tor-forge.com

Tor® is a registered trademark of Macmillan Publishing Group, LLC.

The Library of Congress Cataloging-in-Publication Data is available upon request.

ISBN 978-1-250-86593-9 (hardcover)
ISBN 978-1-250-86595-3 (ebook)

Our books may be purchased in bulk for promotional, educational, or business use. Please contact your local bookseller or the Macmillan Corporate and Premium Sales Department at 1-800-221-7945, extension 5442, or by email at MacmillanSpecialMarkets@macmillan.com.

First Edition: 2023

Printed in the United States of America

0 9 8 7 6 5 4 3 2 1

For David Graeber,
whose legacy is assured

the lost cause

prologue

I thought that I was being *so smart* when I signed up for the overnight pager duty for the solar array at Burroughs High. Solar arrays don't do anything at night. Because it's dark. They're not *lunar* arrays.

Turns out I outsmarted myself.

My pager app went off at 1:58 a.m., making a sound that I hadn't heard since the training session, *GNAAP GNAAP GNAAP*, with those low notes that loosened your bowels offset by high notes that tightened your sphincter. I slapped around my bed for my screen and found the lights and found my underwear and a tee and then the cargo pants I wore on work duty and blinked hard and rubbed my eyes until I could think clearly enough to confirm that I was dressed, had everything that I needed, and then double-checked the pager app to make sure that I really, actually needed to go do something about the school's solar array at, I checked, 2:07 a.m.

2:07 a.m.! *Brooks, you really outsmarted yourself.*

Gramps's house had started out as a two bed / one bath, like most of the houses in Burbank, but it had been expanded with a weird addition at the back—again, like most of the houses in Burbank—giving it a third bedroom and a second bath. That was my room, and it had its own sliding door to the backyard, so I let myself out without waking Gramps.

It was warm enough that I didn't need a jacket, which was good because I'd forgotten to put one on. Still, there was just enough of a nip in the air that I jogged a little to get my blood going. Burbank was quiet, just the sound of the wind in the big, mature trees that lined Fairview Street, a distant freight train whistle, a car zooming down Verdugo. My breath was louder than any of them. A dog barked at me and startled me as I turned onto Verdugo, streetlit and wide and empty, too.

Two minutes later, I was at Burroughs, using my student app to buzz myself into the school's gate, then the side entrance, then the utility stairs, and then I jogged up the stairs. I was only supposed to get paged if the solar array had an error it couldn't diagnose for itself, and that the manufacturer's techs couldn't diagnose from its camera feeds and other telemetry. Basically, never. Not at 2:00 a.m. 2:17 a.m. now. I wondered what the hell it could be. I opened the roof access door just in time to hear a glassy crashing sound, like a window breaking, and I froze.

Someone was on the roof with me. A person, glimpsed in the corner of my eye and then lost in the darkness. Too big to be a raccoon. A person. On the roof.

"Hello?" Gramps's friends sometimes made fun of my voice. I'd hated how high-pitched it was when I was a freshman and had dreamed of it getting deeper someday, but now I was a senior, weeks away from graduation, and I still got mistaken for a girl on gamer voice-chats. I'd made my peace with it, except that I hadn't entirely because I was not happy at all with how it squeaked out over that roof. "Hello?" I tried for deeper. "Someone there?"

No one answered, so I took a step out onto the roof. Glass crunched under my feet. It was dark and it stayed dark when I slapped at the work-lights switch next to the door—they should have been tripped by the motion anyway. I found my flashlight and twisted it to wide beam and checked my feet. Smashed glass, all right, and when I swung the light around to the nearest solar bank, I saw that each panel had been methodically shattered. I took a step back toward the door, and the light beam swung up and caught the man.

He was wearing a head-to-toe suit—a ghillie suit, Gramps's

friends called them—and holding a short four-pound sledgehammer with a handle and head painted in nonreflective black that swallowed my light beam. He was coming toward me. I reflexively hit the bodycam 911 emergency switch on my screen and it sounded its "Warning, bodycam recording" alert in a warm woman's voice that I'd chosen for its nonthreatening tone. Mostly I bodycammed when I was having an argument with someone and the calm voice was a good balance between cooling things out and satisfying California's two-party consent rules for recording.

As he raised the hammer, I wished that I'd chosen the cop voice instead.

"Wait," I said, taking a step back. The roof access door had closed behind me. "Please."

"Shit," the man said. He was using a voice-shifter, either a separate unit or part of the ghillie suit. *His* voice was deep as a diesel engine. "Dammit, you're just a kid." He used the hand that wasn't holding the hammer to flip up his nightscope goggles and peer at me. His eyes, visible in the ghillie suit's slit, were bloodshot and wrinkled and blue. He squinted at my light and brandished the hammer. "Shit," he said again. "Get that out of my eyes, dammit."

"Sorry," I squeaked, and lowered the beam, casting it around. It seemed like 80 percent of the panels were ruined. Why had I said sorry? Force of habit. "Shit." If he could say it, I could too. "Shit. What the hell are you doing, man?"

"You're recording this, kid?"

"Yes. Livestreaming."

"Good, then I'll explain. You just stay there and we won't have a problem. I was gonna have to make a video when this was done, you're just saving me the trouble." He lowered the hammer and let it dangle. I thought about rushing him, but I'm not a fighter, and he was still holding the hammer. Same for turning and trying to get out the door before he could catch up with me.

"'Kay, listen up. This world we're in, it's *debased*. America's been rotted from the inside. First it was immigrants. You might think

I'm a racist, but I'm not. It's not immigrants I object to. It's illegals. You want to come to America, you come in the front door, on the terms your gracious hosts here are offering. You don't skip the line or break in through the window. That's what a criminal does. You let in a criminal, let 'em become citizens, soon enough they're voting for other criminals.

"You know just what I'm talking about, don't kid yourself. The money we're spending now? This Green New Deal? This Jobs Guarantee? These fuckin' solar panels? Bill's gonna come due on this. There's no such thing as a free lunch. Chinese hoaxed us into believing in this climate garbage, then they got us to go into hock to them up to our eyeballs to buy their shiny crap, and then they're gonna charge us interest, and our kids, and their kids, and *their* kids. Mortgaging their future? Shit, what future? They're headed for debt bondage for eternity. Biblical. It's biblical.

"All this mumbo jumbo about 'money users' and 'money creators'—it's just word games. There're two kinds of people in this world, and it's not 'money users' and 'money creators'—it's 'makers' and 'takers.' The makers create all the wealth, the takers elect politicians who confiscate it and *redistribute* it." "Redistribute" came out like another f-bomb.

This was crazy, but it wasn't unfamiliar. I'd heard versions of this conversation around Gramps's place ever since I came to live with him, back when I was eight. More, I'd heard *these specific words* before. I pressed my recollections, tried to put a face to the words. All the faces in Gramps's living room had a sameness, a whiteness, matching haircuts and the same Maga hats, faded and frayed. Who had said those words? I could bring the face to mind now, the rest of the face that went with those blue watery eyes peering out of the ghillie suit.

Now, the name. Mark. Not Mark. Mike. Mike! Mike, uh.

"Mike Kennedy?"

He was so surprised he fumbled the sledge, then squinted at

me. I held the flash under my chin, squinting. "It's me. Brooks. Palazzo. Richard's grandson."

That was when the siren blatted down on Verdugo, *blatt blatt*, two toots, and a crackle of PA. "On the roof, this is Burbank PD."

He did drop the sledge then, said, "Fuck," and produced a water pistol from the suit's marsupial pouch. He handled it with extreme care, shedding a glove to delicately peel away a big blob of some kind of plastic or wax over the business end. His hand shook.

I knew what it was. Hydrochloric acid. It was the weapon of choice for one-on-one white nationalist killings. It worked great, because even if you didn't kill your victim, you'd leave them with skin melted and fused like cascades of melted rubber, a reminder to everyone who saw them that even if President Uwayni took away everyone's guns, the American resistance was still armed and fucking *dangerous*. Gramps and his buddies would some-times make jokes about Medicare for All, and how it was gonna go broke paying for acid burns when the big one came. I'd always found those jokes incredibly gross, but I learned to tune them out. They were coming back to me now. I took a step back and his hand jerked and I cried out, flinching in anticipation of the stream of acid that didn't come.

"Dammit, boy, don't scare me. I don't want to hurt you."

"I don't want to be hurt. Mr. Kennedy—Mike—you know my gramps. He relies on me. He's getting old and frail. I'm all he has." I was crying now. A drop of clear liquid fell from the squirt gun's business end and sizzled on the roof. I whimpered. "Please. Just put that down, we'll go get the cops and—"

"I'm not going anywhere. Listen, kid, turn off your camera, okay? I gotta say some things to you."

"Mike, please—" I was crying harder now. His hand was really shaking, and his finger was on the trigger, and the gun was pointed right at my face.

"Just do it, okay?" He pointed the gun at the ground, and I found I could breathe again. I pretended to turn off my screen and triggered the sound file I had of the "Recording paused" announcement.

"All right, kid. Straight talk. I don't expect to survive this. I knew that was a chance from the start, and it was a sure thing once you got here and sounded the alarm. I made my peace with that possibility a long time ago." He took some deep breaths that the voice-shifter made into the sound of a wind tunnel. He pulled the ghillie suit's mask down and exposed the rest of his face. His lips and chin were shiny with wet sweat in the reflected flashlight beam bouncing up from the roof.

"God dammit, I'm not gonna kid you, this is a stupid thing to die over, but I was gonna die eventually. But you don't have to. You can get out of this in one piece. You can carry on the struggle." His real voice was hoarse with emotion.

Something about his real voice and his real face made me more scared, not less. Gramps's friends were usually just . . . sour. But there was often this undercurrent of violence in them, a bow-string tension that sometimes snapped. Usually that just meant yelling or throwing something or storming out and slamming the door so hard the whole house shook. But every now and then, it turned into punches, and everyone in the room would pull the fighting men apart, and once or twice there had been blood on the floor before they were separated.

I had never been in a fight, not since grade school anyway, and had never thrown a real punch. I found the idea of punching someone literally unimaginable. But I was finding it incredibly easy to vividly imagine this guy punching me.

"Mike, you don't have to die, we can talk to the cops. This is Burbank PD, not LAPD. They'll negotiate. They're not gonna shoot you. Not if you don't give them a reason to. Why don't you put down—"

The roof was flooded with blinding light and the roar of a

quadrotor as a BPD drone rose up over us, floodlights set to max. We both staggered back, hair blowing in the rotor wash, and squinted. Mike involuntarily squirted a small stream of acid that arced over the roof, then got his gun under control.

"THIS IS THE BURBANK POLICE DEPARTMENT. PUT DOWN YOUR WEAPONS AND LACE YOUR HANDS OVER YOUR HEAD. COMPLY IMMEDIATELY."

He swore fiercely and pointed his gun at the drone.

"No!" I shouted. "Jesus, Mike, do you want to fucking die?"

He stared at me. His eyes were wild and unhinged. His mouth worked soundlessly, and then he shouted, "What the fuck does it matter to you?"

"Because—" I almost said, *Because I want to fight on your side and we need you.* I could have sold the line, even though I didn't believe it. Even though he was a terrorist kook whose cause was both idiotic and terrible. I could have sold it because I'm a good actor, even by Burbank standards, where the star of the school play might be moonlighting from their job as an A-lister for one of the studios. But I didn't say it. I didn't want to lie to this guy. "Because there's enough stupid death out there. Because I don't want to explain to Gramps how I saw his poker buddy blown away by BPD on my high-school roof. Because it's a stupid way to die. Because it won't accomplish a goddamned thing." I found that I was angry. God, why did people have to be so stupid? Why was I sitting around with this idiotic person having this idiotic argument, waiting for the cops to storm the roof and maybe kill us both?

"Fuck this," I said. I stalked over to him. The drone dipped toward us, making him flinch, and I was able to grab his stupid water pistol full of acid and wrench it out of his shaking hand and send it skittering over the smashed solar panels. "There," I said, and turned to the drone. "I've disarmed this goddamned idiot. Don't shoot him. And don't shoot *me*—I'm a bystander."

The drone's PA clicked back on. "That was really stupid, kid."

Mike looked like he wanted to cry or punch me.

"This whole thing is really stupid," I said. "But it doesn't have to be violent, too."

"We're coming up. Lace your hands behind your head."

Mike opened his mouth.

"Just do it," I snapped. "I just saved your fucking life, asshole. Do what the nice police officer says."

They burst through the roof door a minute later, and we both laced our hands behind our heads. They cuffed and searched both of us, relieving Mike of a long hunting knife and what I took for hand grenades, but which turned out to be flashbangs.

After patting me down and conferring, they uncuffed me and led me away from Mike, who was looking miserable and scared.

They took a statement from me in the cruiser, tapped my ID to their scanner, conferred a while longer, read messages on their screens that I couldn't see—the cops all had polarizing privacy screens on their devices—and finally let me go.

The cop who opened the back of the cruiser for me was a big, jowly guy, someone who would have looked perfectly at home with Gramps and his pals, rocking a red trucker cap and complaining about "illegals." But he was tender with me as he helped me up and asked me twice if I needed help getting home. I pointed out that I lived a ten-minute walk away—he knew that from my ID, of course—and that I hadn't been hurt.

There had been six Burbank PD SUVs on the street when they led me down, but by the time they let me go, there were only two. The other one had Mike in the back, behind reflective windows. Even though I couldn't see him, I could feel his eyes on me as I turned and started to walk home. It was 3:27 a.m., and I was both completely wired and completely exhausted.

I let myself into Gramps's place by the back door, made my way back to my bedroom, stripped off, and pulled the covers over me.

Who was I kidding? I wasn't going to sleep after *that*. I rolled over and hit my screen. I had a notification that my livestream had been archived and that I could toggle it private if I wanted to, but that it was also going to be subject to FOIA requests because I'd used the 911 option and it had gone straight to Burbank PD.

I reviewed the footage. It was crazy of course—the dark night slashed with my flashlight beam, the screen's night-sight flicking off and on—but the audio was good and once things stabilized, the image was clear enough. I jumped it up to 3X and listened to Mike Kennedy in chipmunk mode spouting his crazy Maga Club garbage. Even at that speed, I picked up on stuff I'd missed, little bits of inflection and vocab, and most of all, how *scared* he sounded. He'd been more scared than me. I guess that made sense, because he was so sure that he was going to die. Look at it that way, I had saved his life.

And as soon as I looked at it that way, I knew it was true. I *had* saved his life. I'd saved a man's life the night before. A man who had been ready to kill me. Or if he hadn't been, he'd said he was.

The realization let something loose inside me and I started to yawn. I pasted a link to the video into my feed and dialed the syndication wheel all the way open because why not, it was freaky and everyone shares freaky stuff wide as possible.

I tapped out a message to the Burroughs High attendance office letting them know I was going to be late for school, then I put my screen down, thumped my pillow, and, amazingly, fell asleep.

I woke at noon, the house hot because Gramps had left the blinds up in the front room, and ever since the big live oak had been cut up and taken away for blight, we'd lost its shade.

I used the bathroom, pulled on shorts and a tee, and went looking for breakfast, or brunch, or whatever.

"Gramps?"

He didn't answer. That was weird. Gramps was a late riser and he rarely got up before ten, and then he took a long time to get going, listening to his podcasts and drinking coffee and sending memes around to his buddies with his giant tablet, with the type zoomed way, way up. He didn't like going out in the heat, either, so in the summer he rarely left the house before four or five, once the sun was low to the hills. He'd left his coffee cup in the sink and his tablet on the table, so I knew he'd gone in a hurry. He hated dirty dishes and hated dead batteries even more.

I put his stuff away and thawed out some waffles and got a big iced coffee from the cold-brew jug I kept in the fridge and started the process of becoming human.

I gobbled my first waffle before the emotional weight of the previous night settled on me. Those emotions were way too big, so big that they all layered on top of each other, leaving me with nothing but numbness.

I did the reflex thing and pulled out my screen, giving myself a brief sear of shame for my mindless screen-handling, just as I'd been trained to do in mindfulness class. That was enough to prompt me to run through the checklist: *Do I need to look at my screen? Do I need to look at it now? What do I hope to find? When will I be done?* I answered the questions (Yes, yes, news about last night, when I've looked at two or three stories), and then unlocked it, but didn't look at it until I'd poured myself another glass of coffee.

Two hours later, there was no coffee left and my eyes hurt from screenburn. I dropped my screen, came out of my trance, and stood up.

I'd gone viral. Or rather, Mike had.

My post had been picked up, first in Burbank, then statewide, then nationally, then internationally. Amateur comedians had edited the footage into highlight reels, moments chosen to demonstrate just how idiotic and hateful he was. Someone made a White Nationalist Bingo Card where every square had a quote from Mike Kennedy. There were lots of jokes about inbreeding, hillbillies, musket-fuckers and ammosexuals, master race masturbation, senility, removable boomers—all the age- and class-based slurs that we weren't allowed to say in school, but that everyone busted out as soon as we were off the property. It was pretty gross, but on the other hand, I couldn't exactly argue with them. Bottom line was, Mike Kennedy had been up on that roof for no good reason, and he'd been ready to kill me to let him finish his stupid, senseless project. So yeah, fuck that guy. I guess.

I was pleased to see that I came off as a hero, with strangers around the world praising me for my cool head, saying I'd saved his life.

I put my plate in the dishwasher and wiped up my crumbs and checked the clock on the kitchen wall—I'd always loved its plain analog face with its thick and thin lines, the yellowing AC cord that came off it. It had belonged to Gramps's own parents, and it was the only thing in the house I considered anything like an heirloom.

It was coming up on two and if I showered fast and ran, I could make my physics class. I decided to go for it, had the fastest shower in history, pulled on whatever was on the top of my dresser drawers, and sprinted for the street.

I was just jogging up to the entrance to Burroughs when I got a screen chime, which stopped me because, like all the students, I'd installed the school app that turned off audible alarms while I was on property during school hours. It wasn't mandatory, but the punishment for having an alarm in class was confiscation, so . . .

I pulled out my screen as I panted by the doorway, mopping my face with my shirttail. It was a text from Burbank PD, informing me that Mike Kennedy was headed for a bail hearing in two hours, and I was entitled to present a victim impact statement, either recorded or in person. I'd known that the police could override the school app (there was a kid in my class whose parole office sometimes paged him, and the fact that he audibly dinged was just part of the package, I figured—a way to remind us all that this kid had fucked up bad), but I hadn't expected them to ping *me,* let alone on school property.

I tapped out a quick thanks-no-thanks, and headed to physics.

A couple of my friends were working on an AP science project—they'd made an enzyme they thought would break down polyethylene at room temperature—and I'd promised that I'd help them after school. Walking home past Verdugo Park, I ran into some more friends sitting in the grass and chatting, so I sat with them, watching the kids on the playground and the dog-walkers and the swordfighting class boffing each other with foam swords, and hours slipped by.

By the time I headed home, the sun was low and the day was finally starting to cool off. I remembered that I'd forgotten to pull the blinds before going out and imagined how hot and stuffy the house would be. Maybe Gramps had gotten back early enough to lower them. Otherwise, I could lie in the backyard in my hammock and do some reading while I waited for the house to air out some.

The blinds *were* drawn. I went in through the back door and dropped my bag on my bed, stripped off my tee and pulled on a fresh one, and headed to the kitchen for a snack.

"Gramps?"

He didn't answer, which I figured meant that he was playing his podcasts through his hearing aids. They were supposed to be smart enough to pass speech through, but they struggled with people shouting from other rooms. I grabbed some more iced coffee and went into the living room.

Gramps was sitting in his spot on the old sofa, staring out the window. "Gramps?"

He didn't look around. I moved into his line of sight and then drew back. His face was set in a mask of rage I hadn't seen since I was a kid and came to live with him, the face he'd make before he'd hit me. He hadn't hit me in a long time, not since he'd raised a bruise where one of my middle-school teachers could see it and she'd called CPS on him. They'd made him do a month of mandatory anger-management classes.

"Gramps?" I reached for him but didn't touch him. He was quivering.

He fixed his gaze on me. Glared.

"What's wrong? Are you okay?"

He stood up. He was shorter than me now, and couldn't quite straighten up, but it still felt like he was towering over me. "Kid, you know exactly what's wrong, and don't pretend otherwise."

Oh.

"Gramps, he could have killed me. I saved his life. I know he's a friend of yours—"

"Shut the fuck up about that, kid. Don't talk about my friends. Don't talk about who I know and who I don't know. You know what that dumb asshole Mike Kennedy is up against? Forty years. Seven felony counts. Most of 'em to do with *you:* kidnapping, assault, attempted murder. Death penalty shit. Don't think that the DA isn't going to use that, the feds have got a hard-on for anyone who doesn't toe the line on their Green New Deal bullshit. They're gonna tell him that either he testifies against his *friends* or he'll get a lethal injection. Kennedy's no genius, either. He'll cave. You just watch."

"Gramps—"

"Shut up, I said. You think saying *my name* on your viral video is gonna help anything. Shit, kid, why didn't you just turn me in yourself?"

"Come on, Gramps. I didn't plan this, Mike did." I wanted so badly to leave, but Gramps was between me and the door. "Tell you what, let's go visit him. They'll let him have visitors in lockup, right?"

Gramps sagged back down into his chair. "Kennedy's not in lockup. They let him go an hour ago."

"Oh," I said. "Well, that sounds good, right?"

He shook his head and gave me a disgusted look. "No, kid, that doesn't sound good. That sounds like he ratted everyone out already. In which case he's a fucking dead man."

I took a deep breath. Gramps was clearly on the brink of losing it altogether and telling him he was being overly dramatic would definitely push him right over the edge. "If that's true, then maybe you should talk to your other friends, or maybe him—"

"Just shut up, okay? Don't talk about shit you don't and can't understand. Look, if Kennedy sold out his friends, then he's got what's coming to him and besides, there isn't a damned thing in the world I could do to stop it. But what's more likely is that he didn't say a word, but they've put him on the street so that people get the impression that maybe he did, and now he's in fear for his life and the only way to save his skin is to run back to the station house and start talking. It wouldn't be the first time they tried that stunt. And the fact is, it doesn't matter which one it is because he's gonna get shut up before he can do that, because everyone understands what's going on here and what's at stake. So me calling that sad sack now would just make me the last person who spoke to the victim before he turned up dead."

"That's terrible."

"No, kid, that's life. What's terrible is that my own grandson is involved in this ugly stupid mess, and that every dumbass on the internet is trading clips with *my name* in them, doxing me, associating me with this ridiculous garbage."

Now *I* was starting to get mad. "I didn't do it on purpose, you know. Your friend threatened to kill me. I didn't tell him to get up on that roof or fill his Super Soaker with hydrochloric acid."

"Yeah, you didn't, that's true." He picked up a beer from the table next to him, finished the last swallow, set it down. "You didn't. But you were and you did and now—" He shook his empty beer. "Ah, shit. Brooks, listen, you know that my friends are okay, but some of *their* friends . . ."

I knew. I'd sometimes spot Gramps's friends marching with the Maga Club groups, carrying ugly signs, conspiracies and racism and "demographics are destiny." Or set up with a table on Magnolia on Food Truck Friday, showing videos about "the great replacement" and "socialist tyranny."

"I know who you mean."

"None of 'em ever liked you. They didn't like your father even *before* he went to Canada with that woman. When he did, well, that sealed it for 'em. To leave America and go work for the socialists? Kid, it's a good thing he never tried to come back here, I'll tell you that much. Far as they're concerned, the only good thing that rabbit flu did was kill a bunch of foreign commies, agitators, traitors, and climate bed wetters. By which they mean your father and mother. And by extension, that means you. Your sex thing doesn't help either—"

My head filled with that buzzing sound I heard whenever Gramps tried to talk to me about sexuality. The fact that I wouldn't call myself straight made him crazy. The fact that I wouldn't say "gay" or "bi" or any of those old-fashioned terms made him absolutely bugfuck. "Queer" was okay with me, or "pan," but honestly, who the fuck *cared*? Why would my grandfather need to know which people I wanted to fuck and which people I *did* fuck? I'd explained this to him calmly and I'd had shouting matches with him about it. My other friends had problems with this stuff, sure, but their parents were able to at least pretend to understand. Gramps was a generation older and not only didn't he understand, he didn't want to. "Just pick one, kid," is what he'd say, and then I'd overhear him saying worse to his friends when they took over the kitchen to play poker or the living room to watch a game.

"Jesus, Gramps"—that buzzing sound was blood, of course, coursing in my ears as my rage built and built—"would you just shut up about that bullshit? I don't care what your asshole friends want. In case you didn't notice, one of them nearly murdered me last night—"

"*Shut. Up.*" Loud, in that boss voice he used when he was getting everyone else to listen to him, whether it was on a jobsite or during an argument over cards. "Yeah, one of my friends just about murdered you last night, but he didn't, did he? You know why? Because of *me*. Because of who *I* am in this community. Our name, Palazzo, it goes back a long way in this town. We're Lockheed originals, thanks to my own dad. That counts for something. You're safe because you're my grandson, that's what I'm trying to explain to you. But it's not a get-out-of-jail-free card. You're not untouchable."

"Thanks for letting me know." I hated it when Gramps acted like he was in the Mafia because he and his friends were the kinds of assholes who periodically got drunk or disturbed enough to commit some act of idiotic vandalism.

"Kid—" he started. I left.

Look, I had weeks to go until graduation. I had a life to live. I had stuff to do.

Gramps and his friends would stew and shout. Idiots on the internet would make dank memes out of Mike Kennedy and deepfake him into a million videos, turn him into a main character whose image would be around long after he left the world.

I just had to keep my head down, collect my diploma, and get the hell out of Burbank. I'd already been provisionally accepted for a Blue Helmets AmeriCorps spot down in San Juan Capistrano, helping to rebuild the city's lower half a mile inland, up in the hills. I was going to do a year of that and then go to college: I had applications in to UCLA, Portland State (they had a really good refugee tech undergrad program), and the University of Waterloo, where my mom did her undergrad in environmental science. They'd let me declare my major in my second year, so I could take a wide variety of courses before settling on something, and if anything, Canada's free college was even more generous than the UC system or Portland's, with a subsidy for dorms and meals.

To tell the truth, I'd be glad to go. My senior year hadn't been anything like I'd anticipated. Gramps's health had gotten a lot worse the previous summer and his shitty sexist and racist remarks chased away any home help worker Burbank sent over within a week or two, so I'd been trying to keep my grades up while picking up after Gramps, getting him to take his meds, washing his sheets and cleaning his toilet—not to mention making sure he made his doctor's appointments and even bringing him into the office a couple of times a month for the kind of exams you couldn't do by telemedicine.

I wasn't sure what Gramps would do without me to take care of him, but at that point, I was running out of fucks to give. Let his asshole Maga Club buddies look after him, or maybe Gramps could figure out how not to offend everyone that came over to wipe his ass and do his laundry. He was—as he was fond of pointing out to me—a grown-ass adult, and this was his house, and he was in charge. So let him be in charge.

I put myself to bed stewing about all of this, thinking of San Juan Capistrano. Some of my older friends had graduated the previous years and had gone down there and I'd followed their relocation of the old mission on their feeds. It looked like hot, sweaty, rewarding work, the kind of thing where you could really measure your progress.

For the second night in a row, I was woken up at 2 a.m. This time, it wasn't my screen, it was Gramps, who'd stumped into my room with his cane, flipped my lights to full on, and started shaking me and calling out, "Get up, kid, get up!"

"I'm up," I said, getting up on my elbows and squinting at him. He was shaking, and he reeked—of both booze and BO, and I felt a flash of guilt for not getting him in the bath that day.

"God dammit," he said, and staggered a bit. I leapt out of bed, pulling the sheets off with me, and steadied him at the elbow.

"Calm down, okay? What's going on? Are you all right?"

"No, I'm not all right. No one is all right. Fuck all right and fuck you." I'd had Gramps tested for early dementia the previous year, by showing his doctor videos of moments like these. The doc had run a battery of tests before pronouncing, "Your grandfather isn't senile, he's just ornery." Which was undeniable, and also pissed me the hell off. "Ornery" was a polite word for "asshole." What the doc was telling me was that Gramps didn't have to be cruel. He was cruel by choice.

I untangled myself from the sheets and piled them on the bed. "What is it?"

"It's Mike Kennedy, that asshole. Someone shot him."

"What?"

He shoved his giant screen into my hands. I tapped the video window. It was from the POV of a car cam, that weird fish-eye view of a self-driving car, split-screen with the passenger in the front seat, and it was Mike Kennedy, looking even worse than Gramps, bloodshot and trembling, with that under-chin camera angle that makes everyone look like they're half dead.

I tried to watch both halves. There was Kennedy, whispering something. There was the cul-de-sac he was parked in, false-lit with IR from the cameras. The timestamp was 1:17. Less than an hour before.

Then the external image flickered for a second and resolved itself into a man, who phased in and out. He was wearing a ghillie suit like the one Kennedy had worn on the roof, covered in telltale CV dazzle stripes, designed to exploit defects in the computer vision system. You had to wear a different specific pattern for every algorithm, but if you got the right matchup, the computer would simply not see you. The man was flickering into existence when his posture crumpled up the ghillie suit and made the pattern stop working, then out again when he straightened up.

He straightened and disappeared and Mike Kennedy's eyes widened as he noticed the man for the first time—computer dazzle worked on computers, not humans—and he started to say something and then a round hole appeared in his forehead, his head snapping back against the headrest, then careening forward. The flickering phantom appeared again as the man in the ghillie suit turned and disappeared.

I dropped the tablet to my bed.

"Jesus Christ, Gramps, I didn't need to see that snuff movie—"

He tried to smack me then. I was ready for it. I was faster. I stepped out of his reach. I was shaking, too.

"You don't get to hit me anymore old man. Never again, you hear me?"

He was purpling now, and a decade's worth of fleeing and defusing his rages rose in me, made me want to apologize. After all, I rationalized, he'd just seen a friend murdered.

But *I'd* seen that friend murdered, too, videobombed with a snuff flick at 2 a.m. without warning or consent. It was a traumatizing, selfish, asshole move. I'd be watching that movie on the backs of my eyelids for years to come. And the friend who'd died? He'd been ready to *kill me*. Gramps had no right. He was a grown-ass adult. He had no right.

"Listen to me, you little shit, you think you can live under my roof, take my charity, and talk to me like that? Now? With all the shit that I'm going through? No sir. No. Get out, you little bastard, get out now. Get out before I kick your goddamned teeth in." He was vibrating with rage now, literally, actually shaking so hard his wispy hair swished back and forth across his forehead.

I didn't say another word. I picked up some jeans and a jacket, put a pair of socks in a jacket pocket, and jammed my feet into a pair of sneakers without bothering to unlace them. I shouldered past him—still vibrating, stinking even worse—and banged out the back door and stomped through the nighttime streets.

My feet automatically took me up to Verdugo, and then

across the empty road. I turned toward school—as I did every morning—and autopiloted in that direction. By the time I reached the Verdugo Aquatic Facility I had calmed down enough to realize that there was no reason to go to school at two thirty in the morning, so I stopped and headed for the playground in the park behind the pool. I sat down on a bench and kicked my shoes off and shook out the playground sand, pulled out my socks and put them on, then put my shoes back on properly. I was still furious, but now I could think straight and my hands weren't shaking.

Gramps and I hadn't had a blowup like that in years, mostly—okay, entirely—because I'd backed down every time we'd been headed in that direction. I wasn't in any mood to back down. Not ever, to be fully honest.

"Hey," someone hissed from beneath the climber and I nearly jumped out of my seat.

"Jesus," I said, and it came out as a loud bark that echoed down the empty street.

"Shhh," the voice said. "What are you doing out there, man?"

"I'm sitting on a bench. What are *you* doing in there?"

"Wait, Brooks?"

"Yeah. Who's that?"

A person climbed out of the climber, then another. As they drew closer to me, I recognized them as Dave and Armen, two goofballs I'd known since grade school, and I knew exactly what they were doing.

"Are you assholes out here in the middle of the night tripping balls?" I couldn't help but smile, though. It was so them.

"No," Armen said, and then Dave spoiled it by dissolving into giggles.

"Just some shrooms," Dave said. They were everywhere, whenever the rains came, all over the hills and even on the verges between the sidewalks and the roads, popping up faster than the city could send out workers to pick them and destroy them (or, rumor had it, to dry them out and offer them for sale, if you knew the right person).

"On a school night?"

"Yeah. Only a month to graduation. What's it matter anymore? The dire is cast."

"The die," I said.

"Die," Armen said. "How morbid." They both dissolved into more giggles. These guys. I mean, they were high af, but they had been like this since the third grade. They were silly, and not all that smart, but they were *nice,* never mean to anyone, never on anyone's side in any kind of feud, even the ones where *everyone* took a side. Armen and Dave were like goofball Switzerland, neutral and always in a corner making each other laugh.

To be honest, they were exactly the guys I needed to see at that moment.

"Got any more shrooms?"

We stayed up all night tripping balls and eating more mushrooms whenever we started to come down. About three thirty in the morning Armen suggested we walk up to Brace Canyon, which is a long-ass walk, but Armen insisted that the sunrises from Brace were incredible so that's where we went.

It turned out he was wrong. It was sun*sets* that were great from Brace Canyon. The sun rose *behind* us, staining all of Burbank—the airport, downtown, Magnolia Park—pink as it crested the hill behind us, and Armen was embarrassed to have gotten it backward and tried to convince us to climb farther up, try to get over the hill and see the sun rise on the other side before it was fully up, but Dave pointed out that the last time they tried that they got stuck because of the monster houses on top of the hills with high fences, and then I pointed out that he was talking about a thirty-minute run and the sun would be over the hill in five minutes, and then Armen pointed out that we'd been tripping and walking all night and we were all tired, so we lay in the grass and watched the city brighten by degrees.

Then it started to get hot, and we were coming down and dozed a little, but then the mosquitoes came out, and then the dog-walkers, and so it was time to drag our asses back down out of the hills.

They walked with me down to Glenoaks, then we split up. There was no way I was going to school that day. I knew the guidance office would give me an excused absence after my traumatic events and all, so I bumbled home slowly, my legs filled with lead, my eyelids drooping. People passing by on bikes or on foot gave me a wide berth that let me know I was giving off walk-of-shame vibes.

I got home and paused in front of the back door. Did I dare go inside? Would Gramps still be awake and "ornery"? Would he be out with his Maga Club buddies planning Mike Kennedy's wake? Or would they be in the living room, ready to give my ass the beatdown Gramps could no longer administer himself?

Hell with it. I was so tired I was about to fall over. If Gramps hadn't calmed down by now, then he and I could just have another fight. I'd let him win. Why not? I was tired and graduation was weeks away.

I let myself in. The house was spooky-quiet. What was spooky about quiet? It was always quiet when Gramps was out, or when he had his headphones on to listen to his podcasts, while he played large-format solitaire on his huge tablet.

But it was spooky. I think I must have known. Otherwise, why wouldn't I have just gone to bed? I mean, I was really tired.

I didn't go to bed. I called out "Gramps?" as I moved from room to room, and I saw that his keys were on the kitchen table and that his shoes were by the door, so I went to his bedroom and whispered "Gramps?" and knocked softly, as though he was asleep.

But I think I knew, even before I opened the door. Otherwise, why would I have peeled back the covers? Why would I have reached out to touch the exposed skin of his neck, felt how cold it was? Why would I have turned him over, boneless and limp, and put my ear next to his mouth, knowing there would be no breath sounds?

I called the nonemergency number and told them my grandfather was dead, that he had died in his sleep, and then I filled the biggest glass in the kitchen with cold brew. I was going to need to stay awake for a while yet.

gramps's secret

I *love* Burbank City Hall. It's the perfect marriage of everything I love about this town: a WPA building celebrating solidarity with beautiful murals and frescoes, but also a *theatrical* building, with an art deco facade that's got this Disneyland-grade forced perspective thing going on that makes it seem twice as tall as it really is. Someone really good at set design had planned the building, and it was impossible to take a bad picture in front of it, whether it was the mayor at her podium giving a presser, or a group of protesters holding signs—it always came out looking like you were starring in some kind of movie.

The first time I'd gone there was in the ninth grade, on a civics evening field trip when we'd all dressed up in our bar mitzvah and confirmation suits to sit in the gallery during a council meeting. The meeting had been boring af, but the building made an impression.

I didn't go back inside for years, but every time I passed it, I got a little squirt of civic pride, so the field trip had done its job. Then in junior year I started hanging out with kids whose parents were in the Democratic Socialists of America and going out with them to the annual Federal Jobs review meetings or other high-stakes council sittings, and I gained a new appreciation for the place, all the old brass and the beautiful wood paneling in the council chamber. I even liked the ground-floor overflow chamber.

But the first time I went back after Gramps died, it was different. I was used to seeing people from his Maga Club there, speaking about why they should get their Jobs Guarantee allocations, and I knew that they'd rat me out to him afterward. But with Gramps dead, I had this feeling like maybe they'd ambush me on the way home, squirt me with acid or put a bullet in my brain.

But I wasn't gonna let them scare me off. I went with a big group of friends—thirty of us, all recent grads from Burroughs—and we met up with a bunch of other groups on those dramatic steps and hung out together on our side, while the Maga Club stood on their side, glowering at us from under their red trucker caps, frayed and faded like badges of honor. Like old battlefield ribbons.

The city held these Jobs Guarantee reviews every year, and every year the Maga Club organized a huge crowd of old white dudes to show up and argue that the Federal Jobs Guarantee should fund organizations devoted to dismantling the Federal Jobs Guarantee (and every other Green New Deal program). At first it had just been a troll, but now they scooped up a third of the Jobs Guarantee positions and it was hurting the city's ability to fund positions for things we really needed, including (ironically) the home helpers that cleaned these old dudes' houses and gave them sponge baths and trimmed their hedges.

When they let us in, we went up the stairs in our separate groups but a lot of the Magas took the elevators and emerged in our midst, so we were all mixed up together by the time we got to the metal detectors, which were always a mess anyway. The old guys started it, shoving and elbowing in the way they did, and then some of our side pushed back and before you knew it, everyone was trash-talking and shouting, and then one of the Maga guys called someone a "wetback" and suddenly the rotunda was a roar of voices.

I was toward the back of the line behind a skinny redheaded guy who had a little notepad that he kept making additions and scribbles on with a golf pencil. When the noise level peaked he looked up from his pad and made eye contact with me.

"What's going on?" he said, craning to see. He was short and had a kind of weird, awkward affect, and he had a huge lapel pin with @DAWGFARTZZZ@LAFFLAND that I wished I'd noticed before I'd caught his eye.

"Politics," I said with a shrug, loud enough to be heard over the roar of voices. "It's Jobs Guarantee night."

He looked puzzled, then he worked out what I was talking about and shrugged. "I don't pay attention to any of that stuff. Just here for the mic. Are you doing a set?"

"No," I said. "I'm here for the politics."

He snorted and went back to his notepad.

The Burbank city charter required that every council meeting include an open comment period where anyone could stand up and speak for up to five minutes. And the city had settled a public records lawsuit decades before by promising to livestream and archive its meetings, originally to YouTube and these days to Gov-Tube, one of the tubes left over from the breakup.

No one knows which of the would-be comedians of the world first got the idea to use these public comment periods as an open mic to work out new material, but the rumors were that half the comedians working today were "discovered" on city-hall cams and boosted over social into fame and fortune.

It was catnip for anyone who thought they were funny, and city councilors and mayors were such a tough audience—to say nothing of the people stuck in the chamber, waiting for a chance to speak about zoning or school funding while some asshole tried to be funny at the podium—that any laughs they got were worth a thousand times more than a laugh in a club.

That's what this little redheaded guy was here for, and why he had his twitter handle on his chest in giant block letters. I had no idea if he'd be funny, but DAWGFARTZZZ with three z's didn't bode well.

The shouting up ahead died down and a couple of Magas stormed past me, evidently ejected for bad behavior, and then a couple of people from our group that I knew by sight, but couldn't name. They went to Burbank High, and I'd seen them at varsity matches and the odd party.

"Everything okay?" I asked a young-looking Latina girl, whose face was set in grim fury.

"What?" She looked at me, seemed to recognize me. "Oh. Yeah. I guess. Those assholes"—she jutted her chin at the backs of the departing Magas—"started shoving at the security checkpoint and so I dropped one of them on his ass." She grinned suddenly, revealing neat, small, very white teeth. "Guess all those years of jiujitsu were worth something."

I low-fived her and she chucked me on the shoulder on her way out, a bounce in her step that hadn't been there before, which I felt good about. It would suck to get kicked out even before the meeting started. She'd taken one for the team.

The redheaded guy gave me a little more space, like he was starting to understand that "politics" wouldn't be the boring part of the night.

We filled both sides of the gallery and lined the back walls and then the security guards closed the room and started shouting at the people still outside to go back downstairs to the overflow room.

The councilors were already seated, along with the mayor and deputy mayor, the city attorney, and the secretary. The big screens showed the streaming view of the room and let us watch as the overflow room filled up. Because we were split in two rooms it was hard to tell whether the Magas were outnumbered by the good guys, but I thought we might have had an edge.

"I guess they were right about demographic replacement," said the person sitting next to me. I knew her name, but it took me a second to place her. Milena. She'd been a couple of years ahead of me at Burroughs and I'd seen her around doing Jobs Guarantee work in the years since she graduated—doing efficiency upgrades to old people's houses, working the shelters during the flood-rains that washed out a couple of the hillside streets.

"What do you mean?"

"Well, they keep getting older and dying off, and no one's making any new Magas, at least not fast enough to replace the ones that are kicking the bucket. Meanwhile, people like you keep on graduating from high school and showing up here. Demographics are destiny." She shrugged and smiled. "Like maybe if we just waited a couple years, these guys'd take care of themselves. They're awfully fond of shooting each other, too."

I must have grimaced.

"Sorry, I don't mean to be flippant. Obviously that stuff is terrible, but—"

"It's okay," I said. "I knew that guy who got shot."

"Oh, shit. Dude, I'm *so* sorry—"

"No, it's okay, really. He tried to kill me right before they killed him."

"Wait—" I saw her putting it together. "Dude, wow. I'm so sorry. I just hadn't made the connection. That's such a fucked-up thing that happened to you. Are you okay? Like emotionally?"

I felt myself grimace again. "Sort of. I guess. It's a long story."

She gestured at the front of the room, where the councilors and the secretary and the attorney were all conferring.

"We got time. If you want someone to talk to. If not, that's cool too."

She and I hadn't really crossed paths much in school—and we'd seen each other even less since, but I'd always liked her and to tell the truth, I'd been pretty isolated since graduation.

"Well, you know. It's just." I took a breath. "My grandfather died right around then, too. He was all the family I had and I didn't actually like him very much but now I'm the last of the family line and I'm all alone in the house full of his stuff, trying to figure out what to do with myself. I'd planned to go down to Capistrano to do a Green New Deal year after grad, but I gotta do something with the house first, and it's just such a big, stupid project that I don't know where to start."

"Oh, man. That sounds intense. Are you okay for money and stuff?"

I shrugged. "I think so. The credit union had just upgraded to comply with the new probate rules, so they let me into Gramps's checking account after he died to pay for expenses and the funeral. Whenever I need a bag or two of groceries I just do some Green New Deal stuff around town, but it's just a holding pattern. I just can't seem to get anything started—not the house, not going down the coast, not getting to university."

"Maybe you should see a counselor. It sounds like you've been through a lot."

"I did some online counseling, and it helped a little, but maybe I should do some more."

"Maybe you should." She gripped my shoulder and gave it a friendly shake. "Maybe you just need a little perspective, you know? Like, I'm still living with my family and I love them and all, but they drive me crazy. And that Green New Deal work you're doing? I know it can feel like shitwork, but remember that you're making an actual difference. You're literally saving our city—our civilization—our species!"

I laughed. "You sound like Hartounian." She laughed too. Hartounian was Burroughs's GND teacher, and her classes were always like sermons. You could sometimes hear them from the next classroom over. Gramps had invoked "freedom of conscience" to keep me out of GND classes in elementary and middle school, but he couldn't keep me out of them in high school and I'd loved 'em.

Evidently Milena shared my enthusiasm, because she busted out a pitch-perfect Hartounian impression: "Yours is the first generation in a century that did not grow up fearing for your future. Do you have *any* idea how incredible that is?"

I laughed. It was the most Hartounian of all possible quotes and she was perfect at it.

"I miss her. Her class was the best."

She shook her head. "She's over there, dude," and yeah, she was, sitting a couple of rows ahead and off to one side. "Ms. H!" Milena called, and she turned around and recognized both of us and beamed, then blew us both kisses.

"It's so weird seeing teachers outside of school," I said.

"Get used to it, you gonna stay in Burbank. It's a small town."

The mayor called the meeting to order and we all settled in.

It was. A long-ass. Meeting.

First there was all the usual city business—the Burbank Historical Society (all white) fighting with families (all brown) who wanted to build extensions on their houses to accommodate larger families; a report on the ongoing plan to reduce the airport's footprint and repurpose the land; another report on how the city was implementing some new California procurement rules—and then there was the public comment period, and DAWGFARTZZZ stood up and did five minutes of terrible material, followed by two more would-be comedians (one of whom had the confusing handle of DOGFARTZZZZZ and had a sincere-seeming beef with DAWGFARTZZZ).

Then we got called up to the mic to testify—first the people who'd got public comment slots, then, after they moved on to the Jobs Guarantee part of the agenda, everyone else.

It was first-come, first-serve and the mess at the metal detector meant that both the pro-Maga and pro-GND sides were all mixed up, and our side put together a chat room so that we could group-edit talking points for whoever was up next. I'd been planning to say something about how I'd grown up in Burbank but didn't think I could get a good GND job so I was planning on going to San Juan Capistrano, but the old Maga guy who went before me talked about all the good deeds the Maga Club did around town and so instead I stood up and reeled off our crowdsourced list of all the ways in which those good deeds were bullshit (for example, the "hot lunches for seniors" was actually a booze-up they threw in their clubhouse for their members on Saturdays).

Not that I minded not getting to speak my truth. My five-minute debullshitification session got a round of applause and some serious old-white-guy side-eye from the Magas, including a bunch of Gramps's old friends.

My heart was thundering when I got back to my seat and Milena squeezed my arm and congratulated me and I whispered thanks. She got up an hour later and talked about the work she did in the community and how much good it did and how many more people were needed, and then more people spoke. And more people. And more people. The people in the overflow room all got a turn by video link, and by the time everyone was done, it was no-fooling three in the morning.

But, then, the mayor called the vote. Over the previous three months, all the different job-allocation proposals had been merged by their proposers into just two: the GND package and the Maga package, and both sides had put in for the full town allocation of jobs. If one side won, the other lost. This was the first time either side had tried it, and once one side got word about what the other was doing, the other side had to follow. This was it, the winner-take-all final round. If we won, the Maga Club would be out dozens of cushy GND jobs and would start circling the drain.

The whole chamber went silent as the mayor called the vote. First they voted on the Magas' measure, to hand every single GND job to the Maga Club. Even as the motion was read out, I knew they were going to lose. They had to lose. That would be totally absurd. The city would be a laughingstock. The Magas had been idiots to even try it.

They were voted down, 4–1, with Claiborne abstaining in a cowardly fashion. The Magas groaned. A couple shouted. We heard more uproar from the overflow room, over the video link. The mayor gaveled for silence and the city cops went and had a quiet word with a couple of the louder old dudes.

The next vote would be for our measure, and suddenly I felt a cold certainty, that we, too, were about to lose. The whole time we'd been planning and campaigning, it hadn't occurred to me that we could *all* lose.

But with Claiborne abstaining, I could see it: they'd vote two in favor, two against, deadlock, and then punt the issue for a couple of months. They'd bill it as "giving both sides a chance to work out a compromise," and the Magas, seeing how close they'd come to losing everything, would offer some kind of split. That's how it would go down. Of course it would. That way the councilors and the mayor could keep their jobs, displeasing everyone equally but without self-inflicting a career-ending injury.

Shit.

My hands were slick with sweat. My armpits. It was so hot and stuffy in the room. The Magas were whispering furiously to each other, turning around to glare at us. Some of them were Gramps's friends. They knew where I lived.

Shit.

The mayor read the motion back into the record and called the vote. Two councilors opposed. All in favor?

Two hands went up.

I could hear my own pulse. My groan of disappointment was halfway up my throat when . . . Claiborne's hand went up.

Chaos.

The shouts of joy and rage made it clear that I wasn't the only one who'd seen that abstention and expected a deadlock. But Claiborne was grinning a little and they put their hand down and said a quick good night and slipped out of the door with a BPD cop behind them. Milena hugged me, then someone else hugged me, and then I was hugging someone else, who turned out to be Ms. H (!), and then someone else, and someone else. There was crazy, sleep-deprived laughter and hoots, and jumping up and down, and the cops were shaking people and sending them out of the chamber. We met up with the overflow crowd in the rotunda, making a crowd so thick that I couldn't even see the doors as we shuffled toward them, so it wasn't until I was right at them that I realized it was *bucketing* down rain outside, just *sheeting,* with streams rushing down the gutter and lapping over the sidewalk. I tried to stop short in the dry rotunda, but the pressure of the crowd behind me pushed me out into the torrent. I was instantly soaked. A cop in a raincoat with a plastic cover over her hat grabbed me and pulled me along so the person behind me didn't run into me. Other cops worked the other doors, sorting the crowd into Magas and non-Magas (for the first time, I envied the Magas their peaked caps), keeping us apart.

A few minutes later, we were spilled out over the stairs, sidewalk, and parking lane in two groups. The rain was so hard that I could barely see, but when I looked over at the Magas, I saw a few of Gramps's old buddies intensely eyeball-fucking me with rage and hatred so pure I took a step back.

Milena caught me; she'd come up behind me in the crowd. "You okay?" she hollered over the rain and crowd.

"Yeah," I said. "Just, those guys over there are friends of my grandfather, the one who died. They're pretty pissed at me and they know where I live."

"Shit," Milena said. "Where *do* you live?"

"Fairview, off Verdugo."

"That's close enough. Come on, we'll get some folks to escort you home."

And just like that, I had an honor guard.

A few Magas followed us, but by the time we got over I-5 and out of downtown Burbank, they'd peeled off. So did the rest of my guardians, a couple every block, until it was just me and Milena, slogging through the pounding rain, soaked through.

"Thank you," I said over the noise, as we waited for the light at Olive.

"Don't worry about it. I'm like six blocks past you, over by Hollywood Way. I'd have to make this walk anyway."

I decided Milena was a good egg. When I got to the turnoff for Fairview, she turned with me. It was coming up to 4 a.m., and I invited her in when we got to my door, and had a flash that maybe we were about to hook up, which was both a terrible and amazing idea, considering what a crazy night it had been. Milena was awfully attractive, too, if not necessarily my type.

But: "Look, can I come in and dry off for a minute? I need the bathroom." And then, inside the door: "Just to be clear, I'm not trying to score with you or anything. Just need a rest."

So I said, "Yeah, no, of course. Hey, why don't you just sleep over? No one is using Gramps's room and I've changed his sheets and turned the mattress since he died—" I heard the words coming out of my mouth and then I stopped saying them. "Or maybe the sofa?"

She laughed. "Yeah, I'd love to sleep on your sofa. Thank you, Brooks."

So she did, wearing a pair of Gramps's old-man PJs, and we both slept in until after noon, and then made a good breakfast together and drank some coffee.

"Hey, Milena?"

She looked up from her screen and picked up her coffee. "Yes?"

"I'm not trying to be weird or anything, but I just wanted to tell you that this was nice. I mean, seriously. I've been alone in this house for weeks now, and it's been hard. I think a lot of it was losing my grampa, but having you here made me realize how much of my bad feelings were just being alone. It was nice to have you over. I know you said you live with your folks and all, but if you ever want a sofa to crash on, consider this place open. And seriously, I'm *not* trying to get with you. Seriously."

"I believe you," she said, and put the coffee down.

Half an hour later, we'd decided to become roommates.

She put her foot down when I offered her Gramps's room, and

I get that, it's super weird to sleep in the room that an old guy just died in, even (especially?) if he wasn't a very nice person most of the time.

So she moved into the box room, which had been Gramps's office when he'd done consulting, but which was just full of old junk that we cleared out and piled on the curb for neighbors to take away and then paid to have the remainder taken to the dump.

One of her old friends, Wilmar, helped with the move. He had a bunch of time off because there was a week of storms that had nerfed all the solar in the Valley and so they'd shut down his factory—it would come online again when the sun was back up and the grid was producing more energy than it could absorb. Wilmar's factory made zero-carbon concrete prefab slabs that they used to build new inland/high-ground cities to replace the coastal cities we knew we'd lose, and its carbon footprint was kept to zero by only switching it on when the energy was free, and then he'd work his balls off. The rest of the time, he got to party or chill or study.

Wilmar had gone to Burbank High, not Burroughs, so I didn't know him well, but he was friendly and a hard worker and funny, and so we invited him to move in, too. He'd dropped some broad hints during Milena's move, about how lucky she was to be moving out of her parents' place and how much he hated living with his parents.

Gramps's dad had paid off the mortgage, so apart from replacing the roof every couple of decades and paying the property taxes and utility bills, the place was basically free, so we all agreed that we'd split the expenses and put 10 percent more into an emergency fund, which made it the cheapest deal in Burbank that wasn't a 100 percent Title 8 subsidy.

Only problem was that Wilmar *also* didn't want to sleep in a dead guy's bedroom, and so, somehow, I ended up moving into Gramps's room, moving out of the back room that my own father had grown up in, and into the front room where Gramps's own father and mother had slept when they built the house in 1949 with Great-Grampa's Lockheed savings.

Which, you know, fine. It's a cycle. And sure, it felt weird, but it also meant that I had to confront the room full of Gramps's old junk and start sorting through it. I bagged up so much stuff for the thrift, and more for the Magnolia vintage stores, and a pile of stuff that I'd give to his friends in case any of them wanted it. I found the family photo albums and lost hours looking at Dad when he was a kid, when he was my age, when he was a young adult, seeing my own face in his, and then finding albums with pics of Gramps at my age and not being able to deny that I looked like him, too. I also got to see all the different decor that the house had had over the years, got an idea of what was under the carpets. Gramps's room had hardwood under it, oak judging by the faded photos, so once everything else was done, I pulled up the ancient, matted blue broadloom in the bedroom. I figured that worst case the oak would be toast and I could just put down some oil or sealant and not have to live with that funky, stinky, gross old broadloom.

Which is how I found Gramps's trove.

The floor wasn't in bad shape, and the carpet wasn't even tacked down on two sides, which should have tipped me off. But it wasn't until I had it rolled up and by the sidewalk for the city to pick up that I walked back into the room and saw the outline of the trapdoor.

I felt around the edge and found a length of floorboard that wasn't stuck down, and beneath it, a heavy nylon loop. I hauled on it and a square of floor lifted straight up, revealing Gramps's secret.

He'd jackhammered away a neat square of foundation slab, dug down about four feet, and poured a concrete vault, which he'd filled with: three AR-15s; forty boxes of ammo; a bag of expired high-strength antibiotics; a wilderness survival kit identical to the one he'd given me for my first Scout sleepout, including the hatchet my Scoutmaster had confiscated before we got on the bus; topographical maps of LA County; and, wrapped in oilcloth, a wooden box like you'd keep poker chips in, but this was full of krugerrands, heavy and glinting dully, dated mostly from the first and second decades of this century.

Gramps wasn't just a crank, he was a prepper, and I'd found his stash.

The first thing I did with all that stuff: I put it back, and moved Gramps's (my!) bed so that it covered the trapdoor (sometime in the hours I'd spent going through his stuff, the city had come and taken away that gross old carpet from the curb).

The next thing I did was try to forget about it.

Look, I had a lot going on. That box of gold, bullets, and guns had been sitting under the house for God knew how long, and a little longer wasn't going to hurt anyone. I had a life to live and I was already spending a fair number of hours dealing with the aftermath of Gramps's death.

After a lot of tossing and turning, I ate some indica gummies and dropped off to sleep. My alarm woke me at 7 a.m. and I found Milena at the breakfast table, eating tamales and drinking coffee. She'd made a pot and I tried some and it was *way* better than the bitter stuff Gramps drank, so I had a cup, leaving my jug of cold brew in the fridge for later.

"What're you doing up?" she asked as I went back for a second cup, finishing the pot.

"I figured I should go and get a job," I said. "I mean, there's money in the bank for now and the bills are okay, but going through boxes of ancestral garbage is getting old. I need to get out there, you know?"

"Sure, makes sense. I was going to say something, even, but I figured it wasn't my place to do so." We were still figuring out what it meant to be roommates, but I was really enjoying having her and Wilmar around, just having people to play Boggle with after dinner or to mix a second cocktail for when I was making one for myself.

"I did a bunch of Jobs Guarantee gig jobs last summer break, just going to the website and taking any day labor they had. I was gonna do that again today. I'm not exactly sure what I want to do, so trying a bunch of stuff sounds smart."

"That's perfect," she said. "Exactly what I did before I settled into doing the solar work. Try a bunch of stuff, get a feel for it. I'm doing the same thing myself today." She gestured with her bandaged hand: she'd sliced it open on a piece of flashing the day before and had needed some stitches. "Doc says no more crawling around on roofs until the stitches are out."

"Huh. Maybe we'll get something together?"

"We can totally do that, it'd be fun. There's always work in pairs if you want it."

Which is how we ended up pulling home help duty for Vikram Sam. He was one of those Burbankers I knew to wave at, even though I hadn't known his name until he buzzed us into his house on Avon Street.

"Come in," he said, wheeling back from the door. "Nice to see you two."

He was in his forties, I figured, youngish, with black wavy hair and a good smile. His house was a typical Burbank 3-and-2 with the odd grab-rail and other accommodations to help him live on his own. He offered us coffee or water and served us ice water from a nice earthenware jug in his fridge with a sprig of mint floating in it.

"From my garden," he said, pointing at the screen door behind him, where I could see rows of neat, raised vegetable beds in boxes. "Raising up the boxes keeps the veggies out of the dirt, which is so contaminated from the Lockheed days, plus I can reach it to work without having to get out of the chair."

"So cool," Milena said. "So, Mr. Sam—"

"Vikram," he said. "Please."

"Vikram, how can we help you today?"

It was a pretty easy list, to tell the truth, mostly light cleaning, changing his sheets, fixing a hinge whose screws had worked their way out of the doorway. He insisted on cooking us lunch—warming up a vegan spinach and cheese curry that was *incredible* ("My father ran an Indian restaurant, but this is all I ever learned to cook")—and generally hung around being pleasant company as we moved from room to room.

When we were done, Vikram made us soda water with an elderflower cordial from his own garden. It was amazing, ice-cold, refreshing, delicious. We were onto our second glass when he snapped his fingers.

"I've got it," he said. I must have looked startled because he grinned apologetically. "Are you Gene Palazzo's son?"

"Uh, yes," I said.

"No. Way. You're *Gene's* son. Dammit, it's been driving me crazy all day. You looked so familiar. Gene and I were really tight. We met in middle school at Huerta, and went to high school together. We used to get into some *crazy* shit." He grinned again, far away now. Then the smile vanished. "I was really shocked when he died. I mean, so many people were dying back then, but mostly old people, you know? He was so young. And of course, no one even found out until things had settled down. I think I went to an online memorial for him and your mom, but I have to be honest, we were having so many memorials back then I might have got that one mixed up. But Gene, man, he was *such* a good guy, and you look so much like him. I can't believe I didn't see it at first."

"It's been a while," I said. I knew a few of my dad's old friends around town, but not many. Gramps didn't like them, blamed them for his decision to go to Canada with Mom to be part of the Canadian Miracle.

He jolted. "Holy moly, I just remembered, didn't your grandfather just die?"

"Yeah," I said.

He shook himself. "I'm sorry, that was really insensitive. I'm sorry about it. It's just—" He looked from me to Milena. "I'm really sorry."

"It's okay," I said. "To tell you the truth, I didn't get on so great with my grandfather."

He laughed. "You sound so much like your dad. He and your grandpa fought *all the time*. Couple times he hit your dad, but then your dad got bigger than him—"

"Same thing happened to me," I said, and Milena looked sharply at me. "I got some social workers involved, too."

"Ugh," he said. "That sucks. I'm sorry, kid. Do you remember your parents much? I think about your dad all the time, tell you the truth."

It was a weird question, not one that anyone had asked me in a long time. I had the feeling that Vikram had transitioned himself from "Guy whose house I was cleaning" to "Dear old friend of the family" the instant he recognized me. He was certainly acting like it.

"To be honest, only sort of. I was eight, and then I was in a foster home for three months until the emergency ended, and then I came here. It's all kind of a muddle. Some things I remember really well, and other things are fragments, and sometimes I don't know if I'm remembering things that actually happened to me, or things that I was told about and that I turned into memories over the years." I shrugged. A couple of my close buddies sometimes asked me about my parents, but apart from that I basically never talked about them. Talking about them with Gramps always turned into a fight, and everyone else wanted to know about things I couldn't remember, and just thinking about that always made me sad.

"I'm sorry," he said. I wasn't sure for what.

"It's okay," I said, because it was the nice thing to say to my dad's old pal.

He got a faraway look. "Can I tell you something? Something private from when I was running around with your dad?"

"Sure," I said.

"Want me to step outside?" Milena was only half kidding.

"No, it's okay," I said.

He got another faraway look. "Gene and I used to cut class all the time together. Sometimes we'd go smoke weed, hike up the hills, ride our bikes together. Your grampa kept him on a tight leash, wouldn't give him any money, and any time he got a part-time job or whatever his old man would start demanding that he chip in for groceries and utilities until he was broke again. So he started raiding the old man's piggy banks, all the cash he kept hidden around the house. It was like some kind of stupid, toxic game."

"Gramps never stopped stashing money around the house," I said. "I'm still finding money between the pages of old books and in the back of the freezer."

He laughed. "I remember! Have you checked his Heinlein books yet? They were always good for a twenty. Your dad thought maybe he was hiding the money there to get him to read 'em." I made a mental note to check the Heinlein shelf. I hadn't gone near it since middle school, when Gramps made me read *I Will Fear No Evil* because I was talking about transgender stuff we'd had in health class.

"Anyway," he said, "one day I was flat broke and your dad was also broke and we were a hundred percent set on getting some pizzas from Monte Carlo and cycling up to the hills to get high and watch the sunset, and your grandfather was at work, so we really tossed the place."

I got a cold feeling in my stomach.

"And after we went through the whole house, Gene was like, 'Okay, the bedroom next,' which was one place we *never* went, but he was on a mission, and after we looked everywhere, he rolled back the carpet—"

Oh, shit.

"—and there was a *trapdoor* under there, like in a movie, and we yanked it up and we found—"

Shit shit shit.

"—a whole stash there, some giant rifles, so much ammo, medicine, and get this, *gold*! Your dad was completely freaked by the whole thing, and we never did get up to the hills."

"Seriously?" Milena asked. "Gold and guns?"

"Totally."

She laughed. "Did you ever go back for it? I bet you could have bought a ton of weed with gold, though you might have freaked out the dispensary people."

"Dispensary? Girl, weed was illegal. And no, far as I know, Gene never went back for it. The next week I had my accident—" He slapped his legs. "—and we had other things to talk about." He looked back at me. "Look, I'm only telling you this because you're on your own, and you're just a kid, forgive me for saying so, and if your weird old racist grampa had a fortune in gold under the floorboards, I figure that rightfully belongs to you, and you could probably use it. I hope you don't find that patronizing or inappropriate."

"No sir, I don't," I said, hearing the tone I used to use when I wanted to placate Gramps coming out of my mouth. "Thank you."

We left not long after and Milena didn't say anything to me as we walked through the driving rain under our umbrellas, boots splashing in the streams running down the sidewalk.

We crossed Magnolia, crowded with rush-hour traffic that raced past and sent up sheets of water from the gutters, and then, after we turned onto California and things got quieter, she finally spoke.

"So, that happened."

"Yeah."

"Your grandfather sure sounds like a character."

I snorted. "You could say that."

"Look," she said, "I don't guess it's any of my business, but I'm not entirely cool with living in a house with unlicensed automatic firearms hidden under the floor."

I stiffened, and my first impulse was to tell her off for bossing me around while living in *my* house, but then I tamped it down. "Yeah," I said.

"I mean, I guess things could have changed since your dad and Vik were teenagers. Maybe there aren't any guns in there." She stopped and turned to me. "I have to be honest with you. Even though the gun thing has me totally freaking out, I am *so excited* that there's a hidden room under the floor of the house I'm living in. That is just *unbelievably cool.*"

I laughed. Ever since I'd figured out what Vikram was about to say, I'd been wrestling with myself, asking myself why I hadn't done something with the box the instant I'd discovered it, and here was the answer. Having a hidden compartment under my bedroom's floorboards was, as Milena put it, *incredibly cool.* "It is, isn't it?" We jumped over a huge puddle and I snapped a pic and sent it off to 311 for flood abatement. "Let's have an opening party when we get home. We'll get Wilmar in, too."

And even though I was pretending to be surprised by each of the things we took out of Gramps's stash, Milena's excitement at this weird relic of a different age was contagious, so by the time we had it all laid out on the floor beside the box, I was just as excited as they were.

Milena straightened out all the stuff, knolling it into perfect alignment, and then she got out her screen.

"No pics!" I said, too loud and too quick.

She put down her screen. "Oh. Sorry. I guess I shoulda asked."

"It's just . . ." What was it? "It's just that it's not nearly so cool to have a formerly secret compartment as it is to have an actual secret that's actually secret."

"Fair point," she said. "Though it's not secret now that I know about it, right? 'Two may keep a secret . . . if one of them is dead.'"

"Okay, that's creepy," I said. "Also, quoting *Pirates of the Caribbean* two blocks from Disney Studios? That's a little on the nose, wouldn't you say?"

"You're thinking of 'dead men tell no tales.' I'm quoting Benjamin Franklin, you ignoramus. God, I can't believe they let you graduate."

And just like that, all the awkwardness drained out of the room, and we were friends looking at this bizarre legacy of my weird, cranky old grandfather.

After we'd finished giggling, I said, "So, I think those are real guns."

"Yup."

"Super illegal."

"Yup."

"I guess I gotta call the cops about them or something?"

"Yup."

"Argh."

"Yup." She smiled.

The back door opened and Wilmar called out hello, so we both rushed out to intercept him and brief him and then he came back into Gramps's room and stared and stared.

"Jesus. Fuckin'. Christ. Your grampa was a terrorist?"

"More like a wannabe terrorist," I said. "I think. I hope. But I'm going to call the cops."

He said, "Maybe you should get rid of the gold first, put it somewhere else so it doesn't get seized." I had the normal background level of mistrust for cops, but Wilmar had that Armenian thing of having been raised on stories of the Turkish genocide and he'd been trained to see every armed official as a potential mass murderer.

"Well now you've said that, I'm starting to freak out a little.

I'm going to put this all back in the box and close it up until I've done some reading."

"Good plan," Milena said.

"Use an anonymizer," Wilmar added.

I decided not to log in to the Jobs Guarantee site the next day. I figured that any wages I missed would be made up for once I figured out what to do with all that gold. I knew the price of gold swung around like crazy, mostly because of blockchain weirdos and stuff happening in the offshore Flotilla, but there was a pretty good whack of it there and it was bound to be worth something.

I half woke up when I heard Milena heading out to work, and then I heard Wilmar take off—he had a girlfriend who'd just rotated off shift at a plant in Sacramento and they were spending a lot of time together—and then I was alone in the house. I got up for a pee and realized it was 11 a.m. and I was hungry and the day was half gone, so I ate and coffeed and browsed headlines and socials on a couple of twitters my friends hung out on, and then I went to go find a full-sized screen and keyboard to do some real research with.

I was just googling which anonymizers were still considered secure when the doorbell rang. I peeked out the cam and saw a couple of familiar faces: ruddy white guys who'd spent endless hours in our kitchen playing poker with Gramps, or turning out on Food Truck Friday with their faded Maga hats to hand out flyers. I couldn't remember their names, though.

The bell rang again. The guys were looking at each other, then back at the camera. One of them waved at it.

I answered the door.

"Hey, guys," I said.

"Hello there, Brooks," one said. He was rail-thin, with a sunburned, deeply lined face. Of the two, he was the one I remembered as being kinder, but I wouldn't have bet money on it. He put out his hand.

"Hi there." I shook. Gramps's generation were big on hand-shakes. He put a lot into this one, drawing it out and I imagined the microbes hopping out of the creases in his palm and finding new roosts on mine.

"It's Kenneth," he said, "Ken. I was a friend of your grand-father's."

"I know," I said. "I remember."

"We're sorry for your loss," the other one said. He was beefier, in that way of old gym rats who've started to sag. His bald head shone with sweat. The rains had stopped, but they'd left behind brutal humidity. I was already starting to wilt.

"Come in, guys," I said.

They kicked off their overshoes at the door and left their um-brellas on the porch and came in, steaming in the cool and dim of the house.

"We're sorry about your grampa," the other one said again, awkwardly giving me his hand. I shook it. His hand was wringing wet. So gross.

"Thank you," I said. "Come on, let's have a cup of coffee." They knew the way to the kitchen but they let me lead them anyway.

After I had coffee in front of them—I saw them smirking as I pressed out three individual cups from the AeroPress instead of making a whole pot—and sat down, the other guy introduced himself ("Derrick") and they got to it.

"You heard anything about the city infill program?" Kenneth asked.

I knew all about it, and had sent a letter of support to the council over it. Anything to get more density in Burbank. Once we hit critical mass, they'd replace our bus lanes with light-rail. I could tell these guys wouldn't like it. Gramps's friends *hated* that kind of thing.

"Yeah?" The question mark on the end would keep 'em guessing.

"Thing is," Derrick said, "it's targeting this area. This *street*. They wanna tear down these houses, all these houses, your house, and put up apartment buildings. No parking, either—they're saying it's part of a new public transit corridor."

Survival instinct kept me from saying *yessss!*

Kenneth took over. "All these houses on this block, they've changed hands. They're not old Burbank, they're yuppies and hipsters who don't care about the city, its history."

I'd heard this business so many times. Gramps's friends were the militant wing of the Burbank Historical Society. To hear them talk, you'd think that Burbank's streetscape was famous for its Revolutionary War battles, not because they shot the B-roll for *Father Knows Best* here.

Back to Derrick. "Thing is, if there's even one holdout against eminent domain, we turn 'em into a martyr, someone who's having their family home stolen out from under them to pave the way for a neighborhood that Burbankers don't want. We can make a case out of it, force 'em to back down. You'd get to keep your family home and the street you grew up on."

I'd been hearing this kind of thing since I was eight years old, these brainwashed dinosaurs were convinced that every idea to save the planet and our species was secretly a plan to turn them gay and force them to live in a slum. It was a miracle I'd come out of it unscathed, though of course it was so obviously stupid that I couldn't see how anyone believed it.

When Gramps died, I'd figured that I'd finally be free of the tedium and unpleasantness of having to put up with this kind of bullshit. But so long as I had the house, it would tie me to these guys. It gave me an idea.

"So, you're saying that if I don't do anything, they'll tear this house down and replace the whole block with high-rises? And once that happens, this whole way of life, Gramps's way of life, it'll die forever?"

"That's the size of it," Derrick said. Kenneth looked alarmed, like he'd just figured out what was coming.

"Well all right then," I said. "You've convinced me. Thanks for coming by, guys."

They looked startled as I took their cups and dumped out the dregs in the sink and headed for the door, but they followed me. I opened the door as they put on their overshoes and stepped out onto the porch to get their umbrellas.

"I'm glad you're doing this, son," Kenneth said. "Your grandfather'd be proud." But he was looking at me through narrowed eyes. He knew. Even before I said it, he definitely knew.

"Guys, I'm not going to help you with this. I'm going to figure out who it is at City Hall I need to call and I'm going to let them know that I am one hundred percent behind the plan. That I'd be *proud* to sacrifice my family home to make Burbank a better city. I know that's gotta disappoint you, but seriously, thank you for filling me in. I've been struggling with what to do with this place when I go away for school. I don't wanna be someone's *landlord,* so this is just about perfect. Seriously, thank you guys."

"Brooks—" Kenneth managed, before I firmly, gently closed the door in both of their faces.

I felt light as a feather.

It was actually the best idea I'd ever had. Selling the house would give me enough money that I wouldn't have to worry about money—for a while—and it would finally get me out of the orbit of Gramps's Maga Club pals. And I wouldn't have to worry about the fucking guns under the floorboards.

I went back into Gramps's/my room and moved the bed and opened the trapdoor. Handling the guns again felt gross and good at the same time. They were relics of another era, when America had been full of these, back before President Uwayni had packed the court and shown the plutes that she wasn't messing around. I was only seven when it happened and we were living in Canada, and I remember Mom and Dad doing a lot of triumphant air-punching and dancing every time the President—our President, as I'd always thought of her—scored another victory. The gun thing had been *huge* and there'd been street parties in Canada and more in the USA when it happened.

President Hart had been a disappointment, though I hadn't realized it at the time. I was living with Gramps by then, still coping with my orphan's grief, and to hear Gramps talk of it, Hart was Uwayni's third term in office, continuing her agenda as he had when he was her VP. It was bullshit, of course. Having lost the Senate and the House, Hart was hamstrung, with neither Uwayni's killer instincts nor her gift for rhetoric. They'd called him President Nothingburger.

Gramps had whooped and woken me up when Rosetta Bennett won in '34, more glad than I could have ever imagined him being for a woman president. For Gramps, the first Republican in the White House in sixteen years was cause for celebration, regardless of their gender. She'd vowed to roll back gun control, but two years into her administration that promise was broken, along with so many others. Everyone thought she was gonna get pasted in the midterms. Certainly, I was planning to do everything I could to make that happen.

So these guns were strange machines, relics out of a historical movie, the religious artifacts of an extinct cult. Everyone knew that America still had more guns than anywhere else, and would for generations, as these old troves were rooted out and beaten into plowshares. I remembered seeing the blacksmith at the county fair doing that, methodically working a huge pile of shooting iron into gardening implements, displaying a permit for the CO_2 emissions from her forge. Gramps had scowled every time we passed her. I'd snuck away and bought a trowel later that day.

I should just call Burbank PD now and say I'd found them in Gramps's closet when I moved into his room. It would be a paper-work nightmare and there'd be a record of it, but this wasn't uncommon. Demographics are destiny, and almost every remaining musketfucker was Gramps's age, and whenever one of them popped their clogs, some unsuspecting xillennial or stormie would discover a trove of high-powered, radioactively illegal guns in their sock drawers. I'm sure Burbank PD wouldn't bat an eye.

Ever since I'd discovered the guns, I'd handled them like spoiled meat, touching them as little as possible, holding them by the barrel rather than the stock. Now, my hand stole over to one of the big rifles and picked it up by the rear grip. It molded perfectly to my hand. I took hold of the front grip and fitted the stock to my shoulder, my finger next to (but not on) the trigger. I posed for the mirror. Okay, this is so stupid, but I did look like a complete badass. Like an action hero (or, I guess, a school shooter). I picked up another one and held them akimbo, like a double-wielding video game character, fully ramboing for myself. I wanted a selfie. They were cool machines. No wonder dudes worshipped these things.

Ugh.

I carefully set one of them down. Then as I was bending to set down the other, the doorbell rang.

I know, in theory, that there are ways that cops can see through walls, using Wi-Fi interference or millimeter-wave radar. In prac-tice, I don't think Burbank PD has those capabilities. But at that instant, I was *sure* that someone was about to put a battering ram through the door. I fumbled out my screen—and nearly dropped the remaining rifle—and then broke out in an allover sweat as I saw the fish-eye view of two Burbank cops standing on my door-step.

I felt light-headed, blood in my ears, cold and then hot. I worked as quickly as I could to get everything into Gramps's se-cret cache, and of course I did a shitty job so the lid wouldn't sit flush. The doorbell rang again. I pulled the bed back into position over the trapdoor and then unmade the sheets, so they hung down over the side that faced the bedroom door. I closed the bedroom door and walked slowly to the front door, breathing deeply, trying to get my thundering pulse under control.

I opened the door.

"Hi there?" I said. My voice came out in a squeak. Shit.

"Are you Brooks Palazzo?" The cop was another old white guy, could have fit right in at a Maga Club, but his partner was young and Latino and a little gender nonconforming, with earrings in both lobes and clear nail polish on their short fingernails.

"Yes?" Not as squeaky.

"Can we come in? We're investigating the death of Mike Kennedy and we wanted to go over your statement from your incident with him."

"Oh." Oh. Right. "Okay, sure. Come in."

And so there I was, back in the kitchen with two more strange dudes, making them coffee and wishing they were gone and I was gone.

The nonconforming one, Officer Velasquez, waited until we were all sitting with our cups in front of us before they started talking, first getting my consent for the officers to activate their bodycams, then having a slug of coffee before getting down to business.

"We're here as part of a second-level investigation at the request of the Department of Homeland Security; their anti-terror office keeps official statistics on white nationalist violence. Based on the footage you streamed, we believe that Mr. Kennedy's attack fits."

They paused, which I knew was a cop trick to get me to say something, but they do that trick because it works. I was so goddamned anxious about the guns, felt like I was going to pit out any second. I just had to say something. "I don't know if Kennedy was a white nationalist. I think he was just a Maga guy who went over the edge."

The other cop, the older white guy, grunted. "Yeah, well, we know that not every Maga Club member is a white nationalist and not every white nationalist is in a Maga Club, but Mr. Kennedy's message board history doesn't leave much to the imagination. Kennedy was an old-fashioned, Charlottesville-type Nazi peckerwood."

It was weird to hear "Charlottesville" coming out of the mouth of someone who wasn't one of Gramps's buddies. They talked about it all the time, but outside of AP history, I never heard anyone else mention it.

"Okay, I believe you. But guys, you've got my video and my statement. I'm not sure what else I can tell you?" My heart was thundering.

Back to Velasquez: "We watched your video, Brooks, and we couldn't help but notice that Mr. Kennedy was pretty good friends with your grandfather."

"He's dead," I blurted. "Gramps, I mean. Also, Kennedy, but you knew that. Gramps died a couple days later, right after Mike."

"We know that too," Velasquez said, looking appropriately grave. "We're very sorry for your loss. We also looked into your grandfather before we called on you. He also had some pretty extreme views."

"He was an old white guy," I said, then involuntarily looked at the old white cop, who glared at me. I was mortified. I caught Velasquez smirking before they composed themself again. "Sorry," I mumbled.

Velasquez smiled. They were handsome as hell and clearly knew it. "It's okay, Brooks. We know it's a difficult subject. How did you and your grandfather get along?"

I shrugged. "We didn't, to tell the truth. He didn't get along with my dad, either. Dad used to make me zoom Gramps from Canada on his birthday and on my birthday and I think we all hated it. To keep telling the truth, it didn't get much better when my mom and dad died and I came here to live with him. I mean,

I'm grateful that he took me in and I guess I loved him, he was family, but we weren't exactly friends, if you understand me."

Velasquez nodded encouragingly. "I get that, sure. Family, right? But Brooks, with all due respect, your grandfather is dead and Mike Kennedy is dead, but there are some people out there who they used to associate with who are bad guys, scary guys, the kind of people who go out and murder people they don't like. Terrorists, Brooks. Our colleagues in the DHS put a lot of energy into finding those guys and dealing with them and we want to help them. So that's why we're here, because you need to help us so we can help them."

"Okay, but I don't know how I can help you."

"Brooks, you lived with your grandfather for a decade. You heard things, saw things. These guys—again, all due respect to your grampa—they're not the brightest guys. They talk a lot. We want you to help us figure out what they might be up to, by telling us everything you heard or saw. Then we'll tell the DHS about it and they'll do their thing."

It was really hot in the kitchen. I'd forgotten to close the blinds at the front of the house and now it was sweltering. I felt like my ass was squelching in a puddle of sweat. "Look, the only thing I heard was that Mike Kennedy might be helping you out with something like this, and then someone put a bullet through his forehead."

The older cop grimaced. "Mr. Kennedy was given some very specific instructions about how to keep himself safe. He didn't follow those instructions. It's very unfortunate, what happened to him, but to be honest, it was his own damned fault. You can't help someone who won't let you help them. Some people are just too damned pigheaded to help. But not you, Brooks. We've seen your transcripts from Burroughs. You're a bright kid. And we can tell your heart's in the right place. Your city and your country need you to do the right thing here."

"Uh, all right. How about this. I'll think it over and write down everything I remember and send it to you."

They traded a skeptical look, like *this kid will not send us shit.* They were right, of course.

"Thank you, Brooks," Velasquez said, and they stood to go. I shook their hands with my damp, nervous palms and felt like they were both staring into my soul as they met my eyes. Once they were gone, I went to draw the blinds to cool the house off, then I realized how guilty that'd make me look and so I left 'em up.

Well, there was no way I was going to tell Velasquez and their partner about the guns under the floorboards now.

I rearranged the guns and stuff until the trapdoor shut properly, washed the sweat off, and pulled out my work placement application for San Juan Capistrano, which I'd abandoned after my run-in with Mike Kennedy and Gramps's death. I just wanted to get the fuck out of Dodge. Let the city tear down the house, get rid of all this crap that was tying me to it, and put in a year or two doing something I could be proud of. I tapped and typed my way through the application but I kept getting distracted by daydreams of what it would be like to visit the new, inland San Juan Capistrano, with its weatherproofed, solarized buildings, public transit, smart infrastructure, and community spaces—to return as a grown man, maybe with a small child, a son or daughter, pudgy hand holding mine as we wandered the streets. Maybe we'd be there for a ceremony honoring all the workers who'd come from across America and all over the world to rebuild the city. Maybe the ceremony would be held in the mission, painstakingly relocated, one brick at a time, to a safer, more permanent site. Maybe we'd go snorkeling through the old city. Maybe there'd be mangroves, like the ones they planted in Florida after they lost Miami.

I was deep in this silly daydream when I got a buzz, from Milena.

> MUDSLIDE. MOUNT UP.

She'd included a pin for a location, way up by Brace Canyon, and for an instant I wondered how Armen and Dave could have triggered a mudslide, but that was stupid. I yanked open Gramps's closet door and tried to remember where I'd put my all-weather work gear when I'd moved into the room. A few minutes later, I was out in the pounding rain in a mud suit, lit up with dangling all-weather LEDs that reflected prisms of light off the fat rain-drops that thundered out of the sky.

I walked as quick as I could through the streams coursing down the sidewalk and streets until I got up to Magnolia, then turned east, making it a couple of blocks before an all-weather bus with EMERGENCY RELIEF on its destination sign pulled over and picked me up.

I recognized a few of the faces on the bus, and we all nodded to each other and tapped at our screens as the bus labored off toward Brace Canyon, winding up the hills and slowing down to drive around smaller slideouts and fallen trees. As we got to higher ground, the wind started to howl around the bus, making it rock whenever it caught like a sail.

The slideouts got bigger and harder to get around, and we passed a house that had shifted off its foundation and slid/rolled down Parish Place, sending up rubble that had shattered the roofs of several more houses. Eventually an emergency captain pulled the bus over and told the driver that was as far as they could go. We debarked and lined up in front of a pair of volunteers who were directing work gangs, squinting at their screens as the rain pelted them. The bus turned around and headed back downhill, its air brakes squealing and its tires crunching as it sought purchase on the slick mud that coated the street.

When it was my turn, I told the dispatcher that I had a couple of housemates already working and I got assigned to Milena and

Wilmar's detail, which was sandbagging at the top of a hillside to try to divert the runoff to detour around a seriously eroded area that was already undermining a couple of houses' foundations and a pretty ambitious swimming pool (these hill houses were pretty chichi). I collected a map-pin and got out a screen and followed it to Milena and Wilmar, detouring a couple of times to get around blockages in the road—overturned cars, fallen trees, racing torrents of sludgy rainwater—and caught up to them on a ridge that had been fenced into several backyards, and was now being energetically unfenced by a wrecking crew that was going ahead of the sandbaggers with wire cutters and chain saws to clear the way.

"You made it!" Wilmar said, and gave me a one-armed hug, then handed me the load of sandbags he was carrying in the other arm. They were black fabric bags filled with hydrophilic "sand" that would absorb several hundred times their weight in water. All I had to do with them was hold them in place until they were wet enough to stay put, then lay the next one, and the next, building up a tall triple-thick wall. Milena was already on it, and had built up a few sections to waist height. She took my armload off me and sent me back with a wheelbarrow to get more. Soon I was working on a line of people bringing the bags out, lining them up, holding them down.

The watercourse we were trying to divert was not so bad at first, but every now and again someone uphill from us would suffer a breach and we'd get a wave of slimy water that could rise to waist height, even sweep you off your feet, and I got knocked down three times before I rotated out to join the fence-clearing crew. That third time I'd hit my head pretty hard and I was feeling too shaky to stay on the line.

I wasn't checked out for chain saws, but bolt cutters were self-explanatory and soon I was snipping away at chain-link, rolling up the fence as I went. I got out ahead of the rest of the crew, into an empty lot, and so I was all on my own when I fell into the sinkhole.

I'm guessing it was originally a cellar or a septic tank, but it had been filled in a long time before, back when the lot was cleared. The rushing water must have scoured it free from fill, leaving only a treacherous borehole that seemed no deeper or muddier than the surrounding area, but which sucked me in to the waist in an instant, even before I could call out. I lost the bolt cutters in the soup, but I was able to lever myself out of the borehole and I limped to Milena to get some hazard stakes, tape, and LEDs to string around it. When I explained to her what I was after, she made me show her the sinkhole, then she sent me off to find a rest trailer, so I stamped through the rain until I reached one and went inside and skinned out of my rain gear in the steamy heat, hanging it all up and then accepting a cup of hot chocolate with marshmallows. I realized that I'd forgotten to bring a whiskey flask. I *always* forgot to bring a flask, even though every time there was a mudslide there came a moment when I was drinking free hot chocolate and relaxing in a folding chair with sore muscles and scrapes and bruises, and the only thing that could make the moment more perfect was some whiskey in my drink.

I groaned and stretched out my back, leaning forward in my chair and then back again. Before I knew it, I'd nodded off.

I woke up a few minutes later, when my head dropped onto my chest, and then jerked upright. While I'd been on the nod, more relief workers had come in and filled up the space, making it louder and more crowded. I stood up to give someone my chair and get back to the sandbag line, but when I did I realized that I was now standing amid a large group of my grandfather's old Maga Club buddies, and they were all staring at me.

I had warmed up in the trailer, but now I was suddenly cold, my clothes clammy and sticking to me all the way to my under-wear. And yup, there were Kenneth and Derrick, hate-fucking me with their eyeballs. I suddenly wished that I'd left them on better terms.

But of course they were out there. The Maga Clubs always came out for emergencies, it was their thing, being "guardians of the community." Some of those guys—the ones who'd worked construction—were strong, too, and knew how to build things well and quickly.

"Chair's all yours," I mumbled, and pushed past them. A couple of them deliberately crowded me, made me dance around them, and they all kept staring at me as I pulled on my rain gear. I was ten paces from the trailer before I realized that I still had my hot chocolate cup. I went back to the trailer and set it on the bottom step, but before I could get away, Derrick had me by the wrist. His rain gear was a lot less advanced than mine, old and worn, and his belly strained at the Velcro down the front.

"Kid," he said, "you got a minute?"

"Actually, I gotta get back on the job, sorry—"

"No, kid, you have got a minute." His grip tightened. "I hear the cops came by your place after we left."

Now how the fuck did he hear that? "Uh-huh."

"I hear they wanna know about Mike Kennedy, about his friends. Your grandfather's friends."

"You heard that," I said.

"I did. And I just wanted to tell you, the thing that happened to Mike was really terrible. I mean, just so damned bad. And because your grandfather meant a lot to me, I feel some obligation to you, to keep you safe."

"Safe."

"I'm saying, what happened to Kennedy was a damned shame."

"And you want to keep me safe."

He grinned. "You get it. Bright kid. You're Gene's grandson, all right. It's good blood. The Palazzos have good blood."

Gramps loved to talk about his blood. Never mind that he died when some of it clotted in an inconvenient fashion.

"I gotta get back to the line," I said. He didn't let go.

"Look, I'm just saying, cops come by, the smart thing to do

is get a lawyer and say nothing. Everyone knows that. Bust Card 101. 'I invoke my right to counsel. I invoke my right to silence. I do not consent to a search of my person or my home. I would like to see your warrant.' That's what smart people say, and you are a smart guy."

I hated this. I mean, he wasn't wrong, which was totally infuriating. I really should have called a lawyer when those two cops showed up at my front door. That was the smart thing to do. Even if you were a nice, middle-class white kid whose family had been in Burbank since the Lockheed days. Even if you owned a nice, three-bedroom, two-bath house in Magnolia Park.

But I hadn't lawyered up, and things had gone okay. I think. And the idea that the next time the cops were at my door, I should call a lawyer because this old mouth-breathing irrelevancy wanted to protect his half-assed white nationalist terror cell?

"Thanks, Derrick. That's good advice."

Still, he didn't let go.

"One more thing before you run off?"

"Sure." God, make it end.

"Your grandfather, he meant a lot to us. I'd meant to talk to you about this at the funeral, but some of his things, things you're not going to want, Maga Club things—I was wondering if me and some of the guys could come and get 'em? So we can have something to remember him by? It's what he woulda wanted."

Gramps had put everything in a family trust in the twenties, during one of the pandemics. If there was any way to beat taxes, Gramps was into it. I was the trustee and the trust's beneficiary, which meant that I got to decide what to do with Gramps's things. I'd been planning on paying someone to truck most of it to a thrift, so maybe Derrick could save me some time and energy. But I also didn't want him and the rest of the Maga Club in my house, going through my closets.

"Why don't you tell me what you're after and I'll put together a box?"

"No, I think it'd be better if we came by. It's what Gene woulda wanted."

The guns. They wanted the guns. That's what they were worried about, why they were freaked out about the cops. This wasn't "snitches get stitches." They just didn't want part of their private arsenal getting sent to the county fair to be beaten down by the blacksmith lady. They needed them for their civil war.

chapter 2
refugee crisis

I eventually found some time to do some private/anonymized search-engine digging, and I learned two deeply disturbing facts: First, I had enough gold to buy one of those new houses they were building in San Juan Capistrano. Second, not turning in Gramps's guns promptly could land me in prison for *ten years*. Worse, it wasn't clear whether the "promptly" mark had already blown past, and the best way to find out would be to ask the cops, but if I did, and it had, well . . .

These two facts intruded on my thoughts regularly for weeks as I did my Jobs Guarantee gigs—playing cards in a seniors' home, playing frisbee in Verdugo Park with an after-school club from Roosevelt Elementary, helping to excavate an old Lockheed fuel dump that had rendered the soil in some poor old lady's backyard toxic.

The inability to concentrate was really getting to me, and it was compounded by the fact that all anyone wanted to talk about was the refugee caravan headed our way. From the caravan's videos, they were ex–fruit pickers from the San Joaquin Valley, where all the farms had dried up and blown away after a solid decade of drought.

Refugee caravans had been leaving the San Joaquin Valley for as long as I could remember, but they'd never come this far downstate—and the caravans out of Mojave and San Bernardino had all headed either south of us, or inland to Nevada. Burbank was about to be the first town in the San Fernando Valley—hell, in the LA area!—to get a caravan.

My affinity group—which I'd been invited into by Milena and Wilmar—had downloaded all kinds of docs on getting emergency fed funding to build temporary shelters and looked up state rules on how to trigger an acceleration of the city's infill plans so we could start work on permanent high-density, high-rise housing for these folks.

We all were half drunk on the idea—seven-hundred-plus new Burbankers, hard workers with brave hearts, who'd come and live with us and help us make a better city!

But of course, the Maga Clubs were wetting the bed at the thought. So much straight-up racist stuff about rapists and gangs and human traffickers. The message boards were *brutal* and the meme warfare was so ugly, full of faked images of "carnage" in other cities that had "accepted" refugees. It was the usual "flood the zone with bullshit" business. No sooner would we get through explaining that federal law didn't even allow the city to avoid "reasonable accommodation" for internally displaced people so there was no reason to be having this debate, than we'd get sucked into a debate about their fake-ass images and the fake-ass stories from other cities.

The Maga Clubs were really feeling their oats. With Bennett in the White House, they were convinced their long nightmare was ending and with it, the obligation to look after one another and acknowledge that the world is a shared space full of living, breathing humans who deserved the same happiness and comfort that you did. They just hated that idea, as I well understood from endless nonconsensual conversations with Gramps and his pals.

I'd left my affinity group after high school when everyone did the post-grad drift-apart, but Wilmar and Milena's group had welcomed me in, and I loved it when we met at Gramps's house, like we were exorcising all the BS he and his buddies had sprayed into the air and sunk into the paintwork.

Two nights after the caravan announced that it was coming to Burbank, we met in my living room. There were a couple dozen members of the group, but it was rare for more than ten to show up for any event. That night there were more than twenty, and I'd brought in folding chairs from the backyard shed and cushions from my bed. After experimenting with various arrangements of fans and swamp coolers, I gave up and closed all the windows and cranked up the AC and lugged out the big beverage cooler and filled it with ice water, balancing it on the sole coffee table I left in the room.

Kiara had called the meeting, and once we were all settled in, they held up their hands for silence. "How many of you ever heard of the People's Airbnb?" People started to chuckle, then laugh, then applaud. Someone hollered.

Milena put her hand up. "Kiara, I think I know what you're talking about, but maybe not everyone does?" I loved that about Milena, she was always thinking of people (like me) who might be shy or worried about seeming stupid.

"Thanks, Milena," Kiara said. They were a decade older than me but their little sister Laila had gone to school with me from elementary to high school and like all the kids with a cool older sister, Laila had always known about the best music and clothes months before us singletons got clued in. Even though I knew it was silly, I was a little starstruck by Kiara, and not just because they looked totally amazing in a shirt they'd cropped and engineered into a kind of box that was both sexy and amazing-looking, offering glimpses of their strong tummy and their outie belly button.

"Back when Burbank kicked out Airbnb, they passed an ordinance that made it illegal to offer short-term rentals, or to rent to more than two people per bedroom. But under the Federal Internal Displaced Persons Act, laws like those are suspended for anyone who uses their private homes to shelter refugees awaiting permanent housing, provided the fire marshal doesn't think there's a safety hazard. The refugees you put up get FEMA housing vouchers and if they give 'em to you, you can redeem these for cash.

"The reason I called this meeting is so that we can start planning on using this to crack the density debate at City Hall. For too many years, we've heard every excuse to keep Burbank from growing up, making it viable for public transit and walking: First they say it'll make social distancing impossible. Then they say it'll make parking impossible—"

"That's the point!" someone yelled from the floor. We chuckled.

"Hell yes it's the point. You know that tired NIMBY song. Thing is, with the caravan on the way, we can crank the density way up and there's nothing the council can do about it."

"And we get to do a solid for our refugee friends." Same guy. I didn't know his name, but this was his regular deal, doing the call and response, and it had bugged me at first, but Milena told me that he just got so excited that he couldn't help himself and everyone was okay with it.

Kiara didn't seem to mind, anyway. "Yes, Samuel, that's right. We get to house people who need it, and fix a structural problem with our city, all at the same time, and the best part is, the city can't say shit about it.

"We're gonna need a lot of rooms though—housing seven hundred people for a couple weeks while we get temporary shelters built, and maybe some of them for a couple years while we start up permanent housing. That's a lot of extra rooms and living-room sofas and backyard sheds. We're gonna need to convince a lot of our neighbors to take those vouchers."

"Food Truck Friday!" Samuel yelled, and now I understood why everyone was okay with him shouting out from the floor. That was a *great* idea.

"That is a *great* idea," Kiara said.

On the last Friday of every month, the cream of Greater Los Angeles's food trucks line a two-mile-long stretch of Magnolia Boulevard, while the Magnolia Park shopkeepers change their windows to display their best wares, and everyone from the Scouts to the Democratic Socialists to the high-school cheerleading squads sets up little tables and tents and performs and pushes literature and sells baked goods, while Burbankers and people from all over LA and the Valley stroll up and down, eating shaved ice and tacos, throwing money into the musicians' guitar cases. Every Christmas, Ume Credit Union brings in an ice machine and creates a mushy tobogganing hill in its parking lot (that struck me mute, the first time I saw that after moving from Canada).

The Burbank Democratic Socialists had a couple of people who made sure that there were always permits available for affinity groups to use when there was a project on, and so, less than a week later, I found myself using a power driver to assemble a model Ikea bedroom that we'd bought at America's Largest Ikea (the city's greatest claim to fame, even if it had been subdivided into a trio of Baby Ikeas) under a People's Airbnb banner, working feverishly with a couple of others to assemble it and make it look pretty in time for rope-drop and the opening of the festivities. We were going to show Burbank how easy it was to convert a spare room to temporary refugee housing.

The furniture off-gassed as I assembled it, a sweet smell from the fixative we applied to the layers of honeycombed cardboard after we had them bolted together. The furniture was cheap, and it would only last for a month at most—less if you had little kids jumping on it—but the fixative that stiffened it and made it waterproof dissolved easily with vinegar, and the cardboard would break down back into the material stream easily.

As I worked, other members of my affinity group were staging the model bedroom with bedspreads, a throw rug, some books, and a clothing rail that we hung with road clothes, a neat line of worn-down shoes beneath it.

"I'd live here," I said, accepting a shaved ice from Samuel, who'd shown up with a tray of them for the crew.

"Me too, man, me too!" He was such an upbeat guy, practically vibrating in place. I loved his energy. Just standing next to him made me feel reinvigorated. And the shaved ice was amazing.

"Is that cardamom?"

"Uh-huh. Cardamom, cinnamon, buncha stuff. Taste of India's doing a popup with Mahalo's. Masala ice. Isn't it amazing?"

I couldn't answer because my mouth was full of shaved ice. He laughed at me and moved on to distribute more of his bounty.

Judging from the crowds and the number of people who took our handouts and scanned our QR, Burbank loved the idea. People were weirdly romantic about Airbnb, the real one, the one that got kicked out of most cities, so the word "Airbnb" brought a lot of foot traffic. They came for the nostalgia, but they stayed for the excitement of having a sleepover party with people who had the grit it took to cross the state on foot in search of a better city. Bur-bankers were proud of their city, and there were plenty of people who were excited at showing some strangers hospitality.

Then Wilmar showed up with a giant banker's box of cardboard sheets.

"What is that?" I asked, as he set it down with a thump that made the cardboard night table shift and creak. I'd stood on that table while I was stringing up the banner, so whatever was in that box was *heavy*.

He grinned. Wilmar was handsome, dark, and always stubbled, with long eyelashes and hair he center-parted like an old-fashioned barbershop-quartet singer. He had something tattooed in Armenian on his collarbone, and he was wearing a V-neck shirt that showed it.

"I had an idea," he said, and lifted the lid off the box. It was full of stiff sheets of cardboard, not the corrugated kind, laser-cut, with laser-engraved instructions. I lifted one up. It was very familiar, though it took a second for me to get it. It was a replica of the bed

I'd assembled, dollhouse-sized, ready to be punched out and stuck together.

I laughed. "What the hell?"

"The designs were all online! I just downscaled 'em and went down to the makerspace and cut a couple hundred sheets. It was easy!"

I punched out and assembled a miniature replica of the room I'd spent the afternoon building, which took minutes, rather than hours. It looked *great*. Ten minutes later, we were mobbed by kids and their parents, demanding the cardboard handouts, which Wilmar had thoughtfully engraved with the QR code for our People's Airbnb pitch, and it worked so well that some of them actually circled back to ask questions later in the evening, their kids clutching the detailed miniature cardboard furnishings.

We ran out of cardboard cutouts by about 9 p.m., just as the crowds were starting to thin. I wandered away and bought a cultured "lobster" roll from one of the trucks, biting into the soft potato roll, and wiping the sauce off the corners of my mouth when I spotted the city manager's information booth, which was half packed up. The woman staffing it was an older white lady, with a kind face and short hair and really cool earrings that could not possibly have been made out of stone because they'd have torn her ears off, but they sure looked like it.

"Hey, sorry to bug you, but do you have time for one quick question?"

She gave me a tight smile that made it clear she wasn't happy about it, but said, "Sure."

"Sorry, sorry—I was working over at the People's Airbnb booth all night and I only just got free. The thing is, I inherited my gramps's house when he died, just last month, and I want to turn the land and the house over to the city for infill. I figured with all the refugees coming in, the city's gotta be trying to figure out where to put some high-density buildings, and we've got two acres on a corner lot at Fairview and Oak, and, well, I just wanted to make sure the city knew it was there for the asking."

She gave me a considering look. "Mr.—"

"Palazzo," I said.

"Mr. Palazzo, if you want to sell your house, you need a realtor, not the City of Burbank."

"Oh hey, no. I'm not looking to sell it—I mean, I guess the city will be paying for houses for any infill, but that's not what I'm asking about. I just . . . I know that when you go and try to do, what's it called, eminent domain, it's expensive. People get angry and fight, you have to go to court, all of that. Well, I not only don't want or need my house, but I also want to help the city do right by the refugees when they get here. I just thought, maybe you folks have a list or something?"

I saw her get it, slowing down from the restless packing up her hands had been doing while we talked, coming into the present moment and looking at me. I nervously wiped my mouth again, convinced I had lobster-mayo on it.

"Oh, I see." She thought for a moment. "I have to be honest, I don't think there's any such list, though you're right that eminent domain is not fun for any of the parties involved." She got a faraway look.

"What?"

She smiled, and she was transformed from a tired city employee at the end of a double shift to someone dreaming a beautiful dream. "I was just imagining what it would be like if we could get all the land we needed for the refugees without having to go to war with Burbankers." She looked up and down at the thinning crowds on Magnolia, the crews breaking down their booths, the food trucks folding down their awnings. "I mean, just between you and me, there's talk of doing away with the football fields at the high schools to build high-rises there."

"No way," I said.

"Oh, I don't know if they'll do it, but it's certainly a measure of how desperate everyone's feeling about this. After that business with the man on the roof of the high school, the whole city feels like a powder keg. Don't get me wrong, I love those old-timers, but they haven't really kept up with the world, and"—she dropped her voice—"a lot of them hung on to their g-u-n-s."

It was her spelling it out like that that got to me. I just loved her, loved the whole city. It was a fucked-up and sick world, but Burbank was full of this kind of person, lifers in the city government with dope earrings who didn't want to say the g-word.

"I know it," I said. I did! "But things are changing. You shoulda seen the folks who came to the People's Airbnb booth. This town wants to welcome in the strangers. I may have been the first one to volunteer his house, but I bet I'm not the last one."

She passed me her card, which was, you know, delightful. Cards!

Carole Burke, Senior Administrator,
City Manager's Office, City of Burbank,
City Hall, 275 E Olive Ave, Burbank, CA 91502.

"You get to work in the old building. How cool!"

She grinned. "It's a creaker, and the air-conditioning's never quite right, but it's a beautiful building, all right. If you're serious about the house, you give me a call on Monday and I'll talk to the manager and see where we get to."

"I will!"

We touched elbows and I left her.

I had to pick up my bag from the People's Airbnb before I went home. I was almost there when I heard the shouting: an angry man's voice, shouting "FUCK YOU!" over and over again. I stepped out from between a Korean taco truck and a barbecue cuy van and saw him: a tall and burly man, iron-gray hair under a red Maga hat, jeans and a tight shirt with tessellated lenticular Punisher logos that animated as he stalked from one member of my affinity group to the next, barking "FUCK YOU!" at them.

Wilmar was mirroring him, almost chest-to-chest, keeping him from getting too close to the smaller members of the group, mostly women, and then Samuel joined him and then Kiara, all four foot eleven of them, also started the dance, like a guard on a basketball court. The shouting man loomed over all of them, even Samuel.

"You want to literally fill my city with rapists and thieves? You want to fill my city with illegals? Fuck you! That's what I say, fuck you!" I was right on them now, joining the guard wall, unsuccessfully stopping him from tearing down our banner and then ripping it with a resounding *RRRRRRIP* sound. That was the thing about using appropriate materials: the banner was only supposed to last for a month or two and then be compostable. If we'd printed on immortal, colorfast Tyvek he'd have needed a knife or he'd have been standing there straining to start the rip.

Of course, plenty of people were recording all this, hands held high, and now the rage man—his neck corded and the color of a hot dog—started to grab for their screens, wrestling with one person, knocking another's screen skittering across the ground. I almost grabbed for his wrist but thought better of it. That's what this guy wanted, a ten-on-one fight where it was young, mostly brown-skinned greenies beating up an old white guy.

Kiara had the answer. "NOT! GONNA! FIGHT! YOU!" they shouted, and we got the idea, joining in: *"NOT! GONNA! FIGHT! YOU!"* We roared it and I heard more people converging, drowning out the guy's hoarse cries of "FUCK YOU! FUCK YOU!"

As the cops finally led him away, he yanked one arm free and pointed a finger at Kiara: "Fuck you, bitch!"

They smiled sweetly. "Not with her dick and him pushing," they said, pointing at me and then Milena, adding some gender-bending to the sick burn. It was cathartic and we whooped with laughter and hugged them. Even the cops grinned.

———

The cross burning started at midnight out front of City Hall. Whoever built it knew how to make quick-assemble, freestanding structures. Lot of that expertise in Burbank, studio carpenters and the like.

They were so quick that the cops didn't catch them. That was the official story: pickup truck arrives, three dudes in ghillie suits jump out, assemble the cross, light it up, speed off. The fact that the police HQ was across the street made this story hard to swallow, but however you gamed out your conspiracy theory, it was ugly: the cops let them get away with it; the cops were so bad at their jobs they couldn't catch them; the cops were in on it. Those were three bad choices.

The refugees were only two days away now, and the forums had gotten *really* mean, but even so, none of us were prepared for this. I got woken up by pings from my screen, it having decided they were important enough to play through my bedtime hours, and then I sat with my screen for a long moment, not knowing what to do. Then I knew what to do. I had to go there and bear witness.

We'd had Wilmar's cowboy beans for dinner and sleep had transformed the delicious residue of garlic and smoke to a vile taste in my mouth, so I grabbed my toothbrush and brushed while I pulled clothes out of drawers. Sleepy and multitasking, I klutzed the little "telephone table" in Gramps's hallway and knocked over the bowl where we collected keys and pens and masks and other lying-around stuff. The racket was terrible and Wilmar and Milena came out of their rooms in PJs and so I had to explain what was going on and show them the streams from City Hall and then I had to wait while *they* got dressed and brushed *their* teeth.

But it was worth the wait to have the company on the ride to downtown. The streets were empty and dark at first, our blinkers bouncing off the houses on Verdugo as we cranked our pedals, no sound but the shush of our wheels and our breath.

We turned onto Olive and stopped: we could see straight down the road, all the way to the rise of the overpass over I-5, and behind that hill, roiling clouds of smoke shot through with blue-red fire-truck lights.

"Well, shit," Milena said, with feeling.

The thing about cross burnings is that they're *historic*. I hadn't ever seen a cross burning before. I don't think anyone I knew had ever seen one, or even met someone who'd seen one. I knew they'd been popping off across America again, both in the run-up to Bennett's election and then any time some culture-war shit kicked off with a Maga Club somewhere like East Bumble-fuck, Texas.

But here was a cross, burning outside of City Hall, in Burbank, California.

"Why haven't they put it out?" I said, pointing to the firefight-ers holding their dry hose, doing nothing with it.

"Magnesium," someone said, another person about my age, vaguely familiar, like maybe they were the sibling of someone I'd gone to school with. Burbank was full of those kinds of familiar faces for me. "They load up the crosses with 'em, that's why it's so bright. You hit it with the hose, it'll go *boom*."

"Jesus."

The person shrugged. "It's effective, give 'em that."

"Yeesh." I moved away. I hadn't liked being near that thing to begin with, and now that I knew that it could explode and shower me with burning magnesium fragments, well . . .

Cross burnings are old, but they're not obsolete. Even though I'm white, even though I was born in the twenty-first century, even though I was in California and not the Deep South, that cross was fucking *spooky*. Magic, and not the good kind. No wonder they burned them. Cross on fire goes straight into your brainstem and down your spine and tells you *Get away from this bad place*.

The firefighters pushed us back behind sawhorses, then mus-cled a big tank off the load-gate of one of their trucks and maneu-vered it into place, so I could see the CLASS D FIRE EXTINGUISHER stencil on its side. A couple of firefighters in armored PPE, complete with oxygen, set up by the tank and propped a couple of heavy metal shields between them and the fire. They weren't screwing around. They sprayed the fire with a cloud of smoky foam that hissed and sputtered as it hit. A few minutes later, the cross was extinguished.

I stared at the afterimages in the sudden dark, wondering belatedly if I'd burned my retinas by looking into the magnesium light and feeling stupid. As the hissing of the dying flames faded, silence descended. I heard irregular, hiccupping breathing and turned around to see a Black guy about my age crying, his face contorted in total anguish, tears coursing down his cheeks.

His face was so distorted by his pain that I didn't even recognize him, and then I did. "Dave?"

He looked up at me and snuffled up his snot and armed the tears off his cheeks. "Hi, Brooks," he croaked. I patted my pockets and came up with the hanky I've carried since my mom drilled into me that you should always have a face covering handy in case someone decided to gas you. I handed it to him, and he thanked me and wiped his face and blew his nose. On impulse, I gave him a hug, and after stiffening for a moment, he gave me a fierce hug back.

"Are you okay?" I said. He smelled of hash oil and laundry soap.

"Oh," he said. "Oh, I guess I'm fine." And then he started crying. I squeezed him harder. Wilmar and Milena came over and caught my eye and I mouthed, *It's okay,* though obviously I had no idea if it was. They gave us space.

Eventually I got Dave to sit on the City Hall steps. I put my arm around his shoulders and listened as his ragged breathing smoothed out.

"You don't have to talk about it," I said, "but if you want to, I'm here."

He snuffled some more. "To be honest, I don't really know. I just took one look at that thing and it was like someone had, you know, like they'd punched me in the gut." He looked thoughtful. "No, I take it back, it's like they punched me in the heart." He wiped his eyes and blew his nose again. He was looking more like himself. "Shit, what the hell was that about?"

"Uh, Dave?" I said.

"What?"

"I mean, it was a burning cross, and you're . . ."

"Yeah, okay, that. I mean, obviously I'd heard about that from my grandparents and I guess my parents, but those were just stories for me. Like, yeah, plenty of racism to go around still, but the Klan? Shit, that's like being worried about ogres or something. It's not 1955. I guess that stuff runs deep."

"I think you're right. I don't want to pretend I can know what this feels like for you, but when I saw that burning cross, it was . . . powerful. Not in a good way. I guess that's why they do it, right? Because it brings all this up."

"Well yeah." He stood and dusted his hands off. "I'll wash this and give it back," he said, gesturing with my balled-up kerchief.

"Don't worry, I got plenty more. Are you gonna be okay to get home?"

"I'm crashing at Armen's. That's how I got here so fast." Armen lived in a condo around the corner from City Hall with his mom, but used his dad's address, near my place, to get a place at Burroughs High.

"You sure? I can get you that far, easy."

He shook his head and stood. He smiled a sad smile. "It's okay, Brooks. I got this. Thank you, though. I'll wash your hanky and get it back to you."

"No, keep it."

"Oh, right, you said." He turned to go, then looked back over his shoulder. "Thank you, Brooks."

"Stay safe, Dave." I watched him go, watched him give a wide berth to the charred remains of the cross. Most of the crowd had gone, but Milena and Wilmar had waited for me and they wheeled their bikes over. Wilmar had my bike, too.

"Oh, hey, I forgot about that," I said. It had been on its stand when I noticed Dave and I'd wandered away from it.

"No problem. Is he gonna be okay?" Wilmar jutted his cleft chin in Dave's direction.

"I guess so," I said.

We all looked at Dave's retreating back, then at the smoldering cross.

"Shit," Milena said. "Well, that happened. What time is it?"

Wilmar rubbed at his sleeve where he had a screen. "It's two a.m. Glad I don't have work tomorrow."

"I was gonna go do some Jobs Guarantee gigs," I said, "but maybe I'll just cancel it and work on the house." Milena and Wilmar were both totally down for me to get rid of the house so the city could build high-rises, even though it meant they'd lose their sweet lodgings. I was secretly a little insulted that they weren't sadder about losing me as a roommate—it played into my even more secret fear that they were only friends with me because I had lucked into inheriting a house they could live in cheap.

"Well, *I* have work tomorrow," Milena said. "We're solarizing Stevenson Elementary, all new panels, and new storage batteries."

"You're doing the lord's work, Milena," Wilmar said with a grin. "But I want pie. Brooks, you wanna go to Chili John's?"

So we ate turkey chili on soft rolls and topped it off with lemon chiffon pie and admired the mural of the original Chili John's favorite hiking spot and debated whether it was in the Sierras somewhere or back in Wisconsin, where the first Chili John's had opened in 1913.

Riding home, stomach full of hot chili and lemon pie, I remembered how I'd worried that Wilmar and Milena didn't really like me, and thought of how foolish that was. Burbank was my town, and these were my people, and we were here for each other.

———

I woke up the next day knowing that I had to get rid of the guns. And maybe the gold, too. I couldn't afford to keep that shit around the house, not with cross-burning crazies out there. I wasn't gonna go to the cops, either. Gramps had a couple of friends who were BPD and a couple who'd been LAPD, and everyone knew there were connections between the cops and the Maga Clubs. Plus I didn't think I could keep a straight face while explaining that I'd only just stumbled on Gramps's secret compartment.

And I knew exactly where they'd be safe.

I had to watch some videos to figure out how to take them apart, but once I did, they fit well enough in my biggest backpack, along with a roll of heavy plastic and some contractor bags. Our cleaning closet was full of heavy-duty, immortal plastic that Gramps had stockpiled when they started phasing it out.

I thought about covering the guns in oil before caching them, like I'd read about in a novel, but decided that was overkill. I was hiding them in the hills of Burbank, not the jungles of Burma. Besides, the bag was already heavy enough to strain the shoulder straps.

The cache box looked weirdly empty once I had its contents loaded up, a sad, cracked concrete cavity that Gramps had stored his most precious belongings in. I looked around the room for something to put in it but nothing seemed right. Then I looked at the folded pile of old clothes on top of the dresser, stuff that no longer fit or had worn out, but that I was keeping for some sentimental reason, and, right on the top, my baby blanket. It was the only thing I had left of my parents, the only thing that came with me when I was evacuated from Canada and sent to my grandfather, my last precious remnant of the dream my parents had chased. I picked it up and smelled it, as I always did, but it no longer smelled of my parents, nor of the scary journey I'd had after leaving them. It had been washed since then. Still, putting my face into its soft, fuzzy, broken fibers triggered a strong memory of what those smells had been long, long ago. I smoothed it out and put it in Gramps's cache, fitting the lid overtop of it. My most precious belonging, in Gramp's most secure cache. It worked.

Once I had the bag on my back and my butt on my bike, I started pedaling toward the site of the flood. It was the middle of the afternoon and it was overcast and hazy and I immediately began to drip with sweat. By the time I started to climb the hill, shifting down to the tiniest cog on both my front and back wheels, I felt like my back was so slippery that my entire shirt might come off and take the backpack with it. I had filled a water bottle before leaving and by the time I was halfway up the hill I'd already drained it dry and was feeling light-headed. It used to be newsworthy when Burbank cracked 15 percent humidity, but today it was close to 75 percent and it was the third day of the month to hit that mark.

The flood site was still taped off, the sandbag walls drooping as some of the water evaporated out of them. I set my bike down behind a section of wall and looked around and made sure I was alone. I was *definitely* alone, except for about ten million mosquitoes. My normal backpack had lots of kinds of bug dope, but not my big pack, which I always emptied and cleaned after camping trips. I slapped at my arms and blinked salty sweat out of my eyes and tried not to dwell on what an idiot I could be.

It took me a while to find the old septic tank, because there were multiple fence lines that had been sliced away and multiple slumped-over sandbag walls along the ridge. After a sweaty half hour, I found it. It still had a stagnant puddle at the bottom and when I bent over to peer into it, a cloud of mosquitoes lifted off from the water, and I ate at least a dozen of them. I tried to console myself with the thought that anything I hid in this thing would be safe because only an idiot like me would go poking around in it.

Breathing through my nose, blinking away more sweat, I wrapped the guns and the gold in multiple windings of heavy plastic, then wrestled the bundles into double thicknesses of contractor bags and nestled them in the bottom of the cistern. I covered them with a few layers of partially dehydrated sandbags, then scrounged for big rocks to fill most of the rest of the cistern, topping it off with another layer of sandbags.

As I stood to examine my work, I felt light-headed and then I stumbled a little and found myself sitting in the grass. I tried to remember what the symptoms of heatstroke were and couldn't and wondered if that was a symptom of heatstroke.

Whatever. I knew for sure that if I *did* have heatstroke, I should get out of the sun and get some cool water as soon as possible. I got shakily to my feet and straddled my bike. I sipped the last slug of water from the bottom of the bottle, clipped it to the crossbar, and started downhill, riding the brakes.

At least it's downhill, I thought, and distracted myself by trying to remember which corner store was closest, and which path I could take to reach it quickest, and which cold drink I would buy out of the cooler when I got there. I had nearly settled on a Burbank Kombucha Co. black licorice flavor (slogan "Better than you'd think!") when I realized I was about to crash into a group of people.

I'd been sticking to the lanes and alleys that ran behind the houses, autopiloting around the odd forgotten street-hockey net or overfilled drain or bold house cat, but I had somehow not noticed these three people until it was too late. I slammed my brakes, leaned over and dropped a foot to scrape the ground and turned my handlebars hard and managed not to crash into anything except the ground, which I hit pretty hard, leg trapped between the bike and the cracked concrete, head bouncing off the hard ground an instant later.

Someone lifted the bike off me, and then I was in shade from the three people leaning over me, staring up at their faces, all concerned expressions.

"Stay there, buddy," one of them said. Someone held up fingers.

"How many?"

My vision swam a little, then resolved. "Three," I said.

"Good," she said. "Open your eyes, let me look at your pupils?" I did, and then submitted to gentle hands that probed me from feet to head, making sure I hadn't broken anything. "Okay, bud, I think you're fine, but if you want, we can get an ambulance, put you on a spine board?"

"Uh," I said. I struggled up onto my elbows, which was a stupendously bad idea, but I didn't think that I'd fallen *that* hard. "I'm okay. Sorry, it was my bad. Have you got anything cold to drink?"

They helped me into a sitting position and one of them gave me a hose from her CamelBak. The water was flat and warm but I needed it. I made myself drink slowly. "I'm really sorry," I said again, once I'd had a couple of good-sized swallows. "That was totally my fault. I went out without enough water and got a little sun-blasted."

"No biggie," the one who'd been talking said. "Your bike's fine, you're okay, and we're okay. I'm Ana Lucía, and these are Jorge and Esai." She offered me her elbow and I dabbed it with mine, then got the other two.

I finally took them in: hard-wearing road clothes, worn hard; ripstop stuff gone the color of dry soil, big packs patched with tape and road-stitching. Deep tans, shaggy hair, dirty fingernails.

"Are you guys the refugees?" I blurted.

They looked at each other. "We're refugees," Ana Lucía said. "I don't know if we're *the* refugees."

"I mean, are you from the Tehachapi caravan? The one coming to Burbank? I mean, obviously you're *in* Burbank, but are you—"

"That's us," Ana Lucía said. I realized belatedly how wary all three were looking.

"No way!" I said. "Damn, look, sorry, I didn't mean to weird you out. I'm *so glad* to meet you." I flung my arms out. "Welcome to Burbank! Seriously!"

They were definitely trying to figure out if I was yanking their chains.

"Seriously," I said. "My friends and I can't wait for you all to get here! We love Burbank and want to show you what a great place it is."

Ana Lucía quirked her head to one side. She was older than me, mid-twenties, with the same vibe as Kiara, that leader/organizer vibe, though of course they didn't look like each other (Ana Lucía is Latina and Kiara is Black), but the expression Ana Lucía was wearing was one I'd definitely seen on Kiara's face. "Listen, uh—"

"Brooks," I said. "Brooks Palazzo." I held out my hand for a shake, which was not usual for me, and she snorted and unclipped some hand san from a D ring on her back and rubbed it into her palm before shaking. Her hand was strong and callused and cold and slimy with the sanitizer.

"Ana Lucía Alarcon," she said. "It's nice to meet you, Mr. Palazzo."

A raindrop, fat and hot, landed on my eye and made me blink. More landed on Ana Lucía and her two friends. Thunder rumbled in the hills.

"Shit," Ana Lucía said, and shucked her pack, pulling a poncho out of a side pocket. Her friends did the same. "Shit," she said again, as the rain began to pound us. I found it a relief, but I was worried that I'd made a bad impression.

"Are you guys in a hurry? My place is like thirty minutes' walk from here—downhill!—and I haven't had lunch yet."

They exchanged looks. The rain battered our heads.

"That's nice of you," Ana Lucía said. "Thank you."

Ana Lucía insisted that she and her friends would cook while I had a shower and found a change of clothes. I insisted that she use *my* food, not the provisions in her pack, because I was hosting, and we made an agreement.

Fifteen minutes later I was sitting at my kitchen table and we were all drinking cold brew and eating absolutely perfect grilled cheese sandwiches.

"How did you get them to go this color?" The sourdough was golden brown, like a menu illustration, and crispy.

"You like it?" Esai said. He was missing a tooth on top, and it made him look like a grinning, friendly pirate.

"Are you fucking kidding me?" I said, trying not to spray crumbs. "It's amazing!"

"My mom's secret," Esai said.

"Oh," I said. "If it's a secret—"

"He'll tell you," Ana Lucía said. "It's not that kind of secret. Right, Esai?"

"Guess first," he said.

I laughed and *did* spray crumbs and they laughed too. I swallowed and had some cold brew. "You toast it first?"

"Nope."

"Extra butter."

"No."

"Uh . . ." I looked around the kitchen, which I should have done in the first place. I spotted the jar on the counter. "Mayonnaise?"

All three laughed. "Yes, mayo! Instead of butter. Makes everything go golden and crackly," Esai said. He crunched into a sandwich. I crunched into mine.

"These are amazing," I said. "You see, that's what I love about all this—" I gestured at them, at me, at their packs. "Cultural exchange!"

They laughed, but this time it was a little forced.

Ana Lucía wiped her mouth with a rectangle of paper towel. "You know that not everyone here feels that way." She flipped open her screen and tapped at it. "Like these guys."

She passed me the screen and I scrolled. It was bad. Really bad. Death threats. Doxings. Screengrabs from other devices, showing how many different people had gotten the threats. Rape threats. Rape threats against kids. Death threats against kids. Signed with names like "Burbank Patriot" or strings of Punisher and U.S. flag emojis. I scrolled and scrolled but I didn't get to the end.

"This has got to be bots," I said. "Or a psycho who stays up all night posting from ten different accounts. There're only a hundred and fifty thousand people in Burbank! And most of them aren't Nazis!"

"Some of them are, though," Ana Lucía said, tapping the screen, landing on a block of text about race-mixing and demographic replacement.

"Some of them are," I said. "God, I hate Nazis."

Esai snorted. "You're a trip, dude."

I laughed. "Sorry. Everyone hates Nazis, but I'm just so sick of these guys."

"They'll die off soon," Jorge said. He didn't speak much, but when he did, it was with real thoughtful gravity.

"Will they?" Ana Lucía said. "Or will they make more?"

I broke out beers next and we sat in the backyard. I learned that they were the advance scouts for their group, coming ahead to figure out how serious all the doxings were. I asked where they planned to sleep and they said they'd marked out a woody spot in Angeles Forest that they had planned to hike back to and pitch a tent in and so I texted Wilmar and Milena to make sure they were cool and then I invited Ana Lucía and her friends to pitch their tents in my backyard.

Milena and Wilmar came back as we were grilling tofu and squeaky cheese and sweet potatoes and Milena got her guitar and Jorge brought out a harmonica and it turned out Ana Lucía could really sing.

"That was beautiful," I said, after a singalong whose chorus went "Y te vas, y te vas, y te vas," and we roared along with it.

"José Alfredo Jiménez," Ana Lucía said. "My great-aunt married a Mexican and they used to play him all the time. The lyrics are terrible, but it's so fun to sing." She swigged beer. "I wish we could just keep going, all the way to Mexico."

"Border's tighter than a frog's ass," Wilmar said, and burped.

"Especially for Salvadorans," Ana Lucía agreed. "We're the boogeymen they scare their kids with when they won't eat their dinners, especially after the Russians got to them." I filed that away. So many people believed so many things about the Russians, and I'd learned the hard way not to engage on the topic unless I wanted to dive way, way down the conspiracy-theory rabbit hole.

"Maybe so," Milena said, "but I hear they're done letting white people in, too. After all the health-care refus, they lost their appetite for 'em."

"Couldn't speak the language," Esai said, and we all laughed.

"All right, it's true," I said. I switched to Spanish: "My Armenian friends speak better Spanish than I do." We laughed some more.

We helped them pitch their tents and loaded their laundry into the washing machine before bed. Afterward, I went into the kitchen to get a glass of water before bed and ran into Milena, who was carrying her own water glass back to her room.

"Those folks are *great*," Milena said.

"Right?"

"I'm so glad you brought 'em here. Can't wait for the rest to arrive, either. It'll be the kick in the ass that this town's needed for decades."

I thought of Gramps's buddies. "You can say that again."

Wilmar joined us in a tee and sweats, a little toothpaste at the corner of his mouth. "We're gonna have to get a lot more Airbnb rooms, though. Last I heard we were short by like fifty beds."

I looked from one to the other. "You guys, feel free to say no to this, but I was thinking, we've got that big front yard and the huge backyard and we hardly ever use it, and all of Ana's people are traveling with tents already . . . We could get a couple porta-potties and set up a field kitchen and—"

"I. Love. That," Milena said.

Wilmar laughed. "I'm gonna rotate back to the factory soon, so I don't guess I should get a vote, but for whatever it's worth, I vote yes, too. Plus, someone can have my room when I go back to Mojave."

I clapped and did a little dance. I couldn't wait for breakfast and the chance to tell Ana Lucía and Esai and Jorge.

chapter 3
chained

Esai and Jorge were super stoked, but Ana Lucía just took it in
stride and started measuring the yards to see how we could lay
out the camp. Milena put the word out to the affinity group, and
people started dropping by with clothes and dry goods and life-
straws and things for a field kitchen.

Ana Lucía, Esai, and Jorge had just headed off to rendezvous
with the rest of the caravan when the doorbell rang. I checked
it and groaned: Kenneth and Derrick, and they looked *pissed*. I
thought about muting the bell but they rang it again and I decided
I'd rather argue with them than have them camped out on my
doorstep, seething.

But I stuck an eyeball on my shirt and turned it on, setting it to
blink red so they'd know it was recording, and opened the door.

"Tell me it's not true." Derrick's tone was belligerent, veins
standing out in his forehead and neck. I forced myself to stand my
ground, though I wanted to recoil.

"Nice to see you, Derrick, Kenneth."

"Invite us in." It was not a question.

"No, Derrick, I don't believe I will."

Kenneth looked pained. "Come on, Brooks, let's not do this
where the neighbors can see and eavesdrop. We're old friends of
your family and—"

"You're old friends of my grandfather. My *dead* grandfather. I
don't think you were ever friends with my father. I *know* you weren't
friends of my mother's. I don't think you're a friend of mine, Kenneth. And Derrick, to be honest, I plain don't like you."

He snorted and Kenneth looked more pained. "Tell me it's not true," Derrick repeated.

"It's not true," I said. "Bye." I started to close the door, but Derrick's boot was in the way.

"Are you going to turn this house of yours into a refugee camp?" Derrick asked.

"Word gets around." I stared into his eyes. He was old, but strong, and he was huffing air out his nostrils like a cartoon bull.

"You have no right—"

"Derrick, shut the fuck up," I suggested. "You and your buddies talk a lot about the sanctity of private property. Well, Gramps left me this house. That makes it my private property. If I want your input on what I should or should not do with it—or who should or should not live here—I will come down to the Maga Club and ask you in person."

"Brooks, you don't want to be a traitor to your gramps, for what he stood for, to this city that took you in. I know you don't. You were raised better than that, by one of the best men I ever knew—"

"Derrick, shut the fuck up. As I believe I already told you, this house is going to be torn down and replaced by a high-density high-rise just as soon as I can arrange for it. My sincere hope is that every lot on this street gets the same treatment, so that this city that took me in can take in a hell of a lot more people. A lot more of my fellow Americans, people who have the bad luck to have lost their homes and the fortitude to come here next. This is how I'm honoring my grandfather's memory, you Hitler wannabe—by doing everything I can to undo every miserable, shitty thing he did in his eighty miserable, shitty years on this dying planet."

Kenneth grabbed Derrick before he could swing at me, hauled him out of reach of me, hugging his arms to his sides from behind.

"You little piece of shit," Derrick said, spit flying. "You want to think *very carefully* about your actions. There're *bad things* that can happen to people who sell out their neighbors, things that none of your antifa pals can help you with. You should be thinking very carefully about the privileges you enjoy as a member of a community, and what your life would be like if you ceased to be a member. Very carefully."

"Dude," I said, really enjoying the moment even though my heart was thudding. "I can*not* believe you're talking about antifa. Aren't you worried about being targeted by a Jewish banker's space-based laser array?" Then, before I could stop myself: "The Antifa High Command is going to be *very* happy when I turn over the things I found under Gramps's floorboards. Very, very happy."

Goddamn did that ever land. He went white, then red, then purple. His face did this fish thing, open mouth, close mouth, open mouth, and I looked at Kenneth, who was clearly quietly freaking out. "Bye, now, boys," I said. "Don't let the door hit you in the ass on the way out." Slam.

So satisfying!

So why were my hands shaking when I got to the backyard where Ana Lucía and half a dozen of her friends were setting up shade sails, a field kitchen, and a kids' play area, with a tree house and some climbing ropes?

"We heard the door slam from out here," Ana Lucía said, hip-checking me as she walked past with some one-by-eight lumber. "Everything okay?"

"Sure," I said, and helped myself to some of the lemonade they'd made with the lemons from the tree on the front lawn. The taste made me think of the lemonade stands I'd set up on the corner at Verdugo when I was a kid. They never made much money, but it was one of the few things that Gramps actually approved of, because of "enterprise."

I drank and stared at the backyard fence; the last of the

Vardazaryans had moved out the year before, when old Tovin had finally gotten too frail to stay on his own, even with help. I hadn't met the new people, but I heard their kids squealing as they ran through the sprinklers on hot days.

"You okay?" Ana Lucía had her own lemonade.

"Yeah," I said. "It's just . . ."

"Crazy times."

"Yeah."

"Things get bad for me, I take a walk. Things are always better when you're in motion."

"Excellent suggestion."

"Can I come?"

"Sure," I said. "I'll show you the neighborhood."

I was about 80 percent sure this wasn't a hookup. She was like seven years older than me, and had more of a big-sister vibe. I wouldn't have minded, she had amazing dark eyes and long lashes, these big cheekbones and fingers that were long and fast-moving, but also, I wasn't in the market for *more* complications and I'd just about learned that dickful thinking was a hell of a lot more trouble than it was worth.

We got parasols and filled up our water bottles and started to walk. The day had slipped by so quickly and I could tell that the sunset was going to be a gorgeous one from the way the clouds were already starting to pinken. There were places in Burbank from which the sunset was an endless, coral-colored plain, and I'd taken a million photos of it without ever capturing it.

"Do you want to see one of my favorite things?" I asked.

She looked skeptical but curious. "It's not weird or gross or, you know, awkward, is it?"

"Ohgodno," I said. "No, nothing like that. I can tell you what it is if you want. But I promise it'd also make for an awesome surprise." I felt confident in the promise. Who doesn't love sunsets?

She considered me for a moment. "Well . . ."

"I'll tell you, it's fine—"

"Shut up, let's go."

"We have to get some bikes." I found some bikeshares on my screen and we adjusted the seats and got on 'em. Mine had a wobble in the front rim that I stopped and tagged before pressing on. Alameda was 100 percent bikes after 5 p.m., so I steered us down there and we started to really work, hitting the biggest cogs. She was *fast*. So strong!

"Okay with hills?" I called as I drew up on her.

"Eat 'em for breakfast," she said, and so I led her up and up to my sunset spot, way up in the hills, a half mile uphill or more. Both of us were a little pooped when I stopped us and we parked the bikes by the road and set off into the brush until we came to the rocky outcropping, not far from the big Burbank "B" (every couple of years someone added "L" and "M" to it, but it was hard to do that kind of landscaping without a crane and a bulldozer and most of the rocks washed away in the rains).

Right on schedule, the sunset turned an infinitely expansive sky ten million shades of pink and red, with the towers of DTLA center-frame and glowing. The insect chorus rose in a wash of sound, and then a flock of Burbank's green parrots screamed past us as they argued their way down into the valley.

"No fucking way," she said. Her face was the most incredible color, dark skin and pink glow, like a saint in an old painting.

"Right?"

"Brooks, this is—" She waved an arm. "Wow."

"Welcome to Burbank. You guys are gonna love it here!"

I had a one-hit in my pocket and we split it as the blaze cooled and the pinks all purpled.

"You really love it here, don't you?"

The one-hit slowed me down so I didn't answer right away. I thought about it instead. "I love so much about this place. It's not perfect. There're a lot of people here who are, I don't know, broken or something. Bad? They have ugly, broken hearts, if that makes sense."

"I know the type."

"But Burbank is a place that's easy to love. It's weird, the thing those ugly-hearts love about this place is that we've got a long history of looking after people. It was always a union town, full of skilled trades from the studios. Then there was aerospace. Lockheed were baby killers, sure, but the people who built the planes here made a good wage and supported the schools and the libraries and built our pools and parks."

She laughed and the pink glow and the laughter transformed her, made her seem young and carefree instead of serious and driven. "You make it sound too good to be true."

"Oh, it's got problems, but the way we solve them gives me hope." I told her about the Jobs Guarantee fight with the Maga Club, and told her about all the amazing jobs I got to pull out of the job bank, along with Milena and so many of my friends. Again, her face changed, getting more and more serious. It was such a transformation that I thought it had to be a trick of the light as the sun sank behind the DTLA towers. I ran down and stopped talking, suddenly nervous, the one-hit totally worn off.

"Brooks," she said, chin up and out and whole manner aggressive. "Do you hear yourself? You think *jobs* are the answer to our problems?"

I almost groaned aloud because I knew *exactly* what was coming next.

"Forced employment cannot deliver human liberation. You've got to see that. All we're doing is creating mountains of debt that'll come due someday, and when it does, we're all going to pay the price. Where do you think money comes from?"

I couldn't believe I was getting dragged into *this* argument, with *this* person. But okay, we're doing this. "Governments spend money into existence." I held up my hand to stop her from jumping in. "I know what you're going to say, 'governments don't have a magic money machine, they can't just make as much as they want,' and yeah, I know that argument, but it's only half right:

governments do have magic money machines, literally, money is just tokens that governments stamp with 'legal currency' but yeah, they can't just spend and spend. If someone at the Treasury types too many zeroes into their spreadsheet and the feds buy too many things, they'll start bidding against us for the stuff we want to buy, and prices will go up."

She was ready: "You think the assholes who did whatever it took to get themselves elected are gonna stop printing money just because they might cause inflation? They have proved so many times that they don't care who they hurt, so long as they're helping themselves and their friends."

I must have groaned because she flashed furious and then got herself under control, taking a deep breath. "Look, money is control. I know your arguments, Brooks. You think that money is only valuable because it's the only way you can pay your tax bills. What's the party line? 'Governments create tax liabilities payable in their currencies so that their citizens have to work to pay their taxes, and that makes their currency valuable so they can spend it to provision themselves with roads and armies.'"

I couldn't stop myself from laughing. "If you know the argument, then why are we having it?"

"Because *you* don't get it, obviously."

And that shut my laughing down, because she was even angrier. "Do you know what happens when governments get to spend their way to popularity? We pay the bill. Sure, maybe you loved President Uwayni and her right-on spending, but now it's Bennett, and *she* wants to spend all that magic money rebuilding the military and invading other countries to take their shit so America can be great again."

I was a little scared of how visibly pissed she was, but also—"I agree with everything you say about Bennett, but how would things be better if we didn't have the Jobs Guarantee? You think people will have more time to fight her if they don't know where their next paycheck is coming from?"

She waved her hand. "Yeah, of course, that's what all the magic money people say. If we had a Universal Basic Income—"

I couldn't help groaning again, even though that clearly made her angrier. "Say it," she demanded.

"Really? Fine. Most of us don't have any savings. You give us money and we'll spend it, and sure, that'll *also* buy us time to fight Bennett and her little plute gang. But what about those plutes? Even after more than a decade of Uwenomics, the one percent still own more than the rest of us by a damned sight. Give them money, they'll stick it in the market or buy bonds or just lend it out and they'll get even richer. Give a ninety-nine percenter a thousand dollars a month and ten years later, they still won't have anything in the bank. Give the same amount to a plute who has all the money they need and then some and ten years later, they'll be a quarter million dollars richer. You've got to see that?"

"I see that. But you don't see the real struggle. You're thinking way too small. The reason the rich are so fuckin' rich is that they bought Congress, bought the state governments, bought the judges and the sheriffs and the town councils for centuries. The reason they were able to do that is we let the government control the money. When governments control money, they can make sure their friends get it. We need a people's money, a money that no one controls."

Honestly, I'd figured out that we were going to get here eventually but I'd held out hope.

"Eighty-seven point six percent of all conversations about blockchain are nonconsensual."

She didn't crack a smile. "Yeah, I know that joke, too. It doesn't change the fact that some of the richest people in the world love your 'Modern Monetary Theory.' I know how that's supposed to work, but do *you* know how it actually works? First, rich people who are scared that someone'll turn off their government money spigots convince a bunch of well-meaning lefties that you can spend and spend without any consequences. Meanwhile, who do you think owns all that debt? They do. Rich people. And when it comes due, they're gonna collect, from you, and your kids and your grandkids.

"And don't get me started on the 'Jobs Guarantee.' It's a guarantee, all right: a guarantee that you'll have to work for them for the rest of your life. If you can't see that there's a dangerously short line between a Jobs Guarantee and forced labor—"

I just tuned her out at that point. A feeling of exhaustion and hopelessness settled over me. I'd just invited this person and all of her friends to live in my house and now it turned out they were blockchain cultists. Fffffuuuu. I could only imagine that Gramps was laughing at me from beyond the grave. Thing was, there were plenty of sudoku addicts in his crowd—blockchain was a bipartisan obsession. He might've gotten along with old Ana Lucía.

I could tell she was winding down.

"You're not even listening anymore." She was still angry, but I could tell that the fury had faded somewhat.

"I don't want to fight."

"Fine. I don't want to fight either." It was dark now. She threw a pebble down the hillside, scaring a critter in the underbrush that rustled as it ran away. "Oh, God, I'm sorry. Look. It's been a day, okay? Like, losing my home, organizing my neighbors, getting on the road. Then all the hate mail and doxings. I mean, you've been amazing, seriously. The way you opened your house up. We appreciate it. Totally. All of us. I'm sorry I yelled at you."

"It's okay. It just means you really care about this stuff. I do, too. That's good. We agree on what's important. Maybe someday we can agree on what to do about it."

She laughed. "You're right, Brooks. Maybe we will. Look, before we go back, I want to tell you one thing. You're totally in your rights to say you're done with this subject, after all that, but—"

"It's fine, go ahead."

"I know you think financial secrecy is just about letting plutes launder the money they steal, but money is power, Brooks. You know there was a time when it was illegal to be queer if you taught in a public school in West Virginia? It was. They got that changed, through a political campaign. Political campaigns cost money. You know who had the incentive to donate to a campaign like that?

"Queer teachers. But if you gave money to the cause, you stood a good chance of getting fired. They got a lot of envelopes of cash in the mail. Ten dollars. Twenty. Fifty. Rich people have accountants and offshore accounts and bearer bonds and krugerrands"—*yikes*—"but regular people don't have any of that. Financial secrecy tools only help rich people a little, make their grift just a little more frictionless. Financial secrecy helps everyone else a *lot*. We gave so much power to Uwayni because she was so right-on, but every one of those powers is in Bennett's hands now. You're going to need financial secrecy to survive in Bennett's world."

"Uh, how do you suppose all that money ended up in Bennett's campaign? It seems pretty obvious to me that financial secrecy is most important to people with a lot of money."

"Didn't you hear me? You think queer teachers in West Virginia—"

And we were off, and even as I was arguing with her and listening to myself say the words, I knew they were a script, a fight that we'd both had before. I just couldn't stop myself, not even as it escalated to real shouting, and then finally—

"Okay, fine, let's agree to disagree. This isn't getting us anywhere." I made myself say the words with a calmness I wasn't feeling. I was in the place I went to when I argued with Gramps, and backing out of that place was hard for me. "Let's go back. It's dark out, and I want dinner."

"Yeah," she said. "Yeah, me too."

Thankfully, no one had claimed the bikes we'd left at the trailhead—I'd figured they'd be safe, this far away from houses and stores. But we rode home in simmering silence. I helped cook dinner—beans and rice with spices and garlic, studded with bits of fake chicken from my big culture-vat. I must have spoken to other people, but when I excused myself to go to bed, I couldn't remember any of the conversations. I looked out the window and made sure Wilmar was still out there, so that our guests had someone to ask logistical questions of.

I pulled the blinds and changed into sweats and a tee and brushed my teeth and put myself to bed. I hated going to bed angry, but it was better than pretending not to be angry in a group of people who'd done nothing to deserve it.

The next thing I knew, I was awake and on my feet, and there was screaming from the backyard. Loud, terrified screaming. I had found my dad's old baseball bat when I moved into Gramps's room and reorganized things, and I grabbed it out of the closet and raced, barefooted, down the hall, banging out of the back door, hand slapping at the switch for the outdoor lighting.

I stopped short. There, in the middle of the camp with its neat rows of tents and tidy camp kitchen—another burning cross. It was the twin of the one from City Hall, right down to the retina-searing magnesium fire. I stared at it with an open mouth for a moment, some distant part of my mind wondering if any of the fire extinguishers were rated for magnesium, when a change in the tone of the shouting around me made me look up. My vision was clouded by green blobs from staring into the magnesium light, but I could see that there was a fat guy in fatigues and a balaclava who'd been grabbed by a couple of my houseguests, and his friends were coming back for him. Someone screamed a Spanish word I didn't quite catch and then there was the impossibly loud crack of a gun and I realized the word had been "*pistola*."

"In the house! *A la casa!*" I screamed, flinging the door open and waving at it. People duck-ran, crouching, crying. I kept waiting for another gunshot, feeling horribly exposed under the lamp outside the door, illuminated by shifting patterns from the flames leaping up from the cross. Finally, Ana Lucía brought up the rear and I slammed and locked the door behind her, then we all crowded into Gramps's room, it being farthest from both the picture windows at the front of the house and the back door where the armed terrorists were. I was already dialing 911 as the last person got in and I started to shove a chest of drawers over the door with one shoulder as I clamped my screen to the opposite ear. Wilmar and Milena got the idea and started pushing, then someone else pushed my bed behind it, and I told the 911 operator what was going on as the people around me tried to stifle their crying so I could hear.

"They're coming," I said, loud enough for everyone to hear.

"Police?" Ana Lucía said.

"Yes."

The color drained from her face. "You shouldn't have done that, Brooks," she said. "Come on," she called to her friends in Spanish, and started to move the bed away from the door. They shoved the dresser aside and rushed for the front door before I could even react. I ran after them and then I was running into them as the people at the front started to shove their way back into the house, everyone talking at once in the narrow hallway, and someone knocked my framed Ned Ludd poster off the wall and the glass cracked on the floor.

"What is it?" I said, catching hold of Ana Lucía as she pushed past me. She turned to me, her eyes rolling white around the irises.

"More of them out front. A *lot* more."

Shit. I'd felt trapped before, but now I felt like I was being crushed, caught in a pincer maneuver between the thugs out back and the mob in the front. Where were the fucking cops? What was going on? When did Burbank get like this?

Thinking that made me remember my sunset on the hillside with Ana Lucía, before we'd argued, when I'd been telling her how much I loved this town. In that instant, my fear turned to rage. How *dare* they do this in *my* city? I grabbed my baseball bat and rushed out the front door.

"Come on, you fucking cowards," I raged into the night, swinging the bat like I was trying for the fences. "Come on you pieces of shit, come and try me. Come on!" I swung the bat some more, spinning myself around a little as it whistled past the lemon tree.

"Brooks?" someone called from the dark. "Brooks, dude—"

I stopped swinging and squinted at the vague forms out front of the house. Someone lit a screen and held it under their chin and I saw it was Brad Turner from next door, and then I realized that I knew all these people—they were my neighbors. Brad held up his hands. "We saw the flames and put out the call and here we are. We thought you could use some help."

There were dozens of them, and more arriving.

"We brought a chem extinguisher," Brad said.

"Fire department says to leave it," said a woman behind him, screen clamped to her head. "They're on the way."

"They're on the way," Brad said.

I let the baseball bat fall to the ground. I heard Ana Lucía and her people talking in hushed voices behind me, and my neighbors talking in hushed tones in front of me, and I had no idea whether to laugh or to cry.

I laughed.

Soon I was doubled over, howling with laughter, and someone was laughing next to me and I turned and saw it was Ana Lucía, and then I heard Brad start to chuckle and Wilmar and Milena got me to my feet and we were all laughing together.

Sirens drew nearer, nearer and I had time to think *The good old Burbank FD, so reliable* before I realized it was the Burbank PD's SWAT team.

They came out hot, weapons in hand, shouting orders, *on the ground, hands where we can see them,* and *clear, clear,* as they surrounded us, swarmed past us, went through the house.

From the ground, I kept shouting, "It's my house, it's my house!," and finally a beefy cop in body armor knelt down beside me and said, "Is this your house, sir?" I couldn't tell if he was being sarcastic.

"I'm going to get up now," I said, because he had some kind of long gun slung across his chest and I didn't want to get murdered on my lawn.

He eyed me warily, a white guy in his thirties, suspicious eyes.

"It's my house," I said. "I'm Brooks Palazzo. Some of these people are my houseguests. Those two"—I pointed at Milena and Wilmar, prone on the lawn, hands behind their heads—"are my roommates. The rest are my neighbors, who came to help when the attack came."

"And the attackers?"

I shrugged. "Guess they've gone. They were out back."

He narrowed his eyes at me. "Are you that kid, the one with the guy on the roof?"

"Mike Kennedy. Yeah, I'm that guy."

"Huh," he said. He seemed to relax a little, put his hands on his hips. "You're kind of a shit-magnet, aren't you?"

I didn't know what to say to that.

"Stay there," he said, and went off to confer with a couple of other cops, including a guy who was clearly in charge, and then ambled back.

"No one hurt?" he said.

"No. I mean, I don't think so. One of the attackers shot at us as they were running off. I only heard one shot and I don't think he hit anyone."

"Can you identify the attackers? How many were there?"

"They were in masks. I don't know how many there were. Maybe some of the folks who were out back when they showed up know."

"These people?" He pointed at Ana Lucía's friends.

I nodded.

"Who are these people, again?" He used the beam of his flashlight like a weapon, spotlighting people as they lay prone, shining it in their turned faces and scared eyes.

I stepped into the path of the beam. "My friends. House-guests."

"All these people?"

"Yeah."

"All these people are staying in your little house here?"

"They're camping in the back."

"Camping."

I didn't answer. I was starting to think I shouldn't say another word except, "I want a lawyer present."

"Wait there." He went back to his commander, then back to me. "These people speak English?"

"Yes." Then I remembered that I was going to say nothing except "lawyer lawyer lawyer" but it was too late.

He cupped his hands to his mouth: "All right people, you stay where you are. We're gonna get you one at a time and talk to you, have a look at things. This is for your safety, you understand?"

"Wait, what?" I got between him and Ana Lucía's friends. "No, I don't give you consent to come on my property. I don't give you consent to search my belongings or the belongings of my guests. I want a lawyer present."

He chuckled. "That's nice, but Mr. Palazzo, we're not here because you invited us. We're here because there was an exchange of gunfire. None of that bullshit matters once you start shooting."

"Someone shot at *us*!" My voice was squeaking and now Milena and Wilmar were by me.

"Cool it," Wilmar said.

"Listen to him," the cop said.

Ana Lucía had risen to her knees, hands still laced behind her head. She was glaring at me and at the cop. "Under the Internal Displaced Persons Act, we are entitled to fair, nondiscriminatory treatment. I am recording you. I do not consent to a search. I invoke my right to counsel."

The commander came over. He was older, and had coffee on his breath. "Internal Displaced Persons Act," he said, and hitched his belt. He nodded to the cop who'd been questioning me. "Get on with it," he said. "You, stand over there," he said, meaning me, Milena, and Wilmar. My roommates basically had to drag me. I was lucky they were there because I was so utterly triggered, this guy was such a Gramps type and was vibing like Gramps always had just before we had a huge screaming match.

My neighbors gathered around me and we watched as, one at a time, they threw Ana Lucía's people up against the wall and patted them down, while some of the cops went out back and tore apart their camp.

An hour later, two of my guests were in handcuffs while we stood around in a furious, helpless daze. "What the fuck?" I kept saying. The cops made a big deal out of the fact that they had "unidentified pills," and refused to listen when the woman insisted that they were her antidepressants and that she'd lost the bottle and the man said he was being busted because his epilepsy prescription came from a cheap Canadian pharmacy.

Ana Lucía had woken up some people from the National Lawyers Guild and she had them videoconferenced in to watch the police as they cuffed her friends. The lawyers asked factual questions about what the charges were and where the prisoners were being taken and when they would have court dates, and recited the Spanish and English standard bust-card advice about not saying anything until someone from the guild showed up.

When they were gone, people filed silently into the backyard. I followed them back and then stood stupidly in the doorway as they disappeared into their tents. The fire department had come and gone during the searches, and the ground was marshy with sharp-smelling chemicals.

Ana Lucía stopped in the act of climbing into her own tent and stalked over to me, so furious that I took an involuntary step back.

"That's why you don't call the fucking police. Ever."

"I—"

She held up her hands.

"I'm going to bed now." Turned on her heel, back into her tent. *Zzzip.*

I lay awake for a long time, turning over all the events in my mind, thinking of the faces of Ana Lucía's friends as they were taken away, then thinking of the half-seen men in the balaclavas who'd lit the cross in my backyard. Did I recognize any of them? Maybe. The body language was familiar enough. Any of them could have been one of the nice old codgers who'd always been welcome in Gramps's living room.

I'd tolerated them when Gramps was alive, and I was still tolerating them now. When Kenneth and Derrick rang my doorbell, I still talked to them, even if I taunted them. I didn't just shout "Fuck off you old irrelevant Nazis!" through the door speaker. Truth be told, I didn't want to do that. Some part of me didn't want to hurt their feelings. The same part of me that hadn't wanted to pick a fight with Gramps when they started saying evil white supremacist shit in my own living room.

Why had I tolerated all of that? Objectively, I knew that the world couldn't survive if these people got their way. They wanted genocide, and if that wasn't bad enough, they had stupid, poisonous ideas that would cook the planet and leave us all to roast, drown, or die of plagues. They were a threat to the fucking species. What kind of commitment to being nice or not picking fights was more important than that fact?

My fists were balled up under the sheets and I made myself relax them. My tolerance for these genocidal monsters was over. They thought it was them or me? Okay, it was them or me. And I knew who I chose.

I was just drifting off to sleep when I remembered my fight with Ana Lucía on the hillside, and I had a moment of falling-off-the-cliff sorrow as I had the same thought about *her*. All that stuff about financial secrecy and dismantling the state to save it from plutes—if there was one thing I was sure of, it's that plutes thrived best with weak states and financial secrecy. The guys in Gramps's Maga Club were sincere in their love of Burbank, but they were still monsters. Ana Lucía was doubtless sincere about her blazing blockchainism, but that didn't mean she couldn't be a monster, right?

Right?

calexit

We had another six days to get ready for the rest of the caravan, and we didn't waste a minute of it. Every gig on the Jobs Guarantee board had something to do with the caravan: setting up People's Airbnbs in people's guest rooms, organizing spaces and carers for daycares, shuttling the medical crews out to the slowly moving column of refus to do health assessments. We started having nightly dinner parties with the caravan, videoing them in to our own tables in small family groups, rotating halfway through so that as many people as possible could get to know each other.

I worked long hours picking up donated clothing and shoes and inventorying them so that the refus could search by size and have their care packages waiting for them when they crossed the town line. A couple of the baby Warners got in a friendly competition with their opposite numbers on the Disney lot and they scoured their wardrobe departments, finding mountains of unworn clothing bought for shoots that either had never happened or hadn't needed them after all.

They were due on Sunday, so by Saturday we were all running around like hyperactive kids getting everything together, hanging banners down Magnolia, scrounging extra beds and food, checking in on everyone who'd promised to cook for the big potluck brunch the next morning.

I was cycling three pallets of eggs from Bret Harte Elementary's coops when I got a big buzz, the kind that meant that everyone I knew was talking about something I should probably go pay

attention to. I pulled the trike over to the side of North Hollywood and got out a screen.

It turned out the refus weren't the only people who'd come to
town. The Flotilla had arrived at Long Beach and was accepting
visitors.

The Flotilla had never made it to LA, so this was a big deal,
and all my feeds were blazing with arguments about whether it
was okay to visit them, and, if not, whether they should be tor-
pedoed where they stood docked in international waters, sending the superyachts and surplus aircraft carriers to Davy Jones's
locker.

I shook my head and stuffed the screen in a pocket. I had eggs
to haul. I'd worry about seasteading hypercapitalist nomads later.

But Flotilla talk was impossible to escape. The kids chopping
sweet potatoes kept goofing off to watch Flotilla videos, especially *Kinetreaders,* the ultraviolent, high-budget, intense drama
adapted from Sutton's awful novel *Those Who Tread the Kine.* It
had raced through my friend group in junior year and the people
who loved it *really* loved it, like it was a gateway to cult membership, and a lot of those people drifted away from my friend
group and never drifted back. It was a scary book that way. Even
scarier was that I could never figure out what other people saw in
it—every time I tried to read it, I just bounced off it hard, like, by
chapter 2. What a snore.

Kinetreaders, at least, had a ton of explosions and fight scenes
and lockpicking and abseiling and all of that stuff, and I found
myself getting half sucked into it, which just made me scared for
the kids. Did their parents even know they were watching it?

I eventually talked the kids into turning off the screen so we
could get all the sweet potatoes chopped and make frittatas. I
tried—unsuccessfully—to draw them into choosing ingredients
for different ones, so I just made them all to suit my taste, with

chilis and olives and farmer's cheese. I put mushrooms in only half because there are some objectively decent people who don't love mushrooms, though I don't claim to be able to reconcile those two facts.

Half a dozen of us got the frittatas delivered to the caterers and restaurants who'd agreed to cook 'em, and then I headed home for a beer and dinner. It was a hive of activity, naturally, with Ana Lucía's friends riding up and riding away as they did all the advance-party stuff, getting clothes and toys into People's Airbnb rooms to order and so on.

I thought about pitching in, but I was exhausted and starving so I made myself a sloppy sandwich—spicy/briny olive dressing, cheese, and chick-n on a big kaiser roll—and carried it out into the backyard with a folding chair.

"Damn, that looks *good*," Ana Lucía said, pulling up a chair. I tore it in half sloppily and handed half to her. "Dude, I can't take half your dinner."

"Plenty more stuff in the kitchen," I said. "If we're still hungry after, one of us can make another one and we'll split that too."

"You are a hell of a guy," she said. She made the next sandwich, and brought it out with beers. We clinked.

"What a day," she said. Everyone was taking dinner now, broken up into twos and threes, fanning themselves, drinking beers. Someone turned on music, and the sun was setting and glorious.

"Best kind of day," I said. "Stuff to do, got it done, and it was stuff that's gonna legit make a difference for other people. Absolutely the best kind of day."

"Hell of a guy," she said, and laughed. I laughed too. "To arrivals," she said, and we clinked again.

"Arrivals! You must be excited, everyone getting settled in. I can't wait to meet them all. Before I found out you folks were on the way, I was getting ready to leave, but now—"

"Dude," she said. "Seriously?"

"Uh?"

"I'm talking about the Flotilla. The caravan is what it is, but honestly, it's just the latest phase in a long, shitty, shitty shit-show of shittiness that's been happening for years—farms blowing away, towns shutting down, water drying up. The Flotilla, though—"

I flashed back on that night, trying to fall asleep after the SWAT team had raided my house, thinking of how tolerating colorful people with funny ideas ended up giving aid and comfort to monsters.

"Ana Lucía, they're not good people."

"No, they're not," she said. "But they've got ideas beyond letting the government take care of everything. They're giving people the tools they need to organize themselves."

Translation: Blockchain.

My mouth opened before my brain got in gear. "They're the worst people in the world. They're fucking war criminals. They drowned the planet and then they literally declared the last mountain peak sticking up out of the Caymans to be a sovereign state and ran away to live on boats around it."

She was getting hot, too. I could see that we were about to fight again, but I didn't care. I was triggered as hell.

"It's easy to sit here in your nice suburb with your nice house and talk about how great it is to trust governments with everything. I don't have that luxury, Brooks. My home is gone. My mother is dead. My father is dead. I've lost everything, so don't lecture me about war crimes. You don't think war crimes are going on here?"

I dropped my beer from my nerveless fingers and walked away. I got out of my backyard and turned right, away from Verdugo and the main road, and struck out blindly, walking fast, tears streaming down my cheeks. Soon, I identified the weird sounds I was hearing as sobs. Then I realized I was making those sounds.

Someone was at my elbow. They were saying something to me. I assumed it was one of my neighbors trying to help me out, so I choked out something like, "I'm fine, it's fine, I'm sorry," and shook my elbow out of their grasp and turned the corner.

The person wouldn't go away. Now they were in front of me and it was Wilmar, blocking my path. "Brooks," he said, reaching out for me. "Come on, man, hold up."

Fuck. I swiped at my eyes, snuffled up my snot. He handed me a kerchief and I blotted my face with it. "I'm sorry," I said.

He looked really worried about me and that made me feel even worse, if that was possible. "Don't be." He gave me a long hug and I was sure everyone was at their windows, staring at us. But I liked the hug. "You can talk about it, or not," he said into my ear.

"Let's walk," I said.

"Good plan." We got onto Olive and then crossed and kept on going to Riverside and then through Warners, wending through the baby Warners' buildings until we got to the pedestrian cut-through that led to the river. It was swollen and clear, running fast thanks to all the rains, mossy rocks peeking out and geese waddling on the banks. Seeing the running water and hearing the geese and the shush of the buses on the freeway instantly calmed me some, made my chest and my fists unsqueeze. I sat down on the concrete at the top of the riverbank and stared down into the water and breathed.

"You don't have to talk about it," Wilmar said, "but if you want to, you can."

I didn't want to talk about it, but for some reason, I did.

"When I was seven, we started to hear about a new strain of beaver fever that was racing around the north, starting in the little towns and settlements and then Iqaluit. Flights stopped. I was really young and my parents tried to keep me from getting scared but suddenly everyone was washing their hands all the time and I wasn't allowed to play on the climbers at the playground anymore. School closed, then we stopped leaving the house."

The geese were honking and it brought me back to reality.

"I'm sorry," I said.

"Don't be," he said. He was a good listener, didn't make me feel like I was having a pity party.

"Everyone has a story like this, I know."

"Doesn't make it easier," he said. "Besides, if this is going where I think it is, your story is different."

I really wanted that beer I'd dropped on my back lawn. "Fuck." I breathed hard. "Mom got sick first, but then she started to get better, just in time for Dad to need her help. Mom had spent a lot of time in bed puking in a bucket that Dad emptied for her, but Dad couldn't even turn his head to use the bucket. There was puke and shit everywhere and Mom couldn't even get the sheets off the bed. She stopped trying, just used plastic garbage bags that she slit open and then balled up and put in bigger bags. When she started to get sick again it became my job to haul them out to the curb. But the garbage wasn't getting picked up either, and every curb had a giant pile of rotting, stinking bags out front. Mom told me I could just put the bags in the backyard, because it was too much work to drag them out front. They made a pile bigger than me."

I patted my pockets and found my one-hit and I thanked myself for remembering to refill it. I toked and shared it with Wilmar. We sat for a moment and then I found it in me to tell the rest.

"Mom died the day after she tried to call Child Protective Services to come and get me. She'd had a long conversation with me before, staring intensely at me and holding my wrist as tight as she could and telling me that some nice people would be by to take care of me and it was really important that I listen to them and do what they said. But when she called them, she couldn't get through, and the website didn't work either. She kept trying and trying, getting weaker and weaker, and then she started crying. I stroked her hair and held her until she fell asleep.

"But she never woke up." I'd told this story before, generally after a couple of drinks with someone I was having a serious relationship with. It never got easier. It wasn't easy then. Wilmar put his hand on my shoulder and left it there.

"You okay?"

I drew a shuddering breath, nodded, let it out. "I couldn't get her out of the bed. I was only eight. My dad woke up but he wasn't lucid, hadn't been in a long time. I got him water and spooned it into his mouth, the way Mom had, held his hand, tried not to look at my mom's body under the sheets next to him.

"He died the next night."

The geese took off. Where were they going? Who fucking cared? Stupid geese.

"I put some food in my little backpack and left the house and started walking, holding my baby blanket. I hadn't slept with it in years, but now I had a death grip on it. I tried walking to the park we used to go and play in, but I kept getting lost, and then I realized that the bad-smelling place with the tall wooden hoardings around it was the park. It was full of garbage now. I pissed against the boards and used some hand sanitizer the way Mom had always told me to and then ate some chips out of my bag and started walking.

"I walked and walked. So many houses were dark. The piles of garbage on the curbs were so high. Finally I needed to take a shit, and I just couldn't bring myself to do it by the road, so I worked up some nerve and rang a doorbell for a house where the lights were on.

"The woman who answered it can't have been much older than high-school age. She was the oldest daughter of the family and her parents were sick, too, but not as bad as mine had been. She was looking after them and when I asked her if I could please use her toilet, she asked me what was going on and I told her and she brought me in.

"She fed me and cleaned me up and kept calling Child Protective Services while I watched a screen and tried to stay quiet. The house smelled weird, that shit smell that was everywhere, but also different laundry soap and different shampoo and different spices in the food. They were from Egypt, had come out for the oil patch and stayed, and the mom would call downstairs in Arabic for the daughter whenever she needed something. Meanwhile, the daughter kept trying to get someone to come and take me away.

"Two days later, they came and got me. I knew my address and I gave it to them and they promised me they'd do something about it, and then I saw a social worker, and for the life of me I couldn't remember my home address even though my mom and dad had made me memorize it and got me to say it aloud every morning at breakfast. They put me in a group home, I guess, for three or four days. There were so many other kids there, always coming and going, some of them fighting all the time, or crying, or hiding and being quiet. One morning, I woke up holding my baby blanket, smelling it, and I could remember my address, so I gave it to someone there and then a lot of time passed and then someone came to get me and tell me I was going to live with my grandfather in California.

"I barely knew Gramps, only videoed with him at Christmas and sometimes on his or my birthday, and from how my parents had talked about him, I knew I wasn't supposed to like him very much. But I was numb from everything that had happened, and I knew all these stories from my dad's life growing up here, and I just—" Suddenly I was crying again, so hard I couldn't breathe for a moment, and Wilmar gave me a hard hug and stroked my hair. I heard someone come near and murmur something to him, heard him tell them no, it was okay, and eventually my breath came back.

"God," I said.

"You can stop," he said.

"No," I said. I tried my one-hit. It was empty. "No. I just wanted to get back to normal. The whole time I was in the home, the enormity of being an orphan just kept punching me in the face. I'd be eating or playing or watching a screen and all of a sudden I'd realize that I was all alone, like that scary feeling of getting separated from your parents in a crowd and not being able to find them, except I knew I could *never* find them. Coming here, to Gramps . . . it meant that I'd stop being an orphan. I'd have a family again. I wouldn't be an eight-year-old, alone in the world . . . forever.

"It wasn't ever going to be easy. I'd seen so much death, gone through so much a kid should never go through. Anyone who inherited me would have had a hard job. But Gramps . . ." God I wanted that beer. "It was not the kind of thing Gramps was good at. If it hadn't been for my social workers here, I think I might have just disappeared. Either run away or disappeared inside myself. Maybe ended up in an institution."

He put his arm around my shoulder and gave me a long squeeze. "Thanks for telling me that story, Brooks. I'm honored you shared it with me." His voice was soft, caring, and sincere. Everything Gramps never was. That was how I remembered my dad's voice, when I could even recall it. I almost never thought about my parents then, except for missing them so hard that it made me want to pinch myself.

"Thanks, man." The geese came back. Where had they gone to? What did they want here? The world was full of people, coming and going, every one of them the center of their own story, each a walk-on for other people's stories. What had happened to that girl who took care of me after my parents died? Did she ever think of me? How long had it been since I'd last thought of her?

"Ana Lucía came by before, when you were, you know. I think she wants to apologize. If you don't want to talk to her, that's okay."

"Really? No, that's okay." I really didn't want to talk to her but I didn't want her to feel bad. Wilmar aimed a two-tone whistle down the riverbank and I realized that she was sitting a couple of hundred yards away. She walked over to us slowly, radiating worry.

"Brooks, I'm sorry," she said. "Milena told me a little about your, uh, parents. I didn't know. I made a bunch of stupid assumptions and I shouldn't have." She was agonized, her big brown eyes brimming with tears, her wide mouth bracketed with deep lines. Seeing her like that, radiating sorrow, made my own tears come back up. I blinked them back.

"Thank you for that," I said, and let her hug me. She smelled of sweat and spice and beer. I wanted a beer so bad.

"I brought you a beer," she said, and fished a pouch out of her back pocket, then found another one for Wilmar.

"What about you?"

"I've had enough," she said.

"You can share mine," I said. I snapped the corner off mine and slurped at it as it foamed over, then passed it to her.

We walked home slowly, the sun setting over our left shoulders, geese flying overhead in formation.

"Two days until the big arrival," I said, as we turned my corner.

"Which means that we've got one day to see the Flotilla before everything kicks off," she said.

I snorted, but she showed me a screen. "I got tickets. Tomorrow. Soft opening. Got an extra. You wanna be my plus-one?"

Wilmar looked from her to me and back, and I knew there was no way I could say no without making her think I was angry about what she'd said to me before.

"I'd like that, thanks," I said, and I may have even been believable.

We booked a minibus to the Port of Long Beach for the next day, meeting it on the corner at 5 a.m. There were a few old guys in Maga hats already on it, and as we crossed the city, we picked up more people, mostly old white dudes, but also some women, some brown and Black people, some people our age. By the time we reached the port, the bus was full and the AC was laboring, and the conversation had grown to a roar, half the bus talking about the Flotilla's big moonshot projects and whether they'd go through with the big geoengineering ones, and, if they did, whether the various militaries that had threatened to blow them out of the water would make good on their threats. The other half were talking about *Those Who Tread the Kine* and how it had changed their life. Ana Lucía was enjoying every second of it. I felt like I was definitely in the wrong place.

We pulled up to the port and were met by good-looking young people in hi-viz VOLUNTEER vests and little nautical hats. They had coolers of iced-coffee cans and bottles of water and they passed them around. The disposable packaging was weird and *durable*— I was used to disposable pouches and bottles that were designed to turn back into raw materials when you were done with them, things you had to be a little careful of because they weren't made of plastics or metals that would last for decades or centuries. These were single-use products that were built to last. They felt so damn weird.

Ana Lucía chugged two coffees and the young VOLUNTEER guy in the sailor hat put her cans in a big white plastic bucket. We were herded into groups of fifty and sent to jetties where sleek hydrofoils bobbed gently in the swell. I noticed that the one we were bound for was called the *Moral Hazard* and was flying the flag of Tuvalu, a flag I recognized only because I'd done a school project on the island nation when it was finally evacuated and its government dissolved.

We crowded into the hydrofoil's cabin, accepting a gift bag on the way in that turned out to contain our own sailor hat, a "smart drink" that advertised its "neurological enhancers," and a little earbead that would play back an audiobook of *Tread the Kine*, read by Theodore Sutton himself. Our fellow passengers were much like the people we'd ridden in the shuttle bus with: mostly old, white, and male, but with a smattering of browner, younger, more female people, many with that manic entrepreneur vibe of the kids I'd grown up with who were unhealthily into their lemonade stands.

While the crew untied us from the pier, a safety recording played over the PA telling us about life jackets and emergency exits, and as we set sail, the voice speeded up into a cartoonish, Mickey Mouse squeal that made a mockery of the whole process, and everyone laughed as it climbed the audio barbershop pole to an impossible squeak and then crescendoed into a hard-rock power chord and a drum fill that segued into some passable rock and roll with lyrics about the open seas and open markets. I snorted, but I got the feeling that I was the only one finding this funny.

The hydrofoil got up to speed pretty damned quick and soon we were skipping over the Pacific at what our captain assured us was 75 m.p.h., headed for the international water line where the Flotilla bobbed.

We all rushed forward to watch the Flotilla growing on the horizon. I knew that the idea had come from a twentieth-century science fiction novel—the plutes that ran the Flotilla *loved* that old futuristic shit—but I hadn't quite appreciated just how *cinematic* it would be as it came into sight, the massive aircraft carrier flanked by a pair of cruise ships, surrounded by superyachts, themselves fringed with fast-moving cigarette boats, jet skis, Cyclones, and other interceptors bought surplus from the world's coast guards, flying flags from drowned island nations and, above them, the flag of the Flotilla, a golden statue of a kneeling man, supporting a glowing blockchain logo that radiated in all directions to the flag's edge.

As our hydrofoil neared one of the cruise ships, the little boats got closer to us, close enough that we could see their grinning pilots and passengers. Some saluted us with boat drinks or beer cans, while some just sunned themselves in little bathing suits. We cut engines and puttered toward the cruise ship—the *Laffer Curve*—alongside a party boat where a DJ spun from an open deck and crowds of people danced to throbbing music. The dancers wore outlandish outfits—long fur coats and sunglasses, glittering jackets cut like military uniforms, kigurumi with strategic cutouts that revealed tanned skin—and were mostly older white men with much younger, much browner women. Someone barfed over the railing as we came to beside the *Laffer Curve* and the hands began to lower the ramps that would let us board.

The inside of the *Laffer Curve* smelled like a casino and was aggressively air-conditioned. A young Asian man handed us hurricane glasses of rum punch and ice and sun visors with the Flotilla logo on the bills. Ana Lucía laughed and chugged half her drink before putting her hat on. I drank mine—it was very good and very cold—and put on my own hat.

It looked exactly like a movie cruise ship, immaculately staged. The large, gilt-edged screens over the elevator banks scrolled a grid of events, and our own screens buzzed as we received our own copies of the schedule, with a flurry of permission requests to mine our data to "personalize" the options. I was pleased to see that Ana Lucía swiped these away as quickly as I did, and we wandered into a large, shop-lined concourse to find a bench where we could page through the schedules manually.

Even though it was only a soft opening, the activities available that day were dizzying, from scuba diving to cooking classes, games and workshops for kids, but the schedule leaned heavily on panels, seminars, and "keynotes" along with tons of "affinity group spaces," a phrase I found more than a little disorienting, since I associated it with my own friends back in Burbank.

We got fed twice in the fifteen minutes we took deliberating over the schedule: first by a waiter with cod sushi hand rolls in ice-cream holders, then by a robot that 3D-printed us ice-cream sculptures on sticks that vaguely resembled our own heads. They weren't great likenesses, but they didn't have to be—not only were they fun to eat but everyone who witnessed the bot's routine lined up to get more, following it when it rolled farther down the concourse, acting as an automated crowd-management system.

"Smart," I said.

Ana Lucía elbowed me. "See, these guys aren't idiots. They've got some weird ideas, but they're not just plutes. Most plutes ended up onshore, got their money taxed away under Uwayni. These are the smart plutes, the ones who figured out how to hang on to it. They're survivors. Maybe the old system wasn't merito-cratic, but this one sure is." Her eyes were shining, reflecting the high buff of the concourse's marble floor.

Listening to her was infuriating and a little scary. Most of the time, Ana Lucía was this tireless organizer for justice and com-munity, and then some of the time, it was like she was channeling Gramps and his buddies. How could she believe both of those things at the same time? I couldn't make any sense of it.

I changed the subject back to the schedule and we whittled down the day to some fun activities—jet-skiing, an m-pop dance party on a superyacht, a 3D-printed caviar buffet—and one big serious one, the Calexit Affinity Group welcome seminar.

"Gotta warn you," Ana Lucía said as she finished off her cone, "depending on how that one goes I might stick around and blow everything else off."

Jet-skiing was first, and after a terrifyingly short orientation from a freckled teenaged girl with an adorable New Zealand ac-cent, I was buzzing around the Flotilla with Ana Lucía. We took a close-up look at the vertical gardens suspended from the sides of the cruise ships and carrier, watched the robots crawl the beds, got misted by the hydration system that ran off a bunch of so-lar desalinators that dangled long straws into the ocean. Then we shadowed a utility crew that was bringing down one of the massive solar kites, which provided both power and motive force as it sailed along in the troposphere. We dialed our screens in to the commentary channel and listened to the insane specs on the kite, half a mile long, supplying a gigawatt an hour at peak performance, each number more implausible than the last, until the actual kite splashed down and we saw it blot out the sun be-fore it floated like a leaf in a breeze to the sea. It was swarmed by utility boats crewed by sure-moving engineers in wet gear who walked across its surface like it was a soft pontoon bridge, doing impossible-to-grasp annual maintenance chores.

It occurred to me that whether or not this was an annual work project, it was also a showpiece. They were going to be parked off the LA shore for a week, and they would spend that week ferrying locals out to their floating playground, and the maintenance schedule meant that everyone who came by for a visit would get a good old eyeful of this marvel of engineering.

Back on the ship, we got coconut water with royal jelly from the ship's hives. Ana Lucía made a face when the handsome Nigerian man in ship's whites offered it to her and then whispered, "Royal jelly? What's next, Reiki? Alkaline water? Crystal healing?" But then she drank a sip from her plastic straw, and her eyes widened. "Oh my God that's delicious." I tried mine and concurred.

The cruise ship was filling up and we were getting close to our affinity group meeting, which was being held on the deck of the aircraft carrier, so we waited for an elevator and rode to the ship's topmost deck, then lined up to cross the suspension bridge that linked the two vessels. As we made our way across, I looked down and saw several more bridges that must have been for authorized personnel, as well as some giant, flexing springlike coils that kept the two ships linked as they bobbed up and down.

The carrier was ex-Indian and had been rechristened *Tanstaafl* by its new owners. They had leaned into the surreal pleasure of turning a giant military vessel into a pleasure cruiser, painting the hull and exterior structure with modernist dazzle, angular shapes that bent the eye, and then coloring it all with bright neons, oranges and pinks and blues and greens. The private aircraft that dotted the deck—choppers and small planes, along with a couple of ex-military jets—were all iridescent, like flying insects come to rest on a cartoon beach.

The affinity group meetings were all being held on the top

deck in temporary pop-up structures made out of tough, reflective quilted fabric with large, screened-in windows. We followed the numbered paths on the deck until we found the Calexit meeting, which was in the biggest of these silvery domes.

We arrived with ten minutes to spare and found a crowd around the entrance, holding up their screens and tuning them in to the spillover sound from the main room.

"Fuck this," Ana Lucía said, and began to excuse-me her way through the crowd, ignoring the stink eye she got. I followed in her wake, muttering apologies, through the spillover and into the dome. Inside there were rows of folding chairs, and of course there were plenty of empty seats, singles trapped between other singles and pairs. Ana Lucía opened the door flap and hollered, "People, there are plenty of seats in here," and then asked-told a florid man in an aloha shirt to shove over one seat so there'd be room for the two of us to sit.

This triggered a shamefaced shuffling-up and an ingress of people from the outdoors, and I could feel all the eyes on us. This was what it must mean to be an "organizer"—the ability to make other people feel uncomfortable in the service of your goals.

More helpers in ship's whites came around and unzipped some windows and zipped up other windows until we had a good cross breeze, and then the first speaker came out. She was a slender, beautiful older woman, wearing a bias-cut, sleeveless hooded blouse that showed off her toned arms. Her hair was silver-white, cut in an angled bob with blunt bangs, and she had great crow's-feet that made her look like she was smiling even when she wasn't. She had a little mic on her cheek done up to glitter like an emerald, and when she tapped it to life, it sparkled and cast a thousand dots of green light on every surface. The effect silenced the crowd in an instant and she smiled, and now her crow's-feet made her look like she was beaming.

"Hello, California!" She held out her arms in an all-encompassing gesture. "It's *so* good to be home!

"My name's Derrida Stephenson, and I was born and raised in the Golden State. Even though I haven't set foot on it for a decade, it's my home. It'll always be my home. I *love* this place."

People giggled at this, but she wasn't kidding. "Come on, guys, do better than that. I *love* this place. Don't you love it? Birthplace of aerospace and computing, cradle of art and culture and music, a beautiful and fertile and wealthy place? A place of opportunity? Come on, let's hear it for California!" And we cheered, clapped, even stomped, though the hard steel of the deck beneath the industrial rug dampened the sound and was hard on the ankles and knees.

"*That's better!*" She had a great laugh. "Thank you for that. Hey, I hope all of you have had a chance to tour the Flotilla, and if you haven't, I hope you'll take the chance. If there's one thing this place reminds me of, it's California—a California of the seas, a place that has attracted the most beautiful, brilliant people in the world around a shared vision of self-determination, free association, and, above all, *ambition*.

"Boy, isn't that what we need about now? With all that's going on in the world? There are parts of India—places people lived comfortably for millennia, were still living in at the start of this century—where an unprotected human body cannot survive for more than a few hours at a time. There're places in Central America that are headed for the same fate. This crisis needs bold people and big ideas, not because it's fun to do big, bold things—" She stopped and beamed at us. "Though of course, it's *really fun* to do big, bold things!" We laughed. She had good timing, and so much raw charisma.

"The crisis needs big, bold people and ideas because *people are dying.* And lots more are going to die.

"So let's talk big, bold ideas. It's no secret that we're working on some ambitious plans to help put this old world of ours back in good working order." Nervous chuckles. China had threatened to literally nuke the Flotilla if it went ahead with either its upper-atmospheric or oceanic geoengineering plans. Uwayni had been a little more restrained when she was President, and after her, Hart—that centrist asshole—had made some noise about "responsible collaboration" with the Flotilla's plans. Bennett—well, who knew what Bennett was thinking. She'd say one thing one day and something else the next, depending on what part of the weird coalition of white nationalists, Christian fundamentalists, conspiracists, goldbugs, blockchainers, preppers, White Horse Prophecy doomsdayers, sovereign citizens, and deplorables that had brought her to power she needed to court. As far as anyone could tell, Bennett's only real principle was that she, Rosetta Bennett, should remain President for at least two terms, erasing as much of Uwayni's legacy as possible during that time.

Stephenson triggered a projector and she became a screen for a projection-mapped image of a spacesuit that covered her from collar to knees, tracking her in real time as she moved. The spill-over light made her face radiate like a flaring satellite catching the sun. She held up her muscular arms and they writhed with space launches.

"We're not stopping there, though. Humanity needs a plan B. Any organism that runs out of room to grow starts to shrink. We've got a *lot* of room to grow, up there." She rolled her eyes up, looking even more saintly. "Guys, you will *go to the Moon*. You will go to *the planets*. You will go to *the stars*." Her outfit flared with incredibly bright light that shook at the edges, turning into the flame from a rocket booster. It dimmed slowly and she stood serene and silent as it did. Somewhere in the room, subwoofers were rumbling the sound of rocket engines thrusting out of the gravity well.

Look, I know space is bullshit. I know there's no plan B. But that was an amazing presentation. Stephenson was really good at what she did. She beamed at us.

"How many of you have heard of 16 Psyche?" There was some knowledgeable chuckling, a few whispers. I had no idea what she was talking about. "16 Psyche is only two hundred and seventy million miles from us right now. That might seem like a long way off, but 16 Psyche's payload of nickel and steel is worth a hundred quadrillion dollars. That's quadrillion with a *q*.

"California has attracted dreamers for centuries, from the forty-niners who came for gold to the techies who flocked here in search of IPOs. You guys, I'm here to tell you that no one has claimed California's true jackpot. From the JPL and Lockheed spinouts down here to the code monkeys upstate, this is the state that could make it happen."

A young woman in ship's whites brought her a tall stool and she dragged it into the middle of the stage and climbed up on it. The young woman handed her an aerogel bottle of water, and she drained it and balled it up so small it seemed to disappear, then tossed it over her shoulder. It moved as slowly as a dust mote in a sunbeam. We watched transfixed. Even me.

"Okay, enough showmanship. How are we going to make it happen, huh? Save the planet, conquer the universe, yadda yadda yadda—what're the actionable, deliverable, meaningful steps that we can take to get our house in order?"

She held up her hand, and an older woman in ship's whites lobbed her another aerogel water bottle, which she caught one-handed and drained, balling it up and batting it over the heads of the crowd.

"Step one, we *gotta* put our house in order. Once upon a time, California was the Golden State, the best place in the world to do business. Today, you can't take a shit without getting an environmental impact assessment. Many of the kinds of people you'd want to hire to get on with this stuff wouldn't dream of living here, thanks to taxes and regulation, and the kind of people the state *does* attract are the kinds of people who benefit from taxes and regulations—"

At this point, I hit my camera and started livestreaming. I can't say why, exactly, except that I'd heard variations on this speech from Gramps and his pals and I had a good idea where it was heading.

"—the kinds of people who take, not make. And this isn't a race thing. I mean, it's true that in California, this historically breaks down on race lines, but I'm here to tell you, the Flotilla is a global operation. We're putting unbanked people on-chain all around the world, starting businesses, accessing capital, creating jobs. This isn't a race thing. It's an *incentives* thing.

"Incentives matter, right? Set up the rules so that anyone who tries to make a dent in the world gets hit with a million rules and regulations, lawsuits about what they can do, who they can hire, who they can fire . . . And if they do manage to make it work, half of it gets taken away in taxes? Who's gonna start a business under those conditions?

"And then, and *then* you set up a system where if you *don't* get a real job, you get paid anyway? Paid for tinkering in the margins with unscalable, fiddling, piddling, useless 'green jobs' that let you feel like you're making a difference even though none of it's gonna make a damned bit of difference in the long run? And you don't even have to do *that* if you don't want to, you can just sit on your fat ass and pretend you've attained fully automated luxury gay space communism.

"I mean no wonder everyone who feels like they could make a difference got the fuck out of Dodge, and so many who stayed behind are takers, people whose learned helplessness means they're destined to enact and reenact the multigenerational pattern of parasitism and self-defeat?

"It can't go on. You *know* it can't go on. You know that there's a reckoning going to come. It doesn't have to be bad news. California may be a little worse for wear, a little scratched and dented, but there's still a tiger in her tank, guys. There's still gold in them thar hills. *California's still got it.*

"And let's be honest, we *all* know exactly what we need to do to make this happen. It's why you're here. We have to take California back. We need to take control of our borders—" Cheers.

"We need to kick out the takers who came to California after they used up their own land and have come to use up *ours*." Loud cheers.

"We need to get the fiscal house in order. If we don't earn it, we can't spend it. California's been dropping helicopter money on multigenerational families of lazy, self-pitying losers for so long we've forgotten that it can be any other way. The way to put Californians to work is to invite in the best people in the world and let them do their thing. California has created billions of jobs, and it could create more if we could just get the state off the backs of the people."

I couldn't help it, I turned to Ana Lucía—who was watching with shining eyes—and whispered, "Dude, they're talking about the Jobs Guarantee—they're talking about me."

She shushed me, though.

"Someone needs to remind California that there's no such thing as government money—"

"What the fuck?" I whispered to Ana Lucía, and got an elbow.

"There's only the money that the government taxes away from the people. Every dollar we spend on 'programs'—" Her finger quotes were razor sharp, sarcasm dripping, like a pidgin ASL she'd developed all on her own. "—is a dollar we take away from people who could be creating *jobs*."

I snorted loud enough that Ana Lucía said "*Be quiet*" in a voice loud enough to carry to the stage.

Stephenson broke off and smiled sweetly at us. "Something you want to share with the rest of the class?"

"Sorry," Ana Lucía called.

"No problem," she said, and gave us a little sarcastic namaste.

"Uh," I said, because my mouth had decided to speak without asking my brain.

For a brief instant, her face showed how irritated she was; then that dazzling smile was back. "Yes?"

"I just—"

"Questions at the end, if you don't mind. Unless it's urgent."

"No, I just—"

"Thank you." She pointedly looked away from us. Everyone else in the room was staring at us, except for the people who couldn't see us and were trying to get a look, craning over the heads of others. "I want you to think for a moment about what a sovereign California could do, once it seized control over its destiny: establish a new, anti-inflationary currency based on distributed consensus, and use that currency to enable free association with others around the world to realize dreams big and small.

"Do a top-to-bottom review of the regulatory cruft that has piled up over the decades. Create charter cities, laboratories of democracy that could take the best of what we've learned from other charters around the world and add to that store of best practices, and create our own. You *know* we'll create our own, don't you? This is *California,* people, we innovate six new ways to do things before breakfast! Every day! Then we wake up the next day and we do it again!"

It got the laugh she was looking for and she was definitely back on her game, soaring as though we hadn't interrupted her. I was getting pocket-buzzes as more people joined my stream and told their friends about it. I didn't stream often, and I never got that big an audience, but after my rooftop encounter with Mike Kennedy I'd ended up on a lot of people's watch lists and the fact that I streamed so infrequently meant that I never got taken off again.

"And boy does this state need some innovative thinking. I mean, just look at what we're doing with our coastal cities, walking away from them, rebuilding them inland. These are the most beautiful cities in the country, beach towns, some of them two hundred and fifty years old, a quarter of a millennium. Cities with Spanish missions that withstood quakes and fires, but they're being torn apart by de-growth greenies who've given up on seawalls, geoengineering, and shore stabilization, surrendering before the battle is joined without firing a single shot.

"We need a different program: Take control of California.

Take control of its borders. Take control of its money. Orient the economy and the priorities around the people who do stuff, not the people who take stuff. Fix our coasts. Fix our forests. Fix our water so we can fix our farms. Do better. Save the state. Save the planet. Save the human race. Leave the planet.

"That's it. Just that." She gave us a gigawatt of smile, spread out her hands. "Any questions?"

My arm had joined my mouth in its mutiny from my brain, and it shot straight up in the air, before anyone else had a chance. What can I say? White guys have a *lot* of questions. Even from my peripheral vision, I could tell that Ana Lucía was glaring at me.

"Hi there," she said, pointing at me. Before I could respond, she raised a finger. "Ground rule, folks, questions, not statements. A question is a short sentence that goes up at the end. *Technically* a long rambling statement followed by 'what do you think of that?' is a question, but it's not a good one." Turning back to me: "With that out of the way, go."

I was suddenly shy, but thankfully my mutinous mouth and hand had cooked up a plan and didn't need help from me. "Thanks. That was a lot. I guess, I just wanted to ask, uh, about inflation?"

"What about it?"

"Oh, sorry," I said. "Didn't want to exceed my sentence limit."

I got a chuckle that time. She gave me a closed-lip grin that clicked off and on like a light switch. "Take a couple more."

"The thing is, we've had more than a decade where we just treated all that stuff you said about budgets as bullshit and as far as I can see, we're doing pretty damned great. We've put everyone who wants a job to work, and the work they're doing makes the people around them happy by taking care of them, and there hasn't been any inflation. So, uh, what do you think of that?"

I got a laugh. It felt good.

"Dude, be serious," she said, and started looking around for another question.

"That's your answer?" I must have said it louder than I intended, because her attention snapped back to me and I caught another lightning-quick flash of rage before she masked up with something more condescending.

"Sir, I don't know what fantasyland you live in, but since the days of Isaac Newton we've been damned certain that what goes up must come down. You can't keep putting make-work projects on the national credit card forever and expect that the bill will never come due."

"Do I get to answer?" I said. Burroughs High has a really good drama department, it's famous for it—we're the *Glee* school! and the *Glee Rebooted* school!—and I can project. It's all in the diaphragm.

"Sure, why not." The smile was all razors now.

"We don't have a national credit card. We have a treasury. It makes dollars by typing them into a spreadsheet. Countries aren't households."

She fired back instantly. "And who owns that debt? China? Venezuela? Nigeria? What happens if they decide to call it in?"

"Uh, China can only buy our debt if we send them dollars. China doesn't have any dollars of its own. It can only get dollars that we give them. So they're using our dollars to buy our debt? And maybe they'll ask us for more dollars? So we could just type some more zeroes into the spreadsheet and—"

"Which is why the dollar is so goddamned *dangerous*. *Thank you,* kind sir, for giving us a little Econ 101. If you let politicians buy their way to glory with the Treasury's printing press, they will, and then the rest of us will get stuck with the bill. Which is why we put our money on-chain, like civilized people, so that economic illiterates and Neanderthals who learned their econ from dank Black Bloc memes can't just make money whenever they feel like it."

"Sounds like you're saying that in your system, if we need money to help sick people, or flooded cities, or people who lose their houses to fire or whatever, we're screwed?"

People were muttering, telling me to shut up, but I was hot, too hot to give a shit about the faces Ana Lucía was pulling in my peripheral vision as she inched farther and farther from me. My pocket-buzzes were crazy, which just egged me on.

A tall woman with a really cool updo—in ship's whites, naturally—scurried (seriously, like a squirrel or something, in that way that tall people who are embarrassed about their heights sometimes do) over to Stephenson and leaned down to whisper in her ear. Stephenson tapped her cheek jewel to mute and listened intently, then nodded. Her face went grim.

"You do not have my permission to livestream this presentation," she said, directly to me.

The sensation I felt then was like falling and falling—stomach-dropping, face-draining, a wind-rush of blood in my ears that made it hard to hear. Ana Lucía had recoiled from me and was staring at me in horror. People around me were jeering angrily. How had they known? Duh. They paid media-monitoring services, I'm sure, and then it was a simple matter of triangulating the camera angle. Or maybe they just got my name off the feed and looked up what I looked like.

It didn't matter. Two big guys—ship's whites, but binding and bulging around their shoulders and necks and tree-trunk thighs—were cutting through the crowd, and the audience was getting out of their way, some of them shouting encouragement, and Ana Lucía stood up and got out of their way, too.

"Hey!" I shouted, as each of them grabbed an arm. "Is this what you call free debate? What have you got to hide, huh? Aren't you proud of what you have to say?"

She was coldly amused. "You have the right to free speech where you live. This is my stage and I say who talks and who doesn't. You're a guest in my house, you behaved rudely, and now you're being asked to leave."

The guys lifted me so my feet dangled. "You call this liberty?" I shouted, a thing I'd wanted to say so often to Gramps's friends but never had. It was all coming up now. "You call yourself an American? You call this respect for the Constitution?"

I was being bum-rushed now, carried backward by the goons through the crowd, showered with abuse. Someone spat on me. It landed on my forehead.

"Dude," Stephenson said. "This isn't America. This is international waters. You're lucky we don't tie an anchor to your ankles and toss you overboard." Judging from the cheers she got, she wasn't the only one who liked that idea.

Right up to the moment they stuffed me, zipcuffed at the ankles and wrists, into a life-jacket closet on the hydrofoil, I was half convinced that I was going to sleep with the fishies. But then we pushed off. Ten minutes into the trip, someone opened the door: a Black woman, in her twenties, holding a pair of snips.

"We're about to enter U.S. waters so I'm going to cut you loose. You gonna behave yourself?"

"Sure thing," I said. She snipped me loose and I went to mingle with the sparse passengers. Most people were spending the whole day, clearly. And why not? It was better than Disneyland.

I realized as we docked up that I didn't have any of the gimmies I'd been given through the day, but, as luck would have it, I got a parting gift bag as I exited the pier, filled with glossy, book-length brochures and my own copy of *Those Who Tread the Kine*.

The day the refugees arrived, Burbank threw a street party. We shut down Magnolia, the way we always do for big celebrations, lining it with kiosks and food trucks from Buena Vista to North Hollywood Way, hanging banners from the light poles, every store window decorated with hand-lettered signs.

The local middle schools and elementary schools had devoted the month's PE classes to long-distance walking and they'd arranged to meet the walkers on Glenoaks—middle schoolers picking them up from all the way in Pacoima, while the little kids walked in from the town line, past the airport. We got a steady stream of social updates from the kids all that morning, and once they turned onto North Hollywood Way a buzz spread up and down the street. A fleet of hobbyist blimps took off from the airport as they passed it, dangling long welcome banners with murals the high-school kids at Burroughs and Burbank High had painted onto massive sheets of perforated mylar that was weighted at the bottom.

When they turned onto Magnolia, the Burroughs band started playing, and fifty people opened their coolers and started handing out empanadas to the new arrivals, kids and refugees, and the misters overhead went into overdrive, bathing us in cool water. The band played "California, Here I Come" and "California Dreamin'" and the conductor timed it perfectly so that as they finished the second tune, they struck up "I Love L.A.," in synchrony with the Burbank High band that swung around the corner from the parking lot behind Porto's, brass bells glinting high in the air as they marched into the crowd, through it, dancing with the arrivals. It was as wonderful a celebration as you could have asked for and it got even better when some of the refus pulled out their own instruments—a couple of ukes, a no-fooling guitarrón the size of a cello, harmonicas and bongos—and started jamming.

I caught Ana Lucía's eye. We hadn't spoken when she got back from the Flotilla the night before, and we'd avoided each other all that day. But as she swung from one friend to the next, laughing and dancing and hugging, she and I made eye contact across the crowd and she shook her head at me, then laughed again, then beckoned me over, and before I knew it, I was in the dance too, being swung around by little kids and old ladies and teens and even some people my own age.

Once the party settled down, it spread out down Magnolia, so all the newcomers got a chance to check in with the People's Airbnb, get a library card, sign their kids up for the schools, get in the Jobs Guarantee database, and have a chance to pose for a pic with one of Burbank's many, many shiny red fire trucks, a remnant of the Lockheed Martin days, when the town was one giant fuel depot and it made sense to have a zillion fire stations.

Walking down the road, grinning like a fool, I got roped into doing a run as a guide, bringing kids and their parents who'd just picked up bathing suits for the short walk down California to the Verdugo Aquatic Facility, where they'd opened up the activity pool with its water slides and fountains. I led a column of five families and learned that Hector was a solar technician and that Laura was a medical administrator and that Hector Jr. really, really liked sharks, specifically lemon sharks, which turned out to be really cool.

I dropped them off at the pool entrance and collected some handshakes and admired Hector Jr.'s screen to watch a lemon shark live birth, which was, you know, *wow*.

When I got back up to the corner of Magnolia and California, I stopped dead. A bunch of the Maga Club guys had a table set up and were standing around, looking stiff and out of place, but as I got closer, I saw that they were handing out Burbank Chamber of Commerce paper fans and smiling at the newcomers who came up to get them. I guess they couldn't just stay home when something like this was going on, and picketing it or burning a cross or whatever would just make them look like assholes. Instead, they could hand out fans covered in slogans written by aggrieved would-be plutes and temporarily embarrassed billionaires and seem like good guys doing good stuff. I wondered if Gramps would have joined them, and decided he'd have shown his face, then gone straight home and drunk beers and complained about the whole situation until bedtime.

I went the other way, giving them a wide berth, and someone tapped me on the shoulder. I turned around and it was Ana Lucía, smiling, holding out a foil-wrapped empanada.

"It's pumpkin," she said. "They're really good."

I took it and bit in: "Oh my God, they're *really* good."

"Right?"

And just like that, all the weirdness from the day before was gone. We walked down Magnolia and turned off onto Avon and sat down on one of the benches that had been put in the curb lane, in the shade of a big, spreading camphor tree.

"So, yesterday," I said.

"That was *crazy*," she said. "I thought they were going to throw you overboard."

"Me too!" We both laughed and I told her about the trip home, being locked in the closet and then getting a gift bag.

"Those people," she said, and shook her head. "You should have heard that lady after you left. She was like, 'An independent California wouldn't be alone—it would be part of a community of sovereign nations devoted to personal liberty and personal responsibility'—and then she listed a bunch and they were all either underwater islands that only existed as flags these days, or poor-as-fuck tiny countries in Asia and Africa that they provide all the banking and governance for with their own private side-chains. It was gross."

"Wow," I said. "So, uh, I'm sorry but I kinda thought you were into it? Now it sounds like you're not?"

"I'm not into *those* guys. Just because I want money and governance out of the hands of people who suck up to rich people, it doesn't mean that I just want them in the hands of rich people! I want something that works for people like me, not people like them."

I grinned. "And you think they don't want something that works for people like you?"

She blew a raspberry. "Think it? I know it. Shit you shoulda heard that crazy white lady after you got eighty-sixed. She was like, 'Let's talk about the Green New Deal' and all the old guys in there started booing, but she held her hands up and made them go silent and said, 'No, no, no, you've got it wrong. Giving people a job, that's good sense, especially if it's work that bootstraps new ventures, clickwork and gigwork, solves all the union problems and all, just underwrite them as a labor commons for all the brilliant ideas you can come up with.'"

"Jesus! Defi for chain gangs!"

"Oh, they *ate that up*. And it got worse."

"I refuse to believe it," I said. It was nice to be on the same side as her again.

"Believe brother. 'We love the Green New Deal,' she said, 'but you have to apply common sense. Like the San Joaquin Valley? Its aquifers have been pumped so dry that it's thirty feet lower than it was a century ago! The San Joaquin Valley's not coming back. We can use it for stuff, sure, like maybe automated manufacturing facilities of the kind you wouldn't want within four hundred miles of a populated area. But subsidizing people to *live* there? Sending them water from the Colorado River? That's just nuts. It's like McMurdo Station without the science!'"

"McMurdo?"

"Antarctica," she said. "I had to look it up."

"Wow. Just . . . wow."

"Yeah. That's her vision of a utopia: people like me in indentured servitude, my home turned into a sacrifice zone that's made permanently uninhabitable by any living thing for a thousand years. So fuck her sideways with a brick."

"Hall-ay-loo," I said. "You're good people, Ana Lucía."

She tore open a pouch of beer and passed it to me, then took it back and swigged. "You too, Brooks." She drank and belched. "Hey, uh, look. I'm sorry I didn't stand up for you yesterday. When they dragged you out. That was weak. I just froze up."

"Aw, it's okay. Freezing up is natural, something like that happens. It was not exactly business as usual."

"No, it's not okay. I'm supposed to be a community organizer. I'm supposed to run toward danger. The way you did, the other night. Freezing up is a luxury for civilians."

"Don't beat yourself up. I accept your apology, if that's what it takes. What I did the other night, it wasn't because I was brave, it was because I was furious, and to be honest, it was mostly on my own behalf. Those asshole pals of my grandfather's, acting like I owe them something, like they're the guardians of Gramps's memory, like they're the guardians of fucking *Burbank* and they have the right to decide its future. I'm done with it. So done."

"Well, that was also a good reason to run towards the danger, Brooks. Thank you."

"Thank you, too. It's been good to get to know you. I'm really glad you and your friends are gonna be my neighbors."

"Me too. You're a great host, but I'm sure you're gonna be glad when we split tomorrow. It's gotta be great to be getting your house back."

"You guys were great houseguests," I said, but even as I said it, my brain was going *yippee!* at the thought of the miniature refugee camp in my backyard being dismantled. Some part of me was a selfish dick. Fine, I was Richard Palazzo's grandson, after all. I couldn't escape that feeling, but I didn't have to act on it.

The Burbank Housing Expansion Project kickoff meeting was held in the big function room at the Buena Vista library. I sat through a presentation from a nice old guy from the city manager's office, explaining that the council had green-lighted three new high-rise buildings on the Burbank Boulevard corridor, right near where the light-rail was going in, and that anyone who sold their land to the project for additional high-density housing would get preference for it, and preferential rates. The way he explained it, it was a pretty sweet deal: I could sell 'em Gramps's house, get market rates for it, then get a cool, well-built co-op unit in a high-rise with all kinds of cool amenities supercheap. I'd be making way for three or four refugee families to live in a low-rise on my lot, I'd get a place to live, and I'd have tons of cash left over.

Oh, Burbank. Always finding a way to do well by doing good.

And then came the Q&A. After a couple of dudes asked rambling questions, a woman stood up. She was Asian, tanned, with broad, strong shoulders, wearing a sort of cut-down, semi-military jacket and wide Thai fisherman's trousers. Her hair was glossy and anime short and prickly, sticking up and out in crazy, cute spikes.

"So, thanks for that, but I've only got one question. Why are we giving preference to Burbankers who own homes, when we're trying to house refugees who don't?"

Well, when you put it that way.

The guy from the city looked at her. Then everyone else did. I felt bad for her. She was supremely cool.

"Well, uh, we're trying to balance out the incentives here. We need infill, and the easiest way to get it is for people to sell us their plots for redevelopment. Deals like this—"

"Deals like this just make lucky people luckier and rich people richer. You don't need incentives. We've got a refugee crisis. Under federal law, you can just use eminent domain, scrape the houses to the foundation slab and get building."

"Well, that doesn't seem very fair—"

"No, that's totally fair. What's unfair is losing your whole town in the climate emergency. Being paid a fair price for your house that you only own because your great-grandfather paid a nickel for it in 1939 isn't fair? Come on."

"Well, that's an interesting perspective. You should come to a council meeting and raise it. I just work for the city manager, and we do what the council tells us to do."

That settled it. She stayed standing for just a few seconds longer than was comfortable for anyone (except, judging from her bearing, her) and then settled herself into her seat, shaking out a screen and tapping away at it. She typed fast and got an awesomely fierce look on her face while she did it—not rage-typing, but so focused. She also looked familiar, I realized, though, of course, most people in Burbank looked a *little* familiar. Maybe I went to school with her younger sibling or . . .

The meeting broke up and she gave the most desultory of applause. On the way out, I found myself next to her. She smiled at me.

Wow. That smile!

"Hi, uh." Smooth, Brooks. Very smooth.

"Hey there."

"So, I liked what you said in there. I mean, I hadn't even thought about it that way, but when you said it, I was like, oh yeah, of course. I mean on the one hand, it's nice to reward people who are being altruistic and making a sacrifice, but on the other hand, isn't it *more* altruistic to do it without a reward?"

"Yup, exactly. I mean, there are so many other ways to do this: needs-based placement, lottos, whatever. We're going to have to do something like that eventually—it's not like this'll be the last caravan of refus that head to Burbank. The way things are going, we could end up housing all of Santa Monica in a decade. These guys are still thinking about this as a problem to solve—not a new normal we have to adapt to."

"Holy shit. I never thought of that. Wow." I scraped up my courage. "I'm Brooks, by the way," and held out my hand.

"Phuong," she said.

Holy shit. "Petrakis?" I said.

"Uh, yeah." She looked surprised and not entirely pleasantly so.

"You were a senior at Burroughs my freshman year. I just graduated. Holy shit, you look totally different." She did—so much *wiser* and stronger, and sophisticated.

"Oh! Hey, that's funny. I guess I sorta remember you? I've been in London for the past two years. Blue Helmets. Working on the Thames Estuary Barrier as part of my engineering practicum. I haven't thought about Burroughs in so long. Is Hartounian still there?"

"Yeah! She's still totally badass. I just ran into her at a council meeting on Jobs Guarantee allocations, when we faced down the Maga Clubs."

"Wow. Good old Ms. H. Badass is right."

We'd reached the corner by now. I wished desperately for the courage to ask her to dinner, but I couldn't find it. Then *she* said, "Hey, have you eaten? I was gonna go to that new Ethiopian on Victory."

"There's an Ethiopian place on Victory?"

"Just opened."

"I *love* Ethiopian food." My heart was pounding and my mouth was watering. Then I thought about getting food all down my shirt while trying to impress this amazing, gorgeous, older woman, and then I remembered again how much I liked Ethiopian food. "Let's find bikes!"

We got a veggie platter and a fake-meat vegan platter and an extra basket of injera. The restaurant was almost empty, which made me sad, so I set a reminder to social it later and took pictures of the food when it arrived, and then set to work demolishing the platters. As always, there was more food than I could eat, and as always, I ate it all anyway. It's the injera, pancakes made from a grain called teff—so spongy and tangy, and the stuff that sits under the curries and absorbs all the sauce is just *the best,* and scooping it up with fresh injera and making an injera-stuffed in-jera roll is recursively delicious.

Phuong ate just as much as I did, making groaning, delicious-food noises and licking her fingers between tearing off more in-jera and going back in for more stew.

"I'm convinced this stuff is hydrophilic," she said, "like you eat it and it fits in your stomach, but then it absorbs all your stom-ach juices and swells up to ten times its size. Every time I go for Ethiopian, I swear I'm going to stop before I get full, and then—" She licked her fingers, gestured at the empty plate.

I looked around and took in the decor. There'd been a period in junior year when I'd been going down to Little Ethiopia three or four times a month, eating my way up and down Fairfax with a group of school friends that I'd cycle there with, taking the LA River Trail along I-5.

"This place is a little different from the other Ethiopian restaurants I've been to, but I can't figure out exactly what it is. It's been bugging me since we got here."

Phuong looked around. "You're right. I used to go to all these Ethiopian places in Kentish Town and Camden and there's something missing . . ." She stared around intently. "Now that you mention it, it's driving me crazy. What is it?"

I grabbed my screen and started tapping through pics of the restaurants on Fairfax. What was it? Then I snapped my fingers. "The pictures! There're no pictures of that guy, Haile Selassie."

"That's it!"

The server came by to take away our clean platter and we told her how much we liked the food and unwisely ordered

138 • cory doctorow

pistachio baklava sweets and coffee that we would have to find room for.

Phuong asked, "How come there are no pictures of Haile Selassie? I think this is the first Ethiopian restaurant I've ever eaten in that doesn't have them."

The waitress—whom I thought was probably the owner, too—a woman in her forties in a bright cotton print dress and a matching headscarf, got a complicated look on her face. When she spoke, I could tell she was choosing her words carefully, and that we'd said something that she wasn't very happy about.

"Oh, we are not Ethiopian, we're Eritrean. Haile Selassie is not . . . He wasn't kind to Eritrea."

"Oh!" Phuong covered her mouth with her hand. "I'm so sorry, I just assumed—"

"No, no, it's okay. Everyone makes that mistake. Ethiopia is much better known than Eritrea. They have many more people—thirty or forty times. And the food is just the same, really. But we don't have such a good relationship with the country."

"I'm really sorry," Phuong said again, and the woman assured her it was fine and brought out a frankincense brazier and roasted our coffee for us at the table, then went back into the kitchen to brew it.

"I love that smell," I said. "I mean, normally I am completely uninterested in coffee before bed, but Ethiopian coffee, fresh roasted at your table—"

"Eritrean," she corrected me.

"Ugh," I said. "Yeah, sorry."

Over coffee, she told me more about her life in London, the time she helped evacuate the Houses of Parliament when the Thames burst its banks, the work on emergency cooling during the big heat wave the previous summer, the time she'd been pressed into service, carrying pensioners' bodies out of overheated blocks of flats where the heat had peaked at 56°C.

"What's that in stupid American?"

"Over a hundred and thirty-five," she said.

"We get days like that most summers," I said.

"But everyone's got air-con here. Lots of that old housing stock, it's just not equipped. They were relying on swamp coolers and fans."

"Damn," I said. "Damn."

We found room for more baklava. The coffee was gritty and strong and so good. She asked me about what I'd done since school, and I told her, a little: Gramps, Ana Lucía, the ship. Then I had to backtrack and tell her about the roof and Mike Kennedy, and for the first time since that happened I loved having the story to tell, loved having a story where I came off as a hero.

"That is fucking *crazy*," she said. "I mean, seriously. Who knew boring old Burbank had all this drama?" I must have had a weird facial expression. "Did I say something?"

"Sorry," I said. "Look, I just really like it here. Burbank. It's my hometown—my adopted hometown, anyway. It's my home."

She smiled a little, and I felt patronized. Trapped. What was I doing here with this near stranger who thought I was some kind of rube? "Sorry, dude. But you gotta admit, that's a lot of drama!"

And then I understood and suddenly felt better, even though my heart was still thudding. "Oh, shit. No, that's not the part I was upset about. Burbank's got all kinds of fucked-up old white nationalists. It's the boring part I was upset about. I love this place. I love Food Truck Fridays. Movie screenings with live orchestras at the amphitheater. Griffith Park. The horses. The Halloween stores. The vintage stores. The schools and the people. My affinity group. All those people who came out for the caravan. Shit, the studios! All those editors and carpenters and scene-painters. The crazy Christmas lawns."

Now she was laughing, but I could tell it was laughing-with, not laughing-at. "You're a one-man tourist brochure." She picked up the last flake of pastry from the baklava plate and licked her finger and I had a little sexy shiver as her fingertip went in and out over her mouth. "You know, all that stuff is true, and it's all great, but I gotta confess, the whole time I was in London, all I could think about was how I wanted to tear this place up."

"Tear it up?"

"You know, infill it. I mean *really* infill it. Not little two-story eightplexes. High-rises. Tokyo-style, earthquake-ready skyscrapers, forty stories tall. Pack in everyone west of Culver City, relocate 'em here, make it as dense as Manhattan, as dense as Kowloon used to be, all pedestrianized, and then extend the Angeles National Forest right to the edge of it, so you go from the middle of this super-dense, urban, walkable city into this wild, massive forest that just goes on and on and on."

"Holy shit," I said. The way she moved her hands while she described it, the way her eyes shone, I felt like I could see it too. "Wait, what about fires?"

She shrugged. "There're *gonna* be fires," she said, "but there's so much rain these days, I'd be more worried about floods. Of course, everything's so fucked that we might get both at once. During an-other pandemic, why not? But come on, think about it. The best way to prevent fires is to decarbonize and the best way to decar-bonize is to put everything close together, maximize how much space we give over to habitat and vegetation and carbon sinks. And it would be *amazing*: with all that weird, gnarly Burbank stuff you love as a seed, we could build the most incredible place here, a city like no other, like Hollywood movies, but real."

"Shit," I said again. "Holy shit."

Let me say right here that Phuong was beautiful. I mean, she'd been beautiful and impossibly glamorous when I was a freshman pip-squeak and she was this tall, smart senior. Four years under a blue helmet had left her roped with muscle and with this amazing world-smarts that was a million times more glamorous. I could have had a crush on her even if we'd never had that dinner.

But when she talked about how she wanted to live, her version of the city, it was like she was this incredibly sexy Joan of Arc, a visionary who made me want to fall in and march. There was a "leader" thing that some people just had. She had it.

"That is just incredible."

She smiled and shrugged and my heart went thud-thud-thud. Did she know she was doing it? How the hell had I ended up across the table from her? I was easily the luckiest guy in Burbank.

"Don't get me started on the airport. After we put in high-speed rail, I want to turn it into a museum of bad habits from a fallen civilization."

"You should run for mayor. I'd vote for you."

"I'd be lying if I said I hadn't thought of it. Because I *do* agree with you, Brooks. Burbank is special. It's beautiful, it's full of smart, creative people who do and make stuff, and it's got political independence. It's not LA, but it's next to LA. They can do what they want, but we don't have to go along with it. We're our own city. Governments are cool toys: they have a lot of power."

I seriously wanted to hug her just then. "Uh, can I tell you something personal?"

She suddenly looked nervous. "I guess?"

"Sorry, that came out weird. It wasn't a swipe-right thing. Though—" I swallowed. "I'd be lying if I said that hadn't crossed my mind. Just putting that out there."

I couldn't bear to look at her face and see what she made of that. I couldn't believe I'd said it! I rushed on. "But that's not what I wanted to tell you. But it is personal. Is that okay?"

"I guess?"

She looked like she wanted to leave. I felt like an idiot.

"Sorry, it's okay, forget I mentioned it."

"Actually," she said, and she smiled and I got so many feels. "Actually, yes, I think I would. Please, go ahead." Another smile. More feels.

"Well, there's a good part, then there's a sad part, and then there's another good part. Just warning you."

"I'm warned." The whole vibe had shifted. Were we bantering? Did *she* want to swipe right?

"Right. The first good part. My dad grew up here, in Burbank. So did my mom. But they both got Canadamania, you know, the Canadian Miracle. They weren't much older than me and they left for Alberta, to work on the Calgary project—wildfires, floods, moving a whole city."

"No way," she said. "That's cool. Romantic, even."

"I think it was! I was born there—"

"You're Canadian?"

"Dual," I said. "But yeah."

"Lucky," she said. "You got an escape hatch."

"Not really," I said. "There's only one planet and—" I realized she'd been teasing. Of course she knew that. "Sorry. Back to my parents. I was born there and it was all totally normal to me, of course, Mom or Dad having to rush out in the middle of the night to help with an evacuation or sandbagging or whatever.

"Now, this is the sad part. They died. I was eight. It was one of the fevers. I was orphaned and then I moved here—" Her face was doing this thing now, and I could tell I was bumming her out. "It's okay, really. I mean, it's not okay. It's fucked. I'm all kinds of fucked up about it, to tell you the truth. But that's not what I want to tell you."

"Okay, but Brooks, that's really—"

"I know. It is. More than I can say. But.

"Okay. Then I came here and I was raised by my grandfather and of course I could tell that things were really different here and there weren't many people like my parents, no one who lived the way they had."

"No shit."

"I mean, back then. None of the adults in my grandfather's circle, they're all Magas. These days, sure, yes, I'm surrounded by people who remind me of my folks, but back then, I wasn't just dealing with being orphaned—I was also trying to deal with this kind of lifestyle whiplash, not just being in a different place, but being with people who weren't living for this big vision of what things could be. I mean, my grandfather, all he cared about was how things had been, and if he thought about where they were going, it was only to be angry about it.

"I fell in love with Burbank obviously, but I never saw myself staying here. I always felt like if I was going to find the kind of cause that made my parents who they were, I'd have to go somewhere else—go help relocate San Juan Capistrano or do what you did, go somewhere drowning like London or Lagos and pitch in.

"But Phuong, the way you talked about Burbank just now—seriously, it gave me goose bumps. What a vision! The idea that we could take all that land all around us and give it back to nature, and then give that nature to *ourselves,* put all the displaced people here, give them somewhere decent to live, give them to ourselves too!" She laughed. I was shouting. The waitress was staring, but smiling. "I mean, don't take this the wrong way, but you don't just have amazing ideas, you have an amazing way of talking about them, a way that makes me want to stand up and salute."

She took my hand across the table and I thrilled from my scalp to my toes.

"Thank you, Brooks. Seriously, thank you."

We were so having a moment. She got all dreamy. "And if we did it," she said, "if we did it, we'd have our own Blue Helmets, people who'd lived through the Burbank Miracle, people who could go across California and teach them how to do it. Make every community that has a future into a haven for the places that don't have one."

Another shiver chased the first one. She had these little flecks in her irises, and a dot of scar on her nostril where she'd had a nose ring. There were a few dark hairs mixed in with the blond ones on her upper lip. Her lips were thick and pouted, like a Greek statue, and her nose had a little hook in it, giving her face so much character. When she was lost in thought, her facial muscles all relaxed, giving her a statue's smoothness, and then when she came back from thought, she animated all at once and a thousand tiny lines and muscles leapt into definition and she was as full of character as a line drawing, crosshatched and shaded.

She squeezed my hand and let go. We split the bill and stepped out into the night. It was cool and there were these giant green fig beetles buzzing us as we mapped our way to more bikes. We hardly said a word as we walked down Victory to the bikes, then we turned to face each other. My hands got sweaty.

"That was a pretty fantastic night, Brooks."

"It was an *extremely* fantastic night, Phuong."

"I wish I'd known you at Burroughs."

"I'm glad I know you now." God, I was so in the *zone*. She laughed.

"I'll call you," she said.

"That makes me happy."

We went in for the hug, and it was a long one and a good one, longer and better than a friendly California hug. A hug with meaning and promise. Then she pecked me on the neck and pulled her face back and gave me a slower one on the lips. Her breath tasted like coffee and spice. My head and hands and feet went numb.

"Wow."

She laughed again. "You're funny."

"Wow."

She rode off, and I just stared after her, hand on my bike's saddle, as her legs flashed through the vents in her trousers and her hair spikes blowing crazy in the wind, the kiss lingering on my lips.

I swung my leg over my bike and cycled home, parked the bike at the curb for the next rider, and stepped into the house. It was empty: Wilmar and Milena were out with friends, and when I got to the back door, I found a gift basket packed with Mexican sweets and a jar of homemade orange marmalade and a huge card signed by everyone from Ana Lucía's advance party of refus, all gone to their People's Airbnbs. They'd completely packed up the backyard, tearing down their tents and infrastructure and installing a pretty little flower bed around the perimeter.

I sat there, reading my card and dipping my finger in the marmalade, which was delicious, spiced with ginger and cardamom, and let the mosquitoes sip at my ankles and calves, watching the stars whirl in their heavens and feeling that kiss again.

People were great. That was something easy to lose sight of because when they were dicks, the experience was so out of the ordinary that you lost sight of just how great they were the rest of the time.

I climbed into bed, thinking of Phuong. Just as I dropped off, I thought about the waitress and my stupid Ethiopia/Eritrea slipup, and just how many of these old grievances there were. Would Eritreans ever stop caring about being mistaken for Ethiopians? Would Gramps's Maga buddies and the seafaring plutes of the Flotilla ever stop nursing their grudges?

impact litigation

Preparing the lot for the new low-rise took three days: working under a master surveyor, we staked it out, got it leveled, and installed the foundation slab. The house had been sitting vacant ever since the original owners—a Lockheed welder and a Warner Brothers archivist—had died in the early part of the century, their estates in some kind of gnarly tangle. They'd been estranged from their kids and the house had been neglected, the roof springing leaks that led to pervasive black mold after a few years' worth of heavy spring rains. The city had scraped it down to the foundation slab a couple of years before, leaving it as an eyesore behind a rusting old fence, that had basically crumbled when we tore it down so we could get the heavy equipment onto the lot.

A structural engineer declared the slab still good, and we used old city infrastructure maps to unearth the gas, power, sewage, and water mains, then worked around them to extend the slab for the new building's larger footprint. The original dwelling was a two bed / one bath on a one-acre lot. The new low-rise would be three stories tall, with six two-bedroom apartments and one four-bedroom apartment on the top story, and no garage. The city inspector had wrangled with the city manager's office for a long time about that, but state rules about internal refugee housing explicitly overrode parking requirements for new housing and even made funds available for developing transit and cycling networks for every garage-free property installed under their rules.

The real excitement started when the panels rolled up. They came from a factory in Mojave, the same one that was providing the materials for the relocation of San Juan Capistrano. The sinterers only fused the concrete and polystyrene balls when the grid was saturated, scavenging solar energy that would otherwise go to waste.

I'd done a science fair project on them in middle school, producing three blocks on my own: one conventional clinker-based block, one low-clinker block cured in a conventional kiln (Gramps's oven), and one that was sintered with focused light—a big magnifying glass I borrowed from Huerta Middle School's science lab. I showed that they were each of equivalent strength, but that the third block had less than 1 percent of the carbon footprint of the conventional block and less than half of the low-clinker block, while weighing only 30 percent as much as either.

I know it's weird to nerd out about blocks, but I was a total block nerd and I knew that the Mojave plant had its own on-site research team that was always tweaking the formula, making them lighter and stronger and more resilient to temperature extremes and quake stresses. I was addicted to their videos of test buildings being subjected to the most awesome tests, watching wrecking balls bounce off them and shake platforms making them shimmy without cracking.

The panels arrived on short-haul heavy movers, slow flatbeds with giant hydrogen cells behind the cabs, in a convoy from the railhead. Then we discovered that the crane that was supposed to arrive at the same time had suffered a breakdown and there wouldn't be a replacement for a full day, which would screw up the job that the heavy movers were supposed to do the next day, setting off a logistical cascade that might take weeks to resolve.

The news sapped our excitement and broke our momentum. The slab was ready, the panels were here, we were all here with our work gloves and our water bottles and our temporary commissary and our shade structure and porta-potties. For the want of a crane, the building was lost?

I scanned the QR code on the tie-down with my screen to

look at the manifest again. The panels—8′ × 4′ concrete sheets—weighed less than fifty kilos each.

"Uh, guys?" I said, tapping my screen.

We unloaded them in less than a day, using our gloved hands, our biceps straining and sweat pouring down our faces, grinning and laughing and ignoring the project manager's pleas to work slower so we didn't hurt ourselves. Periodically, someone would tap out and fling themselves on their backs under the shade structure and get doused in ice water and dosed with electrolyte solution and coco-chocolate energy bars before getting back to the line. The stacked panels filled the lot, turning it into a maze around the foundation slab, just wide enough to get the crane and forklift in the next day, and as we finished a gang of five local massage therapists cycled down the road with cargo bikes carrying their massage tables. They explained that they'd caught us doing the unload on social and decided to come by and say thanks. Everybody got a twenty-minute back-and-shoulder rub under the shade structure and someone showed up with cartons of beer and music and then we all stayed up later than we should have, given that we were scheduled to actually put the house up the next day.

Despite the late night, everyone was back on the jobsite at 7 a.m., this being the earliest the city would let us start—noise abatement was one of the few exceptions to state emergency housing overrides. We slapped at mosquitoes and started to stage the panels based on the order we'd need to slot them in. A couple of the work-crew-mates had spent a Blue Helmet year in San Juan Capistrano and knew the panel construction technique backward and forward. Our foremen were a couple of the refus from the caravan who'd been general contractors back in the San Joaquin Valley. The rest of us had watched the training videos and done the online certification and in theory we knew what we were doing—the panel system was designed to be dead-stupid simple in any event.

Naturally, there was a lot of last-minute delay between the time we thought we'd start standing up panels and the first panel going in: triple-checking everything was level, comparing the panels with the plans to make sure the ones with built-in conduit for plumbing, HVAC, and power services were lined up in the right spot, and so on. But finally, around eight thirty, we were ready to go.

The first panel went in like butter, slotting perfectly into the groove and pin system in the foundation slab. It was now structurally sound, and as the tightening crew gave each of its lock bolts a half turn, it became rigidly fixed in place. This was the keystone, and we cheered as it went up but then quickly broke into the subteams that the apps sorted us into, each with its own piece in the logical path. With twenty-five people, we could finish the main work on the first floor by sunset, and while the upper stories would take longer, that would let interior crews work on the first floor, adding fixatives to the panel intersections, connecting and testing the plumbing, gas, HVAC, and power. Give us ten days, we'd be ready for paint and furniture. It was going to be so amazing, like a magic trick.

And then . . .

Just as we were wrestling the next tranche of panels into place, a Burbank City car rolled up on the jobsite, and an older guy I vaguely recognized from the city manager's office jumped out and sprinted for the foremen. They hit the emergency stop buzzer and we all froze, trying to remember what the protocol was for emergencies. But of course, there was no emergency, so we just ended up jostling around the guy from the city and the foremen, and that's how we learned that a state court had issued an emergency injunction ordering us to halt work.

Naturally we all wanted answers, but the guy from the city kept shaking his head and saying he didn't know any more than we did and to go digging online if we wanted more. In the meantime, he warned us, violating the injunction would put us in contempt of court and we'd face serious legal consequences—including jail time—if we did it.

"So don't do it," he said, staring around at the crowd that had packed tight around him. He still had toothpaste around his mouth, like he'd been shaken out of bed and sent down here by an urgent call at oh-dark-hundred. I felt for him. This wasn't his fault.

"Come on," I said, loudly. "He's just the messenger. Give the poor guy a break. Let's go figure out what the fuck is going on."

One of the women on the crew held up her screen. "Check it out, it's not just here. Every work site in the city has been shut down." People all started to talk at once but she waved her hands and they quieted down. "Looks like everyone's heading to the DSA office on Burbank Boulevard. I'm gonna head there."

"Good idea," I said. I wasn't the only one. It wasn't far, and there was a really good bakery right next to it, the kind of place you had to get to by 9 a.m. if you wanted to get one of the croissants. It had been founded by Lou the French's old head baker and if anything, they were even better than Lou's, which was, you know, wow.

On the walk over, we self-organized. Someone volunteered to stand in line for baked goods and everyone sent them money and orders, while others scrolled their screens and reported on what they found.

Between us and the other work crews, we cleaned out the entire stock of Patisserie D'Or and the inside of the Democratic Socialists' hall smelled like warm butter and rising bread and chicory coffee.

Best of all: Phuong was there. She'd been in a crew building a mid-rise off the downtown strip, on the site of an old gas station on Glenoaks by the library, and they'd all found bikes to ride over. Phuong greeted me with a very warm hug and a dry, quick kiss where my neck met my chin and earlobe, which made me shiver all over. She'd been too late for croissants, so I gave her half of mine and that earned me another kiss, this one on the cheek. It was so distracting I forgot why I was there until Phuong climbed up on a table and tapped into the PA.

"Hey folks, over here!" We all turned to look at her (what a sight!).

"Here's what we know." She held up her screen. "This morning, federal judges across the country granted over seven hundred injunctions to halt emergency housing projects authorized by the Internal Displaced Persons Act and state internal refugee bills. The court orders all responded to complaints under the Climate Emergency Act that demanded environmental impact reviews of the projects."

People groaned and scoffed. I marveled. It was pretty clever, actually. The Climate Emergency Act was pretty fierce when it came to blocking property-development projects—every bit as fierce as the Internal Displaced Persons Act was about greenlighting emergency housing for refus. In hindsight, it was obvious that there would be an immovable object / unstoppable force conflict between these two.

"I know, I know. It's bullshit, as are the claims. They all boil down to 'humans are bad for wildlife, more humans are worse for wildlife, this housing will move more humans here, therefore it's an environmental violation.'

"DSA National and the Alliance for Displaced People have lawyers working on this and they're going to give a statement in a few. We'll throw it up on the big screen when they start. I just wanted to get you up to speed before then. As you were."

The conversation rose quickly to a roar. I helped Phuong down and discovered that she was shaking a little.

"You okay?"

She gave me a tight smile. "I'm okay. It's the combination of being pissed as hell about this bullshit and the public-speaking thing."

"But you're really good at speaking!"

"That's what they tell me, but it always freaks me a little. I secretly think that I might be good at it because I'm a little freaked."

"Ay-yi-yi."

She laughed. "I know, I'm a bit of a mess."

"No way. You're completely badass."

She gave me a hug. "Look, I gotta go, but what about dinner tonight?"

"Yeah! Ethiopian again?"

"Eritrean."

"Shit, right."

"No, what about dinner at my place? You could meet my roommates."

I immediately forgot all about my frustrations with the housing build-out and just about floated to the ceiling as I watched Phuong plunge back into the crowd to caucus with other DSA organizers. I was brought back to ground by a buzz from my screen. I screwed in a bug and answered it.

"Hi, Ana Lucía."

"Brooks, are you at the DSA place on Burbank?"

"Yeah. You heard then?"

"From Antonio and Gabriella"—our refu foremen. "I'm a couple minutes away."

She arrived just in time for the livecast from the DSA lawyer. They were young, with super-short hair that made their big eyes and big mouth seem all the more mobile and expressive. I liked them immediately. I mean, everything was fucked, but everywhere I looked there were these great people who were good at what they did and cared about the same stuff as me.

Ana Lucía arrived with Jorge and Esai and we found a spot where we could see the big screen.

"Am I good to go? Good. Hey out there folks—comrades!—it's been a hell of a morning." They shook their head like they couldn't believe what a morning it had been. "Seven hundred courtrooms! There were lawyers in seven hundred courtrooms filing these bullshit injunctions this morning." They picked up a brick of printer paper and let it thump on their desk for emphasis. The paper was festooned with protruding stickies that vibrated after the impact. "The lawyers work for a lot of different firms, but they're all very expensive, and they all have a long history of working for offshore clients, and I don't just mean non-U.S. persons. I'm also including tax-exiles who bailed during the first and second Uwayni administrations.

"None of these firms are known for their pro bono work. Someone had a *lot* of money to spend on this. The briefs are really similar, but they're not identical. Each one is tailored to the project it was filed against and cites specific details of the local context: endangered species, microclimates, historic environmental designations. These may be bullshit, but they're well-done bullshit.

"What I'm saying is, this wasn't just about spending a lot of money—it was doing a lot of work. A lot. I can't even imagine how many associates they'd have had to put on this, even with AI tools to help with the drafting.

"By now, you may be asking yourself, why spend all this money and do all this work, just to shut down some infill projects? It doesn't make sense. Plutes may spend money on stupid shit, but generally it's stupid shit like superyachts, or Rembrandts, or dark-money political ads. This is off-brand for them.

"Now, none of us know for sure what this is about and we won't until someone on their side leaks it, which will probably happen eventually. But I'll tell you what I think, and this is just me talking: if these turn into cases and they start winning them, they can use them as a wedge to roll back the whole Green New Deal; any high-density housing, high-speed rail, hell, any mass transit will be blocked because it threatens wildlife habitats.

"If they'd tried this five years ago, Congress could have just sat down and amended the environmental protection statutes to clarify things. But no one's getting shit through this Congress, and even if the House and Senate flip in a year and a half, President Bennett's gonna veto whatever they send her on this.

"Comrades, I don't think this is a one-off. I think it's a starter pistol. I think there's a lot more to come."

They switched to Q&A then, taking questions from DSA offices and people at home for an hour. The questions were panicked, the answers were grim. A lot of these injunctions could be killed on the merits, but there were so many, and the DSA and all its partner orgs only had so many lawyers and some of them were bound to slip through. The questions were like a real-time tour of the five stages of grief.

Denial: "This has got to be illegal, right?"

Anger: "Fuck those guys, we shoulda put them all in jail in the first Uwayni administration."

Bargaining: "Can't we just pick the most important cases and use them as precedents to win the rest?"

Depression: "This is it, I guess, we should just give up on saving the planet. The human race is too stupid to live."

Acceptance: "All right, so we're going to be delayed by a decade and lose an extra billion lives, but that just means we've gotta work harder."

Eventually, the lawyer called time, saying they had to get back to fighting the cases, and we were all left sitting around the DSA meeting hall, feeling shitty and angry.

I spotted Ana Lucía leaving and squirmed through the crowd to catch her. "Hey," I said.

"Brooks. Can you believe this shit?" She looked so grim and determined.

"I know. Makes me furious. But I guess we just work harder, right?"

She didn't say anything. Her face was indescribable, this mix of fury and sorrow. It made me feel guilty, like I'd done something wrong. I didn't know why. She just looked at me for a while.

"Hey," I said again. "Hey. This is terrible, but it'll be okay. First generation that doesn't fear the future, remember? We got this."

Fury won the battle with sorrow in her. "*You* have this, Brooks, because you have a home. We don't. And now we're not going to get one. Fuck. Fuck this so much!" She screamed it to the blue Burbank sky.

"Ana Lucía, I know, this is complete bullshit, but we'll all pull through. You do have homes. There're the People's Airbnbs, and we can turn my garden back into a camp, do whatever it takes. Civil disobedience. You belong here, too. You're Burbankers, just like me. I'll fight for you, just like you'd fight for me. Solidarity, right?"

The anger leaked out of her. "Brooks, that's really nice and idealistic, but we can't live in your guest rooms and backyards forever. People have families, both your people and my people. They have lives. Our lives have been on pause ever since we left, and we're sick of it. We need to go somewhere that we can restart them."

"Where? You just heard that every emergency housing project in the country is on lockdown."

"Not in Oregon. The sacrifice zone is wide open."

"The Oregon sacrifice zone? You're going to walk to Oregon to make your permanent homes in a part of the country where they're averaging two hundred days of wildfires per year? And that's better than here?"

She shrugged. "The fires will stop when everything burnable is ashes. All that bullshit about not fearing the future gets a lot less convincing when you have nowhere to call home and everyone you love is sleeping on a stranger's sofa. Brooks, everyone needs a place they belong."

It hurt to hear her say it. I wanted her to call Burbank home—not just for her, but for me. I wanted to be from a place that would welcome people like her. The place that Phuong inspired me to create. But of course, she was right. Jam yesterday, jam tomorrow, no jam today. It wasn't fair for me to ask her to put her faith in a Burbank that might never come. After all, the campaign for injunctions on refugee housing was national, but the complaints for Burbank were all on behalf of locals. Who was to say that their version of Burbank wasn't the true one?

"I'm really sorry, Ana Lucía," I said.

She softened, just a little. "I know you are," she said. "I am too." Her screen dinged. "I gotta go."

I walked home in defeat and when I got there, I took one look at my bed and fell into it fully clothed and zonked out in seconds. I woke, disoriented, to dings from my screen. I found it in a pocket and saw that it was Phuong. I was wide awake in an instant. What did I look like? What time was it? Oh, shit, had I missed dinner at her house? I slapped the screen.

"Hi there!"

"Brooks, hi." She had video on, and looked a little worried. Behind her, I saw other people moving around, clearing plates. I checked the time. 7:30 p.m. I'd missed dinner. Shit. Shit shit shit shit shit.

Shit.

"Oh God," I said. "Phuong, I'm sorry. I fell asleep! Oh God, I'm *so sorry.*" I then realized I had my cam on, because she had *her* cam on, and she was looking like she'd just seen something genuinely pathetic. "I can't believe I fell asleep. I *never* fall asleep during the day. I'm really, really—"

"Brooks, stop."

I did. I'd blown it. Shit. Shit shit shit.

And then, she smiled.

She smiled!

"It's been a crazy day," she said. "Stress like this, it affects all of us in different ways."

Wow. WOW. "You are an incredible person," I blurted, and was rewarded with a laugh.

"All right, Sleeping Beauty. Are you hungry, or do you want to go back to sleep?"

"I'm starving!" I said.

"Okay, well, lucky for you, there are leftovers. Do you like Moroccan food? We've got spinach and chickpea stew and carrot-ginger soup."

"I literally can't answer you because my mouth is full of saliva," I burbled, because my mouth was actually full of saliva. I swallowed. "Sorry, that came out grosser than I intended."

She laughed again. "It's fine. Look, my housemates are all about to play a Mecha Zombie Mecha tournament. It's a nice evening—wanna meet outdoors somewhere?"

Butterflies and bluebirds. "Yes!" I calmed down. "Yes, I'd love that. Really, really love that."

She thought for a second. "What about the back field at Burroughs, by the climbing wall? There're those benches there."

"Totally! I can be there in ten minutes." Which turned out not to be enough time, not if I was going to take a shower and pick out something decent to wear, which is why I found myself jogging toward Verdugo with my cool vintage shirt with the contrast stitching and the disco collar undone, heels and laces flapping on my shoes. I sorted out my shoes at the light and buttoned the shirt while I raced the rest of the way and got there, which is why my shirt was misbuttoned for the first ten minutes after I met her.

"Your shirt buttons are weird," she said.

I stopped setting up the picnic table—disinfecting it with wipes, laying out the containers and cutlery—and looked down. "Dammit," I said, and tried to rebutton it but I'd really screwed it up. She giggled at me and I felt better.

"I'm so sorry," I said.

"Yeah, you said that. Honestly, it's fine. We always cook extra so there'll be leftovers for lunch. If anything, my housemates are disappointed because all this stuff tastes so much better reheated."

It tasted amazing lukewarm, too, one of the best home-cooked meals I'd ever eaten, and I told her so. "That's Miguel," she said. "It's his thing. We all just sous-chef for him and watch in awe. You can thank him when you come by."

"I'm coming by?"

She set down a mosquito vaper and got it running, swatting as she did. "I should certainly hope so," she said.

After I finished eating I wiped out the containers and put them in her bag, and then we just sat in the cool of the evening, with the joggers running the track and the dog-walkers outside the fence, the odd cyclist going by.

"Man, this takes me back," she said. "So many nights sitting out here. This is my first time back here since graduation. It's weird, my friends and I used to hang out here all the time and I don't think I thought about it once for all the years I was in London."

"Well, you musta been busy. Plus, you know, London."

"Oh, yes, London. For sure. It did keep us busy. I got there right after the Hurricane Wendy storm surge hit."

"Jesus," I said. "Wendy!"

"The Thames Barrier barely slowed it down and all of the Strand and the South Bank were underwater. I didn't even get a chance to sleep off my jet lag: we got diverted to Luton, bused into Camden, dropped our bags, and headed straight to the Tate Modern to work on the sandbagging while the art-specialist evac crews got the paintings out the back door."

"I thought the Thames Barrier was some kind of crazy defense system?"

"It is *now*. But they nerfed it down after Brexit, basically said they couldn't afford it and it would have to do, which is like, okay, sure, negotiate with the hurricane and see how far that gets you.

"Anyway, between Wendy and then Hurricane Amrita the next year, they decided that they had to do something about it, and to their credit, once they decided it had to be dealt with, they took it seriously. The new barrier is massive, sixty meters, and then the original barrier is downstream to catch overspill. It's wild to watch it open and close, just incredible. But while they were building it, we had so much to do in the city, relocating people and helping with these incredible old buildings, even Roman ruins. Then there were the plague pits, which kept getting inundated, and you'd get outbreaks, which understandably freaked people out, even if we can treat it with antibiotics now. In the end, they just got everyone out of the riverside lands, everything from King's College to the Tower of London, so they could maneuver machinery in to save the historic sites without having to worry about running anyone over.

"It was incredible to watch that reality settle in there. When I got there, the idea of closing down the riverside areas was completely unthinkable, a joke you'd see in memes. Eighteen months later, it was done. I mean, you still get a lot of urbex kids climbing around in there, and the preservation workers are going at it hard, and they say that with the new barrier, they'll be able to open everything again in a year or two, but that assumes that they don't get more giant surges between now and then. I think that's wishful thinking, frankly, and I suspect most of them know it, but they don't want to accept the reality all at once."

"Well, I can see that," I said. "You gotta eat the elephant one bite at a time."

"Sure," she said, "but think of how many other cities are going to wait until it's too late to act and lose their own treasures because the lesson they took from London is that they can go back and fix their mistakes after the fact. The only thing worse than losing all those beautiful places and all their treasures is not learning anything from those losses so that other people have to lose their treasures, too."

"When you put it that way . . ."

"Yeah," she said. "I get so sad and mad when I think about

being a Blue Helmet. In some ways, it was the most important, most rewarding thing I ever did. Every morning I got up and did hard work. I learned more about civil engineering from working on the barrier than I did in any of my classroom work. I helped people. I saved people, literally saved them, and saved their homes and the things they treasured. I watched them come to grips with a problem so big that it's almost impossible to hold it all in your head.

"But I also got my arms around that problem: not just the climate emergency but also the human-psychology emergency—the fact that we just suck at facing the hard truths, and that even if some of us are ready to do so, there're millions of other people who are still in denial, still fighting."

She got a faraway look. "You know what the worst part was?"

I shook my head. Her expression. Wow.

"The people who'd been on the wrong side all along, the deniers, the ones who'd said the country couldn't afford to do the hard work, whose wrongness had killed people and left the Houses of Parliament to drown—even after we knew they were wrong, even after the Tower of London was halfway submerged, they were still there, still saying that they were right, saying we were overdue for a thousand-year storm, anyway, accusing us of exploiting other people's misery to advance our nefarious political causes.

"Not just a few people, either—this huge cohort of business leaders, politicians, asshole climate deniers and wreckers and their legions of followers. Screaming headlines, all over podcasts and radio, just incessant. At first I thought they were just part of someone's expensive dezinformatsiya and yeah, I'm sure there were some heavies bankrolling the thing, but then I realized that these guys were shouting because they thought they were *right*. They were on the losing side of a just revolution—the generation-long deadlock and inaction they'd fought for had finally ended, and the UK was finally doing what it needed to do to survive the coming decades, and they were *furious* about it.

"And that's when I realized these guys were not going to dig a hole and climb in and disappear forever. Some of these dickheads were going to live for decades, maybe half a century, and they'd pass on all that bullshit to their kids, who'd pass it on to their kids, who'd pass it on—"

"Like the restaurant," I said. "Eritreans and Ethiopians."

She waved her hand. "No, like the fucking Civil *War,* like those Lost Cause crazies who are still angry that slavery ended. It's been centuries and they're still angry."

"Yeah," I said, "that is a much better example."

"Think about it. Who has ever gotten past this kind of thing? My Greek family hate the Turks. Hell, it's the whole reason my grandpa came to Glendale, so he could hang out with Armenians and hate Turks with them. And my Vietnamese family? There's some deep revenge-plot stuff there."

"Purim!" I said.

"Purim?"

"Jewish holiday," I said. "They had a Purim party in middle school one year, seventh grade, and it was supposed to be, like, this costume pageant where everyone dressed up like characters out of this ancient Bible story about a plan to genocide all the Jews in Persia. Like a genocide-themed Jewish Halloween. Anyway, they give you these noisemakers, and any time they said the name of the Grand Vizier who'd planned the genocide, we drowned out his name with the noisemakers. This is over a plot from, like, 400 BC! And they're still pissed off about it!"

"Well, it *was* a genocide."

"Okay, sure. Good point."

"And Christians are still pretty worked up about the Crucifixion and that was two thousand years ago."

"Yes, fine. Exactly. That's my point. Like we're never going to get over any of this shit. Like those people on the Flotilla. They're not going to jump overboard and put us out of their misery. In two thousand years, their descendants will be sailing around the tropical seas of the North Pole, saying we can geoengineer our way out of global warming on our way into space."

"Ugh. Now you're depressing me all over again. This was exactly what got to me in London. It was like, even if we get the barrier built, even if we pump out the city and move everyone back again, we're still going to be fighting with the people who got us in trouble after all."

"But it has to end eventually, right?"

"I dunno. They used to say that they got it right in Germany, but all those Bavarian Nazis say otherwise."

"Now I'm depressed, too," I said. That got me another smile. Wow. "Okay, I lied," I said. She looked a little worried. "I'm not depressed. But only because I enjoy hanging out with you so much."

She gave me a long, considering look and I wondered if I'd misread the room. Then that wow-smile-wow again, and she took my hand, twined her fingers in mine, which felt exactly like being electrocuted, but in a very, very nice way. "Thank you, Brooks," she said. "How would you feel about a kiss right now?"

"I would feel very, very good about it," I said. And, consent negotiated, we leaned in.

Wow.

I actually missed two traffic lights at the corner of California and Verdugo staring bemusedly at the night sky and the twinkling stars. I might have missed a third light but a cyclist waiting to turn right called out, "Hey, are you waiting for the light?"

I drifted home, tasting Phuong on my lips, feeling the phantom of her touch in my hair and on the back of my neck. She was a very good kisser, surprising and slow and, well, you know. Wow.

I was digging for my keys when I heard someone clear their throat and I jumped in surprise. There were two figures on the bench beside the front door, hidden from the street by shrubs, lost in the shadows. I shone my screen on them and saw that it was Derrick and Kenneth, faces grim and set, but they broke out into mean grins when the light hit them.

"Evening, Brooks," Derrick said. "Too bad about your little construction project."

"It's okay," I said. "We'll be back in business before you know it. Nice of you to come by and commiserate, though." I did *not* want to talk to these guys. I went for the door, but Kenneth stood and got right up in my face.

"Brooks, I know you don't believe this, but we want to help you."

That gave me a bad flashback to Gramps, screaming at me, humiliating me, then telling me it was all for my own good. I shrank back, like I was about to get hit. He pressed his advantage, closing on me.

"You need to understand something, Brooks. This—" He waved around at Burbank. "All this bullshit this country has been dragged through for the last fifteen years, it's coming to an end."

Now Derrick crowded in on me too, and his smile was nasty. A snarl, really. I reached to hit the livestream on my screen and he batted my hand away. "Uh-uh, kid, don't even try it. I'm no numbnuts like poor old Mike Kennedy."

Kenneth said, "Kid, you gotta know it's true. All this bullshit, spending like drunken sailors, buying houses and clothes and food for people who couldn't be bothered to save up for a rainy day, inviting every shitbag and loser in the world to come here and crowd us out of our homes. Of course people weren't gonna stand for that."

Derrick took over. "Course they weren't. And you know that Uwayni didn't get *all* the guns. No way could she get 'em all. The real people of America, the patriots, we knew what was coming, and you know, we're not sheep. We don't just let someone show up and disarm us."

Kenneth laughed. "Especially when the cops doing the disarming hated Uwayni's guts as much as we did. You're smart Brooks. Smart enough to figure this out."

Back to Derrick: "But maybe not smart enough to understand that if it comes to war and you choose the wrong side, you're not gonna like how that turns out."

I struggled to get control over my stupid, panicked emotions, to find my voice and yell for help, to punch one of these old Nazis in the mouth. But I couldn't find it.

Kenneth now, trying to play good cop. "Brooks, you love it here. You know, your grandfather showed me that AP English paper you wrote about Burbank. It was beautiful, no bullshit. I read that and I knew that you and me, we have something in common. I don't hate these people who want to come here. That's not why they have to go. They have to go because I love it here, too. When a thousand people wanna share the same apple, nobody enjoys themselves."

"Least of all the apple." Derrick's laugh was a snicker.

"Brooks, I'm trying to explain to you that even though you don't know it, you're on our side. You haven't seen the things we've seen, is all. We want to keep this town on its feet, defend it from people who've ruined their own cities. Sure, people can come here, but by following the rules—let 'em rent a place, or get a mortgage. Not just show up on our doorsteps demanding handouts."

I nearly shot back something about refugees and fairness and all of that stuff, but it wouldn't do any good. It couldn't. These were Gramps's Maga homies, and they'd just say, *That's not my problem, let them take care of their own.* I didn't want to have that argument with these two assholes. I just wanted to go home.

"Those days are over," Derrick said. "You better fucking believe those days are *over*. Kid, you need to understand, this isn't just another political debate. This is a *reckoning*. The people are fed up with all this bullshit, and there's no more Mr. Nice Guy.

There's a storm coming. You're not going back to work on your little refugee fort, ever. That shit's over. All this bullshit is *over*."

Kenneth dropped his good-cop mask. "It is, Brooks. Over. It's a new day in America, as they used to say. Don't doubt it for a second."

I suddenly had a premonition that they were both ready to kill me, that the only reason they hadn't so far was that I hadn't troubled them enough to be worth the hassle of hiding my body. For the first time since my parents died, I feared for my life.

They turned to go, but then Kenneth smacked his forehead and turned back. "Almost forgot, I brought you something. A little consolation prize." He dug in the thigh pocket of his cargo pants and came up with a paperback, worn and dog-eared. "It's my own copy. This book explains *everything*."

I took it numbly, watched them go. I carried it inside and tiptoed past my housemates' closed doors, thinking about how just a few minutes before I'd been floating in a dreamy state of Phuong-infatuation and now I was shaking, scared, and angry.

It wasn't until I got to my room and tossed the book on my bed that I actually registered the title: *Those Who Tread the Kine,* by Theodore Sutton, a fat thing with a line-art drawing of the thrusting prow of a massive ship on the cover, the author's name embossed in flaking gold.

There was no way I was going to fall asleep. All I could think about was Kenneth and Derrick, how they thought this house was theirs, somehow—just like they thought all of Burbank was theirs, how they thought America was theirs, the world, the whole goddamned future. They had guns, I knew it. Gramps couldn't be the only one with a cache of weapons and expired antibiotics under his foundation slab.

The worst part was that there wasn't a single thing I could do about it. It wasn't like going to the cops would do any good—how many of Gramps's pals were cops? All the cops would do was put me on some kind of Maga militia hit list for their next shot at civil war.

I sat on my bed, heart thudding, sweat drying on my armpits, furious and scared and alone. Something was under my butt. The book. I picked it up. There had been copies around the house all the time when I was growing up, it was one of Gramps's favorites and for that reason alone I'd never wanted to touch it. The couple of times I'd tried, to fit in with my obsessed classmates, I hadn't been able to get past the first chapter.

I wished the fireplace in the living room still worked so that I could burn it. Then I felt guilty for wanting to burn a book. Burning books was the kind of thing that was so terrible that every student film at Burroughs High that included some kind of civilizational collapse included a shot of a pile of burning books (there was a freeware deepfake library that would generate them).

Feeling penitent, I turned the book over and read the blurbs, all from billionaires whose names I knew from the businesses their ancestors had founded: Bezos and Koch, Musk and Ellison, Khosla and Mercer. Judging from the blurbs, those guys had *loved* this book. The word "genius" appeared three times.

I changed into track pants and a tee and got between my sheets. I couldn't sleep. I turned on the bedside lamp and opened the book.

chapter 7
taz

Here's the thing: Sutton was actually a pretty good writer. Oh, not on a sentence-by-sentence level, and the way he wrote dialog reminded me of my AP Creative Writing teacher: "Did you type this wearing boxing gloves?"

But the story was actually really good: it started with these incredible amazing, smart, competent people living on a very thinly disguised version of the Flotilla, surrounded by robots that did their bidding and AIs that anticipated their every need before they could even voice it.

The hero was obviously a Larry Stu for Sutton, an entrepreneur/engineer named Brandon Sullivan who was in a polycule with a bunch of hot women half his age, and he inspired everyone he talked to, knowing just what to say to ease the tensions as the ships sailed into a superstorm that all the AIs and other toys were completely not up to the task of getting them through.

It turned out they had to sail through the storm because they were overdue to meet with a group in Indonesia that they had promised aid to—more brilliant entrepreneur/engineers who had been threatened by small-minded, violent, bigoted bureaucrats who resented the fact that they'd come up with this incredibly awesome high-tech way to prevent coastal losses to sea-level rises and were going to arrest them all for having the audacity to build a really cool gated community right at the beach.

These Indonesians were part of a global network of secret societies that Sullivan and his pals supported. Not all of them were genius inventors: to qualify for membership, you merely had to believe that people who were good at what they did should be in charge, rather than having leadership handed out as a participation trophy so that lesser beings wouldn't have hurt fee-fees.

Brandon-a.k.a.-Sutton and his valiant crew help the Indonesians, sneaking them aboard after dark for secret strategy meetings, and using a combination of tactics (laundered money to pay for top-notch lawyers; hackers that dig up kompromat on their political opponents; a bodyguard squad for their leader that kicks six kinds of shit out of the thugs sent after her), the Indonesian allies are triumphant.

I could not put this shit down, and I thrilled to their triumph even though the victory they'd won was the right to tear out a mangrove swamp and build condos. That was the gross and amazing thing about Sutton's work: he got me to root for terrible things, even though I knew they were terrible. How did he do that? Was all storytelling this evil and sneaky and manipulative?

The chapter ended on a cliff-hanger, as Brandon learned that there was a spy in his midst, an infiltrator who was bent on sabotaging his group's valiant quest to rescue the whole human race from these dumb libs and tree huggers who thought they knew everything. He's informed of this by a deep-state informant using a secret back channel, because Brandon and all his friends are censored on online media by giant companies that have been co-opted to be an arm of the corrupt, authoritarian governments of the world, and won't let anyone speak the truth. The whistleblower warns Brandon that his own fleet is filled with traitors, but he can't say who—all he knows is that the world's governments are getting scared of Brandon and his friends and they're ready to do anything, including bombing the fleet, to stop them.

The Brandon scenes were intercut with these scenes from the "default" world where cyberwarriors for Brandon's cause were getting red-pilled in secret forums, then going out to make a difference in the world, picking fights with mindless drones who believed in the Green New Deal and the idea that people should be in charge based on whether they believed the same things, not whether they were good at their jobs. This silent majority caught all kinds of hell from self-righteous, domineering eco-idiots who would jump down their throats at the slightest offense, like one of them who got called a racist for not wanting his grandfather's single-family home torn down to make way for a high-rise.

And here again, I kept finding myself slipping into sympathy for these dumbasses, and filling up with loathing for these caricatures that could have been me and my friends. The weird thing was, I was totally familiar with the stereotypes Sutton was using, they were no different from the ones Gramps and his friends tossed around for my whole life, but somehow having them in this story, especially when I was so (involuntarily) invested in Brandon and his cause, made it all seem so urgent.

I think it was that the story was just really well done: there were all kinds of awesome chases, fight scenes, love stories, super-cool high-tech ninja shit (if the real Flotilla had half as many cool cyberweapons as the one in the novel, it was a wonder that they hadn't seized power) and fantastic acts of bravery. At one point, Brandon's protégé—a plucky, wisecracking teen from Bangladesh—gets into a wingsuit and flies into enemy territory after being lifted and released by a stratospheric drone, and Sutton worked so much cool stuff about aerodynamics and material science and astronomy into the scene that I found myself digging into Astrogoogle and running these little aerospace-engineering tutorials.

I finished the first half of the book and wanted to finally go to sleep—it was after midnight—but I made the mistake of skimming the first paragraph of the second act, and bam, I was sucked straight into it. This one was all guerrilla warfare, all around the world, as all the characters we met in Act 1 ran merry circles around the fat-fingered, slow-footed authorities of the Green New Deal: This is what happens when you promote idiots for ideological purity and ignore their incompetence!

And the more the "good guys" won, the more the masks slipped on the Red Greens of the Green New Deal—faced with unstoppable resistance, they created a police state with genetic checkpoints and mass surveillance and mandatory apps on everyone's screen.

This was the true nature of the "first generation in a century that didn't fear the future": they were so afraid of that fear that at the first sign of trouble, they turned into totalitarian thugs, building concentration camps for their ideological opponents, transplanting refugees—all from poor countries where people had brown and Black skin—to fill the neighborhoods that had been emptied by the roundups.

For all their deep green rhetoric, the enemy would not confront the obvious reality that the Earth's carrying capacity had been vastly exceeded, and that any future for the human race would have to start with getting the population under control. There in the camps, the resistance announced its willingness to put its own fertility under rational control.

People who could demonstrate their objective merit—their intelligence, physical prowess, rationality, and capacity to create things of value—would be awarded the right to reproduce. People who were born to be takers—the dull, the entitled, the foolish, the easily led—would have to join a lottery to win that right. With a finite Earth and a potentially infinite population, something had to be done.

There was even a memorable scene where Brandon agrees to have a reversible vasectomy—he's pretty sure that he'll qualify to reproduce when the time comes—and wins the admiration of a hyperfertile Guatemalan man who's already fathered five kids by five different women and the guy goes and get his tubes snipped, too.

I hated reading this racist trash, but I couldn't stop. It was after two thirty in the morning now and I was coming up to the big climax, and I was involuntarily invested in the massive war that Sutton was teeing up, and which flew past in a series of tight little scenes: dogfights and drone fights, missile strikes and beach landings, space war and cyberwar, ground fighting house-to-house, soldiers turning on their officers and joining the resistance, it's all guns, guts, and glory, flags being hoisted over capital buildings and then . . .

The epilog: starships (of course), all kinds of jobs being created by job creators (not by committees voting on Jobs Guarantee jobs, of course), the climate emergency "solved" with high-tech systems that sink the carbon, protect the shores, and block the sun (no mention of what they do with all those therms sunk into the ocean, melting the poles—maybe they bribed the second law of thermodynamics to look the other way for a century), cars everywhere, and Black and brown people living in harmony with white people, with an end to racial strife and the beginning of a new dawn.

I felt dirty when I finished it, realizing how much I'd been into it, and how gross and just *Nazi* it was at the end, and just, ugh. Besides, it was three in the goddamned morning and I'd just blown up a perfectly good night's sleep on this crap.

I threw the book at the wall and got half a gummy out of the bedside table and turned out the lights. I was just falling asleep when something that had been niggling at me jolted me wide awake and bolt upright. In that second act, when there was all that guerrilla warfare, there'd been a scene I'd somehow glossed over, maybe because I was tired and there was *so much plot* at that part, but—

I flipped through the book and couldn't find it, so I pulled it up on my screen—naturally it was open access, because in pluteland the truth is paywalled and the lies are free—and did full-text search: "solar panel acid squirt" and yeah, there it was.

One of the guerrillas, a minor character, recounts to another how his cell had been getting up on the roofs of public buildings with hammers, smashing the solar arrays, carrying squirt bottles of acid for self-defense.

I read the short passage over and over. The truth was sinking in: this wasn't just a piece of garbage ideology in pulp-fiction form, it was a manual for revolution. Mike Kennedy hadn't come up with his stupid wrecking stunt on his own. He'd been LARPing *Those Who Tread the Kine*. The Flotilla distributed this book by the truckload, and all those Maga Clubs passed it hand-to-hand like it was *Dianetics*.

I switched off my screen, threw the book at the wall again, and turned out the lights. Even with the gummy, it took a long time for me to drop off.

I didn't get up until after twelve, my housemates already gone. Phuong had left me a message telling me she'd really enjoyed our dinner—which made me feel like a clod for not sending *her* a message like that, instead of staying up all night reading apocalyptic late-stage capitalist pornography. I wrote her a gushy note about how much I'd enjoyed it, deleted it, wrote another two drafts, then wisely decided to pause this composition exercise until I could swill a liter of cold brew and heat up some pizza in an iron skillet (that's how you get a crispy crust!).

After I'd fixed my blood-sugar and caffeine levels, I wrote a fourth draft of my text and fired it off and immediately got anxiety sweats, somewhere between schoolboy crush and new-relationship energy, and felt both embarrassed and elated about them. I reminded myself to cool off and not get weird about this and then I nearly broke my neck on the shower tile when she messaged me back and I lunged for my screen.

> Well, now that we've established that YOU enjoyed it and I
enjoyed it, let's do it again! What are you up to this afternoon?

Omg, she was so good at this. Of course, this realization set off a fresh round of panic: What reply could I make that was just as breezily positive, self-assured, and yet not thirsty and weird? I used the rest of my shower to think of something, drafted it twice, then just replied:

> YES!!!

And promptly realized it wasn't a yes-or-no question. I was typing a sheepish reply when she messaged back.

> You are hilarious. okay, I was supposed to be on a building site today but obviously that's canceled. Let's have a picnic in Verdugo Park?

I didn't think, just copy-pasted my last response:

> YES!!!

and then

> I'll bring the food this time. One hour?

> Perfect

I'd roasted a ton of cubed sweet potatoes earlier in the week, so I threw them in a Dutch oven with egg whites and olives and cherry tomatoes and other tasty things, sprinkled feta on top, and stuck the whole thing in the oven for half an hour while I tried on and discarded ten outfits. I found something I hated less than everything else—wide-legged pants a little similar to the ones Phuong had been wearing the night I met her, a vintage Western shirt with contrast stitching and shiny buttons—and moved the frittata from the middle shelf to the top of the oven and turned on the grill, setting a five-minute timer. That was just enough time to toss a leaf/watermelon/pumpkin-seed salad and put some peaches in a tub for dessert and then I took it out and set it down to cool while I found a picnic blanket and extra cutlery.

I was out the door with fifteen minutes to spare and made it to the park just as she arrived, carrying my big picnic bag.

She gave me a hug that was more than warm and friendly and there was a moment there where I forgot what I was doing and just noticed how spicy and amazing she smelled and how smooth and shiny her hair was on my cheek. Then she gave me a kiss on the cheek and a brief one on the lips and I just . . .

Wow.

I set out the picnic, making awkward small talk and wishing I had something perfect to say that would disguise my essential dorkiness. But then I served my frittata and the whole world changed, because my frittata game is super badass. It's the capers. And the caramelized onions, twice cooked (once when I roast the sweet potatoes, then again in the Dutch oven). And the oregano. Also browning it. It's a whole thing.

"This is amazing," she said.

"I know."

"Good. Hate false modesty. Give me another slice."

After wiping her lips with one of the napkins I'd brought, she looked me right in the eyes. "This is good," she said.

"I know," I said.

"Not the food. This." She pointed at herself and at me, and our surroundings. "I mean, in theory, stuff's pretty messed up, but I am seriously enjoying having you around while it's all going to shit."

"Um." I took a deep breath. "Phuong, I am trying to find a way to say how happy that makes me without sounding like a scary weirdo."

"You're not scary."

"But I'm a weirdo?"

"Certainly," she said. The last three (four? five?) times, she'd made the first move. Clearly it was my turn.

"Can I hold your hand?"

"Yes, you can."

It was warm and lively and strong and callused.

"Can I kiss you?"

"Yes, you can."

It went on for a long, long time.

"Wow," I said.

"You know, I was just thinking that."

"My housemates are home today," she said, and gave me a very serious look.

"Mine," I said, "are not."

"Oh, good," she said.

It was so good. I mean, good in that new-relationship-energy way, of course, a new body and a new playmate and playing off all that tension I'd been carrying around for days.

But also, it was objectively good. She was athletic and energetic, surprising and funny—we both laughed really hard at various points, sometimes at the same time, but not always—and, best of all, she knew what she wanted and told me:

"There."

"Lick that."

"Bite that."

"Harder."

"Softer."

"Don't stop now."

Wow.

I'd always struggled with that kind of explicitness. I mean, I'd been raised with all the sex-positive stuff in school—and had it countered by Gramps's mix of squeamishness and gross, sexist jokes—but I could never quite bring myself to tell my partners what I wanted.

Maybe it was because none of them were as explicit as Phuong.

Shyly at first, then with more confidence, I did as she had, and she reacted with such enthusiasm that before long I'd lost all self-consciousness. It was beyond great. It was the best I'd ever had.

"Wow."

"You say that a lot." I'd gotten us ice water from the kitchen, and her lips were cool as she nuzzled me under one ear.

"Not usually," I said. "But you know—" I ran a finger up her flank and she shivered. "Wow."

I yawned, then yawned again.

She bit me in the spot she'd just kissed. "Am I boring you?"

I yelped. "No, sorry. I just didn't sleep last night."

"Ooh, thinking of me?"

"Uh, honestly? No." I told her about my visit from Kenneth and Derrick, and my hate-reading of *Those Who Tread the Kine*.

"I can't believe you read it all the way through?"

"Ugh. I know. I feel so gross. But there's something weirdly unputdownable about it. I mean, there must be some reason for its success."

"Yeah," she said, "it's the same as every shitty fantasy novel: you're part of a group of naturally superior people, held back by a bunch of mud-people and haters who don't want to admit that everything would be better if their social betters were just allowed to get on with being in charge of everything."

"That's the plot of every shitty fantasy novel?"

"Duh. Fucking King Arthur. *Lord of the Rings*. *Ender's Game*. *Star Wars*. *Foundation*—"

"Pretty sure some of those are sci-fi."

"If it's got faster-than-light travel, it's fantasy," she shot back. She got up on one elbow and I sincerely and intensely admired the new play of light and skin and muscle. She clicked her fingers under my nose. "Snap out of it, fella. Eyes up here."

"Sorry."

"It's okay. It's just that you're about to have a revelation. This is the foundational belief behind 'conservativism.' Ever wonder how white nationalists, American imperialists, misogynists, Christian fundamentalists, and finance bros could all fit into one political category? What do all those ideas have in common?"

"Uh," I said. I hadn't ever thought about it, but yeah, those were pretty different ideas. How could they make up one ideology? "Shit, I don't know. That's really weird."

"No, it's totally explicable. Think about what I just said about shitty fantasy novels."

"Oh! Uh." I thought hard. Man I wanted to get it, just to show Phuong that I was in her league intellectually, even though I'd only just gotten out of high school and she'd spent three years hanging out with brilliant, planet-saving heroes in drowning London. "Um."

"You'll get it." She stretched out like a cat, then tweaked me in a sensitive spot. "Eyes up here."

"Uh." It was hard to think. I thought hard. "They all believe that some people should be in charge of other people."

"You are a smart fellow," she said, and gave me a kiss. "That's exactly right. Our side believes that no one was born to rule over others. Their side thinks that some were born to rule and others to be ruled over. That's the difference. That's the change that Uwayni represented—moving away from the idea that the answer to a world ruled over by a hundred and fifty white men was to change things up so half of them were women and people of color to the idea that the world shouldn't be ruled over by a hundred and fifty people, full stop."

"I never thought of it that way."

"Now you can. It's why so much popular fiction over the years has been right-wing garbage. *Harry Potter,* any of those stories about being the Chosen One, *Gone with the Wind, Atlas Shrugged,* so much of it has been just eugenics dressed up as wish fulfillment. No one is born to be The One, any more than you can find The

One that you're supposed to fall in love with. People have different abilities, and they can improve them to different degrees, but no one is born to rule and no one is born to be ruled."

"Wow."

She bit me, but not hard. "You say that too much."

"It's sincere. You make me say wow. I'm sorry."

"No, you're not."

"See? You're so smart."

She made an exasperated noise but it wasn't a real one and then we did stuff for a while.

"Wow."

"Dumbass."

"Sorry, but you know . . . Wow."

"It's just new-relationship energy. Give it a couple months and it'll wear off."

"We get to do this for a couple of months?"

She put her hand over her mouth. "Shit," she said, "sorry, I didn't mean to scare you off."

"Scared off? I'm delighted."

"Now you're scaring *me* off."

I could tell that she was actually a little freaked out, so I said, "Sorry. I'm very happy to keep this up, but I know it's not yet a real thing."

"No, it's not."

"But it might be one someday."

"It might." She smiled a little.

"And if it is . . ."

"Yes?"

"You want me to know that I won't enjoy it."

That earned me another bite and another interlude.

"Don't say wow."

"Okay."

"Stop thinking it."

"Okay."

"I can't *believe* you didn't know about *Those Who Tread the Kine*."

"Oh, I knew about it. Like, I had friends who read it and I'd seen the games and the TV show. I just didn't really get it."

"Brooks, it's been translated into fifty languages. There are major conventions for it. There's a political party named after it in Korea. It is *huge*."

"Jesus, that big?"

"Well, that Sutton guy is a billionaire. He paid for it all—marketing, mass giveaways, the movies. For a long time he was running these cruises, where he'd get thousands of people who just worshipped the book on board and do all these seminars and events with them, 'training sessions' for 'movement leaders.' We'd get tons of them every time there was a bad flood, showing up with ideas for how to 'reopen' all the stuff we were trying to protect on the riverbanks, trying to drum up support from people on the street. They had a crackpot plan for fixing the estuary barrier that was supposed to be cheaper and faster—and it involved a bunch of patented materials that Sutton's companies got royalties on—and they made up little miniatures of it and gave them out to people on the street to convince them to chuck out the Blue Helmets and bring in the private sector."

"Holy shit. That's like a cult."

"It *is* a cult. It's a personality cult, and Sutton is their god-king. The Flotilla started with those cruises of his—he just bought a bunch of cruise ships and then his rich buddies joined up, and then someone thought it would be hilarious to buy an aircraft carrier and take to the sea."

"Man." I thought about my time on the Flotilla, and the bum's rush I'd gotten. "Well, I guess you've got to admit they're good at one thing: convincing everyone they're good at everything."

She laughed. "Yes, they are. I mean, put it that way and they're practically miraculous. I mean, think about what their message is: On the one hand, they say there's no climate emergency and it's all overblown panic. On the other hand, they tell people that they need to side with plutes because the planet is 'over capacity' and the excess people are going to have to be eliminated to save it."

"Ugh. That reminds me so much of my grandfather and his pals. Half the time they'd talk about how the climate was fine and it was all overblown fake news, and the other half the time they'd talk about places like Burbank as 'lifeboats' that were at capacity, and if we let in all the people who hadn't had the good sense to get their own lifeboats, they'd sink ours and we'd *all* drown. All that lifeboat talk, I never really figured it out, but it was basically about genocide, right? Leaving everyone, Ana Lucía and everyone like her, to die, shooting them ourselves if necessary, rather than sharing with them."

"Well, I didn't know your grandfather, but that's definitely what Sutton and his creeps think. Any time you hear someone talking about 'lifeboat rules,' it's just a dog whistle for fascism. They think they're such brain geniuses for coming up with this amazing plan: insist we can't do anything to stop the world from burning and then when it's on fire, insist that it's too late to do anything about it and all we can do is follow orders because an emergency is no time to start taking votes."

I nuzzled her. "You know what I love most about talking to you?"

"Do tell."

"There's all this stuff I've been trying to figure out, ideas floating around in my mind, not quite gelling, and then you come along and, like, *bam,* you've got it."

"Well, I can't claim I thought of any of this stuff—just heard it from other people. And now I'm telling you, and then you can tell other people, too. It's how stuff changes, one conversation at a time."

"Okay, sure. But I also like that it's *you* telling me."

We kissed for a while.

I was sort of floating off into a doze when I started to think about Gramps and his friends again, about my visit from Kenneth and Derrick, about the gunshots in my backyard when Ana Lucía and her friends had been back there. I thought about Gramps's guns, hidden in the hills, along with his krugerrands and his other end-of-the-world lifeboat stuff. I opened my mouth to tell Phuong about the guns, but then I didn't. What if she told me I had to take 'em to the police? What if she *didn't*?

Instead: "Gramps's friends, those guys who visited me, all the ones hanging around here in Burbank, like you said, they're not going to dig a hole and climb into it and pull the dirt in after themselves. They're just going to hang around for years and decades, being assholes, burning crosses, even doing fucking murders, and in the meantime, we can't even put up some refugee housing on an empty lot."

She was quiet for a long time.

"About that . . ."

"Yes?"

"Well, look, my little affinity group, we're kind of the direct-action types. Civil disobedience. Most of us are ex–Blue Helmet, we've seen some shit, we're not playing games. We know it's life or death and we're not gonna sit around and watch these dickheads make it even harder for all of us to get through alive."

"Oh. Oh! Whatever that is, I like the sound of it and I will take three of them, please. Here is my credit card."

That got me a squeeze. "Seriously, though. The city has stopped adding any new People's Airbnb spots, so we're gonna put up a site for rogue ones, we're going to go to all of them and make sure all the kids are signed up for school, that kind of thing."

"Get 'em library cards, too!"

"Oh hell yes. Burbank libraries have already got a lot of good stuff like screens and lawn mowers and electrician's tools and stuff and we're already compiling a list of other needs, using templates from the libraries where we did Blue Helmet service. It sounds radical and all, but it's just replicating stuff that's worked elsewhere. The librarians are *so* into it, too."

"God, that's great."

"It'll drive 'em nuts, too."

I thought about Kenneth and Derrick in fist-shaking, impotent fury and grinned. "I love that." I stared at the ceiling. "You know what would really do 'em in, though."

"What?"

"This place. Knock it down, scrape it to the foundation slab, and build a high-rise. Do it so fast they don't even know it's happening. One day, it's a single-family house that they love because their old white nationalist asshole buddy lived here, then next day, it's got fifteen brown families in it, happily living their lives and existing as human beings in the world. They would go totally apeshit."

She giggled, then I chuckled, then she laughed and I guffawed and before long, we were hooting and crying.

"We could do it, you know."

"What?"

"We could do it," she said. "Small footprint. Just get the right prefab materials, some big lifting tools, some strong backs, and we'd be up in forty-eight hours. It'd take a week to do all the finish inside and whatever, but I've put up bigger buildings in less time."

"Really?"

She told me war stories, then, building on brownfield sites in London to create homeless housing, emergency family housing for refugees, even flats for working families who were precarious. Some places had been so flood-damaged they couldn't be salvaged, and they'd be knocked down, the lot flood-treated and elevated, and then, like a demolition video in reverse, a building would spring up on the lot, almost overnight, whole parts of London being reshaped in days and weeks. After many successful builds in the flood zone, the projects moved all over the city, turning empty, rotting mansions owned by absentee offshore criminals

into giant housing estates with parks and other amenities, building and building, training Londoners on the methods first used
to rebuild most of Calgary off its floodplain, then spread to other
Blue Helmets around the world.

"That was my parents' work," I said. "Calgary. They worked on
those first builds."

"No way," she said. "That's incredible. They were pioneers!"

"They were," I said. "To hear Gramps talk about it, they were
brainwashed by Canadian Miracle propaganda and threw away
their lives to build houses for people doomed by their own stu-
pidity and bad planning."

"Well that's a stupid way to talk about it," she said. "How
about, 'They had the foresight to understand that Blue Helmets
would take what they learned in Canada and spread it around the
world, saving the human race from the sins of their shortsighted
forebears who put the planet in so much climate debt it might go
bankrupt?'"

"I like your version better," I said.

"Me too."

Ana Lucía had invited us to a potluck dinner in the DSA hall, so
I made another frittata and Phuong made a watermelon and feta
salad and we put 'em in a crate that I bungeed to the rack of a
bikeshare bike.

It was nearly as packed as it had been, not so long ago, when
we'd all jammed in to watch the DSA lawyer tell us how badly
everything was fucked. Being back with the same people in the
same space put a damper on my mood, as did Ana Lucía's own
obvious bitter disappointment. We chatted for a moment by the
bar as we waited to refill our beer cups from the keg.

"How is everyone doing?" I asked.

"It's not good, Brooks. I know that in some ways nothing has
changed. I mean, we all expected to be staying in volunteers'

spare rooms"—*People's Airbnb,* I mentally translated—"for weeks or even months while the housing got sorted out, but there's a big difference between a situation like that when it's temporary and you know you'll get a place of your own and when you have no idea if you'll ever get your own place."

"Oof. I hadn't really thought of it that way."

"I mean, honestly, all these people are very nice to take us in, but we can't live in their houses forever. If I was them, I wouldn't want refugees living with me forever, either."

"So what are you gonna do? Are you going to go to Oregon?"

She shrugged, filled her beer cup (we were at the front of the line now). I filled mine. She shrugged again. "I don't know. Honestly, I just don't. The walk here was so hard. You know, there were little kids, old people. It was so hard. People got sick. Walking to Oregon—"

"Yeah."

"But I don't know."

She surprised me by hugging me. "Look, Brooks, this is not just your problem. We're all having this problem together. The fact that you don't know how to solve it doesn't mean we can't solve it. Look, it's a party. We're here to say thanks to you folks for taking us in. Let's enjoy it."

I hugged her back. "Thanks, Ana Lucía. We are all having this problem together."

"I know," she said.

There were speeches and they weren't great. There are some really good DSA speakers in Burbank but they weren't the ones who had the podium that night. And the thank-you speeches from the refugees were so awkward, clearly written before all the housing projects got canceled, hastily edited to thank everyone for *wanting* to help, rather than for *helping.* When they were over, I finished my plate and pitched in at the dishwashing station for ten minutes, before getting tapped out by Ana Lucía.

"Not a great evening," she said.

"It was okay," I lied.

"Thanks for coming. I like your frittata."

"I'll send you a recipe," I said.

Phuong dried off her hands and passed on her apron, too, and we stepped out into the evening, which was cool and clear, with a half-moon rising low in a way that made it look crazy huge.

"Beautiful," she said.

I put my arm around her waist. "Just what I was thinking," and squeezed her gently. She smiled and draped her arm over my shoulders. My heart went thud-thud-thud. She made me completely crazy. New-relationship energy or not: completely crazy.

"How about a drink?" she said. "My housemates just made some amazing bourbon."

"Don't have to ask me twice!"

Phuong's housemates were all ex–Blue Helmets, but they'd also all grown up in Burbank, so it turned out I knew two of them (one from Burroughs High and one from a pickup basketball game I'd been a regular at), and the other two looked familiar.

The bourbon-makers were Don and Miguel, who'd taken an online workshop and built a bioreactor: they used synthetic volatiles that were chemically identical to the expressions of aged bourbon—Pappy Van Winkle 25, a popular choice—and added it to six-day-old grain alcohol they distilled themselves, for a liquor that was indistinguishable from a twenty-thousand-dollar bottle of Pappy.

"It's a little astringent," Miguel said, swirling it in his mouth, passing me the eyedropper full of distilled water to add to my own lowball glass.

"That's how you know it's true to the original," Don said. "I got to taste some in Tokyo. This young guy just grabbed us off the street and dragged us into his mother's memorial service and she turned out to be this rare-whiskey dealer who got novel dengue and died the year before. The son had just signed up to be a Blue Helmet himself and so we sat around with all his friends and relatives, sipping thimblefuls of this stuff and giving him advice. Pappy is supposed to be a little mediciney."

"Well, it is," Miguel said.

I tried mine, first without the water and then with. I thought it tasted great, but then I didn't know anything about bourbon.

"We've got a really nice cabernet-finished Jefferson's coming out tomorrow," Miguel said. "Come back and try that."

They'd rented out a big four-bedroom off Victory Boulevard, furnished with whatever their parents had stored for them while they were overseas and Blue Helmet furniture, a lot of treated cardboard and scavenged materials laser-cut at a community makerspace and decorated with intricate stencils from the Blue Helmet repositories, that supermodernist poster art of brave people doing hard work. I liked it.

I liked all of it: the whiskey, the society of these Blue Helmet veterans telling stories about their adventures (Arina and Jacob had been stationed in Brisbane, and they'd done a long stretch on reef remediation and had wild photos and even better stories), and (especially) getting to snuggle with Phuong on a big, sagging couch with a blanket made from faded denim kimonos draped over it.

When the whiskey was drunk and the conversation had tapered off and Miguel poured Don into their bed and then fell in himself, when Arina and Jacob started yawning and gave us each a hug and a cheek-kiss good night, I found myself all alone on that sofa with Phuong.

She snuggled into me and I threaded my fingers through her thick, straight hair, tickling her earlobes and rubbing her neck muscles, and she preened like a cat, then tilted her face up and gave me a long, slow kiss.

"They liked you," she said.

"I liked them."

"Good."

This time, I kissed her. She tasted like whiskey and spice.

"How about a sleepover?" she said. "I've got a new toothbrush you can use."

My heart went lub-dub-lub-dub.

"Can I tell you something?" I asked.

"Uh, yeah?"

"Don't take this the wrong way. It's just that I have caught such crazy feelings for you that I keep having to remind myself to play it cool so I don't act like a weirdo and scare you off, and then you say stuff like 'I've got a new toothbrush you can use' and I realize that you like me too. I know that's weird, because of course I know you like me too, but I am so totally smitten right now that I can hardly believe it. It's like I know a secret and I don't want to give it away."

"I don't take that the wrong way. I like that you're good at using your words. That is a seriously underrated trait in a serious romantic partner."

"Wow."

"Oh, shush. You still haven't said if you wanna sleep over?"

"Jesus Christ, *yes*! Of course! Yes!"

"See? You're good at using your words."

castles in the sky

By the time we got down to the kitchen, all of Phuong's house-mates had already left for work. I helped her make a shakshuka, slicing the sweet peppers and crushing a little habanero, adding chopped tomatoes and then poaching a half dozen eggs in the bubbling tomato stew, sprinkling parsley and olives over it once it was cooked. Phuong toasted sourdough and squeezed grapefruits from her backyard tree and brewed coffee in a little stovetop vesuvio, making it darker and more bitter than I usually liked, but it went so well with the fiery shakshuka.

"What're you doing today?" she asked.

"I feel like I've barely been home all week. I definitely have a long list of chores I've slacked on, and I should probably do some of my housemates' chores to make up for the ones they've filled in on. Then I guess I'll hit the Jobs Guarantee board and find a new gig—there's no sense in waiting around for the forces of evil to be vanquished and construction to begin again. I've been wanting to get trained on solar upgrading. So much old infrastructure out there waiting to be upgraded."

"It's piss easy," she said. "Assuming the wiring's still good, it's just a hot-swap. Hardest part is not falling off the roof."

"Well, I'm a dead man then."

"Wear a harness," she said, and kissed me.

Just after I turned the corner off Verdugo onto my street, someone called my name. I looked around in time to see Kenneth getting out of a little autonomous cab puffing over to me, his face ruddy and worried.

I thought about sprinting to my house. I could run laps around that old fuck, and besides, maybe he'd drop dead of a coronary while chasing me.

"Wait up," he said, wheezing. He didn't look good. Sweat sheened his face, and his hands were shaking. He was easily seventy, but he looked ninety, barely able to stand upright.

"Hi, Kenneth," I said, making it as deadpan as I could.

"Brooks, listen, I gotta tell you something."

"Okay," I said.

"Maybe we could talk about this indoors?"

"No, I'm good here."

He grimaced. "Okay, have it your way. Look, I know you don't believe this, but I feel responsible for you. I don't want anything bad to happen to you." He looked searchingly into my eyes, his own watery and bloodshot. I realized that he was terrified. I started to feel a little uneasy myself.

"Kenneth, I know you don't believe this, but I don't need you to look out after me. Gramps was my relative, but he was never my friend. We didn't agree about anything, least of all my father and mother, who Gramps thought were idiots who'd wasted their lives. The things you and my grandfather and your buddies stand for? I want to see them dead and buried. The world you want is nothing like the world I want. It's nice of you to come by—"

"Shut up a minute. Let me tell you what I came to say, then I can be done with my conscience and square with your grandfather's memory. I promise I won't bother you again.

"You think me and my guys are a joke, I know, but we are deadly fuckin' serious. The thing your grandfather planned for, the day we all planned for, the day we take this country back, that day is coming. It's almost here. It's going to be ugly and bloody as hell and I know there's a good chance I'll die in the process, but I'm willing to pay that price because I—" He choked up, dug

190 · **cory doctorow**

a crumpled mask out of a pocket, wiped his eyes with it. "I love this fuckin' country. It's the greatest nation the world has ever seen, it's the shining city on the hill, and we're gonna take it back, make it great again."

I looked away. He was snotting now, eyes shining with tears. If it had been anyone else, I'd have been full of sympathy for him, but this guy? He could go fuck himself.

"Look, Kenneth, I know you guys think this. God knows I heard it often enough—"

"Shut up for a sec, okay? This isn't just talking anymore. We're done talking. We're acting. This time next year—hell, next *month*—you won't recognize this place. Things are gonna change."

"Okay, Kenneth, to be honest, I've heard this before too, and—"

"I said, *shut up*." He was intense enough that I did. "Look, kid, Brooks. I know you don't like it around here. Everyone knows that. You hated your grampa, and that's fine, I got relatives I can't stand either. You wanna get out of here, you've made that clear. I have an offer to make you, one that squares up what you want, what we want, and what your grandfather woulda wanted. It's a win-win-win."

He leaned very close and said, "Sell me the house." He named a price. It was a fair price. "It's a fair price," he said. "You sell to me, get the fuck out of town, you get to live your life in peace in a city where you belong, and everyone's happy."

"Yeah. No. Goodbye."

He clamped his hand around my wrist and he was strong, stronger than a weepy old psycho had any right to be. I twisted but couldn't get loose. I was ready to head-butt him or stamp on his instep, but he said, "Listen, this isn't playtime. I am trying to save your fucking life, you little idiot. I'm doing it for your grand-father, not for you. You think we're playing because we never did nothing before? Well before we didn't have the money to buy the stuff we needed for a real change. That is over, all right? There's plenty of funding for the war effort now, enough to buy us all the arms and armor we need to make it happen. We didn't act because we couldn't win. Now we're gonna act because we can't lose. My offer stands. Think hard about it. Someday soon, it'll be too late."

"Goodbye, Kenneth," I said, and wrenched my wrist out of his grasp. As I walked away, I felt his eyes boring into the back of my skull, all the way down the block. When I turned into my walkway, I looked over my shoulder and there he was, at the end of my street, hands in fists, staring at me.

I was shaking when I got into my room and threw my dirty clothes in the laundry, pulling on clean shorts and a fresh tee. It was all that talk about money. There was a lot of money around, that was for sure. When Uwayni had cracked down on plutes, there'd been a ton of money stranded overseas in tax havens, and Uwayni had let it be known that it could stay there, circulate all it wanted, but it would never, ever come back into the USA where it could distort our political process. Now it seemed someone had figured out how to get the money into the country. I thought about Ana Lucía and her blockchainism. Was that how the money was getting here, turning into guns and armor and who knew what all else Kenneth and his fashy army were ready to turn on the rest of us?

It was such a mistake to let Gramps and his friends be harmless cranks, instead of taking them seriously when they muttered about purging the country—the world!—of their enemies. How come our side of the fight had to be committed to peaceful coexistence while their side wanted genocide?

For a moment, I entertained a fantasy—a sick and satisfying fantasy—about lining up all these Junior Concentration Camp Guardsmen and mowing them down with Gramps's guns, but before I knew it, I was shooting down Ana Lucía and her blockchainers and then I felt so angry and sad and disgusted with myself that

I just shut down, sitting on my bed and crying. What a fucking mess. First generation not to fear the future? What a joke. I was terrified.

The fear was an old one, a gnawing one, and I knew myself well enough to recognize it. It was the fear I'd felt when I'd left my parents' house, went wandering off with my backpack and my blanket to find a place where the grown-ups weren't dying, where someone could help. And all of a sudden, I felt an overwhelming urge to hold my blanket again, and I searched for it in my pajama drawer and my keepsake box before I remembered that I'd hid it in Gramps's cache box. I had things to do but at that moment all I wanted was to hold that blanket, bury my face in it, so I dragged the bed over, exposing the hatch, and lifted it out.

My blanket was in tatters. Someone had methodically shredded it, slashing and ripping it to pieces. The pieces were wet. They'd been pissed on. The piss was cold.

Numbly, I dropped the pieces back in the subterranean box and went to the bathroom and washed my hands. Then I washed them again. Then again. I looked at my reflection in the mirror, and it was only then that I realized the mirror was at an angle, partly open. I opened it the rest of the way and saw that the contents of the medicine cabinet were in chaos, shoved every which way. I looked down and noticed that the trash bin was filled to overflowing with things that *had* been in the medicine cabinet.

I stepped into the hall and noticed finally that the pictures were askew, the shoes and coats by the door were now on the floor in a heap. I'd gone into my room through the back door and hadn't even noticed, but now—

They'd punched out the attic hatch by the AC intake and there was insulation foam on the floor. The living room was a wreck, the sofa cushions slashed, the books strewn across the floor. Only Gramps's service trophies, the little statuettes he'd gotten for every five years he spent at the little aerospace company, designing and troubleshooting missile housings, were undisturbed.

The kitchen was a write-off. If they hadn't smashed every plate, it wasn't for lack of trying, and the food they'd taken out of the fridge and freezer had big, booted footprints all over it.

Feeling like I was in a nightmare, I knocked on Milena's door and opened it, switching on the light to discover her mattress slashed open, her drawers and closet dumped out, her vanity mirror smashed. I looked around to make sure that she wasn't somewhere under that mess, then tried Wilmar's room, which was in the same kind of shape. Someone had taken a shit on the floor. Wilmar wasn't in there, either.

I walked numbly back to my room, heart thudding, ears roaring with blood. I found my screen, still in the pocket of the shorts I'd tossed in the laundry—noticing belatedly that the laundry hamper was full of clean clothes that someone had methodically transferred out of my drawers—and called 911.

A bot answered and took my burglary report and guided me through the rooms to take pictures of the wreckage. Halfway through, the system beeped and a person came on, a young woman in a police blouse with a name tag on the chest.

"Sir, there's a high probability that the damages to your property exceed ten thousand dollars. We have already dispatched a pair of officers to do an in-person survey. In the meantime, you and any members of your household are advised to leave your home and touch nothing else, as it is now considered a crime scene. Please let me know if you understand?"

"I understand," I said, and woodenly walked out onto my front lawn.

"Officers are on the way. Please do not disconnect this call."

"I understand," I said again. It was brutally hot, coming up on one in the afternoon, the sky hazy with smoke from one of the inland fires. The smoke created the usual inversion, with the air going yellow and so humid I pitted out within seconds.

Milena arrived a few minutes later. She greeted me warmly and gave me a hug and I realized it had been days since we'd talked properly, our schedules running crosswise. She started inside and I stopped her.

"We can't go in."

She laughed like I was joking. "Why can't we go in?"

"We were robbed," I said. "Or trashed, anyway. They wrecked the place. Wrecked our stuff. Cops are on the way."

"What?" Still laughing, like it was some kind of joke, and then: "*What?*" She seemed to take me in for the first time, reminding me of how long it had taken me to realize that the house had been trashed.

"I—" The words wouldn't come.

"Are you hurt?" She was really alarmed now. I must have looked terrible.

"No," I said, and let her pull me to her so that I was leaning on her. "No, I'm—I'm okay. It just happened. I just got home and—" I waved my hand. "Cops are on their way."

And on cue, a BPD cruiser pulled up and Officer Velasquez and their old white partner got out. They chunked shut their doors, stood on the curb, and did a systematic reccy of their surroundings before approaching me.

"Mr. Palazzo," the old white guy said. His name tag said MURPHY.

"Officer Murphy," I said. "Officer Velasquez. Thank you for coming." I remembered Ana Lucía's outrage when I told her that I'd called the police over the cross burning and the shots, and thought about what it meant that I'd called them again.

"This is my housemate, Milena Perez. Her things were trashed pretty bad."

"I see," Velasquez said. "Are you both unharmed?"

"We're fine," Milena said. "I haven't even been inside."

"That's good," Velasquez said. "You two wait here, we'll go check things out."

At first we stood numbly on the sidewalk, just staring at our home, but then as time went by, Milena said, "I haven't seen you around much lately?"

"Oh," I said. "Yeah. Well, I, uh, met someone."

"Ooh!" she said. "Lucky you. Let me guess, it's all new-relationship energy, right?"

I smiled. "Totally. I'm sorry, I've been out with Phuong—"

"Petrakis? From Burroughs?"

I laughed. Of course Milena knew her. Burbank was a small enough town that everyone sorta knew everyone. "Her."

"Whoa," she said. "Out of your league, dude. I mean, no offense."

"None taken. You're one hundred percent right. I am a very lucky person."

"Damned right you are. I mean, you're a very nice guy and you clean up pretty good, but Phuong Petrakis—"

"I know, right?" The numbness was receding. The Magas had trashed my house, but they hadn't trashed my life. Stuff was just stuff. I was part of the first generation in a century that didn't fear the future. I was going to save the world. I had amazing friends. Phuong Petrakis had engaged in sexual intercourse with me, more than once, and it was extremely likely this would happen again, possibly that very day. Fuck those old, irrelevant mouth-breathing Nazis.

I gave Milena a squeeze and stood up straight. Murphy, the old white cop, came out and formally notified us that we were on bodycam and then took a statement from me.

"And you don't know who might have done this?" he said, giving me a hard stare.

"No sir," I said.

"No suspicions?"

"No sir."

"And what about the box in the bedroom?" How had I forgotten about that? Milena was staring at me now, too.

"The box?"

"The hidden cache under the floorboards. There's kind of a mess in there, some old rags and fresh urine, but it looks like someone's secret hiding place, kind of place you might hide illegal things."

"That box," I said, just as Milena said, "What?" I turned to her. "Sorry, it's just this secret stash my grandfather had. It was just part of his paranoid thing, you know, Maga Club stuff."

She gave me a significant and alarmed look. "*What stuff*, Brooks?"

"I dunno," I lied, and the cop gave me a look like he knew it. "His friends came and emptied it out after he died. I guess whoever tossed the house got excited at finding it and then angry because it was empty."

"Is that what you guess?" Murphy said.

"Yeah, or whatever. I mean who knows why anyone would break in and trash the place?"

"You said you had no ideas, right?" Murphy said. There was unmistakable sarcasm in the question.

"Well, from what I could see, they didn't take anything, but then again, there wasn't really anything to take. I guess it could be political?"

"Political." The sarcasm was getting thicker.

"Because of our support for the refugees. There're a lot of racists who aren't happy about them and don't like the fact that their neighbors support them."

"Racists."

Milena had been quietly watching the exchange but she broke in. "Yes, racists." She gave him a defiant look.

He ignored her, kept staring me down. "And the box was empty?"

"Empty," I said.

"Huh." He scratched some notes on a screen. "Well, there you go. Vandalism. I'll send you the police report for your insurer."

Velasquez came out, wearing a disposable mask and gloves. "I'd get a professional cleaning crew in." They peeled off the PPE and stuck them in a baggie and sealed it. "Any time you're dealing with human waste there's a biohazard risk."

"Someone took a shit on Wilmar's floor," I told Milena.

"And pissed in your box," Murphy reminded me. I thought of my blanket and my stomach lurched.

"I'll call the insurer." I remembered that I'd been meaning to call them since Gramps died, to make sure my roommates' stuff was covered. I hadn't called. What if they weren't covered? What if *I* wasn't covered?

"You should do that," Murphy said. Velasquez got in the cruiser, then Murphy started to get in.

"Wait," Milena said. "Aren't you going to take biometrics?"

Murphy looked pained. "Like what?" Pure condescension.

"DNA?"

"DNA."

"Yeah, DNA."

He shook his head. "How many people's DNA you figure you got going in and out of that house, all the people you've had staying with you, all the people who live there? All the things they've touched?"

"Some person just took a shit in one of the bedrooms and left it on the floor," Milena said, calmly but intensely. "No one touched that shit."

"Is there DNA in shit?"

"Epithelial cells. They line the colon." Milena always did well in bio.

"I don't think Burbank PD has a shit-DNA lab," Murphy said. He leaned into the cruiser. "We got a shit-DNA lab, Velasquez?"

Velasquez made a pinched face, shook their head silently.

"You're just going to leave the evidence there?"

"You mean, am I going the clean up the shit on your floor? No, ma'am, I am not going to clean up the shit on your floor." He got in the cruiser and closed the door.

"Thanks," I said, idiotically, robotically, to the cruiser's rear end as it drove away.

"Fuck," Milena said.

"Yeah."

"Guess I'd better go have a look," she said.

"I'll call Wilmar," I said.

She came out five minutes later holding a small bag. "I'm gonna stay with friends," she said. "I mean, it's not good in there. Did you notice the shower drain?"

"What about the shower drain?"

"Looks like someone filled it with concrete," she said.

Wilmar arrived a few minutes after she left. I barely had time to clean up the shit from his floor, wearing gloves from under the sink, throwing them in the trash along with the turd. He was coldly furious as he packed his own bag. "Who the fuck does this?" he kept saying, sorting through his piled-up clothes, recoiling with a shout when he discovered a layer that had been soaked with piss. He headed for the shower and I shouted at him to stop, explained about the drains. He shouted "Fuck!" and scrubbed his arms to the elbows.

Then I was all alone, with the piss-soaked scraps of my baby blanket and my trashed house. I packed my own bag, not sure where I would go—Wilmar was staying with a boyfriend who had a spare room, but everyone I knew with extra space had converted it to a People's Airbnb. I wasn't going to ask Phuong—I'd rather sleep on a park bench than freak her out by acting like a creeper.

> I just saw Milena-you ok?

It was Ana Lucía. I stared at my screen.

> Not really.

———

Ana Lucía met me at Simply Coffee and bought me a cold brew and swiped through my photos of the wreckage in my house. "What a mess," she said. "Ugh. I'm really sorry."

"Not your fault," I said. I was processing the grief in spurts, ricocheting between rage and fear and heartbreak and cold revenge-obsession. The caffeine helped at first, then soured in my guts and amped up the fury. It was soupy hot on Simply's patio, even with the shade sails and fans, and I had soaked through my shirt and the ass of my shorts.

"Where will you sleep?"

I shrugged. "At home. I can clean up my room in a couple hours, they weren't so bad there. I think they started off thinking they could get whatever they were looking for and then get out easy, and when they couldn't find it, they got angrier and angrier and started smashing the place. I'll just take it room by room." I shrugged. "It's not like I've got anything else to do, with all the construction canceled."

She shook her head. "Stay with us then. At least until you can get it cleaned up. You said you thought your insurance might cover it?"

"Yeah, I'm waiting for them to get back to me."

"There you are, then. You come stay with us tonight, and to-morrow you'll know if your insurance will take care of the house. If they will, then fine, someone gets paid to clean up. If not, we'll get you some help."

"You don't need to—"

"You're right, I don't need to, I want to. You helped me and my friends when I needed it."

"But you don't owe me anything for that. I did that because it was the decent thing to do. It was solidarity, not charity."

"Yes, stupid, that's right. Solidarity, not charity. That's what I'm offering you."

"Oh."

———

Ana Lucía was staying in a People's Airbnb room in a nice retired Indian couple's house downhill from Kenneth Village, near the old Grand View cemetery, with a view of its Spanish tile and white-washed walls. She was sharing the room with another woman, Mason. The room had once housed a daughter, now grown and moved away, and it had a bunk bed with a double below and a single up top. Mason insisted on moving from the single into the double with Ana Lucía, so I could have my own bed. I insisted that I could sleep on the floor. I lost the argument, and then Maneet, the grown daughter's mom, overheard us and produced a trundle bed from under the bottom bunk with the air of a stage magician doing a card production.

"And don't you argue about who will sleep in the trundle bed," she said, wagging her finger at us, but smiling. "Brooks sleeps there. That way he gets clean sheets."

We all laughed and Maneet brought us to the kitchen for chai masala and clucked her tongue at the photos of my trashed house, muttering, "Disgusting, disgusting."

Somehow it was dinnertime, the day whirled past in a chaotic mess of new-relationship energy, fear, rage, and disgust, and here it was, getting dark, my stomach grumbling, Maneet finding me some clean sheets for the trundle.

I sous-chefed for Maneet, and she was patient with me in telling me what went into her quick chana spice mix and how she flash-fried the zucchini from her garden before marinating it in a tangy vinegar mix, while her husband, Kabir, had his regular weekly call with his cousins in Mumbai, them sitting around the breakfast table and waving at me and shouting hello.

After dinner, I found that my eyelids were drooping, and after I fumbled and nearly dropped a plate while loading the dishwasher, everyone told me I had to go to bed and so I did, barely waking when Ana Lucía stepped over the trundle some hours later to climb into the bottom bunk. If I woke at all when Mason came in, I didn't remember it.

I got up hella early the next morning, disoriented at first, then catfooted out of the house and bikeshared to Lou the French's and got a big, fragrant box of croissants and rode them back to Maneet's place, finding Kabir already up in his pajamas making coffee. He helped me find a nice serving basket and some jams and preserves and we laid out the table.

"You didn't have to do this," Maneet said, dabbing crumbs from her mouth and nightshirt.

"But I'm glad he did," Ana Lucía said, tearing the last croissant in half and transferring it to her plate.

"Best in LA," I said. "Maybe best outside of Louisiana."

Ana Lucía said something but it just came out as a spray of crumbs.

I was ready to just head straight home, then I remembered my drain full of concrete so I took up Maneet and Kabir on their offer of a shower and thanked them profusely before heading out, a little jar of Maneet's homemade pickle at the bottom of my bag.

I leaned the bike up on the curb by my house and released it, then started to head around to my usual entrance, the back door, but then I remembered how that had led me astray the day before, caused me to miss the state of the house for crucial moments. Instead, I headed through the front door.

The house was clean! I mean, not spotless, but much cleaner than it had been before I left, the worst of the mess picked up and the pictures squared on the walls, the coats hung up and the shoes in rows. I took it in for a moment, then stuck my head in the living room (still a mess) before taking a trepidatious peek into my absolutely trashed and filthy kitchen.

It was tidied. Some of the cabinet doors had been ripped off, but they were leaned neatly on a cupboard, and the smashed crockery was in large contractor bags along with the ruined food.

The floor, table, surfaces, and empty fridge were spotless. In

202 • **cory doctorow**

the middle of the table was a sheet of paper folded in thirds with my name neatly printed in the middle of the top third.

I unfolded it but even before I read it, I knew what it was.

Dear Brooks,

Sorry we didn't do this in person, but we hope that our help with the cleanup makes it up to you a little.

We're both going to find somewhere else to live. We're intensely grateful to you for being so generous with your home and we'll keep paying rent through the end of the month.

But for obvious reasons—the place getting trashed—and other reasons—you want to tear it down and build a high-rise (which is so cool, seriously!)—it makes sense for us to find somewhere more stable to live.

We hope you aren't too upset. We should all get together for dinner soon, okay?

Take care of yourself.

Love,
Milena
and Wilmar

And below their signatures:

PS: You're seeing Phuong Petrakis?!?!?! You are a VERY lucky guy—Wilmar

I dropped the note on the table and walked the rest of the house. They'd cleared out their rooms and done a good job cleaning them up. The living room and my room needed work, and someone would have to haul all the junk—the bulging bags, the slashed mattresses—to the dump, but the job was three-quarters done. I could probably have just called a plumber to fix the shower drain, paid for bulky item removal, and spent a couple of hours disinfecting and so on, and been back to normal. Add some new roommates and I'd be up and running. Hell, I could just do a big People's Airbnb number.

Fuck that.

Phuong had left me a couple of messages since I'd texted her after arriving at Ana Lucía's People's Airbnb. At first, she was sympathetic, then a little worried, but she'd finished up with I assume you're just dealing with a lot of literal and figurative mess right now so let me know if you need help, otherwise I'll leave you alone.

I texted her and she got back to me in an instant, which felt incredibly good (she'd been waiting to hear from me!) and incredibly shitty (why hadn't I gotten back to her sooner?). I got as far as telling her about the roommates leaving and how I was going to need a plumber to sort out the shower when she all but ordered me to go over to her house and stay there until I'd figured things out.

New-relationship energy made for a weird mixer with enraged terror. The whole ride over to Phuong's, I kept sliding into hate-filled revenge fantasies and then I'd remember that this incredible woman had invited me over to her house for a sleepover and I'd have a moment where I was just on autopilot, lost in a happy daze at my stupendous good luck. New-relationship energy is the best energy.

I knocked at Phuong's door a couple of times but didn't get an answer, and I was about to text her when I registered the loud music coming and thumping from inside and decided to try the doorknob.

Phuong and her roommates were all crowded into the living room, all the furniture pushed against the walls, and loud beats blasting. They were dancing their asses off.

I was thunderstruck for a moment and then I busted out in a huge grin, and then Phuong spotted me and smiled even wider than me and stretched out a hand to me and I jumped into the fray. I'm not a great dancer, but Phuong was, and I was good enough to follow her lead, and the music was so good and her housemates were having so much fun. I got whirled from one to the next, until I'd danced with all of them and I was panting and someone finally killed the music.

"What was *that*?" I asked, as Phuong slipped a sweaty arm around my waist and kissed me where my earlobe met my jawbone.

"Motivational exercise," she said, panting a little. "Every day we do a house-wide, two-minute cleanup called the Two Minutes Hate where we clean as much as we can in a hundred and twenty seconds. But twice a week we do a thirty-minute session and if we get the whole house done in that time, we have a dance party."

"I love you guys," I said. As soon as I heard myself speak the words aloud I realized that I was treading on perilous ground.

But she said, "We love you too," and gave me a smoldering look that made all the blood in my body rush out of my extremities (with one exception).

I helped them move their furniture back into position and accepted a sweating icy glass of homemade ginger beer that was so spicy it made me cough (in a good way).

Phuong plunked down in our snuggling couch and patted the cushion next to her. I didn't need to be asked twice.

"So, you've had quite a day, huh?"

I groaned. "Don't remind me."

"Come on, I wanna hear about it." So I told her: Kenneth's threats and offers, the wrecked house, my baby blanket, the sleepover with Ana Lucía and her Airbnb hosts, and then the note from my house-mates.

"Holy shit," she said.

"Wow," Don agreed. He and Miguel had stayed for the retelling, and then Arina and Jacob had come in midway through. They were all looking at me like I'd blown their minds.

"Your fucking *baby blanket*," Arina said. "I mean, how low is that?"

"What did your grandfather keep in that cache, anyway?" Phuong said.

I shrugged and said, "I have no idea. He was a weird-ass, paranoid old man." I felt like a dick for lying but also didn't think that Phuong and her friends would be excited to hear that I had assault rifles stashed in the Burbank hills. I liked these people so much and I wanted to be someone they'd like, too.

"I bet you can fix up the blanket," Miguel said. "Get the scraps out, hand-wash them, then fit the pieces together on a backing. You could frame it." He patted the worn, stitched-together denim kimonos that covered the sofa. "That's basically how I made this. I could show you."

It was such a nice offer I nearly cried. The welling up of emotions made me realize how fucking hurt and angry I was at the Maga militiamen who'd defiled my house and chased out my roommates.

"Hey," Phuong said. "Hey. You're shaking. It's okay, Brooks, it'll be okay." She stroked my hair. They were all looking at me, staring at me, and the rage all bubbled up.

"These fuckers, these fucking . . . *fuckers*. They think they're the future of California, of America, of the world. They've got rich psycho friends who'll arm them and pay for their lawyers and organize them, and they're planning some kind of paramilitary coup. They're not going to stop at vandalism and cross burning. They want a war. We have to do something, you guys. We *have to*. It's them or us. They want to steal the world from us. We can't let them. The world needs defenders. Who's going to do that if we don't?"

"Sit down, okay, Brooks?" Phuong said. I almost snapped that I *was* sitting down and then I realized I was pacing the room, fists clenched, and they were all staring at me.

I sat down. Don looked at me with soft concern in his eyes. "Brooks, I get it. After what you just went through, you've got a right to be angry like this. But don't let them turn you into what they are."

"Translation," Phuong said, "forget all the macho 'defenders of the homeland' shit. We're not going to get into a *firefight* with these assholes. They're not a militia, they're a criminal conspiracy. They've got big money behind them, but Brooks, they're *nitwits*."

I couldn't help myself. I snorted.

"So what do we do, call the cops?"

Now she snorted. "You've called the cops on these assholes how many times now? Three? Four? Has it helped even once? It's no good to do the same thing over and over again and expect a different outcome?"

"So what, then?"

"Let's figure it out."

Miguel brought out his cabernet-finished Jefferson's, which I liked a lot more than the Pappy. We had it on ice with spicy bitters and citrus peels and it took the edge off everything. Phuong stuck a whiteboard up on the wall and got some markers and we drank whiskey and brainstormed. Her housemates really took the brainstorming rule that no idea is too stupid to throw out seriously. I found it a little bewildering when Arina suggested finding all their addresses and chalking their sidewalks with personal testimonials from people who'd been rescued by GND programs, but Phuong added it to the board and everyone nodded so I rolled with it.

"Send their dox to Watanabe's office," I said.

"Who?" Arina asked.

"The state attorney general. She hates these fucking militias."

Phuong gave me a quick headshake before writing it down. I guess calling the AG was basically the same as calling the cops.

"And the National Guard. My history teacher had all kinds of stories about Grizzlies fighting off rioting militias after Uwayni's election."

Again, that little headshake, but she wrote it down, too. Guardsmen were *definitely* just cops by another name.

Getting that disapproval from Phuong—especially when Arina's dumb sidewalk-chalking idea hadn't gotten any—fired me up, so I fished around for a more out-there idea.

"Let's tear down my grandfather's house and build a high-rise there before anyone notices."

She didn't write anything down this time, just looked at me. Soon, I realized that they were *all* looking at me.

"I think we have a winner," Miguel said.

"Seriously," Don said.

"Dude," Jacob said.

And Phuong? She kissed me.

The brainstorming session made me think they were just dreamers, but Phuong and her housemates were all ex–Blue Helmets. They were used to getting up in the morning, meeting with a community group about the destiny of some brownfield site, and building a new residence there in three days flat.

Don and Arina got onto some next-generation modular slab designs and then Arina realized she'd been in the field with the woman who'd led the project to create them, so they bridged her in.

Miguel had a contact in Simi Valley who coordinated GND Housing Guarantee builds for the whole region, and he took all of ten minutes to find us a flock of cranes, bulldozers, forklifts, and other heavy machines.

Meanwhile, Phuong was crawling these databases of parameterized build plans, dragging buildings of various sizes onto Gramps's lot to check out the shadows, seismics, and whether they needed more water infrastructure than the city could provide from the nearby mains and sewer.

I had said "high-rise" but honestly, I'd never really thought about anything more than five or six stories. The tallest building in the neighborhood was only three stories tall. Plus, even with all my GND trufan energy, I couldn't imagine a ragtag group of guerrilla builders erecting an honest-to-goodness skyscraper.

Phuong had other ideas, and she clicked and dragged a bunch of legit high-rises onto her rendering of the lot before settling on a building that could be scaled up as high as thirty floors, though she'd settled for twenty, earmarking both the top and bottom floors for community spaces.

"How're you going to sink the pilings?" Don asked, looking over at her screen. She tapped and showed him a picture of a machine with an auger bit on it that was insane, like something you'd use to drill to the center of the Earth.

Don laughed. I laughed too. It was absurd.

"That's two, three days of drilling," Miguel said. He tapped at Phuong's screen to bring up a time-critical path chart. He dragged the top story of the building down to eight floors and we watched as the time ticked down. "Ninth story is always the killer," he said.

Phuong stuck her lower lip out. "I want a skyscraper!"

"I know baby, I know," Don said, distractedly, tweaking the floor plans to create more flexible configurations, either a three-bedroom and a bachelor on each floor, or two two-bedrooms. I mirrored his work on my screen and started tapping around, finding a mode that let me tap into the city street plan and start dragging that around, and before long, I was transforming the whole Verdugo corridor into high-rises with a light-rail line down the middle of it, anchored to a subway station where the old strip mall was currently languishing, part-occupied, mostly used as a skate park and a weekend craft market.

I zoomed out and saw that my own crude high-density corridor was being polished by Phuong's housemates, who abandoned their work on the hypothetical high-rise we were going to build on Gramps's lot in order to create green roofs, vertical farms, parkettes, a community center added to the main branch library at Buena Vista. I watched with my mouth open as they worked together, like musicians improvising a jam session, except they were improvising a whole neighborhood, and I could tab over to the spreadsheets where there were build plans, bills of materials, critical path and building-code variances we'd have to file for.

Jacob shoulder-surfed me. "It's cool, isn't it? It's just Blue Helmet stuff, though; kind of thing we used to do in-country, helping people think through what their neighborhoods could be. We'd do a couple training sessions, turn 'em loose for a week to come up with designs, get into revert-wars, and then we workshop 'em and do it again. A month later, you've got some incredible designs, and all that stuff gets trained back into the model so it hints the next group who try it. That's why it's going so fast—it's hella trained."

"Don't say 'hella,'" Arina said. "It makes you sound stupid."

"I am stupid," he said, and crossed his eyes and stuck out his tongue. Then Arina took away his screen and wiped out and reshaped a granny flat he'd been sticking on top of a garage off California, tapping the seismic rating box when she was done.

"There, not a death trap anymore."

"Aw, *man*," he said, with feeling.

I grabbed a screen and dug in, snuggling up to Phuong, who'd sometimes look over at my screen and show me a faster or more elegant way to do what I was trying to do, and the neighborhood took on a polish and veneer that made it seem like a real architect's rendering. I was flying around when I realized I was looking at the building we'd started with. Gramps's house. My house.

It was beautiful, eight stories tall, roofed over with photovoltaics and a couple of eggbeaters, a courtyard with vegetable beds and ornamentals. The apartments were neat, thoughtful, weatherized for cross breezes, with charming, self-adjusting shades that kept them cool.

I flew through it, one apartment after another, the utility spaces and infrastructure, and I realized that we were the last ones in the room, and Phuong put her fingers over mine and guided them as we flew through the house, through the neighborhood, through the city, flying off the edge of the map into the undefined places of Cartesian grid lines. Phuong swiveled us around so that we were looking at my neighborhood, the place that had been my home since I arrived in trauma and bewilderment when I was eight years old. It glittered with photovoltaics that picked up greens from the roof gardens. Trolleys glided down the arteries, and people thronged in and out of the subway station. The Warner and Disney lots were opened up with pass-throughs for foot and bike traffic, and the LA River wended its way along their backs and through the equestrian district.

I felt for a moment like I'd lost my body, like my mind had separated from my flesh and flown into the screen, a world I'd conjured up with my friends that was so real that I could disappear into it, soar into it, accompanied by the untethered spirit of Phuong, whose nearness stayed with me even as my body drifted away.

Slowly I returned to the world, and Phuong's fingers were on mine.

"Oh. My. God. Aspirational urban planning is so fucking *hot*," she hissed in my ear.

We barely made it to her room before we tore our clothes off.

chapter 9
atlas shrugs

I've often thought of how the world changed for my parents—how one day it was out-of-control fires, rising authoritarianism, rampant disease, and the sense that no one cared and nothing could make it better, and the next day: the Canadian Miracle. A new government, a city moved from its floodplain, a job for anyone who wanted one, and the funding needed to service the terrible debts of the country: the inequality debt, the infrastructure debt, the climate debt. A nation unleashed upon itself, building high-speed rail lines connecting every major aviation route, weatherizing homes, restoring habitats, caring for those in need.

How strange must it have been to go from total hopelessness, the feeling of the world's doom as a flywheel, spinning faster and faster with no way to slow it, and then, all of a sudden, someone found the brake. The wheel that had only ever accelerated began to slow. It halted. It *changed direction*.

Hope in such a dark place. What can it have been like?

I don't know, but I can tell you how the reverse experience goes.

Phuong was up before me for a change. I'd been up late, hanging out with Don and Miguel, tasting whiskeys, and she'd turned in at a sensible hour. I dozed in her bed, smelling her pillow and pretending that I didn't need to pee, that I could just stay there all morning. She came in and rummaged quietly for a battery and I cracked one eye and then smiled at her. "Cuddle?" I suggested, turning back the sheets and patting the bed next to me.

212 • **cory doctorow**

She looked at me and I stopped smiling. Her face was a pinched mask, etched with worry. I sat bolt upright. "What is it?"

"A shitshow," she said, and handed me her screen.

It was a video showing a militia; they had all the trappings, the Gadsden flag and the camo ghillie suits and the AR-15s and plastic AR-3DPs, and, of course, white skin, blazing eyes, 3D-printed rank insignia like a cartoon general.

There were a dozen men on the screen, ranged in two rows behind a man at a desk. He was shiny-bald, old, with turkey-wattle skin hanging off his neck; wire-rim circular glasses; a saber and a swagger stick in front of him on the blotter. In the window behind them, a familiar view: the Port of Los Angeles, long spits of squared-off landfill supporting ranks of precisely arrayed cranes; giant container ships motionless at their docks.

"This is Commander Vinton G. Ritzheimer, speaking for the California Irregulars and affiliated militia groups. This morning, we seized control of the Port of Los Angeles at Long Beach in a smoothly executed martial maneuver that resulted in minimum loss of civilian life.

"Make no mistake: this action was *lawful*. The State of California has long pursued an unconstitutional program of private property seizures under color of so-called environmental protection and remediation, and our do-nothing federal government has sat by, playing King Log, and courts, presided over by Marxist-appointed judges who sit beneath fringed flags in packed courts, let them get away with it.

"This. Ends. *Now*." He thumped his desk, making his saber literally rattle. "We California Irregulars call upon all California patriots to converge on the new Free Port of Long Beach to defend liberty. California depends on its imports and exports. This is a key strategic acquisition for the forces of freedom: if we hold this port, we will bring the state to its knees. America, your day of liberation is coming!"

On cue, the men behind him lifted their guns. One of them

let off some rounds into the ceiling accidentally, flinching and ducking as plaster dust rained down on him and his comrades in arms. The look of disappointment on the commander's face was fleeting, but heartfelt.

"What a bunch of assholes," I said, handing Phuong her screen back. "But it's just a bunch of knuckleheads. The National Guard'll shake 'em out in a day or two."

Phuong tucked the screen away. "I got a really bad feeling about this, is all."

I got up and hugged her. "I'm sure it'll be fine. And if it's not, we'll do something about it. All of us. Those guys are dead, they just don't know it. Their time is over."

Three days later, it wasn't over. The cops arrested three guys who tried to take a cab to Burbank Airport. Their AR-15s were detected by the lidar in the cab's trunk and it drove them into the old Fry's parking lot where they were met by a SWAT squad and a bomb-sniffing botswarm that picked over them and their belongings before the cops got within twenty-five yards of them. They were under snipers' crosshairs the whole time, and were periodically reminded by bullhorn not to twitch an eyebrow unless they wanted that eyebrow—and the face it was attached to—turned into a pointillist painting.

Burbank PD must have war-gamed this scenario, because they materialized a million sawhorses, movable suicide-car bollards, and millimeter-wave body scanners and set up checkpoints all around town; anyone crossing the city line, entering the studios, coming in or out of downtown or entering the Magnolia Park strip had to clear a checkpoint. Most people got waved through, but Ana Lucía and her refugee friends—and anyone who looked like them—had a high probability of being searched and IDed.

"You are fucking kidding me." I'd been waved through the checkpoint at North Hollywood Way and Magnolia with nothing more than a body scan, but as I turned to continue my discussion with Ana Lucía, I realized that she was getting a pat-down and an ID check. I stalked back to the checkpoint.

"What the hell, guys?" I said to the cops. I couldn't believe it.

"Please wait behind the line, sir." The cop was older than any cop I'd ever seen in uniform, like he was some kind of reservist or desk guy they'd pressed into service. His partner, the woman patting down Ana Lucía, was young and white and stony-faced.

"I'm behind the line. But seriously, what the hell? The terrorists holding the port hostage look like me, not like her. The terrorists who tried to seize the airport looked like me, not like her. How come I sailed through but she gets the date with Doctor Jellyfinger over there?"

"Sir, if you have a complaint about our procedures, you can scan the QR code on your left and someone from public relations will be in touch with you."

Ana Lucía was rigid with anger as the cop completed her pat-down. "You're free to go," the cop said, peeling off her gloves and dropping them in a bin. "Thanks for your cooperation."

The old cop and I locked eyes for a long moment while Ana Lucía cleared the body scanner and collected her bag from the belt.

"We both know why she got scanned and I didn't," I said.

He snapped upright, eyes wide. "What are you trying to say?"

"I'm saying that being a racist is a worse sin than calling someone a racist."

I turned and walked away with Ana Lucía. "Hey!" the cop yelled behind me. I heard the woman cop say something indistinct to him, and he said something angry back, and she said some more words, and then we were out of earshot.

"Assholes," I said, spittle flecking off my lips. I was furious. White Nazis were taking over California and "law enforcement" was shaking down brown refugees.

"It's all over town," Ana Lucía said. "All the time now. Like I was telling you."

"I'm sorry," I said. "That's not who we are."

She stopped me, turned me to face her. People on the sidewalk swerved to go around us. "Brooks, this may not be who *you* are, but it's what this city is. Otherwise they'd all do something about it." She waved an arm expansively at the shoppers around us under their sun parasols, aiming their little battery-powered fans at their sheened faces. The wet-bulb temp was spiking again as a blanket of humidity settled over the city, driving us up into the 110s. It was the kind of weather that made everything frustrating and enraging and all this bullshit wasn't helping. Being told off by Ana Lucía made me briefly but seriously angry, and the fact that she was clearly right didn't help any.

She searched my face, apparently decided whatever she saw was acceptable, and started moving again. "Let's get froyo," she said. "It's too hot."

In the line at the froyo co-op, she got some screen buzzes and tapped for a while, her face furious. She crumpled it up and stuck it in her pocket. "Fuck," she muttered. An old white lady in the line gave her a stink eye.

She didn't notice. Instead, she squeezed her eyes shut and ground her jaw and I had to ask, "What's going on?" I tried to make it soft and nondemanding so she'd have space to tell me to shut up if she needed to.

"The new People's Airbnbs," she said. "They're shutting down. At first it was just a couple but now it's dozens of them. All this terrorism bullshit has people freaking out."

"Wait, *what*? People who've been hosting refugee families are suddenly worried that they're *terrorists*? That doesn't make any sense—I mean, leaving aside that all the terrorists are crazy white people—" The old lady gave *me* a stink eye. I stuck my tongue out at her and she flinched back, shocked. I felt disgustingly good about it.

"No, the hosts don't think that, but their asshole neighbors do, and they're making life hell for anyone hosting a refugee family.

Fuck it. I can't blame 'em. I mean, if you've gotta live next to someone for the next twenty years, do you really wanna get into a feud where they think you've got mass murderers crashing on your sofa?"

"They're cowards. Who cares about your asshole neighbors? Who cares about assholes?" The old lady was about to say something, and I tensed up, but she got called up to the counter.

"It's so much bullshit," I said. "I mean, move whoever you want into my house, for sure—" I twinged, thinking of the plan to scrape it to the foundation slab and build a high-rise. But that was a fantasy, right? This was reality, and people needed housing. "But we've got to do *something*."

"They're calling us up," she said, gesturing at the froyo kid. The old lady was still glaring at us.

Three days later, I was delivering my twentieth tent. I'd put out the call on social for people's camping gear, and we'd cleaned out the library's stock of tents and camp stoves. Every park had become a tent city, and my DSA chapter had assembled a ton of swamp coolers with twelve-volt fans and ten-gallon buckets, running off of surplus solar cells.

The tent cities were a shock and a rebuke to Burbank, a reminder that our city had denied these people the homes it had promised them, and then put them out on the streets. Every time I saw them, I felt terrible. The composting toilets stank and the city showers at the Verdugo Aquatic Facility were crammed from the moment it opened to the end of the swimming day, and the swimmers were all pissed and being dicks to the refus who were just trying to keep clean.

The LA County DSA found our local chapter a lawyer to draft a petition to the city to ignore the injunctions and get to building housing for our refu friends, and we staked out the city checkpoints, gathering signatures, staffing all of them 24/7 in an effort to gather heroic numbers in short time. Forty-eight hours later, we had twenty-five thousand verified signatures, one in five Burbankers, and we decided that was enough to take to City Hall. A friendly councilor called an emergency session, got our petition agendized, and we packed the house.

The Magas were there, of course, but our side had lost all restraint. We didn't let them push into line, we closed ranks around anyone small or old or young that they tried to crowd around and intimidate, and we got the one asshole who was open-carrying arrested and jeered as he was thrown in the back of a cruiser.

The idea that this was a polite battle of political viewpoints was over. The mask was off. Magas were accelerationists, accelerationists were separatists, separatists were fascists, fascists wanted to murder us all. We were done playing. The councilors, mayor, treasurer, chief counsel, and secretary were visibly nervous, spooking every time a voice in the gallery rose over a mutter, flinching like they expected an outbreak of violence.

After some opening statements from our friendly councilor—Tony Yiannopoulos, a DSA-endorsed guy who'd been on the right side of every local issue—the president of the Burbank DSA came up to the mic. I knew Huey Wilkins from the annual DSA picnic in Griffith Park, where he'd show up and barbecue endless platters of tofu and vat meat and give a closing benediction after the last band played, exhorting us to all help pick up the trash.

I'd never seen Huey in full flight, but here he was, in his neat black suit and bow tie, rolling out preacher oratory that had these amazing tones of righteousness and anger. It made me half scared, in a good way: he could have called on us to charge the cops lining the chamber walls and half of us would have done it. All that, and he was just reading the lawyer's case citations about why the city had the legal authority to overrule the injunction and start construction again! Then he got to the good part.

"Ladies and gentlemen, I have read you a whole lot of legal arguments tonight, chapter and verse on state and federal case law. The lawyer who prepared those arguments is damned good at her job and I'm sure that every one of those arguments checks out good.

"But let's be real here. The reason you should lift the injunction isn't legal, it's moral. We have a city full of people who came here because the law of the land and the custom of civilized people told them that we'd take them in. We have a city full of people who *want* to take them in, and we have a small, bitter minority of people who don't care about the will of the majority—no more than they care about human decency. These people are allied with violent terrorists. They tried to take over our airport. They have us cowering in fear, here in our own homes, in our own city.

"*You* are the people we elected to manage this city. You have already heard that you have the legal authority to overturn this vicious minority of terrorist sympathizers. Now I am appealing to your *moral* sense.

"We all know Burbank has a *history*. We know this was a sundown town. The 1930 census listed *six* Black people residing in Burbank. We know that there were Black people in LA County then. The reason there were only six Black folks inside the city limits back then? It wasn't safe for them." He checked his notes. "1940 census? Twenty-two Black people. 1950 census? *Twenty-nine* Black people. All those Black people building bombers for Lockheed? Not welcome after dark. All the Black women inking and painting cels at Disney? We kicked 'em the hell across the city line before the sun went down.

"Burbank can't do anything about those past injustices. Nothing you do or say will ever change things for the Black people who were redlined, terrorized, and excluded.

"But you can show that Burbank has *changed*. That it has learned from its sins. You can show repentance. You can show *growth*. You can stand up and by God you can *lead* because you are our *leaders* and if you aren't running at the head of our movement, you're gonna end up way behind it, wondering what the hell just happened to your moral authority. To your legal authority.

"So, Madam Mayor, Councilors, city officials, Chief: I ask you tonight to listen to the people of Burbank. Listen to the still, small voice of your consciences. Listen to the voices of history. Think about your history. Think about the people who will come after you. Think about where *you* will fit in history and what side of it you will be remembered for upholding."

He stopped so abruptly that it took a minute for the audience to realize that he was done and to start cheering. The cheers were so loud that my ears buzzed, and it took me a while to realize that the Magas were booing, because they were inaudible over the roar.

Now Huey was holding his hands up for silence and the mayor was pounding her gavel. Huey had a screen someone had passed him and he said something to the mayor that we couldn't hear because his mic had been cut. The mayor shook her head like she couldn't understand and he repeated himself and then his mic came back on abruptly:

"—a message from the office of the undersecretary for the interior, who was contacted by Congresswoman Beverley Carr on this matter. It's a longish letter, Madam Mayor, so I'll just read the final paragraph here.

"'It is the judgment of the Department of the Interior and the Office for Internal Refugees that, in light of the circumstances and the urgent humanitarian crisis on its doorstep, the City of Burbank can and should exercise its authority to permit additional shelters such as are needed to alleviate the pressing and immediate needs of unhoused persons. It is the legal judgment of the General Counsel of the Office for Internal Refugees that the City of Burbank has this authority, notwithstanding any injunctions issued by California state court. Further, it is the opinion of the Office and its counsel that the City of Burbank may have a duty to act under the Internal Displaced Persons Act of 2026.'"

The room was perfectly silent at first, people looking from one to another, *Did that mean what I thought it meant?*

Then, a buzz of whispers that quickly grew to a roar of conversation, and the mayor started banging her gavel again, but no one was listening, and then there was an ear-piercing alarm in the room that was impossible to talk over. The mayor tapped her screen and the sound died, leaving behind a ringing in our ears.

"That's enough. In light of this, I move that the council go to an in-camera session so that we may confer with the city attorney. Do I have a second?"

Within moments, we were ushered out of the chamber, down the stairs and out onto the sidewalk. The Magas and the rest of us kept our distance, overseen by the cops. We wondered how long it would be, exchanged messages with people in other parts of the country undergoing similar fights. A few people sat on the City Hall steps and played cards. Someone ordered a couple of boxes of doughnuts. An hour went by. It was 10 p.m. We texted our friendly councilor inside the chamber and got a terse answer that deliberations were intense.

The Magas got burgers delivered. We got coffee. Someone organized a tennis-ball soccer game with backpacks for goalposts that was briefly hilarious and then the ball rolled down a sewer. The Magas laughed. We laughed at them thinking that this was some kind of epic dunk.

Midnight came and went. The *Burbank Bugle* account reported leaks from inside the council chamber that said they were split and the city attorney was taking the side of the people who wanted to start building again. Our friendly councilor texted us to say they were taking away all the councilors' screens because of the leaks.

People slept on the sidewalk with rolled-up jackets for pillows. It was sweaty and gross and there were so many mosquitoes, and no amount of bug dope could keep them all at bay. The waking slapped the bugs off the sleeping. Some people went home, but not many. We all understood that if they thought they could fuck us over without facing an angry crowd, then fucking over would happen.

At 1:15 a.m. we were readmitted. The people who'd been asleep shuffled up the stairs, supported by the people who'd drunk all the coffee. We went back through the body scanners and found our seats again. As soon as I saw the council and the mayor at the front of the room, I knew it was going to be terrible. The long delay and the leaks had suggested as much but I'd been nursing hope. One look at those faces—furious and frightened, by turns—and my hope was vaporized.

The mayor gaveled us in.

"Thank you for your patience. The council has carefully weighed the petition and the supplementary materials our friends in the federal administration were kind enough to provide, and, after extensive consultation with the city attorney, it is the judgment of the majority of this council that we cannot, in good conscience, expose the city to the kind of legal liability that ignoring a court order would entail. To be perfectly frank, the civil penalties from suits by citizens of this city who would have standing to seek compensation for such a course of action could render this city bankrupt. In light of that grave peril, it is our conclusion that we will not permit construction on emergency refugee housing to resume at this time."

Our groan quickly turned into a roar. The mayor let it go for thirty seconds or so, but when it showed no sign of abating, she hit her klaxon again. I swear it was even louder this time. Once she switched it off, she gave us all a second to recover from the ringing in our ears.

"However, in light of the humanitarian challenges this presents, the council has unanimously voted to allocate three hundred thousand dollars from the city's emergency fund for humanitarian supplies, including food relief, tents, and additional temporary toilet and bathing facilities."

The roar came back. They were going to make the tent cities permanent. Our parks were now refugee camps, forever. The smiles on the Magas who'd stuck around were just the last twist of the knife. I caught sight of Huey and he just looked . . . crushed. That broke me. I shouted "FUCK" into the roar of hundreds of other outraged people and stomped out of the chamber, out of City Hall, and home to my stupid bed in my stupid house.

The terrorists who'd tried to seize Burbank Airport were the Maga Club's new heroes and there were signs all over the place that read FREE THE BURBANK THREE. Local social was full of the video they'd planned on releasing once they seized the airport, a kind of low-budg version of the Commander Vinton G. Ritzheimer and the California Irregulars Long Beach Port Seizure video. Not only did it have low production values (a sin in a town that was once home to three movie-studio monopolies and was now home to dozens of plucky indies the DOJ had created when it split them up), but their central demand was reopening the airport to private jet traffic. Not small hobbyist planes—jets. Private jets were such a weird remnant of a long-buried world, it was like they were demanding the right to park zeppelins or autogyros.

My roommates were gone, but my house was full again, with eight of Ana Lucía's friends sleeping in the two spare bedrooms and the living room. They were all really nice—some of them had been in the advance party that had camped in the backyard—but still, I found it impossible to relax at home. The crowded spaces and lines for the bathrooms were a constant reminder of how screwed up everything was and how much the city and its people had let me down.

All that made me hate Gramps's house, that cursed place, that anchor dragging me down to this stupid city that my parents couldn't get out of fast enough. I wanted to tear it down and build a high-rise. I wanted to tear it down and dig a hole and push the remains inside it. Fuck that house and fuck the people who thought houses like this were a good idea.

One night as I lay in bed, unable to sleep, listening to the shifting and muttering of my very full house, I decided I needed to get out and do something, something that would make the world in some small way better. I grabbed a screen and tapped up a chore-board, looking for a useful task I could go and do and get my ya-yas out on.

SOLAR MAINTENANCE—BURROUGHS HIGH

Huh.

Well, it made sense. I was checked out for solar, I knew Burroughs, and I lived close by. I mean, the last time I'd gone up there someone had tried to murder me, but as far as I knew, no one had attempted to murder anyone else on the Burroughs roof since. Plus, it had a nice view. I hit the lights and found some clothes.

The panels hadn't been cleaned in a long time. I lit up the roof and got a squeegee and pressure hose and got to work cleaning the layers of ash and gunk off them, then reapplied some dirt-stop stuff that was supposed to shed most of that gunk. Maybe it did. Maybe all the gunk I was hosing down the drains would be a thousand times worse next time if I didn't apply it.

Working in the middle-of-the-night silence was relaxing, and for the first time since the City Hall meeting, I felt the knots in my shoulders loosening. I put the cleaning gear away in its shed and stretched out and realized that I could see the sky going pink in the distance. I moved to the edge of the roof and dangled my feet and watched the sunrise turn the sky deeper pink, then red, then orange. Some people swear by sunsets, but I'll take staying up to watch the sunrise anytime. I'd been feeling pretty rotten about Burbank lately, but the sunrise filled me with warm feelings. I was finally sleepy and it was definitely time to get home. My legs were asleep and I had the sudden realization that maybe having numb legs while perched on a roof edge and suffering from sleep deprivation wasn't the safest thing to be doing. I leaned way back, rolled slowly onto my belly, and *slowly* came to my hands and knees. I looked up to make sure I wasn't about to split my skull open on the edge of a solar panel's frame and saw something weird.

It was still dark, of course, the sun low in the sky. But what rays were available were coming in nearly horizontally, and they made the weird thing glint. It was a steel case, ruggedized, the kind of thing you'd use to protect a fragile musical instrument in shipping. Burroughs High had a bunch of them, including some really massive ones for double basses. But this one was square, and its seam had been welded shut, the weld a kind of drippy line blackened with scorch marks.

That was weird. But what made me scuttle back a step—my left toe going off the ledge and just hanging out there in space, sending a jolt up my spine—was the little project box attached to it by an umbilicus of wires that penetrated a gasket that had been hacked into the case's edge. The project box had a cheap OLED screen displaying one word: ACTIVE.

The weird thing was a fucking bomb. What the hell else could it be? Inside that case would be a proprietary blend of explosives and shrapnel—ball bearings or lug nuts or roofing nails. I crept away from it sideways, not wanting to move toward it and not wanting to back myself off the edge of the roof.

I pelted down the stairs three at a time and nearly tripped at the second-floor landing, and *did* trip at the first-floor landing, but caught myself on the wall before I could break my neck. I ran like hell down Verdugo, putting a block between me and the school before I shook out my screen and hit 911. I told the robot I'd found a bomb and half a second later I was talking to a human. He was Asian and had a Southern accent and told me he was Specialist Jeong in the Fort Worth antiterrorism center. He was disappointed that I hadn't taken any pictures, but he took my detailed description, asking me to hold for a moment while he dispatched Burbank PD, then came back to me and made me describe it all over again. I was just getting to the end when BPD arrived and fenced off the block. Specialist Jeong told me to go introduce myself to the officers and I looked over at them.

For an instant, I was convinced that the cop on the sawhorse closest to me was my old friend Officer Murphy, but he was just another chunky white guy out of central casting. He watched me approach through his heads-up goggles. I reached him just as a big white van screamed up and more cops jumped out, moving stiffly in head-to-toe armor, carrying awkward armloads of armor that they handed to the cops on the barricades.

My cop—name tag SCHLOSSMAN—held up a hand to me while he struggled, grunting, into a vest and buckled a helmet on.

"Uh, should we move away?" I asked.

"It's fine," he said. I mean, okay, but you're the guy with the body armor. I guess I could use him as a shield?

"You're Brooks Palazzo?" he said.

"Yes."

"Radio says you found a bomb up there?"

"Yes." Another van arrived and three people in *much* thicker armor got out of it. A bunch of drones lifted off from inside it and headed over to the roof.

"Do you need me to go show them where it is?"

He shook his head. "You just stay put. They'll let you know if they need you."

My pulse was finally returning to normal when there was a loud, sudden ruckus near the van the drones had lifted off from, and the cops who'd been operating the drones were joined by a bunch of cops, with the specialists shouldering through the rubbernecking guys who'd come off the sawhorses. My cop, Schlossman, gave the scene a considering look.

"Guess they found your bomb," he said.

"It's not my bomb!" I said.

He tilted his head at me. I wondered what he'd read in my file when he'd been told to expect me. He cocked his head to listen to his radio. "Okay," he said. "Let's move."

"Where?"

He pointed. "One block down," he said. "They just scanned your bomb and it's a big one."

There was a weird transition where for a while I was waiting at the sawhorses Schlossman was ferrying a block down the road to set up his new barricade, then I actually pitched in for a while and helped until another cop told me I wasn't allowed to be behind the lines (even though the lines weren't actually established yet), and then I was waiting, bored, for Schlossman to finish humping up his sawhorses while sweating buckets in his armor.

And then, once we were all set up one block farther along, he called me back to him and made me stand, just a few feet away. I asked if I could go sit on the curb and he said no.

"What? Come on, I've been standing here the whole time, it's not like I'm gonna run away."

He just shook his head and listened to his radio. I inched away from him and he snapped his head to me and shook his head. "Don't play games," he said.

I got out my screen and texted Phuong.

> Get out of there then!

          > I can't, the cops say I can't go

> What?!!? Are you under arrest?

          > No

> Are you being detained?

          > Uh I am not sure

> Ask!

          > ??

> Just say, AM I BEING DETAINED?

          > Really?

> BROOKS!

"Am I being detained?"

Schlossman rolled his eyes. "No, you aren't being detained."

> I'm not being detained

> Say AM I FREE TO GO?

> Really?

> DUDE

"Am I free to go?"

"Really?"

I reread Phuong's texts.

"I guess so?"

"Sir, you are free to go. But if you go, that might constitute probable cause. We're having kind of a tense moment here, in case you haven't noticed, and if you make things complicated or difficult, it's hard to say how that'll work out for you. I don't know who's texting you a bust card there, but I seriously recommend that you just sit tight until we're done with you."

I looked from the screen to the cop. "How about you let me sit on the curb over there, then?"

He shook his head and puffed out his cheeks. "You do what you gotta do, kid," he said.

> They're letting me sit on the curb

> This is a load of bullshit you should just go

The ruckus from the drone van rose in pitch and intensity and I stared at them. So did Schlossman.

The hubbub died down then, and Schlossman listened to his radio. "They got it," he said. "All done."

"Really?" I asked.

He shrugged. "That's what they tell me."

But I still wasn't free to go. I sat back on the curb and texted Phuong and posted about the bomb and waited for one of the bomb specialists to come by. After an hour or so, I got a call from the SPECIALIST JEONG FT WORTH ANTITERRORISM CENTER and I picked up.

"Well, that's all done," he said.

"What is?"

"The bomb. Thank you for phoning it in. I have to gather a little more data from you and you can be on your way."

I stared at Specialist Jeong. He wasn't much older than me, and he'd helped disarm an IED from three states away.

"Hey," I said. "Before we begin, let me just say thanks, okay? That was scarily efficient. It feels good to know that even with everything going wrong right now, people like you are keeping us safe from the whack jobs who want to send us back to the 2020s."

He grinned and ducked his head. "That's really nice of you to say, Mr. Palazzo, but that one was *especially* easy. It's a standard design, the militias just download the plans and build 'em. I've dealt with eleven of them this week. Yours was my third for the day and it's just after lunchtime here."

"Oh." So much for my warm feeling about the competence of my government in the face of a wave of terror attacks. I felt suddenly hopeless and tired. So tired.

"All right," I said. "Well, that's a hundred percent terrible."

He shrugged. "At least they're not very creative. At this point, we know exactly what to do when one of these things pops up. Now, let's get you out of here."

Three bombs went off across the state of California that day: Sacramento, San Luis Obispo, and Mendocino. Eighteen more were caught and defused.

I thought it was bad before, but by the next morning there were bomb-detector drones zipping through the sky and the bullshit checkpoints got much less bullshitty, with hardcore bag searches and pat-downs for everyone, not just people who fit the profile.

"How long can they keep this up?" I said to Phuong, as we cooked dinner for her housemates.

"Judging from past experiences, a hell of a long time," she said. "I mean, put yourself in their shoes—how'd you like to be the police chief or the mayor who says they can stand down . . . and then a bomb goes off?"

"You make it sound like they'll *never* stop, then."

"Brooks, do you know how long this country made people take off their shoes to fly? One failed shoe bomber, twenty years of business travelers wading through slush at airport checkpoints in their socks."

I scraped the habaneros I'd been mincing into a little pinch-bowl and washed my hands three times to get the oils off my fingertips before I forgot and picked my nose or (yowch) wiped my butt. "But they stopped eventually, right?"

"Eventually. *After* they came up with body scanners. As far as I can tell, we're still operating under the presumption that shoe bombs are a thing, even though they've literally never been a thing, or at least not a successful thing."

Dinner was a success in that the food was good—green Thai chili over zucchini noodles—but even Phuong's housemates were too glum to make much of a meal out of it. It didn't help that the house got buzzed by bomb-detector drones twice during the meal. I'd made coconut cream to put over mango for dessert and everyone made a show out of enjoying it, but we all knew it was just a show.

Arina floated the idea of watching a movie or playing a game after dinner, but Miguel said he had to work early the next day and was going to bed after he finished dessert. I didn't blame him. The sooner this stupid day ended, the better.

Jacob and Don were just clearing the table when all our screens started going crazy.

They'd bombed City Hall.

The first impressions were crazy: aerial shots of City Hall with its facade and east wall just *gone,* rubble and smoke all around. On-the-ground shots from the sawhorses, smoke and dust and people on stretchers. Later, we found out that this wasn't a gigantic bomb going off, but rather six or possibly seven well-placed demolition charges planted by someone bent on maximum damage.

The Net of a Thousand Lies swung into full effect, with conspiracy theories and secondhand hot takes piling up, and we all did our bit by pitching in on a Reality-Based Community channel that vetted the social flurry and boosted the stuff that was well-cited and factual. This, of course, attracted brigaders who created their own channel that supposedly showed our bad faith in downranking the conspiracy theories about this being a false-flag op, citing examples where Blue Helmets had supposedly set off bombs and made it look like it came from plute-backed militias to drum up support for their cause. I tried wading in there to argue with them but Phuong pointed out that I kept holding my breath whenever I typed in those channels and told me that if I was having rage apnea, I had to step back.

The bombs went off during a committee meeting. They killed a councilor and the deputy mayor and hospitalized the mayor and the city attorney, along with nine city employees, including two people from planning, a security guard, and a cleaner. One of the bombs was hidden in the supply cupboard where they kept their cleaning products. They lost an eye and a hand.

Riverside's city hall was bombed, too, almost at the same time. Anaheim's city hall had *twelve* bombs, but they didn't go off and after the Riverside and Burbank bombings, every city hall in the state got a top-to-bottom search by millimeter-wave drones. Six more had bombs in them, though in the case of La Jolla, they later determined that the bombs were years old and were left over from an unsuspected, long-failed bombing plot. No one could figure out if that was cause for alarm or relief. Or both.

The next day, militias seized a solar farm in Mojave, a decommissioned Camp Pendleton auxiliary armory, and a desalination plant near Santa Barbara and declared them sovereign territory. There was a lot more viral video nonsense about fringed flags and deep states and the need to get back on "sound money": the gold standard or at least gold-backed cryptocurrency.

Compared with LA, we had it easy in Burbank. Across the city-limit line, there were National Guardsmen and whole neighborhoods ordered into lockdown when "credible threat intelligence" indicated some shit might be about to go down. The LAPD officers mobilized for the emergency were clearly incredibly glad to be back in command of the streets after more than a decade of being sidelined by social workers and addiction counselors and child and youth specialists. Finally, a public emergency that demanded a massive show of force.

Burbank PD took its MRAP out for a single spin down Magnolia but the stunt generated so many downvotes that it got parked for the duration. But the checkpoints got more serious still, and then we got a notice saying they were overflying with high-altitude scanners as well as low-flying drones, and cautioning us to steer clear of sewers and other utility spaces as these were now also drone-patrolled and we didn't want to create false alarms.

Heaven forfend.

I'd been spending so much time at Phuong's place that Ana Lucía texted me to tell me that my houseguests were worried that they'd crowded me out of my own home and I felt horribly guilty and then stupid about it. I decided to channel all that anxiety into something productive and invited Phuong's housemates and Ana

Lucía over for a big dinner at mine, with all my sleepover guests as guests of honor. I made three kinds of stew: lentil, tinga, and chili with cornbread dumplings. The kitchen was still a wreck, but I'd bought some standalone induction burners and I set them up on a couple of Gramps's card tables and borrowed big pots from the library, along with some long folding tables and plates and chairs that my houseguests helped me set up in the backyard.

A woman called Emily—shy, hardly said a word to me since moving in—emerged from her room with hand-cut colored streamers, like paper-doll chains but more intricate and beautiful, and she strung them from tree to fence to tree in the backyard, making it look enchanted. She taught Moises, who slept in the other room, how to make paper flowers, and they created one for each place setting.

Phuong's housemates brought whiskey (of course), but also some actual brewed booze, a ginger-habanero kombucha that they warned me was 7 percent and that was so spicy it made my earwax runny (but in a good way).

The dinner was a good reminder of just how funny and fun my new housemates were, and to make things even sweeter, Milena and Wilmar came by for dessert, with homemade granita in a huge cooler that they lugged into the backyard from a three-wheel cargo bike they'd booked. It had real chunks of lemon peel in it and turned our faces into delighted, sour puckers. Guitars came out, people clapped time, some people danced.

Drones buzzed us, first a couple, then a flock of about twenty, because I guess we fit some kind of AI profile or because someone who was watching their feeds wanted to get a better look at the gathering. As they got louder and lower, we all took out our screens and started livestreaming them and then someone must have gotten the message that they were coming off like assholes and the drones pulled back.

We brought out washtubs and everyone took turns washing the dishes—they'd go through sterilization at the library anyway—

and wiping down the tables and before long we had it all packed up, and my houseguests went off to bed, and Wilmar and Milena gave me long goodbye hugs.

"Still some granita left," Wilmar said, grabbing three bowls off the dry rack and dishing up the last of it for me and Phuong and Ana Lucía, before setting off.

The bottom of the granita was the most sour of all and so we washed it down with the last of the fiery ginger beer, and the spice and the sour and the sweet just *wrecked* our mouths, again, in the very best way, and then the booziness of the kombucha settled over us and we just lolled there for a while on our folding chairs, sweating in the nighttime heat, mouths afire and apucker, until Phuong said, "Wow. That was a hell of a dinner party."

Ana Lucía and I giggled. A drone buzzed us and just hovered for a long time. It killed the mood. They had mics and cameras, millimeter-wave, and some of them did gas chromatography, looking for black powder residue. Supposedly nothing we said was listened to by a human, but if something happened later, a judge could issue a warrant that let the cops go back in time and listen in on us.

"I want to throw a rock at it," I said, after it had hovered for five minutes.

"Don't joke," Ana Lucía said. "It's listening to you."

"I. WANT. TO—" That was all I got out before Phuong clamped a hand over my mouth, then she turned it into a caress and ruffled my hair.

The drone flew off. Ana Lucía picked up her chair and brought it in close to ours, so she was facing us, making a knee-to-knee triangle.

"I need to talk to you guys." In the dim light of my backyard, her face was all shadows and planes, cheekbones and hollows.

We nodded in the shadows. She looked up at the sky, checking for drones, then brought out a screen and turned on some white noise. I got a premonitory thrill.

"Look," she said, then drew in a deep breath and stared at her hands for a moment. "Look. It's not a coincidence, you know. How could it be a coincidence? Things being what they are, people like us losing our homes and coming to places like this, it was always going to be a trigger. There are plenty of people in government and especially in the police who have been playing nicey-nice with all your GND stuff, but who never believed it—whose version of saving America is kicking all the people who look like me out of the country and squatting on top of all the wealth they stole from us."

She broke off, stared at her hands some more, cranked up the gain on the white noise. "I'm not saying white people, middle-class people, they can't be allies. I mean, obviously. Look at you two. I mean, that's why I'm talking to you now. But before I say the next part I need to know that whatever I say, it's not going to spread without us all agreeing on who it spreads to."

"I promise," I said, and waited for Phuong, whose face I couldn't read in the dark.

"Ana Lucía, I agree with everything you just said but now you're asking me to make promises without my being able to understand what I'm promising. I take my promises too seriously for that. I trust you to be reasonable and to stick to your personal code of ethics. Will you trust me?"

Ana Lucía thought it over. I felt like a nitwit for making a promise instead of saying what Phuong had just said.

"I trust you," Ana Lucía said. "God dammit. Okay, here it is. This isn't the ending, this is the start. First burning crosses. Then takeovers. Then bombings. They're ramping up, escalating. There're so many guns out there, and mostly in their hands. And this is us-or-them time. Us or them. They want to push me into the ocean, me and everyone else like me. Then they'll make you clean their toilets. And the world will burn. They've got money, they've got organization, and they are making their move.

"When it's you or them, you have to choose a side. There aren't any bystanders. I've chosen a side. There're some of us, lots of us, all across the country, who are ready to do this thing. Hide in the hills. Fight back. Resist. Fight. Fight like our lives are on the line, because they are. Fight like we can't depend on the cops and the government and the army and the National Guard to stand up for us, because they won't. You know they won't. When have they ever stood up for us?"

"What about when they kept the polls open for Uwayni?"

Ana Lucía gave me a withering look. "*We* kept the polls open. Brown people. Black people. They showed up because there would have been a civil war if they didn't get out in front of it."

"Okay," I said. "Good point." I felt stupid and white.

"Yes, it is." I couldn't tell for sure, but it sounded like maybe she was choked up. She took a few deep breaths. "They've never changed. Uwayni didn't change them, she just made it socially unacceptable to call for genocide. For a while. No more. Genocide was hibernating, not dead. It's coming for us. Think about Florida."

There'd been so many bombings in Florida, I'd lost count. All targeting the seawalls and pumps that protected the reparations zone, and there were thousands of Black and brown families on their way out of the state, looking for somewhere to live now that their homes were ankle-deep in water. But that was Florida. The South. This was California, right? I thought of the Flotilla, all those Californians. This was California.

This was California.

Phuong said, "What, exactly, are you asking? Like, will we join a militia and shoot people?"

"That's what I'm asking, Phuong. If they come for your homes, if they come for your future, will you defend it?"

"Ana Lucía—"

"Phuong, I know you've been overseas, you've seen people lose everything, but I *have* lost everything. Twice. I was six years old when my parents lost their place in Washington State to the fires.

Both of my uncles and my grandma died. Then we came here, built up again. Lost it. Lost it slow and hard. First my parents' farm went, dried up because they couldn't afford water rights. They were doing everything right, permaculture, passive atmospheric moisture capture, rotation, drought-resistant crops. Meanwhile, the big farms nearby just outbid us on water and grew fucking *almonds,* making a big deal out of the fact that their drip irrigators had reduced the water need to half a gallon *per nut.*

"Have you two ever fought and fought, knowing that the cause was lost, but fighting on anyway, because surrender isn't an option? That was us on our farm, going without, working such long hours, taking the train to Sacto to beg the Department of Food and Agriculture for a bridge loan and having the nice man look you right in the eyes and tell you that a bridge loan was just going to put off the inevitable, because it's a bridge to nowhere.

"When the bank took the farm, they sold it to the big guy next door, Mr. Moneyball, who promised he'd leave it fallow and collected a big, fat carbon credit. He generously let us live in a trailer on his farm, and he generously gave us piecework picking for him, and my mom and dad picked like they had on their own place, but they never could get ahead. Never could afford to take care of me or my brother—not just things like college admission prep or school trips, but real basics. Clothes. Food. The Jobs Guarantee was just getting started and we lived on unincorporated land, so there wasn't any city government to do outreach to people like my parents, not for years.

"By the time anyone came around to tell us about it, it was too late. My dad's heart condition, my mom's diabetes. We were still stuck in single-payer land out there, and the clinic didn't bother to tell them that they could apply for Medicare for All to get their procedures and meds covered. They both got good care once Uwayni just socialized the motherfucker, but by that point all they could hope for was a halfway comfortable death.

"That's when I became an activist, and of course the landlord didn't want a mouthy brown girl living in his trailer anymore. The Jobs Guarantee meant I could get decent work as a community organizer, and so that's what I did, getting all those other people in their trailers up to speed on their rights, but everyone knew it was too late for the whole county. We lost rights to the Colorado River water, then the deepest wells went dry, and then there were seasons of such heavy rain that everything washed away—crops, topsoil, houses and trailers.

"So we came here. My idea. I did my homework, found the places with affluent tax bases, active DSA chapters, low density and room to build in and up to absorb us. I got DSA lawyers to help me figure out the internal refugee stuff, convinced the other kids in town that we had to go, and then they convinced their parents."

She heaved in a huge sigh. "This was my fucking plan, okay? This plan that left us sleeping in tents in parks while Nazis light up crosses and fire guns and set off bombs? My stupid plan." Her shoulders shook.

Phuong put a gentle hand on her knee. "You did the right thing. This thing that's going down right now, it's statewide. It's national. Hell, it's global. Go or stay, you'd be caught in the avalanche. Here, at least, you've got solid bedrock to stand on. People who care about each other. Decent people."

Ana Lucía snorted. "Decent."

"Yes," Phuong said. "Decent. Some of them are scared and some of them don't know what to do when things go wrong, but the mean ones, the hateful ones? They're loud because they have to be, because there just aren't that many of 'em. Babe, the shit you lived through, it's hard trauma, and all this stuff, it's gotta be triggering. How could it not?"

Ana Lucía pushed her hand away. "Don't patronize me."

"I'm not patronizing you," she said. "Trauma's the real deal, and there's a lot of it around here." I felt her eyes on me in the dark and my heart went thud-thud-thud as I thought about my parents' death, the shelter, my journey to Burbank. "But you're talking about a war, Ana Lucía. A war, right here. Is that what you want?"

"Listen to yourself," she spat. "We *have* a war. They're out there with guns and bombs and they are about to *steal your revolution back,* you fucking complacent idiots! You think you get a *choice* about whether it's going to come to fighting? You think power ever gives up without a fight?"

Her voice had risen to a shout. We were all shocked by it, including her. She muttered "Sorry" and looked at her hands.

"Ana Lucía," I said, then swallowed hard, feeling the lump of grief I got whenever my parents were on my mind. "I, shit." I heaved breath against tears, got them under control. "I've been through death. Mass death. The people out there, the bombers and the shooters, they're a death *cult.* They'd rather die, rather drown or cook or shit themselves to death of some disease than give up the 'freedom' to pollute, to destroy the planet, to wreck everything. They want to kill us. We want to *save* them. That's the difference."

"So what do you want to do, Brooks? Show them your belly when they come for you, dare them to shoot you? They will shoot you, Brooks. They'll shoot us all."

"They can't shoot us all," I said. "Even they don't have enough ammo for that."

She smiled and sniffed back tears. "Okay, not everybody. But a lot of us. Makes no difference."

"It does make a difference," I said. "It makes all the difference. If they get their way, it won't be by killing everyone who disagrees with them—it'll be by convincing people that resisting will hurt worse than it will help. If they can't scare or demoralize or traumatize us into submission, they *can't* win."

Phuong slipped her arm around my shoulders and it felt so good, like a handrail at a cliff's edge.

Ana Lucía shook her head. "Just words, Brooks. What the hell does that mean? How is that a plan?"

I made a set of balance scales out of my hands. "It's an equilibrium. The better the alternative seems, the harder they have to fight to crush it. If we want to preserve what we've made, if we want to save the world, we can't just hide in the hills and take sniper shots at these fuckers. That's the world *they* want. If we go and build the world that we want—"

"What does that *mean* though, Brooks? What do you want to *do*?"

"We should live the fucking revolution, that's what I want to do. I want to go rebuild City Hall, whether or not the city is there to help us. I want to tear down this idiotic house and build an eight-story mid-rise for families. I want to put streetcar tracks down the middle of Verdugo. I want to rebuild Burbank so it has the capacity to house every displaced person from San Diego to Santa Barbara, and build bomb sensors into the fabric of every road and sidewalk and building so that we can catch these fuckers the instant they start mixing some black powder. I want to stop fighting with these assholes and start fixing the world, saving the country and rescuing our goddamned species."

I realized I was pacing, declaiming to the night, waving my arms.

"That's what I want to do, Ana Lucía. I want to stop being afraid of the future."

"Shit," Phuong said, and though her face was lost in the shadows, I could *hear* her smiling. "That sounds way better than starting a war."

Ana Lucía looked at the sky and said "Aaaaah" but in a theatrical way that let me know she wasn't angry, just *overwhelmed* with all the bullshit. Fair enough. There was a lot of bullshit and it was seriously overwhelming.

Phuong got up out of her chair and went around behind Ana Lucía and rubbed her shoulders. She let her head slump and groaned in pleasure.

"Babe," Phuong said, "don't let Nazis live rent-free in your head. If you want to exterminate those fuckers, start with fumigating your brains. Brooks is right. They win if we let them define the terms. We win if we show everyone that their terms are bullshit. I've seen what happens when you let those fuckers decide what the fight is about and how it's fought. My first Blue Helmet placement was in Victoria, Australia. Barely lasted a month before they airlifted us all out. It was the wildfires, but not the fires themselves—it was the disinformation machine that said that us 'greenies' were setting the fires to prove that the climate was fucked, to clear out the cities and turn them over to refugees, to sell out to the Chinese. A million theories, none of them made any sense, all of them mutually exclusive. Today, you've got the militias saying the fires in Oregon and Sonoma are being set by refugee arsonists. I've seen how that movie ends. We can't let it turn into a shooting war or people will choose sides and let fly.

"Today, there are more Blue Helmets than ever in Australia and no one will even admit to having chased us out the last time around. That's because Australian comrades did the hard work, the solidarity work—evaccing people, building camps, and land care. They backed the Aboriginal landbackers *hard,* reestablished the controlled burns. They didn't fight for the revolution, they *lived* it."

All the while, she'd been kneading the knots out of Ana Lucía's shoulders and now worked her way up to her scalp, burying her fingers in her hair as Ana Lucía went limper and limper, the fight draining out of her with the rage. She lolled her head forward, exposing the tension at the base of her skull, and as Phuong went to work on those steel-cable tendons, she said, "Hard to live the revolution with a bullet in your back."

"It is," Phuong said. "But it's also hard to live the revolution when you're playing Che Guevara in the hills."

I'd had a feeling coming up in me ever since I'd gotten out of my chair and started pacing, a wild feeling. It was all the fear and sadness from the last days of my parents, mixed with all the rage and helplessness I'd felt in my years under Gramps's roof and under Gramps's thumb. It was all the joy and the ferocious new-relationship energy I got whenever I was near Phuong. It was the taste of Don and Miguel's whiskey and the feeling I got when I slammed the door in Kenneth's and Derrick's faces. The feeling I got when Ana Lucía tore a strip out of me for calling the cops when the Magas burned a cross in our backyard and the feeling I got at City Hall when the council came back from their closed-door session and fucked us all. It was the feeling I got when I buried Gramps's guns and the feeling I got when Phuong and her roommates showed me how to design a fantasy Burbank, one that would support people and the planet.

A wild feeling. Such a wild feeling.

"Let's just *do* it. Come on, we can *do* it. If we're going to get popped by the cops, let it be because we were doing guerrilla refugee shelter, not guerrilla warfare. 'If I can't build, I don't wanna be a part of your revolution.'"

That made them both laugh. Or maybe it was the wild feeling and the way it had me jerking around Gramps's backyard like a marionette with a seizure.

"You're an idiot," Ana Lucía said around her laughter.

"He's *our* idiot," Phuong said, and tackled me to the grass, covering my body with hers and my face with her kisses.

I'd been worried that Ana Lucía's mysterious countermilitia friends would dismiss our plan as weaksauce. Instead, they threw their backs into it. Lots of people did—more than I would have imagined. The DSA was the hub for it, and people circulated the ideas to their affinity groups. I'm sure there were snitches in those groups, people reporting back to the feds or maybe even the state, but none of it got to the city. Or if it did, the Burbank city people who got snitched to decided they'd rather let us fly than ground us.

Taking over Magnolia was easy. We still had all the stuff we'd used to build booths for the refugees' arrival fair. We had the floor plan showing where each pavilion or table or easy-up would go. It was late fall, with shorter, blustery days, so everyone needed a wind and/or rain backup plan, but we knew all about those. You didn't do community organizing in Southern California without being prepared for heavy winds, sudden rainstorms, or wet-bulb temps over a hundred. Sometimes all in the same day.

And of course, all the affinity groups were filled with bored, angry people who'd cleared their schedules to work on building refugee housing, until the Flotilla (or maybe some other plutes, no one was sure) spent all that lawyercoin on shutting us down. In other words, the Magas and the plutes created the ideal conditions for our little street fair.

The only tricky part was getting through the checkpoints with all our stuff. That took some doing, and it involved a seventy-two-hour period starting Wednesday morning of people carrying stuff past the cordon in small sub-suspicion loads and stashing it with friendly merchants—or merchants who had friendly staffers with a key to the stockroom. By dawn on Saturday, everything was stashed on Magnolia and waiting for us.

The drones got *super* interested as soon as we started setting up, of course, but the sniffers didn't whiff any volatiles and the lidar didn't spot anything that looked like a firearm, so they just kept buzzing us, having a good old sniff-and-peep and then lifting off. But then they'd do a couple of high circles and their algorithms would say "Uh-oh, why are there all those people handling un-wieldy objects on Magnolia?" and they'd come in for a closer look. Drones are not smart about false positives—they're a lot more worried about false negatives. I get it. Better to take two or three good looks to make sure that thing isn't a bomb than to buzz off after the first pass and only discover your mistake when every-thing goes boom a couple of hours later.

We hustled. By the time the first cops showed up we were curtain-raiser ready, with all our booths up and the big screens shook out and powered up, showing displays of the new Burbank, first cooked up in Phuong's living room and then wikified and edited by a couple thousand Burbankers, mostly affinity group members and their friends, whose designs got polished up by in-fill urbanists all around the world.

Burbank wasn't the first city to have a virtual doppelgänger that people could project their dreams and hopes onto, but it was the first one since the injunctions against emergency housing went into effect across America, and the rolling mass hackathon had this air of melancholy (this is our lost dream) and urgency (we can't lose this dream).

The cops were clearly not expecting us and had no idea what to make of us. I mean, they'd been on high alert for terrorist bomb-ers and mass shooters, not whatever the fuck we were. An urban vision street fair? Wildcat design fictioneers? To make things even better, everyone who got questioned by the cops insisted that they were farmers getting set up for a permitted farmer's market, all appearances to the contrary notwithstanding.

We'd had all our comms ready to go out from the moment the cops turned out, and as the word spread up Magnolia that they were on the scene, everyone mashed their go buttons that messaged every friend they had in every way they had to let them know that something big was happening in Magnolia Park and they had to get there *right now,* as in, don't stop for coffee or a pee first.

Burbank's not that big and it's well-supplied with bikeshares and scootershares and private vehicles of every description from old muscle cars (even gas ones) to mobility vehicles and autonomous taxis, and so the first people were on the scene even before the first cop had radioed in a report about an improbable "farmer's market" and asked their boss to see if anyone at City Hall (which was a crater and whose functions had been distributed around other municipal buildings) knew about the supposed permit for this thing?

Then the cops had *two* weird things to worry about: our farmer's market and the hundreds, then thousands, of people who showed up for it, and while it was possible that this was all a prelude to a militia uprising or mass bombing campaign or armed occupation, it sure didn't look like one.

Then Tony Yiannopoulos showed up in his councilor suit. No one had briefed him—we all knew it would have compromised his position if he'd had foreknowledge of our weird plan—but Tony was a quick study and he found a BPD sergeant and conferred with him. After a minute, the cops withdrew back to their checkpoints and I heard Tony telling a DSA organizer that he'd explained that this was a City Hall thing, not a cop thing, and the cop was relieved to hear it.

Phuong sent me a drone pic of the neighborhood that someone had stitched together from multiple angles, showing the lineups at the checkpoints. No wonder the cops had been glad to get back to those metal detectors, the lines were stretched around the block.

I called her. "This is crazy," I said. "All these people!"

"All these people!" she agreed. "It's because everyone was sick and stuck and scared, sitting at home waiting to find out if California was going to secede from the USA and become a stationary Flotilla territory. They were all rightfully afraid that their kids would have to recite from *Those Who Tread the Kine* every day at school. There is absolutely nothing worse than the sense that things are going wrong and there's nothing you can do to fix them."

I had a file of vlogs my dad and mom had uploaded before they moved to Canada, just ten or twelve that the Internet Archive had scraped and preserved, and there was one where my dad said nearly exactly the same words, explaining why they were leaving everything behind. *The world's on fire, we just got through a plague, and floods just washed away half the town. No one here will fucking do anything about it.* He'd teared up. The only other time I saw my dad cry was right at the end. *I feel so helpless. It's like we're driving as fast as we can toward a cliff edge and no one will grab the wheel or hit the brakes.*

"You are a brilliant woman," I said to Phuong.

"Awww," she said. "Thank you. What did I do to earn that?"

"Just made a connection for me, is all." No wonder I'd been in such a fucked-up space. I was experiencing the helpless apocalypse anxiety syndrome that drove my parents out of the country, twenty years before. Naming it felt instantly better, and it also explained the crowds. I looked at the drone shot again. They were crazy. Totally crazy. Then Phuong found me in the crowd and grabbed me in a massive hug. What a wild feeling.

Every booth displayed a different aspect of the New Burbank. One group had done transit, another had done libraries, another had done schools. The big action was in the neighborhoods, displayed as big-screen flythroughs that you could view or modify, either from your own screen or by just dragging stuff around on the big screens. The kids did a lot of the latter, while their grown-ups were more interested in the former. I eavesdropped on a lot of conversations, hopping from booth to booth, and I started to see a pattern:

Rando: "Come on, you've gotta be kidding me. This is crazy, it's not what the city is about."

Guerrilla planner: "Did you see this park?" (or stadium, or rink, or subway station, or library, or business strip)

Rando: "Sure, sure, but come on. Be serious."

Guerrilla planner: "Did you see the lake? The lake's super cool, it's part of the runoff system. All the road grades run toward it; if there's a flood it'll absorb all the water and then most of that will end up back in the water table."

Rando: "Yeah, that's cool, but come on. Be serious."

Guerrilla planner: "Did you see the solar capacity? Total energy independence, and we've got this concrete factory over here, it'll just sinter prefab any time there's more power in the grid than we can use. Then any time someone goes on the job guarantee, one of the gigs'll be building one of these buildings, using that prefab. It's carbon-neutral mass-scale construction—"

Rando: "That *is* cool. How the hell does that work?"

And then they were off. The excitement was infectious, not least because of all the social we were getting, with tons of cross-over between all the different twitters and fbs the work crossed over. A big Armenian twitter—the hub of Yerevan drought rebuild—went crazy over it and then half of Glendale got calls from their cousins and aunties and showed up at the checkpoints. The people who couldn't get to Burbank, especially other Californians who'd been in a fury about the injunctions and the bombings and the seizures, started building out our map, overlaying huge swaths of LA and the San Fernando Valley with their own dreams.

Even better: the Magas fucking *hated* it. This was culture-war clickbait times a billion, and it seemed like half the world's reactionaries, trolls, bots, and assholes were determined to vandalize our virtual space (we had good anti-vandal, plus a swift revert-squad that the little kids on Magnolia joined in droves, cackling as their tiny hands smacked the screens to undo the damage faster than the irrelevant hunt-and-peck typists of the fallen past could wreak it).

The Magas came down in person, first in a trickle, then in larger numbers, glaring at people and asking booth staffers if they had permits, though it wasn't clear whether they meant permits to have a booth or permits to tear down and rebuild all of Southern California. We didn't have either of course, but then again, they didn't have a permit to fucking bomb City Hall.

There was something magical about having the Magas there. When they were running around in the hills with long guns or semtex or whatever, they were terrifying. In person, they were a remnant, a rump, a vestige. Not numerous, not scary. Sad. Frightened. So angry. They'd been doing death-cult shit for a generation and it showed. Looking at them was a reminder that the only reason half of them were alive today was the socialized medicine they all professed to hate. Before they arrived, it all felt like defiance. Once they got there, it felt like *victory*.

> The mayor is here

Ana Lucía's message was decorated with raised fists and animated victory dances, more than I'd ever seen her use before. A second later, a picture of Mayor Phyllis Friess and three councilors in the crowd, looking awed and tired and excited and scared, all at once.

She dropped a pin for me, so I followed it to get to her and saw the mayor and her posse in person. They were starting to draw stares, getting stopped for handshakes and selfies and also getting their share of stink eye and middle fingers. I wondered what it must feel like to have your office blown up by terrorists, your coworkers killed or maimed, and then to have to come down to all of this, and I felt a little bad for them.

"We should go rescue them," I said. "It's not cool. We want them on our side, right?"

Ana Lucía gave me a pitying look. "They're on *their own* side, Brooks. Haven't you been paying attention?"

"Come on," I said. "They've had a rough week—" I held up my hand to stop her from getting angry at me. "I mean, a seriously rough week. They were *bombed*. If all of this is going to get anywhere, it's going to have to get through them."

"Not if it runs over them."

"Fine, maybe we'll run over them. Why don't we see if we can get them to lie down to make it easier?"

Which is how Ana Lucía and I ended up approaching the posse and introducing ourselves.

"We just wanted to make you feel welcome," I said, hearing Ana Lucía's quiet snort only because I was listening for it.

"That's very kind of you," Mayor Friess said. I'd only ever seen her at city council meetings, dressed in her skirt-suits and perfectly composed, no matter how long the night dragged on or how terrible the stand-up comics who zoombombed the public comment period were. In person, she was smaller than I'd have guessed, and maybe a little frailer, though that could have been the terror of the week's events. She had worn athleisure for her stroll down Magnolia, or maybe she'd been called to it from a dog-walk or something, and in her warmup jacket and sweats, she could have been a swim mom at the side of the Verdugo pool, cheering on her kid and swigging from a coffee thermos.

The councilors with her were similarly attired, and seemed no more able to come to grips with what was going on around them than the mayor was. Everyone touched elbows and introduced themselves, the city officials sneaking peeks around them, acting like they knew they were on camera because they were totally, definitely on camera.

"Can we show you around?" Ana Lucía asked, waving a hand expansively down the street, taking in the booths, the crowds, the chatter.

"Uh," the mayor said, clearly *not* wanting to be hitched to Ana Lucía, an obvious refu and also some kind of DSA radical involved in a takeover of the city's main retail strip. But the mayor *also* didn't want to be a dick, and Ana Lucía had a seriously winning smile on, so she finished, "Sure, that would be lovely."

And it was, you know? I liked Mayor Friess, despite hating more than half the decisions she'd made since taking office. For all that she was smaller and frailer up close, she was also *magnetic* in that politician way that Ana Lucía also had, as well as Kiara and a few of the DSA organizers I'd met, especially the regional and state reps. You just *liked* them and you wanted them to like you. The mayor had that. And she could do that thing where six people were all in a circle around her, seeking her attention, and she could load-balance all of them, giving them nods and other signals when it was their turn, shutting down people who interrupted without making them feel like they'd been rude. This was politician stuff, and I could recognize it even if I didn't know how to do it myself.

We got the mayor and her posse to a rest area—a parklet with little tables and loungers to catch the weak autumn sun, where people made space for the City Hall gang and us, unfolding more chairs and making space by shifting some of the potted palms off the parklet and into the street.

"So?" Ana Lucía said. "What do you think?"

"It's certainly visionary," the mayor said, and I couldn't hide my smile. "Visionary"—what a great, noncommittal adjective. She was *good*. Phuong found me around then, pecked me on the cheek and squatted on her haunches beside me, turning down my offer of my chair. I took her hand and we all looked at the poor mayor.

Ana Lucía made a little mime out of having a great idea. "Folks, do you know what? There're all these people here, learning about this stuff for the first time, taking it all in, and I know they'd really like to get your take on it. Can I do, like, a five-minute mini-interview with you? We'll put it on all the booth screens and—"

The mayor shut her down with a polite, firm smile. "I don't think so," she said. "We only just got here ourselves and it wouldn't be right to comment—"

Ana Lucía's polite-interruption game was strong. "You don't have to comment on the proposals—there're way too many of those anyway and it's all changing anyway. But Mayor Friess, we've all been scared and angry and didn't know what to do with ourselves, and it all just seemed to be getting worse, day after day. These folks decided to do something positive with all that fear, and looking around, I think you'll agree that it was something the community was hungry for."

"Well, certainly, it's good to see people directing their energy to positive—"

Ana Lucía interrupted. "This is perfect, just let me get my screen."

The mayor looked around at all the cameras already pointed at her, did a quick gut-check about how it would look if she stood up and walked away now, what that viral clip would look like. Then she gave a shy, wry, game-recognize-game smile at Ana Lucía and put on her mayor face.

"Mayor Friess, could you say a few words about what you see here today?" Ana Lucía's face and voice came out of every booth down Magnolia, the big screens clicking over to her in unison, the sound echoing a little as the crowd went quiet so we could hear the out-of-phase audio from down the block (the signal was moving at the speed of light minus network lag, the sound was traveling back a lot slower).

The people around us recognized themselves in the video, then turned their heads to find the camera, then spotted Ana Lucía, then spotted the mayor, and then Ana Lucía swung her screen around to the mayor and her posse.

The mayor mayor-faced the camera, gave the crowd a beat to settle down, then smiled. "You and your friends have done something really remarkable here. After the violence, fear, and tragedy of the past week, your, uh, project, has really helped with our healing." A smattering of applause from the crowd.

"Thank you, Mayor Friess," Ana Lucía said. "As you know, the internal refugees who came to Burbank for shelter have been stranded by terrorist violence and legal dirty tricks. We've come together here today not just to celebrate a vision for what Burbank might become in the future, but for what it should be now, if it's going to survive the months and years ahead of us. The designs that Burbankers have imagineered here come from a global database of climate-hardened structures that can withstand extreme heat and floods. They're structures that can see us through the coming century, and they'll support the populations that move inland from the LA flood basin. Don't you think it's time that we stopped tinkering with planning guidelines and engaged in a coordinated effort to future-proof our city?"

I loved watching her work. The mayor's face was perfectly composed for all of this, but the councilors' poker faces needed work. They were clearly taken aback by the ambush, and affronted on the mayor's behalf. Tony Yiannopoulos emerged from the crowd and stood next to me, and the mayor's posse gave him surprised, none-too-friendly looks.

"Burbank, like all of California, is going to have to adapt to a changing world. I'm proud of our track record, both when it comes to making our city future-ready and when it comes to welcoming in people who've been brought our way by the climate emergency." I nodded when she used the phrase, and so did most of the people around us. The willingness to say the words "climate emergency" had become a litmus test in the election that brought us President Bennett, and the "emergency" side had lost that election. Politicians who'd still say the words got automatic points. "And we're going to do more. We were all traumatized by the terrorist attacks on our city and our state, but no one should live in fear. That's just giving in to the terrorists. So of course I'm glad to see you here, putting your imaginations to good use."

Another smattering of applause, and a couple of boos from some Magas who'd found their way to our parklet. Ana Lucía pointed her screen back at herself: "Thank you, Mayor, but that's not what I asked. I asked if it wasn't time to stop messing around with tiny tweaks to the way our city looks and runs and instead confront this emergency that we're all facing? Terrorists don't want us to do it—" She pointed at the Magas, and they got even ruddier, and the crowd glared at them. "—but we don't give in to terrorists, do we?"

"No we don't," Yiannopoulos said, subtly shifting so that he made himself part of the mayor's posse. "This city government has a job to do, a duty to the people who live here. That means *all* the people, not just a few violent psychos with too many guns and not enough brains."

"We *are* the people of Burbank," one of the Magas yelled, right on cue. "We have a right to our city. If the people who come here begging for handouts don't like what's on offer, let 'em go look for charity somewhere else."

Tony inclined his head at the Maga. "That's what I'm talking about. People who think that because they got here first, they're better than the people who got here next. Buddy, Burbank is for Burbankers, and a Burbanker is anyone who wants to live here. That's the way the law works, here in America. If you don't like it, you don't have to stay."

That got a cheer. More Magas were arriving and so were some

cops, preceded by a trio of BPD drones in a holding pattern. The Magas were all yelling now, and Ana Lucía thumbed up the gain on her screen's mic.

"Councilor Claiborne, you lost a good friend in the City Hall bombing. There are thousands of people who were supposed to be building themselves new homes here in Burbank, now living in tents in the city parks. What do you think the city should be doing now?"

Claiborne opened their mouth, closed it. One of the other councilors moved to answer, but Claiborne waved her away, and they had bright tears standing out in their eyes. "What should we be doing now?" They drew in a deep breath. "You know what we should be doing now. You're already doing it. Right here." They waved their arm to take in the whole street fair. "You're doing our job for us, the job we didn't have the courage to do." A moment of stunned silence, a cacophony of cheers mixed with boos from the Magas, and Ana Lucía thumbed the gain higher, so that when Claiborne spoke again, their voice *boomed,* rattling the storefront windows and our fillings. "You're doing what we should have done from the start: ignoring the illegitimate, vicious, cruel court orders to abandon our duty and getting on with giving people a place to live and a life to live in it." Their voice broke on the last word and Tony gave them a hug. It was an intense moment. Even the Magas shut up. For an instant. Then they were shouting.

The mayor was doing a slow fade, backing away from the scene, banking toward the cops who were standing uneasily between the crowd and the city officials.

"Exactly," Ana Lucía said. "You gave them everything they wanted, and they bombed us. They didn't ask you to shut down construction because they wanted to deprive us of a place to live: they did it to see if you could be pushed around. Once you showed them you could—" She made a *boom* sound/gesture and people cheered again. The Magas started to look uncomfortable. They were clearly outnumbered, and being publicly associated

254 • **cory doctorow**

with terrorist attacks that killed people's friends and family and blew up beloved city buildings was no fun.

Claiborne disengaged from Tony's hug and took a step back themself. They didn't like that they'd lost their cool in public, not at all. It looked like we were done, but then they stepped up to try and put a smooth edge on the roughness. "I want to thank you— thank *all* of you—for this remarkable show of community spirit. We know that this is a rough time. We know that as well as any of you. This thing you've come together to do today has made me proud to be a Burbanker."

Ana Lucía sprung her trap. "Will you agendize these plans at the next meeting?"

The councilor was caught by surprise and had nothing to say. On the screens all around, their eyes flicked back and forth as they looked from the camera to themself on the screens and back to the camera. I felt sorry for them.

"I, uh, don't know that this would be the best way to proceed with all of this—"

Tony shook his head. "Come on, Rafi," he said. "These are the people who voted you into office, and they're telling you what they want you to do with the power they've given you. This is your job. It's my job. I will commit, right here, that I will agendize this at the next council meeting, and then I will by God *vote* for it because this is what our city wants. The people have never spoken so loudly and so clearly. If we can't hear them, we don't deserve our goddamned paychecks."

He'd started quiet but then he'd straightened up as he rolled along until he was *thundering* and by the time he got to *goddamned paychecks* he was thumping his chest loud enough that the mic caught it, boom, boom.

Claiborne went from deer-in-headlights to engaged to furious in the space of six sentences. They were either a terrible politician or an amazing one, putting on a virtuoso performance that could have landed them a leading part at any of the studios. By the time

Tony was done chest pounding, they were cheering along with the rest of them. Ana Lucía pounced.

"Councilor Claiborne, I see you cheering, does that mean you'll commit to agendizing our question at the next meeting?"

"Hell yes!" They weren't acting. They'd been bombed that week, after all.

Ana Lucía wasn't letting up. "And will you vote for it?"

"Goddamned right!" they said, and Tony clasped their hand and yanked it into the sky like a ref announcing a prizefight win. The crowd was going wild. The mayor wasn't quite at the police line.

"Madam Mayor!" Ana Lucía shouted, and all eyes were on the mayor now. People cleared a patch so Ana Lucía could get her screen's mic in range of the mayor. "You know what the question is, Madam Mayor. The people want to know."

The mayor straightened up and gave another game-recognize-game smile to Ana Lucía. "The people know what the answer is. At Friday's meeting, the agenda will include a resolution on these proposals. We will task the city attorney and our head of planning to work with you and, uh, Mr. Yiannopoulos"—Tony saluted her—"to prepare and circulate the motion. I will hear arguments for and against it. And, I have to warn you, I will hear arguments that we can't vote on these proposals unless they have been formally submitted and exposed to public comment and expert review from structural, architectural, and environmental consultants. This is California, friends, and we have learned our lesson when it comes to 'move fast and break things.' That's not what you elected us to do. You elected us to move cautiously and fix things. That may not be what you were hoping for today, but it will have to be enough."

"It's not enough," Ana Lucía said, and her voice was so serious and ice-cold I got a shiver. "But it's enough for now."

———

There must have been seventy people at my house.

Between beers, hard spicy kombucha, and these crazy super-old bourbons (none older than six days, but with the molecular structure of an extrapolated bottle after 150 years in oak staves), the party was really good. Someone brought watermelons, someone else brought guitars, and the kitchen supplied a rhythm section in the form of pans and spoons. It was about fifty-fifty refus and locals, with my houseguests beaming with pride as they showed their friends around. Someone gave me a vegan empanada.

I danced with Phuong. Oh my God she was a good dancer and so unbelievably sexy while doing it that I kept nearly tripping. Everyone watched us and I didn't mind at all: they were watching her, and if they noticed me, it was only to wonder why someone as gorgeous and sexy and amazing as my girlfriend was hanging around with a clod like me. That sounds like it would feel bad, but it felt so, so great.

We collapsed, sweaty and grinning, onto the backyard grass, the long desert grasses I'd planted after Gramps died, replacing his water-hungry turf. We propped ourselves on our elbows and watched the festivities, heads touching. Ana Lucía loomed over us, all nostrils, chin, and underboob from our angle.

"Pull up a seat," Phuong said, and she joined us.

"You were *amazing* today," I said.

She smiled and held up a fist for a dap. "Couldn't have done it if everyone else hadn't played their part. Those Magas were perfect, really made it clear what the question was."

We snorted. She had a one-hit and she loaded it with a dab of oil and blew out a plume. She reloaded it and passed it to Phuong, who hit it and then mimed for me to get a shotgun. As she blew the vapor into my mouth, I felt like a giddy teen. The weed and the erotic charge mingled and I was instantly, pleasantly buzzed.

"God, I hope it works," I said. "I mean, it'd be terrible if the Magas win, if the Flotilla wins, terrible for millions of people.

But I just keep thinking of how terrible it would be if you moved on, Ana Lucía, you and your friends. You folks are just *great,* you know. And you—you're a force of nature. The way you ended up here is terrible, but we're so lucky you came."

I tried to read the expression on her face. It was weird. Sad? Angry? I rewound what I'd just said. "I mean, shit, sorry—I didn't mean to say . . . Sorry. Oh God, I'm sorry, Ana Lucía. I can only imagine what it's like to be in your situation. Of course you just want to go home if you can. I just meant—"

She cut me off with a gesture. "I don't want to go home," she said. "You have to understand, we didn't just get bored or sad and leave Tehachapi. We tried. We tried *so hard.* People worked until they dropped. My parents dropped *dead.* We begged the state and the feds for help, money and water rights and health care. We wrote letters to big companies telling them they should locate a call center in Tehachapi and give us jobs. Out here in Burbank, you've got an incorporated city, a government that can administer the Jobs Guarantee. In Tehachapi, it's just the county, and it's all sewn up by good ole boys with red hats under their white hoods, and they keep delaying any kind of GND program kickoffs.

"It wasn't easy to convince people to leave. First we had to convince them not to stay, convince them that there wasn't anything for them at home, and never would be. Some of my people, they've been in Tehachapi for generations, born and grew up and met and married and had kids there. It was their home. It was like the land was part of their family. It's beautiful country there, a wild place with real sky. Like a member of the family.

"When the town started dying, it was like your grandma getting sick, slipping away, getting worse and worse, until the pain was unbearable and everyone knows that she's never coming back this time. When that happens, you say your goodbyes, do you understand?

"We didn't just leave Tehachapi, we buried it. It's dead. We can't go home. We don't have a home anymore. Going back? It'd be like digging up Grandma's bones and sitting her down at the end of the Thanksgiving table."

Phuong reached out and squeezed her arm. "So it's Burbank or bust, huh?"

Ana Lucía shook her head. I couldn't read her expression in the dark. "I was ready to leave a couple days ago, but no one else wanted to go. I did a lot of research to pick Burbank, got the data on how much room there was for infill, what the city government's uptake had been to other GND programs, the demographics, everything. I sold it hard. Too hard, maybe, because half of my folks think this is the promised land."

"It's a good town, and it's trying to be better," I said. "And you can't blame people for wanting to stick with the devil they know."

"Oh, I sure *can* blame them for that. That's the sin that nearly wiped out the human race and may kill us all still, sticking with the system we had even though it was destroying us, because we couldn't know for sure that whatever we built to replace it would be any better."

"Fine," I said. "But do you really think it'll be better somewhere else?"

"No," she said. "No, that's what I figured. Once I saw that the injunctions were nationwide, I gave up on finding somewhere easier. Once I saw that they were setting up a world where there were winners and losers, people with the good luck to live inland, or on high ground; people with the money to relocate, they're fine. The rest of us? We can drown or starve, so long as enough of us survive to wait on our social betters, cook their dinners, raise their kids and mow their lawns. That's the endgame and the dumbasses here think that they'll be rewarded for helping out, when the best they can hope for is to be allowed inside the compound to serve as a butler or a dishwasher."

"Grim, but fair," Phuong said. "Whatever the reason, *I'm* glad you folks are staying here. You class the joint up. Plus, we're going to end up absorbing a hell of a lot more people in the years to come, so it's really good that we get to sort out the process with such a kick-ass bunch of new neighbors."

Ana Lucía clucked her tongue, but in a friendly way. "You two are such GND goody-goody Kool-Aid drinkers."

"I'm a believer, all right," Phuong said.

"I'm second-generation," I added.

Ana Lucía groaned and refilled her one-hit and passed it around again.

We were getting pretty mellow by then. It had been a very long day—I'd set my alarm for 3:30 a.m. and I'd woken up before it had a chance to go off—and emotional, too. Then there'd been the whiskey and the food and a couple of lungfuls of Ana Lucía's lethal indica oil and the warm, good smell of Phuong next to me and I felt like a turkey that's come out of the oven and had all its strings cut, spreading outward as my very muscles relaxed right off my bones.

And that's when the Magas showed up. They'd clearly been drinking, too, having their own parallel house party in someone else's backyard. They came with tiki torches, which was meant to be scary but it was such a throwback that I snorted when I figured out what they were brandishing.

"Brooks!" one of them shouted. Kenneth? No, Derrick. He looked every one of his seventy-something years, stoop-shouldered and florid, wearing a big windbreaker with one hand behind him, where you'd tuck a pistol if you were the kind of person who really liked old action movies and didn't mind the risk of literally shooting your own ass off.

He was at the head of a gang of men, many of them I recognized as Gramps's friends, but there were some strangers in there. Most were his vintage, but there were younger dudes in there, with that look: big beards, shaved heads, belligerent stares. Some wore long coats, the kind you'd hide a long gun in. Some wore warmup jackets, and I spotted a couple of armpit bulges.

A weird calm settled over me. These guys were here with their guns, and that meant they were ready to kill me. You didn't need that many guns to scare someone. So that meant I could very well be about to die.

That calm, though. I'd seen death before, seen it up close, with the people I'd loved the most. I'd always been on borrowed time. And at that moment, in love and surrounded by the best people I knew, having won an improbable victory against a vastly better-provisioned enemy force, I was absolutely prepared to die. To be a martyr. We would all die eventually. Why not make it count? If these militiamen gunned me down on my sidewalk, in front of all these witnesses, it would shock the city. It would absolutely break down any support they had left after their bombings. The bombings were anonymous, deniable. A gangland hit in cold blood? Not even close.

I stood up. They puffed out their chests and raised their chins, squaring off. Someone said something, probably Phuong or maybe Ana Lucía, but I couldn't hear words anymore. Someone was grabbing my arms, but I shook their hands off. I took a step toward the mob. They grinned and patted their weapons' hiding places. I grinned right back, nodding, taking another step. Another. Another. They were shouting words. Derrick was saying something. Who had time for words.

Another step.

They looked at each other, scared now. What did I know that they didn't? I'll tell you what I knew: that I wasn't afraid to die. That I wanted to die in a state of grace. Another step.

They took a step back.

And I took a step forward.

"Go away," I said. The words were clear and loud and they rang out.

Another step.

They jeered and threw hand signals and patted their bulges, but . . . they left. They turned and walked back toward the corner and I stood there at the edge of my property line and the sidewalk, chest out, head back, watching the shadows absorb them, feeling incredible.

Someone touched my arm. Phuong must have been scared to death. What had I done? I turned to say something, and it wasn't Phuong at all. It was Dave and Armen, who I hadn't even known were *at* the party, both with huge, sloppy-stoned grins. Suddenly, the white noise around me turned back into words, crowd sounds, Dave and Armen shouting *Dude, that was AWESOME* and laughing, and I laughed and kept turning around and realized that everyone had been standing behind me.

All of them. My friends. My neighbors. My houseguests. Burbankers. Refus. Ana Lucía and Phuong, with linked arms and chins high. Vikram in his wheelchair—jeez, how many people had been at my house that night that I hadn't even noticed? I was a shitty host. He had a fist in the air.

The crowd noise was a cheer. That's what it was, a cheer and we were all cheering, loud and wild and cut loose, and I raised my voice and *howled* my victory call, raising my hands over my head like a prizefighter.

It was an amazing night after that. Dancing. Singing. Cuddling with Phuong in the grass and having an intense conversation all about my dad with Vikram, things I'd never heard before. Milena and Wilmar sat with us, cuddling too, and I realized they'd become a couple.

I went to bed beside Phuong and fell immediately into a satisfied, warm, satiated sleep.

I woke a few hours later, the clock said 3:17 a.m., covered in sweat and heart thundering and one thought in my mind: *I attempted suicide tonight.*

I sat bolt upright, shaking. Phuong made sleepy noises and stroked my back, felt the shivering there, woke up. "You all right, babe?"

"No," I said. "Yes. Shit. Sorry. Bad dream. Let's sleep."

She pulled me to her and we wrapped our arms around each other and she was all I could feel and all I could smell and I kissed her scalp through her hair and she was all I could taste and I fell back asleep.

free as air

I woke up choking, laboring to breathe. I opened my eyes and the room was hazy. I sprang out of bed and ran to the back door, putting my hand on it to confirm it was cool before opening it. The smoke outside was much thicker. I closed the door, closed the windows, put a dirty pair of jeans at the base of the door, and grabbed my screen, which was plastered in wildfire warnings. The San Fernando hills were burning, Angeles National Forest was burning, and there were burns in Griffith Park.

I pulled on boxers and a tee and ran around the house slamming windows shut, stuffing towels beneath the doors, and taping plastic around the windowsills. Phuong caught up with me and I told her where the thermostat was and got her to switch it over to recirculation and close the intakes, and hit my USN95 mask stash, knocking on my houseguests' doors and making sure everyone was equipped, telling them to talk to any friends who were sleeping in the parks and inviting them to come shelter with us.

Our screens were already filling up with details about emergency shelters in libraries and schools, warning us to stay indoors and avoid exercise, telling us schools and nonessential businesses were all shutting until the fires were under control or the winds shifted. There were pics of the tennis courts and the pool on Verdugo, the former under a carpet of ash, the latter stained tea-black by settling ash as lifeguard kids in masks struggled to get a big weighted bubble-wrap blanket over it.

"Fuuuuuuck," I said, as we gathered in my skeletal, ruined

kitchen for coffee and toast. The house air was better now, though my little air-quality meter was still warning us all to wear our masks if we could to spare our fragile pink lungs.

We all doomscrolled and ate our toast. Dolores, one of my houseguests, gasped and shared her screen, and we all looked at ours. It was a screengrab from a neighborhood social channel, a Burbank-filtered version of a militia-centric federation that Gramps was always forwarding me messages from.

I could see why Dolores was worried. On the one hand, it was your basic unhinged racist Maga stuff, but on the other hand, it was highly specific about the fires:

> gnds know that a fire will keep the population pliable, which is
> why we get so much arson. means they can force majeur us out
> of our houses, build refugee slums, round us up and ship us out,
> make us into refugees too

That was the most polite version of it. There was lots more, stuff that didn't hide behind polite terms. Racial slurs, in combination with "eco-fascist," "eco-terrorist," "invaders," and then, the calls to rise up.

That's where it got *really* ugly: these elaborate fantasies about "wiping out the roaches," and "destroying the nest," and I was just thinking *Shit this is straight out of* Those Who Tread the Kine when I came on a post that was just a huge pastedump from the apocalyptic final chapter, this giant orgy of violence that my eyes had kind of skated over when I'd read the book. It had been three or four in the morning by then and I'd been more concerned with just getting to the end and finding out how the hero emerged victorious and getting my head down on my pillow than on the gory violence, but . . . wow.

Just wow. I felt embarrassed for not having paid more attention to it at first, and then grossed out by the incredible detailed violence, descriptions of flesh ripped by bullets and explosives, of knives slitting throats, of skulls caving in under heavy clubs, narrated with detail and relish.

And then, reading it over again, I got scared. I was staring into the raw id of the Magas, the things they didn't even say aloud when they were hanging out with Gramps and talking shit—things so dark they had to write them down. This was what they thought: we were headed for a war, and when it arrived, they wanted to fill the streets with our blood. They *wanted* a war, because that would give them the excuse to do it.

I could see Dolores and Phuong and the others getting antsy, too. I looked around the taped kitchen windows and beyond to the orange sky and gray air of the outside world. "Anyone mind if I close the blinds?" I asked, and when no one answered, I closed them. Then we all went around the house and closed all the rest.

We were trapped indoors along with the rest of the city, with nothing to do but hang out on social and keep refreshing for status updates on the fires. At least they were moving away from us. The big rains the previous spring and the long, hot dry summer had led to an explosion of underbrush that had then all died and dried out, creating a bumper crop of fuel. There had been some controlled burns in Angeles National Forest over the past few years, but it was just getting started and everyone who understood fire remediation said it would take a decade of serious burning before they could create the "checkerboard" of burned and unburned sections that would prevent wildfires from spreading. In the meantime, there was lightning, careless campers, the old PG&E power lines that were slowly but surely being replaced, and, just maybe (?), arsonists.

I had enough USN95s for each of us to have four. With careful washing and air-drying, we could swap them out every six hours. Luckily there were tons of leftover food from the party, enough for all of us to eat for a couple of days without braving the smoke.

Every now and again we'd pull back the blinds and look at the ash coating every surface: trees, lawns, the cacti and desert grass in my front yard. The few taxis and emergency vehicles that went by ran their wipers, clearing away the ash that sifted relentlessly out of the sky.

The forecast was improving by bedtime, with the firefighters making tentatively optimistic projections about the winds and the progress of the fires, but I woke in the morning with streaming eyes and a sore, dry throat and after I chugged water out of the tap I looked at my screen and confirmed that the winds had shifted in the night all right—toward us. And the fire crews had been caught flat-footed when the winds shifted and lost ground. A second fire had followed the shifts and merged with the first one, creating a front that was gobbling its way toward us. The hill fires were nearly out, but there was so much smoke coming off the Angeles fire that it didn't matter.

I got out the ladder and climbed up into the attic crawlspace and changed the HVAC filters, taking hits off canned air and noting with a grimace all the places where light shone through cracks in the roof, letting in the smoke. No wonder the house was such a gas chamber.

Breakfast was leftovers in the kitchen with Dolores and the rest of the houseguests, a glum meal where everything tasted like ashes and smoke. Phuong made a halfhearted joke about bottling some of it for Don and Miguel's next peaty whiskey and we all chuckled dutifully. The houseguests finished up and went back to their rooms to lie down and breathe through wet face cloths, and Phuong and I were left on our own.

"I hate this place," I said.

"Burbank?" Phuong sounded surprised.

"No, this house. I mean, fuck this place, seriously. I am so sick of it." I told her about the roof. "We'll have to take down all the solar to fix the roof. That's a twenty-five-year investment. I'll be in my forties by the time it's time to replace it again."

"God, it's weird hearing you talk like that."

"What?"

"I sometimes forget that you are a nineteen-year-old who owns his own house in Magnolia Park. That is some seriously weird shit."

"It is," I said. "I hate it. I mean, I know I'm incredibly lucky, but that's *why* I hate it. I don't deserve this place, any more than Dolores deserves to be a refu. It's just pure, dumb luck."

"Well, you were owed some good luck, after what happened to your parents and all."

"There're plenty of orphans out there, most of them didn't get multimillion-dollar houses."

"Multimillion. I guess I knew that but man, it's weird."

"I hate it."

"You said that," she said. "Well . . . What about giving it away?"

"I tried that. Back when the city was looking for sites for infill. That's why I was at the meeting where I met you, at the library!"

"So *that's* why you were there," she said.

"Best public meeting I ever attended," I said. "Anyway, then the city found enough empty lots to start building on and I got on a build crew and was taking people in here and fighting with those Maga psychos and I just kind of lost sight of it. Maybe I can do it now—just give the place to Ana Lucía and tell her to put as many of her gang in as will fit, for as long as they want. Like a permanent People's Airbnb. I'll sign over the deed and walk away."

"And do what?"

I shrugged. "Get on the Housing Guarantee list. Do Jobs Guarantee work. Join the Blue Helmets and see the world."

"You'd make a great Blue Helmet," she said, squeezing the back of my neck and pulling my face toward hers to touch foreheads. I loved how she smelled, especially her hair, and I was suddenly and utterly horny. She must have sensed it, because she gave me a smoky look and then said, "Easy, tiger. No heavy breathing in this air." Our masks rasped against each other. I got myself under control.

"I hate this," I said, snapping my mask against my face.

She shrugged. "It's a lockdown. Can't do anything about 'em." She lifted her mask to drink some coffee, seated it again.

"Not just the lockdown, though. It's the lockdown and the shutdown. If I knew that once the smoke cleared we'd be heading out to do something positive, then yeah, I could just hunker down and read a book—" She poked me in the ribs. "Ow. Or roll around with you while keeping our breathing slow and regular. But I just feel *helpless* here, like we're just going to go from one kind of lockdown to another."

"I hear you, but it's not over. It's just getting started. Once the fires clear we'll have that city meeting, remember? We can talk them into just steamrollering over those Maga fucks and getting us back on the job. I know it's frustrating but you've got to pace yourself, Brooks. This is a marathon. This is just the first wave of refugees that're headed this way. There will be so many more. Just these fires, I mean, they're talking about evacuating La Cañada and Flintridge already. Things get bad enough, they could lose a big chunk of the city, and I bet a bunch of those people would head this way. It's like when Miami went—one neighborhood at a time, then the Keys and some of the smaller towns up the coast, and then the whole city, *bam.*

"This crisis is just the dry run for all the crises we're *gonna* have. These guys'll all croak soon enough but their ideas will live on. There's big money being spent on it."

I smiled, recalling a treasured memory. "I'll never forget what you told me at the Ethiopian place on our first date, about the people in London you'd meet—"

"These people aren't gonna dig a hole and pull the dirt in on top of themselves. Yeah, that's a thing I say a lot. Also, it's an Eritrean restaurant."

"Right," I said.

"Right. So here's the deal, Brooks, the thing you'll figure out if you ever do become a Blue Helmet: this isn't the end, it's the beginning. Things are gonna get so much worse in the years to come. More fires. More floods. More trauma, and that means more of this shit, people lashing out, looking for someone else to blame because they can't punch their ancestors in the face for failing to act a hundred years ago."

"Is this supposed to make me feel better? Because it's not working."

"It should make you feel better, Brooks, because you're getting to play the easy levels before you get to the boss levels. Believe it or not, this is the low-stakes version. The fires are miles away, not right here. The militias are blowing shit up and planning war, but we still have a government that is invested in preventing them from marching us into the sea. All that stuff is in the future, and some of it may never happen, depending on how well we do here on the training missions.

"There's some stuff we can't change. The heat we've sunk into the ocean? It's gonna melt the ice caps. No one's gonna repeal the second law of thermodynamics. Habitat loss is going to keep pushing animals into new territories where they have no predators—and where no one has any resistance to the diseases they carry. All of that is going to happen, the same way they used to get bad blizzards up north every couple of years. Those blizzards were brutal, but they weren't fixable—instead, you had to fix the people who lived through them. Good insulation. Backup power. A plan to shut down schools and offices when the plows couldn't get through the streets.

"That's what this is—a fire and a militia uprising and a coordinated courtroom fuckery campaign against the people trying to fix it all. It's a blizzard. You don't fix blizzards, you figure out how to cohabitate with them. This is our chance, here in the easy levels, our chance to try out all kinds of tactics for coping with them."

"Holy shit," I said. "You learned all that as a Blue Helmet?"

"Learned, figured out, got taught. Yeah. It's a weird gig, because half the time you're so busy you can't think, and a quarter of the time, you're just exhausted and basking in the feeling that you've personally made an actual difference in the world, and the other quarter of the time, you're totally convinced that you'll never make *enough* of a difference to make any difference at all."

"Shit," I said. "Does that feeling ever go away?"

"Yes. No. Maybe? I mean we're literally on fire here and I'm comforting myself that maybe we can win this tiny little zoning battle and put up a couple of buildings and that maybe that will snowball into bigger, bolder things. Like, I'm dreaming of the promised land that we'll reach if we live a pure enough life where we are brave and eternal soldiers for the righteous cause."

"It's pretty hard being the first generation in a century not to fear—"

"Don't say it."

"I'm finally starting to feel better."

"Really?"

"No. Yes. Maybe?"

"You're an idiot."

"You're a goddess."

"Shut up," she said, but she led me into my bedroom. We kept our masks on. It was both literally and figuratively steamy.

"I can hear the hamsters running behind your eyeballs from over here. What are you thinking, boy?"

I looked away from the ceiling, which, I realized, I'd been staring at hard enough to bore holes into.

"Sorry," I said. "Just trying to get hold of a thought." It had been eluding me ever since we'd rolled onto our respective sides of the bed to pant away at our masks and let the sweat dry on our bodies. Just a thought that was riiight . . . *there*. "So," I said.

"Uh-oh."

"Shh. So. This is a practice level, and it only gets harder from here."

"In some ways."

"Right, in some ways. In other ways, if we win a decisive victory here, it carries over to the rest of our lives."

"You mean, if we beat the militia."

"If we *break* them. Show them that the harder they push, the more they lose. If we *demoralize* them, sap them of their will."

"You're scaring me."

"It's from *Those Who Tread the Kine*."

"Jesus, seriously?"

"Seriously," I said. "It's how they think so it's *what* they'll think. When they try to imagine what it'll take to beat us, they imagine that they *are* us and they imagine what it would take to get us to dig a hole and pull the dirt in after ourselves."

"Plagiarist." She gave my stomach a light, stinging slap. It fluttered in response.

"Amateurs plagiarize—"

"—artists steal. Do go on, Mr. Palazzo."

"They're showing us how to beat them, you get it? Like it's idiotic what they're doing to us because you and I know that the climate emergency's not going to let up, so no matter how beaten we are, there's always going to be a reason for us to fight some more, because it doesn't matter how pissed off you are, when your house is on fire, you gotta figure out how to put it out.

"They'll never beat us by stopping us from building emergency housing because next year we'll need twice as much emergency housing. We aren't digging holes and pulling the dirt in after us, and neither are all the people who are gonna lose their homes— their whole towns—in those fires out there." I pointed out the window. The sky was more yellow than orange now and I could see the outlines of the trees in my backyard, which was a serious improvement over just a couple of hours before. Maybe things were getting better. Maybe not.

"But they don't understand that. They just know what would demoralize them, what would make them stand down: being boxed in, having a one-two punch of being legally outgunned and having everything you care about in total chaos thanks to direct action. If we want to beat them, that's what we need to do."

"You want to blow up City Hall?"

"No," I said. "I want to blow up this house."

Not literally, of course. But knocking down a house and building an eightplex is a solved problem, as they say on the DSA socials. It takes a lot of heavy equipment and prefab slabs and a lot of people, especially if you're in a hurry. But with every project in limbo, we had all the materials and equipment we needed standing by and most of it was in depots that were managed by friends and friends-of-friends, and there were also lots of friends and friends-of-friends standing by with nothing to do and a lot of pent-up nervous energy.

"You're seriously serious?" Phuong asked me.

"Once again, yes. Seriously, seriously serious. What are they gonna do, fine me? Fine, I'll be broke, except for the building. I'll go bankrupt, they'll seize the building and then it'll be public housing. Why the hell not? I'm nineteen years old and I own a house. It's stupid. Burbank is stupid. We've got all this space, all this misallocated wealth, and there are so many people who need it, and we could oversee a nice, orderly transition, but no, we're in this clusterfuck. Ana Lucía got the mayor to commit to debating overturning the order, and now I'm just gonna give them a nudge in the right direction."

"And you wanna do this *now*? In the middle of the fires?"

"Definitely right now. The fires are perfect. Everyone's locked inside, the cops are doing emergency service for old people having respiratory distress, the inspectors don't want to leave their houses—"

"Okay, but what about us?"

"What about us?"

"How do we breathe?"

"Masks. Oxy, if we need it. Everyone's got an emergency stash. We just put out a call, get what we can."

"Brooks, people need their masks and O_2 right now. There's a fire emergency. That's what the emergency stash is *for*."

"People just need to make sure they've got a bit left over in case the fire lasts longer than expected. But you read the same stuff I did—there's no way this'll last more than a week."

"Unless it does."

"It won't."

"Now who's in denial? Brooks, I'm not trying to yuck your yum here. I agree that this is an extremely fun fantasy to have, like a very specific version of our new-city fair, but you can't make it happen with wishful thinking. If you're going to do this, you need to be solid. You're going to be asking people to stick their necks out for you. You can't do that unless you're sure you can succeed."

I shot back, "Nothing's sure." I could feel that I was getting furious with her, that arguing-with-Gramps feeling of getting shit on from a great height. She must have seen it in my eyes, too.

"Hey," she said, pulling back but putting her hand on my shoulder. "Hey. Look, let's rewind. I love this idea, seriously. But I don't want to fuck it up. It's only tactically sound if it's structurally sound. So let's figure it out."

I breathed and breathed. The air tasted like smoke and I couldn't get my lungs full enough to calm down. She just waited it out. That waiting made the difference. Made me feel understood in a way I never felt understood. In a way that reminded me of my parents. "Jesus," I said, once I was halfway back under my own control. "I'm sorry, Phuong. You're right. I just got overexcited and then everything got all . . . triggery. It was just a crazy idea. Let's go figure out what's for lunch."

"Dude, are you kidding me? It's a *great* idea. We just don't know if it's a *practical* idea. Look, we're locked in here for days at least, and we're gonna run out of board games and movies to stream and my Spanish isn't good enough to play charades with Dolores and Camila and Santiago. What the hell else are we gonna do?"

I grinned behind my mask and then kissed her cheek through it. She yanked it down and then mine and we did some serious, smoky smooching. "Whew," she said. "You're right, we should eat first. I'm hangry."

The turning point came when we got an alert telling us that the winds had shifted again and the firefighters were withdrawing back to the next valley to clear a break while the bombers worked the fire line.

"That's it," Phuong said. "Minimum five more days before they get this under control, barring a miracle. There's another outbreak in San Diego, which is going to split the force. We've got all the time in the world, my friend." She skipped from foot to foot and I laughed so hard I snorted.

"We're really doing this?"

"We're really doing this."

We'd told Dolores and company what we were thinking of over lunch and asked them what they thought. We made sure they understood that they had a veto over this, because we weren't about to turn them out into the smoke while we did our weird-ass shit. They were completely cool about it, though, excited once we'd conveyed what we had in mind and wanting to help out. They found friends who talked their host families into letting them double up, and pored over the floor plans for the new building, talking about how they'd furnish their places. Antonio was a finish carpenter and pulled up pictures of some of the kitchen remodels he'd done and we all noodled around with superimposing them on the renders of the interiors.

Phuong, meanwhile, had been exchanging disappearing/ deniable messages with friends around the DSA, which led her to Tony Yiannopoulos, who found us a mole inside the Department of Public Works—a former shop steward who got promoted to management but never switched sides. After a couple of texts, she jumped on video and did this mind-meld thing with Phuong, in-gesting her project manifest and locating available equipment at DPW lots all around the city. There was a lot of idle gear in town, thanks to the double whammy of the fires and the moratorium on emergency house construction—the city had requisitioned a lot of extra equipment from the county when the caravan first started heading our way.

I was supposed to be finding us air—oxygen tanks, masks, goggles, ruggedized bunny suits, whatever would let us do taxing physical labor in smoke so thick you couldn't see your hand in front of your face at times. I struck out, of course. All that stuff was in heavy demand, because, duh, there was a fire on and you couldn't see your hand in front of your face.

But then Milena returned my call and got that twinkle in her eye when I told her what we were planning, and she told me to leave it with her. An hour later, she beeped me while I was hav-ing yet another useless call with a podmate from the DSA and I switched calls to catch her dancing from foot to foot and an-nouncing that she'd found a stash of forty full suits of smoke gear in a DSA stockpile for delivering meals during crises.

"Don't we need to deliver meals during *this* crisis?" I asked.

"The forty are leftovers. They've got like thirty people out there in full gear. Someone ordered way too many of these things. How many do you need?"

I got up at five the next morning and started packing. Phuong's housemates had agreed to let me store as many boxes as would fit in their living room, but as I went from room to room, looking

276 • **cory doctorow**

at the things Gramps and his father had accumulated, the things my father had left behind when he went to Canada, the relics of my nineteen years on Earth and eleven years in Burbank, I found very little I wanted to keep: Gramps had thrown out Dad's baby clothes when Gramma died and there wasn't anyone around to insist that he keep them. Gramps's books were shit. The art was terrible. There were family photos; I kept those and put them in a box to donate to the Burbank archives—they'd scan them and I could access them whenever I wanted them, and I wouldn't have to pay to store them or back them up. The Magas had smashed Gramps's family china. By 7:30 a.m. I'd come to the realization that I had lived nineteen years and accumulated virtually nothing worth keeping. It gave me mixed feelings: On the one hand, I was an orphan with nothing of personal value in the world. On the other hand, I was a democratic socialist who could check any tool, table, appliance, or vehicle out of the public library, a citizen of the twenty-first century who could access every book ever published and every song ever recorded with a few taps on a screen; a member of my community who could find a bed to sleep in and a change of clothes just as easily as I could call up those books and songs and paintings.

I was free. If Burbank caught fire and burned to the ground, I could go anywhere and start over, so long as there was a library, solar panels, and good people. The world was on fire, and the fires would burn every year for many years to come. This might be the best year for wildfires we'd have for the rest of my life. When things weren't on fire, we'd be harrowed by plagues, scoured by storms, flooded and droughted.

And yet . . . And yet. I had arrived at a place of circulating abundance amid all of that tragedy and terror. Wherever I was, I could be happy, fed, surrounded by good people and hard work.

I was *so* ready to tear down my fucking house.

————

Phuong touched my shoulder as we stood before the gates of the DPW storage yard. "Babe, are you okay? We don't have to do this, you know." The others around us, lost in the smoke, murmured their agreement.

I was confused for a moment, then I realized that Phuong couldn't see my face because of my breather mask. I undid one of the clips and flipped it up, holding my breath, letting her get a look at my massive, uncontrollable grin, then flipped it back, blew out the air and the smoke, and went back to breathing.

I rattled the gate and shouted, "Who brought the bolt cutters?"

A figure loomed out of the smoke on the other side of the gate, bulky and shambling in a grayish, worn hazmat suit. "Don't you cut my goddamned gate, child, or I'll make you whittle a replacement." The voice, muffled by the mask, was gravely and gruff, but affectionate. "You Brooks?"

"That's me," I said.

"You know how to drive a forklift?"

I shrugged. "Just a little I picked up on jobsites."

"Uh-huh. How about a crane? Backhoe? Excavator? Boring machine?"

"Nope," I said. "But they do." I jerked my thumb over my shoulder at the gang we'd organized over the DSA socials. There were fifteen of us, and with current certifications for all those and more.

"How about a tractor cab?"

"Uh," I said.

He snorted. "Trick question, boy. Thing drives itself. It's got fifteen hundred prefab slabs on it and all the electric and plumbing fittings on your bill of materials."

"Bruce," I said, "this is just amazing."

Bruce—the big guy in the dirty suit—just shrugged. "Look, it's all just sitting here, collecting ash. It's been beached since those assholes sued to stop all the city projects. I got stuff piled up under tarps in the goods yard because we're out of outdoor storage. Just don't tell anyone I gave it to you."

278 • **cory doctorow**

"No problem," I said. "We'll get so much more cred if people think we hacked the locks and swiped all this stuff. Having an insider hand us the stuff is pretty small-time."

He snorted again. "Be careful with this shit. Those panels are light, but jobsites are a good way to lose a limb if you space out. All this smoke won't help, either."

"Thanks, Dad," I said. The DSA crew chuckled.

He punched me in the shoulder, but softly, and his next words were gentle. "Seriously, son, go slow, observe safety protocols, and then observe 'em again. You build this house in the smoke before anyone catches you and you'll be a hero. You maim or kill someone trying to do it? You'll be an asshole, and the whole project will look bad because of it. You got that?"

Phuong put her hand on his big shoulder. "We hear you, Bruce. I've bossed bigger projects like this with the Blue Helmets. I know what happens if you get lazy. We are one hundred percent committed to being heroes here."

"Not assholes," Bruce said.

"Definitely not assholes." Phuong released his shoulder and put her hand to her heart.

"Not assholes!" I called, and the DSA crew echoed it back.

"Not assholes," Bruce said, and got us set up on the gear.

Step one: unload and stack the slabs: Step two: clear everything out of Gramps's house that could be salvaged and load it into the big 16-wheeler to be driven to the Glendale recycling center. That took the rest of the morning. After a lunch break in the hollow shell of the house, the wrecking crew started wrecking, working from the side of the house that didn't face the road, to hide the work. I'd seen houses go down to the foundation slab before, but this was still different. One second, it was a house, the next, it was rubble. I regretted that we hadn't been able to salvage the windows or the copper, but fuck it. This omelet was going to take a *lot* of broken eggs.

A fence crew put up hoardings around the jobsite, unrolling chain-link and lashing tarps to it. Working in the smoke was hard, but we heeded Bruce's warnings to keep safe, and Arina showed us a protocol for setting up emergency shelter in a sandstorm, adapted from gun-range safety, where the "downrange" had to be fully clear of people before any machine could be activated. It made things slow, but it was a good slow, knowing we were all safe. And anyway, my time sense got all weird, like I'd feel as though no progress was being made and the next thing I knew we'd be sinking these monster pilings for the new structure, and I'd be like, whoa, when did *that* happen? The last thing we did before the sun set was load up the second truckload of building waste, using the backhoe and the forklifts, and a couple of comrades drove it off to the dump. There was still a huge pile of debris, but the dozers got it off to one side and left us room to work.

We had night lights, and I was pumped to keep going, but Phuong talked me out of it. "You have been up since five in the morning, Brooks. Call it a day. Otherwise you're going to hurt yourself—and that's if you're lucky. You'll probably hurt someone else, too. Let's go. Dinner and bed."

The folks around us nodded. It was full dark now, and smoky. Neighbors had passed by during the day, but in our environmental suits, we could have been anyone. There was nothing on the main socials about it, and nothing on the Maga socials that the public could see. So we'd be able to build tomorrow. I was suddenly ravenous and exhausted.

"Shit, I'm inside-out with hunger," I said.

"Stressful times," Phuong said. "Let's go eat our feelings." Much of the crew had already drifted away. We hugged the ones that were still there and walked to her place.

We took a shower together, making jokes about saving water, but really because we just wanted to be in the shower together. We soaped each other and it was only partly sexual. Mostly what it was, was *tender*.

"It *has* been a big day," I said, as I toweled her off.

"Crazy," she said. "But good crazy."

We wrapped the towels around ourselves and I picked our discarded clothes up off the floor. "Oof," I said. "Jesus, they smell like a trash fire."

Phuong sniffed. "You're not kidding. Straight into the washing machine, please. Don't want those in my hamper all night stinking up my room."

Her housemates had already eaten, but Arina had saved us some jerk tofu and spiralized butternut squash noodles in puttanesca sauce. The tofu was lethally spicy, as was nearly everything Arina cooked, but yogurt made it delicious again. My scalp sweated. I chased it with Don and Miguel's best whiskey, an "impossible" wheated bourbon that was "aged" in a Chablis cask (Chablis is aged in steel, but Miguel and his whiskey-nerd pals had made a guess at what a hypothetical Chablis cask would do to whiskey if it existed and you aged whiskey in it). I drank way too much of it, way too fast, and the next thing I knew I was half asleep on the sofa, nodding off to the buzz of Phuong and her housemates talking among themselves. Everything I owned was in a short stack of mover's boxes in their corner: a box of photos for the city archive, a box of clothes, a box of knickknacks; on top of them, my backpack with a couple of chargers and batteries.

I dropped off with my head on the headrest, then woke myself up with my own snores. Everyone laughed at me, but in a kind way, and Phuong put her arm around my neck and put me into a friendly headlock. "Come on, fella, time to put you to bed."

Just as I was dropping off again, I had a waking thought: "Set the alarm," I said. "Four a.m. We'll get there early and get a start."

"City doesn't allow construction to start before eight a.m. You do that and someone will call noise enforcement and we'll get busted on the spot."

"Why are you so smart?"

"Blue Helmet school. They teach us how to do the job without pissing off the locals. It's literally like the first week of training. Most important lesson of the Canadian Miracle. Your parents' legacy."

She kissed my forehead.

"Okay, six thirty a.m. alarm."

"Brooks, it's a ten-minute walk and you don't own enough clothes to dither over what you're going to wear. How long, exactly, do you think your shower and breakfast are gonna take, fella?"

"Seven, then."

"See you at seven." She turned out the lights and then my body turned out mine.

My body spent the next seven hours getting ready to punish me. When the alarm went off, I sprang out of bed and promptly fell over.

"Jesus, are you okay?" Phuong scrambled around the bed.

"Ow," I managed.

"What is it?"

"I overdid it." My ribs hurt. My arms hurt. My legs hurt. My neck? My neck hurt *so much*. My *hips* hurt. "I'm nineteen years old. My hips aren't supposed to start hurting for years and years."

"I'll fill the tub," she said. "We've got tons of rainwater in the cistern, so it won't cost anything."

"Ohhhhh," I said.

"Hang in there, Grampa," she said. "I'll get you some painkillers, too."

We barely made it out at 7:50 a.m. I had soaked about 30 percent of the ache out of my joints and muscles, the painkillers had done for another 20 percent, and the Tiger Balm that Phuong slathered over every part of my body had accounted for 10 percent more, getting me into an upright and ambulatory state.

"I'll feel better once I warm everything up," I said, as we walked quickly toward Gramps's house. I was limping a little, but I was limbering up.

"Remember," Phuong said, muffled by her mask, "it's only a learning experience if you learn from it. Go easy today, okay?"

Blue Helmet prefab buildings are fast, but word gets around faster.

We were able to recycle the foundation slab, which meant that once the pilings were in, one crew could go to work fitting and locking panels while a second crew added structural members for the next stage. Wilmar was in charge of double-checking the building against the plans, making sure that panels with inset plumbing and electrical components were seated correctly and had good interconnects with their adjacent panels.

I was on a panel crew, which was easy when we were doing the first layer, but when that was done we had to work on ladders and it got awkward. Working in the smoke gear was idiotic, something no one should do. It started off difficult and quickly became unbearable as my clothes got saturated with my sweat and started to chafe. I sweated under my goggles and the sweat got in my eyes. When I reached inside my goggles to scratch, they filled up with smoke, and the grit on my filthy fingers added to the sting that made my eyes water.

With all that, it was inevitable that I'd fuck up, and I did. I was passing a panel up the ladder and I zigged when I should have zagged and the people above me whom I'd been handing it to lost their grip, then I lost mine, then Milena, who had the other corner, lost hers, and the panel tumbled, clanging off my helmet and knocking me on my ass as it shattered on the foundation slab next to me, showering me in sharp, hard fragments.

"Ow, *fuck*," I said, as I rolled around, holding my helmet.

"Idiot, stop moving," Phuong said, clamping me still. "You could have a spinal." I stopped struggling. She was right. Every

Blue Helmet on-site was fully up to date on basic, advanced, and wilderness first aid, and within seconds there was a whole god-damned committee probing me, asking me to count their fingers and tell them who was President ("She who must not be named," I said, and they laughed. Bennett was the *worst*), working my joints from the bottom to the top.

"How do you feel?" Phuong said after the exam was over.

"Okay. Stupid. Clumsy."

"But it's an adorable clumsiness," she said. "Your pupils are the same size. Headache?"

"No. My ears were ringing at first, but that went away quick. I think I'm okay."

"I think you're engaging in wishful thinking. You should be strapped to a spine board and taken for X-rays."

"Come on," I said. "That looked worse than it was. It just clipped me and then made a giant mess. Let me walk it off."

She and I locked eyes through our goggles. I was *not* current on even basic first aid, but I knew she was right. Technically. Also, she was just right. I didn't *think* I'd hurt my neck, but history is filled with people who "walked it off" and then never walked another step after the precarious arrangement of bones and nerves running through their fool necks reached a (literal) breaking point.

"If I go to the hospital, they'll want to know how it happened. That'll be the end of it."

"We'll lie."

"I'm needed here."

"Brooks, don't take this the wrong way, but you're probably the least skilled person on this jobsite."

"Ouch."

"Sorry, dude, but facts don't care about your feelings."

"It's my house."

"Not anymore."

I closed my eyes. My neck really didn't hurt. "Please," I said. "Please. I need this. I'm fine, Phuong."

"You're an idiot."

I looked into her eyes. Darkest chocolate, only a shade or two off the black of her pupils, made a little milky by her goggles. Normally she'd call me an idiot and I say something silly and we'd shake it off. I just held her gaze. "Please, Phuong."

She looked away, then looked back at me. We had an audience. Someone said, "I saw it hit him. Just caromed off his head. Didn't see any compression or stress on his neck."

"Slowly," she said. "Move slowly. Snail-pace. Anything hurts, anything feels funny, you stop. I need you to promise me."

"I promise."

"You paralyze yourself, I'll kick your ass."

"You'd kick a paralyzed guy's ass?"

"Sweetie, that'd just make it easier."

They gave me a round of applause when I got to my feet and slowly rolled my head to one side and the other.

That's when my neighbor Brad came through the gate in the work fence. "Brooks?"

I froze. He was hard to read behind the mask and goggles, but his body language was pretty astonished. I looked over my shoulder at the jobsite, and for the first time, it all sank in: a day before, this had been Gramps's house, which had been *his* father's house, and had stood on this site since 1939. Now it was a completely new building, the backyard piled high on one side with prefab slabs, and on the other side with rubble from the house that had stood for more than a century.

"Yo," I said. Someone on the jobsite groaned audibly.

"What's, uh, what's going on?"

"Emergency housing," I said.

He stood for a long moment. Almost everyone on the site had gathered around to check in on my accident, but now the others who'd kept working stopped.

"Right," he said. "Only, I thought they'd stopped all that?"

"Not this one," I said.

"You got an exemption?"

"It's an emergency," I said. I liked Brad and I didn't want to lie to him. At least not overtly.

He put his hands on his hips. "What're you building here?"

"Four stories, eight apartments. Mix of three- and two-bedroom places. Fully solarized, weatherized, with vertical farming, a roof garden, and a courtyard."

He looked around again. "That sounds nice, Brooks. Thought there was something about a parking requirement? One spot per bedroom? You're not excavating a garage?" He said it like a joke, but I could hear that he sounded concerned.

"Emergency housing doesn't have the same parking requirements. These are transit-oriented homes."

"Ah."

More silence. So much silence, even the small noises of the city were absorbed by the drifting smoke.

"Someone told me this was a city crew. Didn't realize you were out here."

"Well, it's a municipal project," I said. "Easy to get confused."

He straightened up and locked eyes with me, in a way that reminded me of how I'd locked eyes with Phuong. He was old enough to be my dad, eyes a little tired behind his goggles. I had known him most of my life. He'd come to my house when he'd heard gunfire. He wasn't a member of the Maga Club, but there were plenty of people who admired them and didn't make a big show of it. They tended to be middle-aged guys. Like him.

"I guess it's easy to get confused," he said. All the tension went out of my body.

He looked around. "Looks like I'm gonna have some new neighbors," he said, and waved goodbye to us all. He turned and disappeared into the smoke. I watched him go, relieved . . . until I asked myself how long it would be until my *next* neighbor came by.

We locked the gate.

———

The second set of visitors came by at noon, a group of about five or ten who crowded the crack between the gate and the fence to get a look. We ran our noisiest machines and pretended we didn't hear them calling "Excuse me!" and "Hello!" They left, and moments later, there were drones flying over us. We pretended we didn't see them.

We got a respite from the smoke as the sun began to set, just enough to make the sky turn an astonishing, bloody red, but thin enough that we could pull down our masks and air out our moist, chafed faces.

Over the course of that day, progress had been amazing, then agonizing, then amazing again. The first two rows of slabs clicked into place quickly, accelerating as the work crews got into the rhythm of the job. There'd been a moment when I stepped back from sealing a slab into place and looked around and realized that there was a *brand-new structure* there, just like that, a magic trick in three dimensions.

Then there'd been a long period of agonizing slowness as all the services were checked and rechecked—electrics, plumbing, data. It all had interconnect and integrity sensors built in, but we had to activate them and get them initialized and chained before they could start working. Time crawled as we troubleshot per-snickety problems, sometimes using Blue Helmet socials to conference in experts who could suggest fixes to thorny problems.

Then everything lit green and crews went to work snapping on the joists and locking them in, laying down the floor slabs, and putting in scaffolding for the second story and we were off to the races again, half of the next story racing around the building's edge even as a crew added exterior and interior doors and other fittings to the first floor. We even got the plumbing working, and the jobsite got a sink and a toilet. With the door closed, the windows fitted, and the first-floor ceiling in place, we got filters running and then we had an indoor space with breathable air, just like that.

Now it was sundown and I was so fucking proud and tired that I wanted to do a jig and then collapse. Phuong was huddled with some of the other senior Blue Helmets on the site, the ones who'd taken on foreman roles, goggles on her forehead, mask under her chin, a sooty line between them on her glowing, sweaty, beautiful face. I ambled over to her, grinning and groaning and feeling that good ache of a good day's work done good.

As I got closer, I realized they weren't just relaxing after a long day. There was something . . . intense going on.

"Guys?"

Phuong motioned me to sit down with them and get my head into the close circle.

"It's not gonna work, Brooks," she said.

I started to answer, but she kept going.

"The neighbors, the drone. It's a miracle we lasted until sunset. We're gonna have code enforcement out here first thing tomorrow, soon as the office opens at eight. Then it'll be cops."

"Shit," I said.

"Yeah, well." She squeezed my hand. "It was always a long shot. And at least we got this much done, one and a half stories out of four. At this rate, the simplest thing will be to finish it. It'd be crazy to knock it down. We made a point. Maybe we get everyone down here tomorrow, just throw caution to the wind and go wide-public with messaging on socials instead of DMs and group chat, make it a spectacle. That'll up the odds that it'll get finished."

I felt slammed. All that good tired was now bad tired. I'd knocked down Gramps's house. The house my dad grew up in. The house I'd been raised in. The house I'd been sheltering half a dozen unhoused refus in. That house was gone, and what would replace it? A half-built shell. Not even half-built. Maybe it would sit that way for months. Years. Maybe they'd knock it down.

I must have made a sound, because Phuong said, "Shh, now,

we're gonna tell everyone before they go home for the day, give them a say in how we handle it tomorrow."

I closed my eyes, imagined the scene, the people, the cops, the building. In my imagination, the building was a lot more . . . built.

"What if we don't go home?"

Phuong started to say something, then saw I wasn't done, and waited. The other Blue Helmet elders took her lead. They all radiated intimidating levels of competence, so I chose my words carefully.

"Building inspectors aren't going to come out overnight. They work regular work hours. We have outdoor lights. Cops aren't going to arrest us for unverified building-code violations. No one is going to get a judge to order an injunction after six p.m. for unlicensed construction. What if we stay and keep working until they *make* us stop? Finish the second story. Finish the interior services. Start on the third floor. Maybe *finish* the third floor?"

Phuong unsuccessfully hid a smile. "That's a lot of work, and we're all exhausted. You're amazing, Brooks, but tired people and jobsites don't mix. Remember your little near-spinal-injury?"

"Wait." The Blue Helmet elder was a woman whose name I didn't know. She had an Italian accent, or maybe Greek, and I'd gathered that she was romantically involved with a Burbank Blue Helmet she met on an overseas project and came home with. She gave off scary competence-vibes and always seemed to know the answer to thorny technical questions that came up in the build. She got a faraway look in her eyes, then stood and walked away from us, entering the half-built first floor and taking a walk around inside. We looked at each other, shrugged, and waited until she came back.

"Okay guys," she said. "I think we could split into five or six crews, each working separately: three utilities crews, one more doing fit and finish on the ground floor, one more completing the structures on the second floor. Sixty, seventy people. Now we've got a second floor, there's much more space for people to work without getting in each other's way." She sucked her teeth and looked the structure up and down. "Between now and eight a.m. tomorrow, with meal breaks, two shifts, I think we'll have the third story done and be working on the fourth."

We looked at her, at each other, at the building. Everyone's faces were naked and glowing in the sunset.

"Fani," Phuong said, "where do we get seventy people from without blowing our cover?"

Fani rolled her eyes. "We already said our cover's blown, yes? Building inspectors at eight, cops at eight fifteen. Not before."

Josh, another elder Blue Helmet who I remembered from Burroughs, said, "Unless there's a noise complaint. Cops come out for noise."

Fani shrugged again. "Do they write tickets or do they arrest you? If they write tickets, we crowdfund them in the morning."

"It's tickets," Josh said. He giggled. "Definitely tickets. Maybe twice, three times, then they tell you arrests are next if you don't keep it down." He giggled again. "Don't ask me how I know."

Phuong gave him a friendly shoulder-sock. "I remember that party too. Dumbass."

I bounced on my hunkers, looking at all of them but mostly at Phuong. They glowed. She radiated. Holy shit I was in love with her. "Are we doing this?"

The Blue Helmet elders played eyeball hockey, doing some kind of mind-meld. "Fuck yeah," Phuong said. "Someone get the coffee going."

We got a noise ticket at 10 p.m. Then some drone flyovers, then more. Another noise ticket at midnight. The cops marveled at the building and complimented us on our workmanship but told us to stop pissing off the neighbors. "People got kids," they said. We gave them coffee. Half the DSA kitchen was set up under an easy-up outside the new structure, including its excellent bulk-coffee apparatus and its emergency batteries.

The drones got thicker and more aggressive. Someone got one inside of the house and flew it around until someone swatted it out of the air with a fifteen-ounce claw hammer, rousing a cheer all around.

I took a catnap at 2 a.m. and swore I'd taken another at four, but the next thing I knew, the sky was getting lighter and there was another pair of cops at the door—and one of them was my old friend Officer Velasquez.

We showed them in and offered them coffee. They weren't interested. Velasquez gave me a long look and then said, "Brooks Palazzo, right?"

"Nice to see you again," I said.

They shook their head. "This is the third or fourth time I've been here, but I see you've done some renovations."

I shrugged and tried a grin. It felt pasted on. My shoulders and sphincter were tight. Officer Velasquez might have been the good cop in the Burbank PD's good cop / bad cop pairings, but right now, they were looking at me in a way that freaked me out a little. Or maybe it was just the lack of sleep. "Just making some space to move in some friends from out of town."

Their partner, an older, no-nonsense white woman with gray in her red hair and a good five inches on me, gave me a hard stare. "I'm not in the planning department, but I had the really strong impression that a federal judge in Sacramento ordered that all refugee construction had to be shut down."

I shrugged again. *Don't talk to cops* was an easy thing to say, a harder thing to do. If I said, "I'd like this interview to stop while I call my lawyer," would they just haul me in? Their bodycams' activity lights winked at me.

Some of the elder Blue Helmets drifted over my way and both cops tensed up. They just sipped their coffee and kept it neutral. It was a standoff.

Velasquez sized up the situation and made a call. "We're going to wake up someone from planning," they said. "In the meantime, your neighbors are trying to get some sleep, and it would be a kindness of you after what seems to have been a full night of construction to give it a rest until we've had planning on the site and cleared up any confusion. Does that sound like something you all can live with?"

"Absolutely," Phuong said, speaking for the elder Blue Helmets. "Sure you won't have a cup of coffee?"

Velasquez smiled and their partner scowled. "No thank you," Velasquez said. "We've got to figure out who's on deck at planning."

"Good luck," Phuong said, and sprinkled a wave at their departing backs.

The inspector goggled. Or maybe she boggled. I've seen both those words used before and never had an idea of what they might actually refer to but then this thirty-something Chinese-American woman with bedhead and a giant oxygen backpack showed up on the doorstep of Gramps's lot and just stopped dead, eyes wide, looking up, then down, then up, then down, then straight ahead, hands out at her sides, palms out, like she was a telekinetic trying to use her powers to levitate our brand-new, three-story building.

Finally, she spoke. "What. The. Fuck." She put her hand over her mouth, smashing herself in the mask, then shaking her head like a cartoon character and saying, "Ow," loudly.

"One of you want to come and talk to me about this? Like, maybe the property owner if that person happens to be present at this time?"

Everyone looked at me. I took a big step forward and stuck out my elbow. "Hi, I'm Brooks Palazzo. I'm the owner."

She bumped elbows with me. "Mr. Palazzo, I'm Olivia Chin, with Burbank Code Enforcement. I think you probably can guess why I'm here."

I thought about playing dumb—*No idea, why don't you tell me?*—but it would have been a dick move. "I guess I can."

"Mr. Palazzo, you appear to have built a multifamily unit on your lot, which is zoned for a single-family dwelling. Do you have a permit to carry out this construction?"

"I do not."

"We were relying on the Internet Displaced Persons Act waiver," Phuong said. I looked around. She and her elder Blue Helmet posse had formed up behind me, literally getting my back. That got my heart to stop thundering. "We are in the midst of a declared refugee emergency."

"Ms.—"

"Petrakis. Phuong Petrakis. Hi, Olivia." She pulled her mask down.

The city inspector took a closer look. "Shit," she said. "Phuong? From the Slammin' Coyotes?"

"Not since high school, but yeah. You're looking good, girl." To the rest of us: "I know Olivia from roller derby."

"Phuong, it's, uh, good to see you, but—" She flapped her arm at our apartment block, which appeared and disappeared in the blowing smoke. I was so sweaty in my gear, and my face and scalp itched like they were covered with fire ants. "I mean, *come on.*"

"Olivia, it's done. I mean, by sunset we'll have the roof on. You know as well as I do that the Magas' injunction is bullshit, and you know as well as I do that a building like this, put together by a crew of Blue Helmets from regular slabs, it's gonna pass all the inspections. We just need a couple more hours to finish the exterior, then you can padlock the site."

"And what, you'll jump the fence and do all the interior work? I know how you play, Petrakis. I mean—" She flung her arms out again. "*Come on.*"

"Okay, I get it. You've got a job to do. So what comes next?"

Olivia paced the perimeter, got to the front door. "Can I?"

Phuong made a go-ahead gesture. She made little noises as she moved through the building, going from room to room, then up the scaffolding to the second and then third floor. Finally, she leaned down out of an unglazed third-story window. "Jesus fucking Christ you guys. *Seriously?*"

A few minutes later she was back with us on what was left of the lawn. "How did you keep this all under wraps while you built it?"

"We didn't," I said. "I mean, we did, a little, but it only took forty-eight hours."

"Forty-eight hours for what?"

"For you to show up."

I watched that land on her. "Wait . . . You built this over the last *two days*?"

"Well, the first day was mostly demolition and hauling. Most of this is day two. Phuong tells me it'll take forever to finish the interiors, but like she said, we figure we can do all the structural work including the roof by tonight."

Olivia opened her mouth. Closed it. Repeated the procedure. "Bullshit."

Phuong laughed. "Girl, it's only because you went into planning instead of going overseas with a Blue Helmet brigade. This is how we do it, when we're working fast after a flood or a famine— the time it used to take to put up a bunch of tents and build some shithole refugee camp, now we can build a whole fucking *city*. We could do it here, if we had the same rules of engagement as we do in the field."

Olivia slumped and I felt kind of bad for her. She was only trying to do her job, and clearly she cared about it. Listening to Phuong deride California's safety and planning rules reminded me of Gramps and his pals and their crazy, knee-jerk opposition to any kind of regulation, how they'd call all the exceptions to those rules in the Internal Displaced Persons Act "Green Shock Doctrine" and say it was a plot to exclude their concerns from the fate of their community. Gramps and his Maga buddies were evil psychos, but maybe they were right about that.

"Look, you know I can't let you keep working on this. I mean, *seriously*. I've got to write you a citation, immobilize all your equipment, and shut the site down. You haven't done an environmental impact assessment, you don't have a first aid plan, you have no workplace monitors, and, in case you haven't noticed, there's a gigantic fire about ten miles that way and near-zero visibility and extremely poor air quality that make doing *any* work of this kind totally unsafe. Oh, and illegal."

Phuong shrugged. One of the elder Blue Helmets said, "You gotta do what you gotta do."

Olivia looked hard at him. "And you do what you gotta do?"

"Something like that."

Up until then, there'd been some camaraderie in their discussion, but now it evaporated. *Wrong thing to say, bro,* I thought. "Look, people. Word of advice: there's a world of difference between wildcatting your own construction project and violating a workplace shutdown order. That difference *starts* with criminal penalties, and goes up from there. You are clearly doing this because you believe in a good cause and I want to help you get it built and opened. So, take my advice: go get some breakfast, then get some sleep, then get some lawyers. Don't push this one."

"We hear you," Phuong said. Every single person on the jobsite, including Olivia, noticed that this was not the same thing as "We agree with you." Olivia flapped her arms helplessly.

"I tried," she said. "We'll have the immobilizers on-site in fifteen minutes, maybe half an hour. Don't give that crew any trouble, please and thanks. They're just doing a job."

"Take some coffee for the road?" Phuong suggested. Olivia turned on her heel and walked back to her car, back stiff.

"I feel bad for her," I said.

"Me too," Phuong said. Other people nodded and made agreeing sounds. There were seventy of us on the site, all gathered around the building, all looking at Phuong to say something. I had a moment where I thought it was weird that no one was looking at me, because it was my property. Then I realized how stupid that thought was, given that I had gone to such great lengths to get rid of it, and these people, my friends and comrades, were only honoring my stated wishes.

And then I felt proud because everyone was looking at Phuong, and Phuong was standing with me, and she thought I was great. She loved me.

"Okay, people, finish what you're doing, especially anything that needs the heavy gear. Immobilizers in thirty minutes tops. Hop to!"

And they did, but Phuong and the elders didn't. They huddled up and called over a few other people. I hesitated, not sure if I should join their huddle or get to work with the crew that was craning more slabs and roof joists up to the third floor. Phuong settled it for me by waving me over.

"You still got the list of names you contacted for the alternative street fair, the city-planning thing?"

"Yeah," I said. "Somewhere in my screen. Shit, do you think I should delete it? Is it evidence?"

Phuong giggled a little. "Oh, I'm *sure* it's evidence, but no, don't delete it. We're going to get in touch with everyone we seeded the street fair call-to-action to and ask them to get over here and provide support."

That surprised me into silence. Finally, I managed, "Why? Support for what? Everything's gonna be immobilized in minutes."

"Immobilizers can be removed," Fani said. She rocked her head from side to side. "It's been known to happen."

The immobilizer crew was businesslike and efficient. They showed up, logged into each machine, did some stuff to it using their city-issued fobs, and then double-checked it. They waved off our offers of coffee and split.

The first support crew showed up within half an hour, as the Blue Helmet elders sweated over each machine in pairs, one looking up online tutorials, the other following their instructions. There were about ten of them, and they drew out more of my neighbors, including Brad. They brought cold coconut water, sandwiches, mask filters, Tiger Balm, and hand-lettered signs: BUILD IT! HOUSING NOW! GND! UP AND THROUGH!

I took a vat-tuna sandwich into one of the rooms on the ground floor—I realized as I sat down on the floor that it was right where my old bedroom had been and felt like such a creature of habit—and stripped out of my mask and overalls and goggles and got ready to eat and drink, but then I gave in and leaned back against the wall and shut my eyes for just a minute and when I opened them again, hours had gone by and the air quality had gotten noticeably worse. My throat felt like sandpaper. I was still holding my water flask (and my sandwich) so I took a slug and then a bite and then masked up again. I found that I was a little short of breath and realized that the fog I was seeing wasn't sleep in my eyes but drifting smoke. I got out my oxy can and gave myself a couple of deep shots of O_2 until that feeling receded, then stood and stretched and went to find Phuong and my next work assignment.

Instead, I found a mob scene. Fairview Street had been transformed into an outdoor, smoky street fair, with what had to be *hundreds* of supporters who'd poured into Magnolia Park and found their way to our building site. They'd brought folding chairs, coolers, and more signs.

And tools. The new building was swarming with more volunteers who were hard at work on it. I looked up and up and up and though the smoke was thick, it seemed like they were actually putting on the roof. A stranger gave me another sandwich and a pack of ice-cold ginger beer that I gulped down, coughing at the fire. I put the sandwich in my toolbelt.

It was a crazy scene: the smoke, the people. There was a crash from up above me, a serious one, making the whole building shake. There was a part of me that knew that the building was *supposed* to shake, that the slabs were built to shimmy and give rather than shatter under seismic and wind loads, but there was a second where I had this conviction that the whole fucking thing was about to collapse and kill us all. How the *hell* had I and a bunch of friends built an *apartment building* in two days? Or was it three? I was so tired.

I couldn't find Phuong anywhere so I got out my screen to call her but when I opened it, it was just a wall of notifications from main socials, DSA socials, Blue Helmet socials, and Maga socials.

I'd been named. Derrick had outed me as some kind of radical socialist redgreen who was engaged in an act of eco-terror, building a refugee slum without an environmental impact statement. He had a whole playbook for making *me* sound like the right-wing asshole, hammering the fact that it wasn't a union jobsite.

"This is the kind of cult GND bullshit that leads to arson. They don't care about the environment. They don't care what species they disrupt when they build without a permit or an environmental impact statement. Starts with disrespecting your neighbors' right to live in a city of laws, goes to disrespecting those laws, and then it's whatever it takes to advance your radical agenda, whatever it takes to dismantle the country and make it into a coast-to-coast refugee camp where no one productive has anywhere to be and nothing to do."

It got worse after that: the comments on Derrick's post weren't just angry, they were *unhinged*. More than one person called for me to be put to death, and of course, these guys had *lots of guns* and they had my address, so that was intensely worrying.

One thing that took me a minute to notice was how much crosstalk there was between the different socials. Everyone had their own house rules, of course, but more important than that was just how *icky* distant socials' conversations were. No one from DSA wanted to go hang out in Maga land, and vice versa.

But both camps had been heavily screenshotting the other ones and pasting them into their feeds, which almost never happened, in part because mods hated it—it tended to kick off raids that turned into massive flame wars and sometimes even nuisance legal threats against users and mods. The twitters were mostly co-ops, and they bought media insurance, but the insurers weren't going to keep writing them policies if they spent all their time in court.

That explained the crowd: there was all this Maga chatter about coming down and, you know, lining us up against our own freshly built wall and opening fire. Most of us were normies and never went into Maga socials, so this was pretty shocking (not for me, I'd heard enough of it from Gramps and his pals over the years), and so everyone who saw it went to bring back more and whip up people to come to our defense.

And my mentions on the Maga side were full of threats, over-heated fantasies about a hive of terrorists, arsonists, illegals, and socialists whose masks had finally slipped, revealing their intention to literally rebuild cities out from under their homeowners, turning them into hives filled with freeloaders and losers and whiners.

What's more, all this stuff had burst the regional socials and escaped all over California and even out of state, and there were people calling for new construction to start on every frozen refu housing project that had been mothballed by the wave of injunctions. And naturally, there were Magas promising to dynamite any building that got restarted, under the banner of "helping our overworked, overwhelmed city planning officers."

That actually made me snort because how many times had I heard Gramps gripe about "red tape" and the "statists" who enforced it.

I had found a bit of unoccupied wall and sunk down on my

haunches to paw and swipe at my screen, tuning out the world around me so that I could read faraway people writing about the stuff that was happening right where I was sitting.

The thing that snapped me out of it was getting tagged in a picture of myself, all bedhead and construction dust, crouched against the wall, still holding my pre-nap tuna sandwich in the same hand that held my screen. I had forgotten it was there and I'd also forgotten that I was starving. I wiped the tuna salad off the back of my screen and stuffed the screen into a pocket, then lifted my mask and tore into it. It tasted like tuna and smoke and construction dust. I was about to spit it out and then I remembered that someone was photographing me and decided that wouldn't be a good look so I forced myself to chew and swallow. Then I remembered that I had another sandwich, given to me by a stranger, so I switched and got the taste out of my mouth.

My eyes started watering and then it got worse, so I found my goggles and put them on. They were filthy and the smoke was getting thicker. I felt my way back inside. I wasn't the only one—everywhere I looked someone was testing network integrity or running water through a pipe-join or probing an electrical outlet, and shooting filthies at the growing army of would-be helpers asking what they could do.

I climbed the temporary stairs up to the second floor and then the third, and then the fourth, but retreated from its unglazed windows and choking smoke.

Back on the third floor, I found another corner to eat my sandwich—a wall in a small kid's bedroom that I remembered personally dragging into place on a screen in Phuong's living room. It was wild to be leaning against that wall!

"There you are!" Phuong's mask hung under her chin and her goggles were up on her forehead. The skin between it was soot- and sweat-streaked and she looked fucking amazing. I collected a very long hug and a frustratingly short smooch. "Where have you been?"

"I fell asleep," I said. "Right after we unlocked the equipment. Sat down for a sandwich and zonk. Then I woke up and all this"—an arm wave—"was going down."

"You missed some pretty wild times," she said. "Have you looked at the socials?"

"Ugh. Scary. You think they mean it?"

She looked puzzled. "What? Oh. The Magas. Who knows. There're tons of cops on the way, from what I can tell, though whether they'll defend us from yahoos with ARs or line us up to make the shot easier is anyone's guess. No, I was talking about all the stuff happening in other towns."

"The construction? I couldn't tell if that was real—"

"Oh, it's real, but the wild-ass part is the munis and unis."

"I sorta know what those are—"

"Local currencies," she said. "It was a big idea in the early GND days, when unemployment was up at thirty percent and the fed wouldn't spring loose any more relief money. Towns and universities started minting their own currencies, managed by credit unions. The FDIC said it would yank their charters and the cities said they didn't give a shit, they'd keep using them, charter or no, and then Uwayni got elected and it didn't matter anymore, because she started the Jobs Guarantee."

"Right," I said. "Before my time."

"Mine too, but it was a big deal for the OG Blue Helmets, those Canadians, who said that it was the threat of wildcat money that gave their prime minister the leverage she needed to get the Bank of Canada to give in. It's been this kind of legendary weapon ever since, like a lost mystical doomsday sword that no one dared to use."

"Until now."

"Yes! Well, they're not using it either, but they're threatening to."

"It sounds kinda blockchainy to me," I said. "I mean, gross."

"Well, it could be—I mean, the money can live anywhere, but they're doing it old school, with the credit unions leading.

Credit unions already know how to create money, they do it every time they issue a loan. They're just threatening to do it without following the FDIC rules. Spend the money into existence to pay for GND projects, annihilate it by charging everyone in the system an annual fee to keep using it so they can control the money supply. And they say they've got their local governments on board, so—"

"So it's a big deal!" Ana Lucía was also covered in ash and dust and sweat, and had a wild look in her eyes. "Taking money back from the plutes, holy shit, it's all kicking off!"

"When did you get here?" I asked.

She shrugged. "Hours ago. I would have come yesterday but things are fucked up right now out there and my people needed help—not enough beds, too much smoke."

I felt suddenly awful. "Shit," I said. "I'm sorry."

"Oh," she said, "oh, no, I don't mean it that way at all. Yeah, it was hard to find six more billets, but Brooks, are you kidding me? This is amazing." She did a little shuffle-step. "I gotta say, when I first got here, I wasn't sure what to make of you, of all this talk. I mean, you have so much to lose here, and all the things you stand to gain are so . . . *hypothetical.* But this isn't talk. This is a fucking *building.* Eight apartments! Eight!"

I was still holding my sandwich. I snuck a look at it.

"Why aren't you eating?" Ana Lucía said.

"Because we're talking. I *was* eating, then—"

"Eat your sandwich, *flaco,*" Ana Lucía said.

"Administer sandwich, stat!" Phuong said.

I ate.

As I got to the last bite—both Phuong and Ana Lucía declined to try a bite of their own—I became aware that there was a weird sound on the jobsite, coming from downstairs but also outside the windows and also maybe the next room. Phuong and Ana Lucía noticed it around the same time I did. An older man and woman—maybe a married couple—had been working across the room from us, sealing the joins between the slabs, and now they were both looking at a screen.

"What's going on?" Phuong called to them.

"It's Strentzel," the woman said. She said the name with reverence. Juliet Strentzel was one of the heroes of the GND, the first American to join the Canadians in Calgary, whose vlogs and newshits had inspired a generation. She'd been Uwayni's deputy secretary of the interior and had run circles around the Beltway lifer who was nominally her boss, creating a lot of drama and getting a lot of shit done.

"I thought she was done," I said. It was famous. She'd gotten sick of being a celebrity, told every interviewer to fuck off and get a shovel, and disappeared into the mangroves of Florida to try to stabilize what remained of its landmass.

And yup, there she was, on my screen, once I followed the links ricocheting all over my socials and DMs. She looked so much older than my mental image of her, and had buzzed her hair. With her thin face, high cheekbones, intense stare, and fine-formed skull, she looked like a swamp apparition, standing in the mangroves, face sheened with sweat, her naked arms all ropy muscle beneath her bug-net suit, broad shoulders and prominent collarbones. She was leaning on a shovel, gesturing at a screen someone else must have been holding, since the frame followed her as she waved her arms, paced, moved restlessly around her swamp.

"Like I said, I don't like that I have to do this, but I guess I have to do this. We started something, back in the thirties. It was always gonna be too little, too late. That's what no one understood back then, because the human mind is a coward and it can't confront the future. We knew that we couldn't save most of the cities, most of the animals. We knew there would be mountains of dead, from disease and famine and fire and flood. We knew all that. The mission was never to avert that future, because it was too late for that.

"The mission was only ever to *confront* it. Do what needed to be done. Like a doctor figuring out which organs were too cancerous to save, doing what it takes to save the rest. I never went in for that bull about 'the first generation not to fear the future.' The future is a fearful place. It's going to get a *lot* worse before it gets better, and forgetting your fear is how you get a sociopath like Bennett in the Oval Office who sits by and watches as dark-money ops try to slow us down, stop us from our emergency scramble to save whatever we can.

"I don't do a lot of screen time down here. I'm pretty much done with the socials. You all can talk about what needs doing. I'm going to do it, until I can't. Only got so many years left in me and I plan on spending them in action, not talk.

"But someone sent me a stream of what those kids are doing up in Burbank—" and then I figured out why everyone around me was watching Strentzel in her swamp and I jolted like I'd been pinched. This was about us. About me. This living legend was talking about *me*. "—and I was like, *that, that* is what this is about. We won this argument. We fought for half a century and we won this argument, and now it's what, twenty years later and we're ready to forget about it? To pretend that this is about a difference of opinion and not about whether someone's idiotic fantasy about 'market-based solutions' is really about whether we're going to doom billions of people to grisly deaths.

"So someone sent me this stream and asked me what I thought and then I had to go and dig through all the bullshit about why they couldn't just build the refugee housing that the laws we passed demanded, and I learned about all the courthouse bullshit you all let some offshore plute wreckers get up to, and was all, 'Yeah, I'll tell you what I think.'

"So here goes. Build that building. Build as much emergency housing as it takes so that everyone gets a roof and a bed and somewhere halfway decent to come home to after a day's hard work saving our species and our planet and all the species we share it with.

When they tell you to stop, tell them to go to hell. When they arrest you, fight it. If the building next door gets shut down because the crew building it was all arrested, show up and finish the work. They can't arrest us all."

She sat down on the bulbous knuckle of a mangrove, let her shovel fall behind her. She looked very tired. "You guys, there's a lot of work we have to do and time is running out. I toiled in the bullshit fields for a decade, and now I'm out here, doing what I can in the actual world. The minutes they're stealing from you are minutes you could be spending doing the work."

She looked out at her swamp.

"There is so much work." She dropped her head. Without lifting it, she said, "Show them, Murph," and the camera person (Murph, I guess) showed us the mangrove swamp, and I realized that it was a city. I was looking at the ruins of a three-story motel, only one end of it still intact, the rest sunk into the marshy ground.

"Welcome to Miami, people," she said. "Eighty billion dollars' worth of real estate, a couple million people's homes. Memories. Achievements. People think we don't love these places. I fuckin' *loved* Miami. The food, the music, the people. Even the people. Love my Floridian friends.

"We lost Miami, Jakarta, every one of those cruise-ship towns in the Caribbean. Havana. Gone. Lives ruined. The evolved cities that human footfall and desire and rage and striving built, washed away and left to rot. That's what's coming for us all. We are out of time."

She lifted her head, her cheeks streaked with tears. "This shit is why I left. I just couldn't stand talking anymore. We've talked this thing to death. Right now, the only talking anyone needs to do is to ask 'How can I help?'

"So you comrades out there in Burbank, you're doing it. Don't let anyone tell you different."

She looked around at Miami. The day was drawing to a close there, and a shaft of red sunset caught her face, made it golden and highlighted every line and wrinkle. For an instant, she looked like a bronze, a statue commemorating a long-dead war hero, a legend.

"Ah shit," she breathed. "It's beautiful, sometimes, if you can forget all the other stuff, the blood that fertilized the soil, the obscene floating islands of wealth that will spill more blood still for no reason except that they don't want to face the future. Do me a favor, all of you? Next sunset that comes your way, stop for a sec and really *look* at it.

"All right, that's me done. I love you all, even the sociopaths. Don't write, don't DM, don't call. You want to shout back to me, pick up a shovel." She got heavily to her feet and pulled work gloves out of her back pocket and put them on, then bent down with a groan to get her shovel. She looked up at the camera. "Don't be a dick, Murph. Turn that off, shit." And the feed died.

"Well, that happened," Phuong said, and laughed. Ana Lucía laughed too. I couldn't laugh because I was crying too hard.

"Oh, babe," Phuong said, slipping an arm around my shoulders, "what's all the tears for?"

"She reminded me of my mom," I said, and sobbed.

After I'd had a good cry, we went looking for chores that needed doing. I was asking "How can I help?" and the answer was "Get out of my way, I'm working here." I took the hint. I went with Phuong back to her house to augment my too-short nap and smoky sandwich with a real lunch and a solid eight hours' sleep.

Okay, it wasn't all my idea. Phuong may have suggested it. And by suggested, I mean, she may have literally twisted my arm behind my back and marched me away from the jobsite.

We got between the sheets next to each other, smelling of soap and toothpaste. "Shit, we forgot to look at the sunset," I said, as I started to drift off.

"Too much smoke today anyway," Phuong said. "Tomorrow."

It was tomorrow before I knew it, albeit four in the morning. I got up as quietly as I could but I still woke up Phuong, who smiled sleepily at me as I used my light from the screen to find a T-shirt and boxers to wear down to the kitchen.

"Four a.m., huh?"

"Sorry."

"Don't be. My sleep schedule is just as messed up as yours."

We made big bowls of granola in the kitchen and crumbled dehydrated citrus fruit over it along with fresh apple slices, and Phuong made Greek coffee, which she only made on serious days (regular days were strictly sweet Vietnamese coffee), and we sipped it carefully so we didn't get the grounds in our mouths, talking in whispers so we wouldn't disturb her housemates.

Inevitably, I got up to pee, and inevitably, I brought a screen, and that's when I found out what I'd slept through. I barely managed to flush, zip, and wash before rushing out to find Phuong.

"Did you see?" She was on her screen, too, of course. What else was she going to do while I was peeing?

"See what?"

I shoved my screen under her nose and danced from foot to foot, drinking too much coffee at once and getting grounds in my teeth.

"No way."

Just as we'd been getting ready for bed the night before, a federal judge in Alaska had lifted all of the Flotilla's anti-construction injunctions in the whole Ninth Circuit—Alaska, Arizona, Hawaii, Idaho, Montana, Nevada, Washington, Oregon, and California. Within an hour, another judge—this one in Honolulu—had reinstated the injunctions, and her order contained a "sharp rebuke" for the Anchorage judge whose order she was overturning. I read the order and discovered that "sharp rebuke" was the phrase that legal reporters used when they meant "vicious personal attack."

Well, that kicked off a shitstorm up and down the whole Ninth Circuit, as it experienced the long-feared "massive intracircuit split" that those same court watchers made sound like the big quake everyone in California quietly dreaded in the backs of our imaginations.

One thing led to another thing and the chief judge of the circuit summoned ten more judges to a federal courthouse in Pendleton, a small town deep in inland Oregon—which also happened to be the only federal courthouse in the circuit with breathable air. Small planes and helicopters had been scrambled, backup judges had been tapped, and right at this moment, grumpy judges were being brought breakfast at the Umatilla Indian casino that had reserved a whole tower just for their use.

Even grumpier—but far better paid—lawyers for the DSA, the Flotilla, environmental groups, law societies, environmental law societies, human rights groups, refugee rights groups, housing rights groups, real estate developer associations, and many other orgs were finalizing their amicus briefs for the hearing.

And the curtain would rise on the whole thing in a mere three hours.

We were just about the last ones to learn about the courtroom fight, and there was already a plan to gather at various places around Burbank for viewing parties: the DSA hall, Burroughs High's gym, and the house we'd been building on Gramps's lot. It was obvious where we'd be watching.

Only we almost didn't make it. The smoke had gotten worse overnight, as bad as I'd ever seen it. The screens said we were getting it from multiple fire systems now, from the Angeles National Forest but also from Mendocino, from Oregon, from Washington State. We had to stop twice to take O_2 hits, and I began to question the wisdom of leaving the house at all. I could have done the walk from Phuong's to Gramps's blindfolded, but the smoke screwed up my whole sense of place and orientation, till I couldn't tell where I was or where I was going. I realized that some of my shortness of breath came from panic, not smoke, and worse, there was no way I was going to take deep breaths to calm down.

"Come on," Phuong said. "Almost there. I got ya."

The smoke cleared a little as we turned the corner and I was suddenly disoriented again. That couldn't possibly be Gramps's house, could it? I mean, not Gramps's house, but the building we'd started building, what, three days ago? Four?

It had curtains. I mean, curtains. All the way up to the fourth floor. Even the construction waste had been tidied, a lot of it hauled away, and there was some rudimentary landscaping on the lawn, French drains and drip-irrigation pipes and a raised, slightly humped walk up to the door. The door! We'd added some scrap lumber onto Gramps's door to fit it into the wider, accessible doorway, but someone had found a real door and put it into place. It was painted a bright, deep green with enough gloss that it shone through the smoke, a porch light over it illuminating a sphere of smoky air like a lightning bug in a foggy swamp.

Phuong was just as blown away as I was. We stood there at the foot of the walkway in the fence gate, gawping, until I started to cough.

"Let's get in there," she said, grabbing my arm and dragging me as she skipped and I coughed my way to the door.

It was obvious that crews had worked through the night: not just putting up curtains, but getting the HVAC working—its hum was loud in the entrance hall—and fitting switch plates and receptacle covers to all the electrics. There were two apartments on the ground floor, a thousand-square-foot, two-bedroom place and a seven-hundred-square-foot one-bedroom, and each had its own door (the one-bedroom had the door from my old bedroom, I saw, and smiled). There were voices coming from inside both, and we poked our heads into a few rooms, happening on work crews that were busy painting, assembling storage, and doing other finish work.

We said hi and made approving noises, then climbed the stairs—still temporary stringer stairs—up to the second story, which was a lot rougher than the ground floor, and then up to the third floor. Up on three, the rooms were much barer, and the work crews were thinner still—mostly, it was pairs of people unrolling big screens and setting up stools to use as chairs so we could watch the hearings. Phuong checked the job board on her screen and we picked up the task of ferrying food from the kitchens down on the first floor up to the viewing rooms: electrolytes and coffee, freeze-dried fruit and granola mixed with powdered oat milk that could be wetted with water from the faucets in the two apartments' bathrooms and kitchens, which had been jury-rigged with buckets instead of basins.

Ana Lucía found us as we were making our fifth trip together and pitched in, and soon there were more people on the stairs, heading up to the third floor, and they pitched in too, so we were all able to settle in with coffee and cereal, like it was a pajama party where everyone wore construction overalls and USN95s.

The hearings were not as dramatic as I'd hoped. Courtroom dramas had apparently misled me about how these things went down. It was cool to see that Constance Ming, the DSA lawyer who'd briefed us on the injunctions a million years before, was on the call, though they didn't get to argue. Instead, there was this old guy who seemed to know the judges all personally, who got on the call and presented the most bare-bones, straightforward version of our case I could have imagined.

"Plaintiffs argue that the lower court erred in its interpretation of the Internal Displaced Persons Act, which clearly contemplates that emergency refugee construction might require alternative environmental assessments and ex ante compliance with other rules and regulations. Indeed, the statute exists solely to balance these important priorities against other, more immediate ones—to allow us to put out the fire before we fix the roof. As our briefs and support from our amici make clear, the injunctions should not have been issued because they are counter to the statute's plain language, to precedent in every circuit, and to regulatory determinations made at the affected expert agencies. My clients ask for an immediate lifting of the injunctions and clemency for those who soldiered on with the firefighting the situation demanded in spite of an adverse ruling from the lower court."

I liked that he used the fire metaphor, what with all the smoke outside the windows, but I was pretty shocked by how *mellow* his whole delivery was. Like, he was talking about life-or-death stuff here, a horrific act of sabotage against the planet itself, and he was just laying it out like he was reading the weather. Admittedly, the weather was pretty political, but this was way more political, as far as I was concerned.

When the judges started questioning him, my dread worsened. They were really grilling him, making it sound like he thought that people should be able to do *anything* if it meant helping climate refugees, even committing violent acts. But he fielded all their questions with the same calm, and now he started quoting sections of the Internal Displaced Persons Act from memory, citing cases, even correcting one of the judges' citations in a very calm way that let the judge save face, and I got to understanding that he was a walking encyclopedia of this stuff, and the reason he was so cool about it all was that he had nothing to worry about. It was gratifying to watch the lawyer for the Flotilla dark-money groups watch *our* lawyer being so utterly, coolly badass.

But if the judges were impressed, they did a good job of hiding it. Once it was clear how cold our guy had it, they started interrupting his answers to ask him other questions and then more questions on top of those, sometimes talking on top of each other. Fundamentally, they wanted to know how the Internal Displaced

Persons Act wasn't a "lawbreaker's charter" that allowed "vigilantes" to "decide which laws they were going to follow and when."

It was weird to see our guy being so unruffled by all of this when it seemed so clear that the judges hated him, and then it was the other guy's turn. He was much younger, and Latino, with movie-star looks, and even though he did a much more lean-forward delivery—literally and figuratively, speaking with real passion about how we couldn't afford the risks from "private citizens making unilateral decisions about the environmental impact of permanent structures"—he seemed every bit as self-assured as our guy had been and someone googled him and learned he'd been tops in his class at Stanford Law and did a postdoc at Oxford.

The judges were as easy on him as they'd been hard on our guy, just lobbing these softballs at him and putting on these serious, thoughtful faces while he answered. It wasn't obvious at the start, but a few minutes into it, it was clear that he wasn't getting the same treatment, and people in the room with us started groaning and catcalling the screen, and we heard the same thing coming from other rooms.

Then, suddenly, it was over. We all looked at one another as the courtroom feed winked out of the screen, like, *Was that it?* The buzz of conversation rose, and then Constance, the DSA lawyer, popped onto the screen. They were grinning broadly.

"Well folks, thanks for tuning in to that. I thought I'd pop on to the channel and give you a rundown on what happens next. The judges are going to meet and deliberate, and we expect to get a judgment within twenty-four hours. That's a *lot* faster than normal, but this whole thing is abnormal, and when there's an emergency hearing, they can move fast." They looked down at their screen, their eyes flicking as they read the chat. They frowned and then laughed.

"Oh, man, sorry. I see a *lot* of you are worried about the way that hearing went down, like why were they so hard on poor old Kuby, and why did Guzman get the white-glove treatment?

"So here's a dirty not-so-secret of this kind of hearing—appeals panels, en banc review, the Supremes. They know they've got history's eyes on them, that law students are going to debate what they do and what they don't do. That means that when they're about to make major law, they want to prove to posterity that they're not being sloppy about it. The upshot of that is that if the judges really lay into you, it's often because they're in the tank for you."

"But not always." That was Kuby, now leaning back in his chair with a sandwich in one hand, tie missing and jacket off, feet on his desk, revealing that he'd been wearing striped pajama bottoms and slippers from the waist down. "Sometimes, they're hard on you because they hate you."

Constance grabbed the video feed back from him. "Come on, don't scare 'em. Yes, sometimes they act like they hate you because they hate you. But mostly, it's because they want to prove they're not playing faves. I'm a glass-half-full kind of lawyer."

Kuby popped back. "Takes all kinds." He took a huge bite of his sandwich and we watched in fascination as he chewed and swallowed. "Sorry, court makes me so damned hungry. I just couldn't sit here while Constance sung their sweet song of a rosy future assured to all."

"Sir," they said, "I am reliably informed that my generation is the first in a century that doesn't fear the future."

He snorted and gestured with his sandwich. "Translation: 'Okay Millennial.'"

We spent the next three hours on a troll counteroffensive, flagging content, fact-backing fast-moving threads, outing botmasters by publishing screengrabs from their command-and-control servers that got leaked by confederates, the basic socials firefighting that

I got sucked into all the time, but this time with a global audience, as our fight sprawled past the local socials, going statewide, then national, then everywhere that the Flotilla was drumming up meme warriors to smear us.

I was really getting into it when Ana Lucía sat down next to me and said, "Dude, there's a verdict, come on."

I stood up—I'd been sitting on the floor up on the fourth floor, having moved from room to room every time a work crew showed up to do something useful, and my knees and back and neck were tight and sore. I did some toe-touching, and when I took a deep breath, my lungs ached, way down low, in the way that told me I'd been careless about smoke inhalation.

As I walked on shaky legs down to the third floor and back to the empty bedroom where I'd watched the hearing—now equipped with a built-in wardrobe and new light fixtures—I felt like a salmon that had been swimming upstream to its spawning ground, arriving at last with one and a half fins, only one eye, and most of my scales missing.

Phuong was already there, looking as tired as I felt, as did everyone else in the room: paint- and plaster-spattered volunteers, streaked with soot, masks around their chins or dangling from one ear. The air was close and sweaty, body smells and smoke smells and paint smells. A couple of hours before, there'd been a palpable sense of defiance and hope, and now that seemed gone, replaced by exhaustion. I'd known so many of these people for so long, since middle school, grade school, even, and many of them were part of Phuong's cohort, older cool kids I'd idolized for their skateboard skills, amazing fashion, and, later, political activism. Seeing them in this state was truly dispiriting. I felt like someone had cut my strings. Ana Lucía and I squeezed into seats to either side of Phuong and I took her hand.

"You okay, babe?" she said.

I tried for a smile. "Just beat," I said. "Probably hangry. Screen-burn."

"When this is over I'm going to go to bed for a week and then I'm going to go and sit on the beach for a week."

"Can I come?"

"To bed, or the beach?"

"Both," I said.

She squeezed my hand and gave me a quick kiss, and then the big screen at the front of the room came to life.

It was Constance Ming, in some kind of DSA war room, a boardroom in what I took to be DC, walls covered in screens and heavily marked-up whiteboards, table littered with coffee cups and water glasses. They were huddled with a group of DSA activists, some of whom I recognized as elder statespeople, but many as young as me. It was basically exactly what I figured life must be like at DSA HQ, like it had been set-dressed and cast over at one of the baby Warners.

"The verdict came out faster than we thought it would," Ming said, without any kind of greeting. "And it's long-ass, which suggests that there were clerks who were pretty anxious to get their ya-yas out on this issue and had a lot of draft text in the can. Before I say anything else about it, I want to get to the headline: all the injunctions are lifted. All of them, effective immediately." Whatever they said next was lost in the cheers, which bounced off the unfurnished room's hard walls, and also rang in from the rooms down the halls and below us.

I was part of that roar, but even as I cheered and stamped my feet and clapped, my body was sending me these heavy lethargy messages, like, *soon as we're done with this, I'm gonna go lie down,* and I realized how much of my ability to stay vertical over the past several hours had been tension, waiting to hear what was going to happen next.

They were still talking and people shushed each other and then a guy my age in their war room showed them his screen and they said, "Shit, sorry, I shoulda given you all a chance to finish cheering. That's all right, you deserve to take a moment to recognize what just happened. We just beat back one of the most expensive, powerful, and coordinated assaults in Green New Deal history. We did it by putting our bodies on the line.

"Here's a thing about the law: there aren't enough cops to enforce the law if people don't believe in it. That means that society's primary law enforcement tool isn't cops, it's legitimacy. And that goes double for judges: that's why they wear the robes and use all that Latin and do the whole all-rise business: to reinforce their own legitimacy, to remind you that we, as a society, hold them in high esteem.

"The reason for all those reminders is that if the esteem goes away, then so does their legitimacy. Remember when Uwayni just ignored the Supreme Court for her first term, just kept signing these wildly popular GND bills that they struck down, until they stopped? Everyone had been on her to pack the court from the start, but she was like, nah, I'm gonna hit these old fuckers where it hurts, right in their legitimacy. I'm gonna pass all kinds of super-popular legislation and dare them to void it, because every time they do, it makes me look like the true representative of democratic will and makes them look like an obstructionist relic that no one should take seriously.

"It worked. Today, we did a version of that. Well, *you* did. When you occupied those building sites, when you whipped up a nation to see that the court had got in the way of doing the obviously right thing, you put the fear into those judges. I'm a hundred percent convinced that this is why they ruled the way they did. That's the good news."

They took a deep breath, then slugged some water. "Now, the bad news: the injunctions are lifted *prospectively*, but not *retrospectively*. That means that anyone who violated them is liable to civil penalties—fines—and in some cases, like if you were ordered to stop and then went back to work anyway, you might face criminal penalties.

"There're three million-odd people on this stream, and now's the time when I ask you to open up your wallets. I'm not fundraising here, this is a defense and bail fund, because there're gonna be a *lot* of arrests and we're going to need to start retaining counsel up and down the country for our comrades. Link's on the screen. You know what to do."

Suddenly, they looked very tired, raccoon-eyed and slumped and ten years older. "Folks, our work only just got started. I know a lot of you are thinking, 'When do we get to stop fighting this fight?' I'll tell you what a wise friend told me, before she took up full-time work as a swamp-witch: Some fights you fight because you plan on winning them. Some fights, you fight because the minute you stop, you lose ground. For reasons that I can't even pretend to understand, there's a large cohort of people out there who think that we should bury our heads in the sand, or worse, fight each other rather than the fires around us. I mean, it's a cliché to say some people just want to watch the world burn, but after a lot of years doing this, I have concluded that this is just a statement of fact. Some people seriously do want to watch the world burn.

"Some of you are going to go to jail for your good work. I don't think anyone will serve a long term, and we're going to fight like hell for each and every one of you. I don't think anyone in the wild-fire zone has to worry about cops until the smoke clears, but whatever you do, stay put, don't run away from the cops, that'll just make our job harder. We can probably beat the rap for failing to respond to a noise ticket or stop-work order from a building inspector, but evading law enforcement is a much more serious charge.

"In the meantime, don't forget that we won a hell of a victory today. Yes, all it did was get us back to where we were a couple weeks ago, but I'll take that win—beats the shit out of going backwards." They blew out a double cheekful of air and shook their head. "I'm gonna go take a walk. We can do that here in DC, for now. For those of you stuck in the fires, I recommend taking a nap. You've earned it."

I spent the next twenty-four hours at Phuong's place, mostly in her bed or on the sofa, hacking my lungs out and catching up on my sleep and nutrition. But I wouldn't call it rest: whenever I could focus my eyes, I was on a screen, giving advice to the crews that had swarmed every work site where the injunction halted things, putting up fresh emergency buildings in the smoke, which only got thicker. Erecting permanent prefab housing with zero visibility and unbreathable air turned out to be a relatively new field, so new that I was one of the leading experts, despite the fact that I felt like I didn't have a single clue.

But the buildings needed to go up because we needed to get people indoors. The homeless refugees in their tents were choking to death, literally, and the community centers, libraries, and school gyms had been turned into emergency shelters, but they were bursting at the seams, especially as people whose houses were in the fire's path rode or cycled or marched into town, eyes streaming, lungs clogged, desperate and scared.

When my eyes couldn't focus on my screen anymore, I tried to rest, but that's when my brain replayed a greatest-hits reel of everything screwed up and awful from recent months, always coming to rest on the same thing: Constance saying, *Some people seriously do want to watch the world burn.*

The thing is, I think they were wrong. I grew up around those people, Gramps and his friends. They didn't want to see the world burn. They thought *we* wanted to destroy the world. They didn't always act in good faith, but they thought the same of us. Gramps and his Maga buddies didn't deny climate change (not anymore, though I could believe they had, once upon a time). Some of them thought we were exaggerating it, but there were plenty of them who believed in it as much as I did.

Mostly, we agreed on the facts. What we disagreed on was what to do about them.

318 • cory doctorow

Some of the Magas thought that it was hopeless, most of the world was already lost, and the job was to make sure that the patch they were on survived, along with the people they cared about. They hated refus because they were bigots, but also, they hated them because they saw themselves as living in a lifeboat, and saw every refu they hauled over the gunwales as one more mouth to feed from the dwindling supplies, and believed that if they let enough refus in, the boat would sink.

And then there was the gospel of the Flotilla, the idea that we could just nerd our way out of the emergency with geoengineering and asteroid mining. The thing was, this wasn't so different from the GND, which had built zero-carbon factories across every American desert that ran only when the sun shone, turning out all the material and technology we'd need to relocate every coastal city inland, retrofit all our housing stock, and solarize every home.

The difference was that Uwayni had nationalized all the knowledge and practices that went into building these factories, just shunting aside the big asset funds and patent trolls that stood in the way of the whole human race coming together to solve its problems.

The Flotilla believed that some of us were born to be wise kings, and that winning in the market was the modern equivalent to pulling a sword out of a stone, and that Uwayni and the GND were doomed because they had defied the natural order of things, like trusting toddlers to run the factory.

The Magas who believed this were a combination of pathetic and outraged: convinced that they were inferior to the superheroic "inventors" and "founders" they worshipped, but also sure that they were smarter than the rest of us, because we were too stupid to recognize our betters.

The smartest Magas actually understood our arguments, they just thought we were lying about what we truly believed and intended: they thought we were so offended by the idea that some people were just better than others that we'd sacrifice the whole human race and its only planet to prove the point.

All of this was gross and wrong and the years I'd spent arguing with Gramps and his buddies over it had been miserable, but one thing it had made me sure of was that the Magas didn't want to watch the world burn. They sincerely wanted to save it. They weren't wrong because they were cruel.

They were cruel because they were wrong.

Smoke-out builds—as they came to be known—were literally and figuratively the new hotness. Everywhere the smoke blew, there were fresh refus: unhomed people who couldn't find shelter, refus from towns that were afire or in the fire's path, people who'd built emergency buildings in their neighborhoods only to abandon them when the wind shifted and the flames licked at their boundaries.

A decade before, Uwayni had created powerful tools to liberate idle real estate from tangled legal ambiguities, absentee owners, and lost deeds. But as good as those tools were, they weren't perfect, and every town and city—including Burbank—had empty lots and abandoned houses dotted through it, properties whose legal status was so snarled that even Uwayni's legal tools couldn't unpick it.

We built on those lots. I mean, I didn't, not at first, not while I was recovering, but I cheered them on. Even when they talked about being in a lifeboat, and the need to throw the old rules overboard during an emergency. Even when I thought that this was exactly what Gramps's friends thought they were doing, the Green Shock Doctrine, seizing on emergencies with direct action that literally bulldozed through the rules they couldn't change through democratic means. Even when I thought about how this was what the Magas had done, a Flotilla-funded shock doctrine that shut down all the building they'd opposed all along. If it was going to be Dueling Shock Doctrines, I'd take the green one. If it was going to be Lifeboat Rules, I'd take a captain in a green hat, not a red one.

If your house is on fire, you pull the firehose to it by the shortest path, even if it crosses your neighbor's lawn. Even if he howls about his property rights. Fuck property rights, we were defending human rights.

Back to work. Three days of nebulizers and O_2 cannisters and rest and—especially—watching everyone else putting in the hours in the smoke, and I was so eager to get out there. Phuong, too. We'd been rattling around her house like change in the bottom of your pocket, clanking and clicking and getting nowhere fast and driving her housemates nuts.

But on the fourth day, we listened to each other's chests and declared ourselves fit for service and suited up, put on our masks and goggles, and hit the road. We had our choice of building sites to work on, but of course, we went back to Gramps's place, to do finish work: solarizing, paint, carpet, fixtures, staircases, exterior fire escapes. We did it for sentimental reasons, of course, but also for good reasons: the HVAC worked, meaning any indoor work we did would have filtered air, sparing our abused lungs from searing smoke, while still challenging us with a huge variety of new tasks that we had to learn from videos and mentors and remote experts.

The first day was incredibly rewarding, but we nearly got lost on the way home, the smoke was so thick, and so we decided the next day that we'd bring bedrolls and go fully live-work until the smoke cleared or the house was done, whichever came first.

There's a Blue Helmet truism that the last 10 percent of any project takes 90 percent of the time, and that was certainly my experience with the building that had once been Gramps's house. The early stages had involved standard parts—slabs, infrastructure, glazing, insulation—but now that we were doing fine work, things had to be just right—exactly right modular kitchen cabinets, the right sliding doors for balconies and locks for internal doors. More than half of the work was just hitting the screens, wrangling with other crews nearby to see who had the part you needed and then figuring out how to make rendezvous and acquire it.

But over the next four days, things took shape, and a couple of the apartments got real furniture, a mix of prefabs and donated pieces, and it was wild to see the rough structure I'd left a week before with my lungs on fire and my arms so heavy I could barely lift them now looking ready for human habitation. And habitate it we did, as parts of our crew left to work on other buildings that needed more work, until there were fewer than a dozen of us on-site at any moment, many of us couples like Phuong and me, so that we ended up with our own temporary, personal apartments (though people on the third and fourth floors had to borrow facilities from their downstairs neighbors because the city hadn't been able to upgrade our main water service yet).

We started every day with an all-hands meeting up on the fourth floor, which had been laid out as a one-bedroom and an efficiency so that there could be leftover space for community use, with tall windows that afforded a commanding view of the rest of Fairview Street—the big camphor trees and ash-coated backyard furniture and pools. We'd put some easy-assembly stools in there made of glue and cardboard suspended on tight lengths of tensegrity monofilament, and we'd make a circle and get our screens out and plan the day's work over coffee.

There were eight of us up there on the eighth day, and we were just coming to the consensus that there wasn't enough work for all of us to do that day when Armen—who'd moved in with Dave and kept us all supplied with after-work vapes—interrupted us, pointing out the window and saying, "Hold up, hold up, what the *fuck*?" He didn't sound at all like his usual laid-back, unruffleable self. He sounded scared. We all followed his finger.

Six men were moving down the street, masked and goggled like anyone you saw in the smoke, but through the haze you could see there was something different about them. They were in body armor, and two of them had automatic rifles I recognized as siblings to the guns I'd found in Gramps's cache. All of them wore holstered squirt guns, doubtless full of acid, and one carried a baseball bat; another, a hatchet.

"Oh, shit," someone said, and then I realized it was me. They were in a wedge-shaped formation, swinging their gaze from side to side as they quick-marched down Fairview Street. As we watched, they split into two groups, one heading for our front door, the other for the rear entrance.

Phuong smacked the big screen on one wall and then we were looking at their livestream, chyroned SHERIFF'S WARRANTS SERVED ON ENVIRONMENTAL CRIMINALS.

I started to say, "You've gotta be fucking kidding me," but Phuong cut me off in the middle of "gotta" and cranked the sound, which was narration from the camera at our front door.

"—don't have a lot of situational data about the interior, but we're presuming up to about two dozen hostiles. We've got our warrants here but we're not counting on compliance, which is why we're going in hot. In the event that our suspects are watching this feed, we want you to know that we intend for you to face justice and that means we won't use more force than is warranted for our own safety." He'd been creeping steadily up to the front door through all this, and now his helmet cam showed him looking to the two others in his squad, one of whom had his rifle up and ready; the other was holding his squirt gun, a mini Super Soaker he was methodically and enthusiastically pumping up.

Now he stood on our doorstep and raised one hand to knock at the door, but before he did, he said, "Rear entry team check in." Another voice on the stream: "Ready Leader One. Awaiting your signal."

He nodded curtly, the camera going up-down, and then

pounded on our door. "Self-sovereign sheriffs serving an arrest warrant. Open up in there. You have ten seconds."

"The door's not even locked," Phuong said. It broke the horrified spell that had frozen us all in place.

"Fire escape," I said, and bolted for the hallway. Every Blue Helmet knew the story of the Levant Company fire, an Istanbul warehouse conversion that had burned down mid-construction, after the rusting exterior fire stairs had been removed but before the emergency internal staircase had been built, trapping more than forty people on the upper floors. From the moment that our building had acquired a second story, it had a set of scaffolding running down one side, with steep stair/ladders, each landing kept clear in case of another fire.

I was closest to the door, so I was the first person to reach the fire escape, and the sound of my boots thumping on its landing was incredibly loud in the morning quiet. The smoke made it hard to see the ground floor and the militiamen, but I was sure they were craning their necks up at me, aiming their guns straight up. Not the squirt guns, of course. Not even the Magas were stupid enough to fire acid straight overhead.

Maybe.

I crept as quietly down the stairs as I could manage. The scaffolding had been well-constructed, but it was still made of bolts, pipes, and boards and it had a certain amount of flex and sway, and as more people piled out of the window above me that flex grew more pronounced, and the whole thing creaked like a windmill with a bad bearing.

I touched down on the ground just as more smoke rolled in and looked up to see how far away Phuong was. She was two landings up, helping someone else—I couldn't make out who it was. The smoke was really getting thick. I looked up at her and thought *come on, come on* and then took a step away from the scaffolding toward the neighbor's fence. Then I took a step back toward the scaffolding. What the hell was she doing?

Someone up on the landing, or maybe the one above it, started to cough. Real, old-fashioned, hacking spasms, the kind you got after weeks of smoke, when your lungs were so enflamed that they wanted to sue for divorce. Whoever it was tried to muffle it, but it wasn't working. I heard voices from around the corner as the "sheriff's deputies" heard the sounds, and then calls, and then running feet. I hopped from one foot to the next, put my hands on the ladder to scurry up again, and then decided not to and bolted for the fence, scrambling over it as the militiamen barked orders at me: *Freeze! Hands where I can see them! Stop or I'll shoot!*

The chain-link tore my shirt and the skin of my hands as I cleared it, and all around me, liquid sizzled on the ground as someone emptied a Super Soaker full of hydrochloric acid toward me. A drop landed on the back of my work boot and began to eat through the sole, dissolving part of the stitching and making my boot feel loose and wobbly as I pelted off through the smoke, down Fairview Street, turning the corner onto Verdugo as I heard the first rounds of AR-15 fire tear through the air, back at the construction site.

Standing in Verdugo Park, a sense of unreality wafted over me with the smoke. All around me were the abandoned tents of the refus whom Burbank had finally welcomed indoors once the smoke got too thick. My lungs burned from the run, and my panting was loud in my ears.

But apart from the breathing and the smoke, everything seemed normal. Not like an armed militia gang had just tried to murder me. Not like they weren't holding an unknown number of my friends and comrades hostage. Not like Phuong wasn't in terrible danger. She might be dead. How could that be? So sudden. So irreversible. Like knocking a house down: one minute it's there, eternal, the site of a million memories, the central node of a network of people and things and deeds. The next minute, it's gone.

Forever. Nothing can ever be done to put it back. If Phuong was dead, I would never talk to her again. Never see her again. Never kiss her again. Never resolve our misunderstandings. Never create new memories together. I might find someone else someday, but it wouldn't be her. No one would be her.

What do you do when an armed militia wants to murder you? When they've taken your friends hostage?

Go to the cops? Fuck that. The militias had fully infiltrated law enforcement, obviously. The cops were no friends of mine. They'd had lots of opportunities to deal with the terrorists who'd blown up our buildings and instead they'd spent their time enforcing against the people putting up new buildings.

Go to the DSA? That was my first impulse: for weeks I'd been a cyber-militiaman for the Green New Deal, fighting in a flame war over what we were doing, what it meant, and who the bad guys and good guys were. The war was fought with screens, but it wasn't virtual. Like Constance Ming said, we would have lost our court battle if it wasn't for the undeniable truth that more people supported our side than the side of plutes, militias, and wreckers. They have the money, but we have the people, and the people have to show up if they're gonna get shit done.

My impulse to go to the DSA was immediate, but short-lived. I was rasping, sweating, cut up, scared, and, above all, furious. My lover and my friends were being held hostage by *monsters,* and it was all happening in *my* house, and the experience of being run off the property I'd been raised on by masked, armed cowards had humiliated me and made me so furious I couldn't see straight, literally. My vision had gone black and red around the edges, and between that and the smoke and my tears, I could barely see.

It was there in Verdugo Park, staring at the unseeable, heart thudding with rage, that I had a wicked, terrible, *amazing* idea.

———————

If standing in a park moments after getting shot at felt weird, touching in to get on a bikeshare felt even weirder. But after walking a couple of blocks in the smoke, I realized that I was in a race between how long I had to spend outdoors and how hard I had to work while I was out there, and decided that I was going to have to ride if I was going to make it up to the Burbank hills and back again without rendering myself so lung-sick that I wouldn't be able to fight when I got back to the house.

With Gramps's guns.

I stuck to the sidewalk for the first two-thirds of the trip, but when I got to the steep uphills where the sidewalks petered out, I rode nervously on the shoulder, hugging as close as I could to the curbs, but then I dismounted and walked the bike—as soon as I hit that steep slope and started breathing hard, it was like someone had filled my lungs with broken glass. I only got passed by a single car, semiautonomous and lidar-guided. It gave me a wide berth.

The ash from the fires, the rains, and the sunshine had turned the flood zone into a weed-choked riot of shrubs, scrub, and grasses, and for a while I thought I wouldn't be able to find my cache. But then I found the fence line and walked it carefully, squinting through my goggles, wheeling the bike, then leaning the bike down in the weeds and hacking my way to the cistern. It was smaller than I remembered.

The top layer of sandbags had been exposed to successive waves of rain and sun and the fabric had started to disintegrate. Many of the bags split as I tossed them into the brush. Then, as I remembered, a layer of rocks. What I hadn't remembered was how heavy they were. How had I lifted these into the cistern? The sand from the leaking bags had infiltrated the spaces between the rocks, turning into a dry cement that sucked at them as I wrestled them free. Then there were more sandbags, these ones intact, damp, and *heavy.*

And then my fingers scrabbled over the slick plastic of the contractor bag. It was slimy from the water that had seeped through the sandbags, and therefore slippery, and it was *big,* but I got it free and used my key-ring knife to slice through the tape. There were two more layers of bags inside of it, slice, slice, and then I was looking at Gramps's guns.

The wireless up in the hills was too janky for an anonymizing tunnel. I used the most performatively privacy-respecting Baby Google—Duck Duck Goog—to search a tutorial on how to operate an AR-15. The clips were full, and I laboriously assembled and disassembled one gun, just so I knew how to do it. Then I used the roll of tape and the extra contractor bags I'd stashed in the cache bag to rewrap everything and created a cross-body sling for it all. It was awkward and it weighed a ton, but I'd be going downhill.

I rode the bike brakes cautiously down the steep parts, nearly falling off on the first three corners as my arsenal swung wide and dragged my center of gravity way out. Then the plastic started to tear and I had to dismount and cocoon the whole thing in tape.

I was bathed in sweat by the time I hit the lowlands, eyes so swollen and red I could barely see, breathing in ragtime, head swimming. I pumped at the pedals like my legs were made of wood. And attached to someone else's body. I kept trying to wipe the sweat out of my eyes and punching myself in the goggles. The skin around my eyes was already sore from weeks in goggles. Each smack in the face was a fresh outrage.

Pocket-buzzes from my screen reminded me that I'd descended into civilized zones where the wireless was strong. I wheeled the bike into a 7-Twelve, trash-bag-o'-guns smacking into my hip, and bought a huge bottle of ice-cold black licorice kombucha and guzzled it outside the store, not caring that it sluiced down my face and chest. My shirt was already soaked through.

As the kombucha soothed my throat and cooled off my core, I had a moment of disembodiment, this picture of myself as seen from above, soot-streaked, sweat-soaked, panting, half blind, armed to the teeth, carrying enough gold to buy a two-bedroom condo in my neighborhood. What the actual fuck was I doing? I should be calling the police—there was no way I was going to go in there with guns blazing. God, how much time had I wasted already?

I had to call the cops now. Could I call the cops now? What about the guns? I could just stick them in a trash can, I guess, or admit to them, say that I knew that Gramps had cached them and I'd gone for them and then thought better of it . . . It would be messy, but the DSA had good lawyers. Hell, I had enough gold to pay for my own lawyer.

I shook my head. What had I been about to do? Jesus. I got out my screen and got ready to call the cops, and just as I was about to hit send, an alert popped up. Ana Lucía was calling me.

"Ana Lucía? Where are you? Are you okay?"

She looked worse than me, no goggles, eyes streaming, a big bruise on her cheek and a fat lip. "I got out," she said. "I got out and I ran. I'm by the high school. The one you went to. Big football fields?"

"You're at Burroughs?" We were basically across the street from each other.

"Yes, that's it. Where are you?"

"I'll be there in two minutes. What do you need? Food? Drinks? Goggles?"

"Yes, all of that." Her voice broke. "Oh, God, Brooks—"

"Just sit tight," I said. "Two minutes."

We sat down at the same picnic table that I'd sat at with Phuong a million years ago, by the climbing wall. She tore open the 7-Twelve bag and sorted through the goodies I'd bought her: a filter mask with integrated goggles (I'd upgraded my own at the same time, because why not?), energy bars from the co-op, more ginger booch, aspirins, and a couple of snap-to-activate cold packs.

She chugged one booch and crumpled the pouch, then cracked the other one and washed down a bunch of painkillers with it, and then peeled the energy bars and gobbled two. Finally, she snapped her mask back over her face, mindful of her bruises, and looked at me.

"Are you hurt?"

"No," I said. "How about you?"

"Superficial," she said, pointing at her face. "Mostly just my lungs. After they'd started shooting, we all surrendered. None of us wanted to take a chance. They took all our masks and herded us into a room on the third floor, posted a guard. They bickered constantly. And streamed. They have a big audience of crazy people out there, and they kept calling on them to 'rise up, rise up, take back America,' and do more of these stupid so-called arrests. That was another thing they fought over, how to arrest us, like what words they had to read us, like they were playing some weird RPG where they had to get the words right or it wouldn't be a real arrest."

"Arrests?"

"Yeah, that whole 'sheriff's deputies' thing. I'd run into that bullshit before, some weird conspiracy about 'sovereign citizens,' a complete delusion."

"But they weren't actually deputies? Like LA County cops?"

She chuckled. "Of course not. Those idiots? No, no way." She paused. "Actually, a couple of them really talked like cops, so maybe they were cops of some kind, but not the kind they said they were, if that makes sense."

"Not really."

"Yeah, okay, it doesn't make a lot of sense. Maybe it makes sense to them. I think there were three groups there: the ones who really believe in this whole sovereign-deputy conspiracy and think they're actually following the law; the ones who don't give a shit about all that nonsense and just want to murder our asses; and then there're the toddlers with the shitty diapers, the little boys who were just in it because they hero-worshipped the other ones and didn't really think anyone would go through with it. They scared me the most, because they had no idea what was going on but they still had lethal weapons."

"How'd you get out?"

"Broke the toilet. Then they had to start escorting us next door for piss-calls, and when that started to interfere with their streaming, they got fed up and decided to move us to another apartment. I waited until we were in the hallway by the fire escape and I jumped out the window."

"You—"

"I'd installed those windows and I knew they were designed to pop out if you hit them in the top corners to make it easy to get out in an emergency, so I just ran for it, hammered those releases and followed the window out full-body, like surfing on it. It turned into little glass cubes when it hit the scaffold landing, and I rolled over them and just kind of tobogganed down the stairs, dived off the next landing, hopped the fence, and disappeared into the smoke."

"Ana Lucía, Jesus Christ, you could have killed yourself."

"Yeah, and they could have killed me too. They tried, with those squirt guns—the guys with the rifles were downstairs, thankfully. That's why I made my break when I did. But Brooks, those guys are going to end up killing everyone, eventually. They're ready to be martyrs, and they just want to take some of us with them when they go."

"Fuck," I said. "What about Phuong?"

Even with the mask, I could tell she was frowning. "She

thought it was a mistake to run. We talked about it and she said no, she said to wait for the cops, that you'd get them and we'd get loose."

"We gotta call the cops then." I remembered my moment of clarity outside the 7-Twelve.

"Any kind of standoff is going to get our people killed. They don't want to get out, Brooks. They kept saying, 'Waco meant something, Malheur didn't.' You know what that means? It's two stupid armed standoffs with the cops and right-wing militias. Waco was the one where nearly everyone died, along with a bunch of non-combatants, mostly kids. Malheur was the one where practically nobody died and then a judge let them all walk free. These guys want to go to Valhalla, not court."

She lifted up her mask and swiped away the tears standing in her red eyes. "Brooks, I think they're going to kill everyone in that building, and then themselves."

I'm not sure what happened right after that. It was like my hearing and vision just . . . went away, replaced by a kind of hissing white noise and fog, as my overloaded brain processed what I'd just heard.

Then I was back, at the table, in the smoke, sitting opposite Ana Lucía, and in my hands was the taped-up contractor bag that was full of Gramps's guns. I was gripping it so hard my hands hurt.

"Brooks? Are you okay?"

My brain had recovered from its vapor lock and now it was running at triple speed, plans and counterplans slotting in so quickly and surely that I felt almost like a spectator at someone else's strategy meeting.

"Brooks?"

"We know that building. We *built* that building. We can get in and out in ways that no one else can. I know which windows can be removed, I know where there're HVAC access panels, I know where the breakers are and how to flood the whole fucking place. If we want to get into that place, they can't stop us."

She shook her head, her face unreadable behind the mask, her body language unmistakable. She thought I was out of my mind. She might have been right, but I was right, too: this was the only way.

"I don't understand, Brooks. We get inside to do what? They have guns. Big guns."

I got out my pocketknife and slit the plastic.

She lifted her mask again, holding the disassembled rifle pieces up to her face, turning them this way and that, until she started to cough and reseated the mask. *"Hijo de—"* I passed her one of the clips and then a box of ammo. "Holy. Fucking. *Shit.*" She clicked the rifle together carefully, did a thing with the slide that seemed competent and safety oriented, squinted at one part and then another. "Where the fuck did you *get* these?"

"It's my inheritance." I laughed and it sounded weird and angry. "My grandfather had these stashed under the floor." I had a sudden realization. "That day I met you, riding on my bike? I was coming back from stashing them in the hills. I'd just found them and I didn't want them in the house."

"But you didn't want to turn them in to the police, either?" She'd found the krugerrands and was turning them over in her hands. Even in the smoky half-light, they had a rich, dull gleam. She hefted them in one hand and then the other. "These are—"

"My grandfather had a lot of weird ideas," I said. I hadn't thought about the gold in months, and even when I'd recovered it from the cache, it had just been another thing to pack up and sling. Now, looking at it, thinking about what it could buy, seeing it in Ana Lucía's callused hands with her bruised thumbnail, I had two absolutely contradictory feelings at precisely the same moment: *That's my gold, give it back* and *what the hell would I do* with a small fortune in gold? And then, just as quick, *Phuong could be dead soon, why am I even thinking about gold?*

She put them down on the table with a deep *thunk* that I both heard and felt. "How many of these are there?"

"A little over two hundred. Most of them are rolled and wrapped, but there are a few loose in there."

She stared at the coins for a moment and then swept them back into the bag. Then she took one out again. "Do you know how long my parents would have had to work to earn these?"

"I've got an idea," I said. "I figure this is a sizable portion of Gramps's pension savings, plus whatever else he could liquidate. I don't know what those guns go for, but they're probably almost as valuable, ounce for ounce."

"Not quite," she said. She got out the pieces for one of the AR-15s and looked around. We weren't visible from the street, and the smoke meant that even people in the school would see us as only blurs. Moving with sure, economical motions, she snapped the gun together, looking just as competent as the guy in the video I'd watched.

"You've done that before, huh?"

"Country girl," she said. "Out in the San Joaquin Valley, everyone knows someone who's got a couple long guns cached somewhere. I had a friend growing up who knew where her dad kept his guns. We watched all these old movies about it, practiced putting them together blindfolded."

"*Why?*" I blurted. Like the gold, the guns hadn't been real until I saw them in her hands. Watching her handle the rifle, it seemed unimaginably dangerous, like a nuclear bomb.

She pulled up her mask again. Her eyes were red, furious. "Why? Brooks, why? Because, asshole. Because this is why. Because there are a lot of angry white guys out there who would rather see me dead of smoke inhalation than share their city with me. Because I'm only useful if I'm picking crops or cleaning someone's house, and if I'm not willing to settle for that, there's an *army* of these guys out there, and *they've* got guns. An *army*, Brooks, an *army*."

I looked away. "I don't want to kill anyone."

"Me either," she said, and pulled her mask down. "But if someone is going to die, it's not going to be me."

I almost stood up and walked away then, but then I thought of Phuong. If it was me, she wouldn't hesitate. Would she?

Now Ana Lucía was exploring the rest of the bag, unwrapping the weird semirigid fabric wraps that had been around the guns, but that I'd been unable to get perfectly back into place. "Body armor," she said.

"Shit, is *that* what that is?"

Even with the mask, I could tell that she was making a face at me. "Brooks, come on, be serious."

"I'm serious," I said. "I mean, when I found the guns and the gold, they kind of ate my brain, everything else was just kind of . . . blurry. Like if you saw a plane crash and then someone asked you whether it was cloudy out that day."

She unwrapped and unfolded it and as she did, I understood the topology: it was a vest with plates that fit into pockets. In my defense, Gramps had removed a bunch of plates and doubled them up in some of the pockets. And even Ana Lucía struggled a little with which plate went where, but after a minute or two of Tetris, she had two fully operational battle rattles, and she pulled one of them on and awkwardly tabbed the Velcro together under her armpits to hold it in place.

"Here," she said, handing the other one to me. It was lighter than I'd guessed it would be, and I had to take off my mask to get it over my head, and Ana Lucía helped with the Velcro. But once it was on and I was holding a rifle—assembled and checked over by Ana Lucía, who made me work the safety three times before she took her hand off it—I felt embarrassingly badass. "This is ridiculous," I said, turning this way and that to see how it felt.

She had been getting herself sorted out, distributing spare

clips around her armor's pockets, adjusting the straps, checking the rifle over. She turned and, well, "posed" isn't the right word, but there are only so many ways you can stand in body armor with a giant assault rifle and all of them have become tropes, visual staples of adventure movies. The thing is, she looked *terrifying,* like a warrior-goddess, like she had assumed an aspect that she had always been poised to embody.

I thought about her girlhood, the sickness and the terror, the humiliation, and her friendship with the girl she'd gone shooting with, who taught her how to handle a firearm. To be totally honest, I couldn't imagine what that must have been like. Here I was, picking fights, giving away my house—she hadn't had any choice in the matter. And to come through it as an organizer, pulling together your neighbors for weeks of marching, and then getting stranded in a city that reneged on its promise of refuge. For a moment, I had a flash of an inkling of a hint of what she might be feeling then, and it did something to me.

In that moment, it all swirled together: that day my mom didn't wake up, the years of being screamed at and belittled by Gramps, the threats and humiliations, the hope snatched away again and again, and above it all, the thought of Phuong in that building we'd built, held at gunpoint by suicidal, Maga-addled would-be murderers playing "sheriff." I knew that they'd get away with it: either they'd die as martyrs and inspire other killers to do the same, or they'd make it out and be heroes with their legal bills covered by laundered cryptocurrency from the Flotilla's plutes.

These were the people who'd spent half a century telling us that we didn't need to do anything about climate change, and the next half century telling us it was too late to do anything about it. Where we had confronted the vast, destructive forces they'd set in motion and decided to meet them head-on, they wanted to retreat, head for high ground, leave the rest of us behind.

Ana Lucía was looking hard at me, holding her gun, warrior queen, avatar of destruction.

My body armor no longer felt stiff. It felt magical, a hard layer that would let me stand up to these men who wanted to take my love, my building, my future, and my world. I'd been prepared to coexist with these monsters. They insisted that it had to be me or them. It would not be me.

I slid the rifle's safety off and on, adjusted the shoulder strap, double-checked the ammo clip and the spare clip Velcroed to my vest, and nodded at Ana Lucía.

"All right," I said.

"All right," she said.

The smoke covered us as we crept along Clark, off the main road. My feet felt spring-loaded; the rasp of my breath under my mask was deafening, a whole world of white noise. My vision had irised down to a narrow aperture, centered on Ana Lucía's back as she glided along the sidewalk.

We circled around Gramps's neighbor's house and slipped through a hole in the fencing around the new building, one that we knew about but the Magas didn't. I almost laughed. How could they think to defend themselves in a fortress I had built, whose every flaw and secret I knew intimately?

For example, I knew which corner of the lot could not be seen from any of the building's windows, because all the windows that looked down on it were frosted glass in the bathrooms. Ana Lucía and I padded up to it. From there, we could crawl around the building's perimeter to the HVAC intake on the left and the unlocked patio doors on the right. Ana Lucía and I communicated in terse whispers, deciding that she would have an easier time with the smaller HVAC grille, while I'd take the patio doors. Once that decision was made, all that was left was to hug. It was a long, hard hug, our body armor rubbing together, masks clunking. I didn't care. All I cared about was this brave woman, this comrade of mine, who was going in with me to save my future and the love of my life.

"I love you, Ana Lucía," I whispered.

"I love you too, Brooks," she said, and squeezed me harder.

Finally, we had to let go. We maneuvered our rifles around the front of us and got our hands on them. Ana Lucía hissed: "Three. Two. One—"

But before she could say "GO!" I heard a person turn the corner behind me. I whirled and—

Nearly blew Phuong's chest open. I actually tightened my finger on the trigger, seeing her eyes widen, her mouth open, and for a moment, I thought I'd just murdered my lover, when my brain realized that though I was squeezing my trigger and aiming my gun, nothing was coming out of it.

The safety was on.

I gasped and dropped to my knees, the world reeling around me. Two simultaneous thoughts—*You just murdered Phuong Petrakis* and *You* almost *murdered Phuong Petrakis*—chased each other around and around in my mind. Someone roughly grabbed my gun away from me and I let them have it. Then, the same hands took my mask, and I reached for it, too late, and I heard Phuong gasp in just the same way I had, then say my name.

"*Brooks,*" she hissed. "*Jesus fucking Christ, Brooks.*" She dragged me to my feet and we embraced, clinging to each other like we were afraid it would all be taken away from us. People moved around us and I gradually became aware that it wasn't just Phuong that had come around the corner, it was a whole *group* of people.

"You got out?" I whispered in her ear. My eyes were streaming and my nose and throat burned from the smoke, but I didn't care.

"We all got out," she said. "And they don't know it. Let's get the fuck away from here, fast."

We got to the neighbor's property line and paused only to stash the guns and body armor behind a cracked prefab slab that had arrived defective and been set aside for rehabilitation. Then, choking and coughing, we ran up to Verdugo. The public toilets there were still open, and had filtered air.

Phuong had led the escape. The Magas had all retreated to the ground floor, all except a single guard, Kenneth, who'd been given one of the water pistols full of acid and left behind. After an hour or two, he got terminally bored and distracted, as the guys down on the ground floor sent him the social media martyr videos they were shooting to post when the cops arrived, and she'd snuck up on him with a tack hammer and smashed his wrist, knocking the Super Soaker to the ground and then clamping her hand over his mouth and bearing him to the ground before he could holler. They'd efficiently bound and gagged him with electrical tape, networking cabling, and rags from the jobsite and then gone out the fire exit.

Phuong and the other escapees washed up as they told us the story, eyes glittering, still pumped up from their daring escape. I was excited too, but for another reason. I still couldn't get over the feeling that had come over me when I'd squeezed the trigger on the rifle at the exact instant that I'd recognized Phuong.

"Are you okay?" she said, patting up and down my arms and shoulders as if checking for a broken bone. "Brooks?"

"I'm—" I couldn't say it. I started to sob. I wasn't okay at all. She hugged me, and then Ana Lucía joined, and then it turned into a group hug, some of us crying or just rocking.

Once I disentangled myself, I felt a little more distance and calm. "I'm sorry," I said, miserably. "It's just . . . Phuong, I thought I'd murdered you. If I'd remembered to take the safety off, you'd be dead now. I can't believe what I almost did."

She squeezed her lips together. "Where did you get those guns, Brooks? Ana Lucía, they weren't yours, were they?"

She snorted. "No, Rambo Jr. here had them when I ran into him."

"Where the fuck did you get *guns,* Brooks?"

I told her as quickly as I could, explaining about Gramps's cache, my decision to hide the guns rather than hand them in, the Magas' obsession with recovering their ordnance, which I thought probably antagonized them into their raid.

"No," she said flatly. "That wasn't it. They are angry about *everything,* Brooks—the construction, the refugees, losing your gramps's house, all of it. They're convinced that they're an endangered species, the last free people in America, and they're just furious that no one else can see it.

"And now we've got a problem. I was thinking that once we got away from the building we could call the cops. Without us there, they're the hostages, holed up with no leverage to stop the cops from moving in. They don't get a long-armed standoff, they'll just get droned or blown up or shot if they don't surrender.

"But now there're the guns, with yours and Ana Lucía's fingerprints all over them. Whatever happens between the cops and those assholes, the cops are bound to find them, and when they do—"

"Shit," I said. "God, I feel like such an asshole."

"Not gonna lie," Phuong said, "all that bullshit with the guns was an asshole move from the very start. You should have turned them in as soon as you found them." She looked pissed.

"It's simple," Ana Lucía said. "We just sneak back over there, clean the guns and armor down, retreat, call the cops, and wait. Those dumbasses are already fully tooled up, it's not going to be hard for the cops to attribute any additional guns they find lying around to them."

We all let that sink in. Phuong broke the silence: "That's a good plan," she said.

"It's a good plan," I agreed. "I'll sneak over and wipe everything down, meet you back here, and then we're good to go."

Phuong held up her hands. "You'll go? Why you?"

I was ready. "The fewer of us who go over, the less chance we'll attract attention. Most of us don't have masks, but I have this amazing one I bought at the 7-Twelve." I hefted it.

"Fine, so give it to me and I'll do it. Why should you take all the risk? Is this some weird thing about it being your grandfather's house so you have to do this work?"

"No," I said. "It's some weird thing about me knowing where I hid the third gun."

"The third gun?" She looked a little angry and a little bemused. It was one of her very best expressions.

"There were three rifles but only two of us. The third gun is in a taped-up plastic bag I stashed on the way in." Along with a fortune in gold, I realized. Truth be told, I'd forgotten about that third gun until I'd needed an excuse to go back on my own, because yeah, I *did* have some weird thing about it being my grandfather's house.

Ana Lucía nodded. "That's right."

Phuong made a fake-mad face, which was another of her very best expressions. She had a lot of those.

"Go," she said. "Be quick. If it looks dangerous, pull back here. Don't risk anything. I'd rather explain your unlicensed guns than mourn your bullet-riddled corpse."

"You have a way with words," I said, trying to keep it light, but when she grabbed me for a fierce goodbye hug, some of that fluttery, terrified feeling I'd had when I'd thought I'd murdered her came back.

The guns were exactly where I'd left them. I used hand sanitizer and my T-shirt to clean all the guns, working stripped to the waist, methodically, crouched down, in a state of eerie calm.

As I worked, I managed to forget all about the armed men in the building just a few meters away from me. I was too busy turning over a new thought: all my life, I'd felt like a fake. I was supposed to be in the vanguard of the first generation in a century that didn't fear the future, but I'd always been afraid.

I'd been terrified.

Deep down, I'd always been *certain* that I would die defending the GND, that I'd be a martyr. It was what happened, wasn't it? That was what happened to my parents. That was what my grandfather had raised me to expect: a final confrontation, an all-out war, a battle for the future of the human race and its planet. That was what he was planning for, and right up until that moment, as I cleaned off his guns and hid them in the construction waste, I had never really considered the possibility that he'd been wrong. I'd thought there'd be a war with two sides: Gramps's side and mine. I'd never thought that the real war would be between the people who refused to go to war and the fools who thought they could shoot climate change in the face.

God, I'd been an idiot.

The smoke cleared a little and the building I'd helped build came into sharper focus. It was a beauty, a miracle, a lifetime of dignified shelter for dozens of people, built by dozens of people, in a handful of days.

I crouched there, transfixed, and I realized that for the first time in my life, I genuinely did not fear the future.

chapter 12
cavalry

The police met us in Verdugo Park, rapping on the bathroom door. We opened it cautiously, smoke quickly infiltrating the little space, and we passed around the emergency USN95s the officers supplied. The masks came from Velasquez, who let me know that they'd made a point of answering the call when they heard the address. "You're one of our best customers, Mr. Palazzo."

Burbank PD had rolled up with a single cruiser, but Velasquez told me that there were more vans waiting on Clark: drone support, SWAT, snipers. They were ready to move into position but they wanted to know as much as possible before they went in. Phuong and I agreed to get in the cruiser with Velasquez to tell them what we knew about the Magas' locations and arms, and to help them plan an entry.

We talked quickly. I let Phuong take the lead, since she'd actually been inside with the Magas. I listened intently, rethinking the entry plan that Ana Lucía and I had come up with based on her information, realizing that if I'd gone in through the patio doors I'd planned to use, I'd have been completely exposed to the main body of them. They'd likely have shot me dead before I could have gotten out a single word.

I was digesting this fact when Velasquez's screen beeped and they grabbed it and started tapping. Their face went tight, then they touched their earpiece and had a terse conversation full of "yes, sir"s and "I understand"s.

"We've got to move," they said, getting out of the car. "We've got to get all of these people out of here."

We followed them hastily. "What's happening?" I said, chasing after them. "Is it more militiamen? Should we get back into the bathroom?"

They kept walking until they reached our group. Their partner, a young female cop who'd been interviewing them, had already crowded them together. Velasquez held their hands up. "Listen up," they said. "I said *listen!*" There was a note of urgency that bordered on panic in their voice. We fell silent.

"About an hour ago, the fires reached Sun Valley. Firefighters hit it hard, but the winds picked up and it reached a large chemical refinery there. None of its fire suppression and fail-safes were rated for this kind of fire. The smoke plume is now considered lethal, full of things like dioxins that you do *not* want to breathe, not even through a mask. Not through *two* masks.

"Now the winds have shifted and that plume is headed right here, right *now*." That's when the civil defense sirens kicked in, blaring from the community center and lampposts, an eerie moan, then three blats, then a synthetic voice repeating "SHELTER IN PLACE, SHELTER IN PLACE." Velasquez raised their voice. "Our vehicles are not considered adequate for this kind of chemical hazard. We need to get indoors, *now*."

Phuong had her screen out, tapping furiously. She brought it to Officer Velasquez and stuck it under their nose. "These are the filters on the HVAC in our new building. Will they do?"

They squinted at the screen, lifting their goggles briefly. They got out their own screen and tapped at it, comparing the two. "Are you sure?" they asked. Phuong nodded. They looked at us, then at their partner, and then off into the smoke, now blowing from the north.

"Fuck it, we're going in."

Phuong and I got to ride in the cruiser. Everyone else jog-walked as fast as they could to the building. The streets had been mostly empty since the fires started, and now they were totally deserted except for emergency vehicles crawling through the low-visibility smoke, sirens blaring and lights staining the sky red-blue-red-blue.

We met two SWAT vans at the corner and turned off Verdugo and down the street, a convoy that filled both lanes, making incredible noise.

The vans rolled right through the fencing we'd put up around the jobsite, and I watched a third one crash through the fence at the back of the house on the cruiser's dash screen.

"Get down," Velasquez said. "Get right down on the floor." Their partner was already unlocking the shotgun that stood between their seats. I saw pop-ups snap out on the roofs of the SWAT vans, rifle muzzles pointing through the windows, just as swarms of drones lifted off and surrounded the building, so that within seconds, every window had at least one drone at it. That was the last thing I saw before I curled up on the floor of the cruiser, next to Phuong, tightly clutching her hand.

There was a *SNAP* sound like a bolt of lightning and then a rasping boom—it took me a second to realize that I was hearing a *very* high-powered public address system. "YOU HAVE ONE MINUTE TO SURRENDER. LETHAL FORCE HAS BEEN AUTHORIZED. LOWER YOUR WEAPONS, LACE YOUR HANDS BEHIND YOUR HEADS, AND WALK SINGLE FILE OUT OF THE FRONT ENTRANCE. YOU HAVE FIFTY SECONDS TO SURRENDER."

The sound literally made the car shake, and I pressed my hands over my ears.

"THIRTY SECONDS. LETHAL FORCE HAS BEEN AUTHORIZED."

"I hate this place," Phuong whispered. "Fuck, I hate this place." She was crying. I squeezed her hand harder. "I want out. I'm re-enlisting. I just can't be here anymore. I know it's the same everywhere, but it's different when it's people you know. I know those imbeciles in there, about to get their brains blown out. Jesus. I hate this place."

"TWENTY SECONDS."

I swallowed hard. I loved Burbank. All that had happened, it only made my love stronger. Right? But what did I actually love? I loved the building project. The solidarity. Phuong. God, I loved Phuong.

"I'm coming," I said, and she looked at me with what might have been alarm. "If that's okay," I said. "I mean, I understand if you—"

"Shut up, you idiot," she said. "Of course I want you to come!"

"TEN SECONDS."

"NINE."

"EIGHT."

And then there was an indistinct holler, and then shouting, and then . . . it was all over.

They'd marched out with their hands over their heads, slowly, the cops' weapons trained on them, drones hovering nearby, and it wasn't until the last one emerged that someone shouted "GUN!" at the same instant that someone else shouted "WAIT!"

I uncurled from the car floor in time to see Kenneth, one hand bandaged, slowly and awkwardly putting an AR-15 on the ground. He'd been holding it on the rest of them.

The cops swarmed the Magas just as the rest of our group arrived, masked and out of breath. Phuong popped her door and got out to check on them and so I did the same, spotting Ana Lucía at the front of the group and making a beeline for her.

"What happened?" she said. "Is everyone okay?"

Phuong threw her hands in the air. "Who the fuck knows? Who the fuck knows anything? It looks like they surrendered, or possibly that guy I hit with the tack hammer forced them to give up? Who the fuck knows anything?" She gave a wild laugh and I grabbed her hand.

She gave me a hug as wild as the laugh and then Ana Lucía dragged us apart. "Come on, you two, they want us to get inside."

Velasquez's eyes were hooded and worried behind their goggles. We filed into the building and Velasquez buttoned up the door. "Do you have anything we can use to seal the windows and doors?" they asked. "The word on the chemical plume keeps getting worse. We don't want a single whiff of that stuff in here."

Ana Lucía nodded. "There's some two-way fiber tape and insulating sheets up on the third floor," she said. "I'll go grab it."

"Wait," Velasquez said. They hollered down the hallway, toward the two-bedroom ground-floor apartment, where the cops had taken the militiamen. "Three more coming in," they said. "Friendlies." They turned back to us. "Okay," they said. "Can you get the plastic and tape and we'll seal off this level? Weather office thinks we'll be in the plume for two to three hours, then we can move out."

We ripped off our masks and bounded up the stairs two at a time. Ana Lucía led us quickly to the plastic and tape. "There's food up on the fourth floor," she said. "Snacks for meetings. I think we should bring them down. I'm starving."

I was about to say that I couldn't imagine eating when I realized I was also ravenous. What a weird goddamned day it had been. "Do you need help?" I asked.

"Maybe one person," she said.

"I'll go," Phuong said.

I hoisted one of the heavy insulation rolls over my shoulder and thudded down the stairs with it, dumping it in the lobby and running back up the stairs for another one before Velasquez could ask where Phuong and Ana Lucía were. Back on the third floor, I unrolled foot-long tongues from the tape rolls so I could hang them from my body, then I humped the second spindle of insulation down the stairs, handing it to Velasquez, who took it with an *oof.*

"Where are—" they began, as Phuong and Ana Lucía arrived, hauling stacked eighteen-gallon tubs of snacks—dried fruits, nuts, popcorn, and bite-sized chocolate chip cookies that someone had baked by the hundreds and donated to the jobsite.

"Food," Phuong said, heading for the ground-floor apartment door. Velasquez hustled to get ahead of her. They knocked first, announced themself, and then entered, waving the rest of us in.

I love my crew. They efficiently self-organized to seal off the apartment, working room to room in threesomes: two people to unroll the insulation and hold it over doors and windows, one person to tape around the plastic's perimeter. They treated the cops and the hangdog, handcuffed militiamen like they were furniture, stepping around their captors without even acknowledging them. Phuong and Ana Lucía floated from room to room, making sure everyone got snacks and topping up their water bottles.

Once everyone was fed, they brought the leftover food to the kitchen, where the militiamen were lined against the walls, alongside the major-appliance hookups, cuffed and furious-looking.

"You guys hungry?" Ana Lucía said. She got sullen glares in return. Kenneth shook his head in disgust.

"I'm hungry, thank you," he said.

Ana Lucía nodded briskly. "Popcorn or dried bananas?"

"The bananas," Kenneth said. Then he added, "Please."

"Can you please cuff him in front?" Ana Lucía asked one of the three cops in the room—the dozen-odd SWAT members had taken over the bedrooms and were resting against the walls there with the eerie patience of armed people with nothing to shoot.

The cop she'd addressed—a Black guy not much older than me—looked at the other two and they played a quick game of eyeball hockey before they all nodded minutely at each other. The Black cop went around behind Kenneth and the other two flanked him as he was recuffed with his hands in front of his body, so he could take the little sack of freeze-dried banana chips.

"Anyone else?"

"Uh," said one of the other Magas, whom I recognized as the squad leader who'd been on point at the front door. "Uh. Do you have more bananas?"

"Of course," Ana Lucía deadpanned.

What with the uncuffing/recuffing rigmarole, getting everyone their food took a good ten minutes. The banana chips disappeared first, and the last three men looked disappointed with their popcorn. I had to resist laughing at them. An hour before, they'd been holding us hostage, now they were sad because they had to take second-choice at snack time? The master race was pretty disappointing.

"Ma'am," said one of the popcorn guys. In a group of middle-aged and old men, he stood out as especially old, like an apple doll in a red trucker cap. His hands shook as they'd recuffed him.

"Yes?" Ana Lucía said.

"Thank you, ma'am," he said.

Ana Lucía gave him a guarded look. "You're welcome."

"Might I ask you another favor?"

She snorted. "You can *ask*."

He looked wounded. "I just wondered . . . would you please call my wife? I'm sure she's worried about me and—"

Ana Lucía gave him a very long, stone-faced look. Then she rolled her eyes. "Why not? Give me the number."

She dialed and clamped her screen to her head. "Hello? Is that Marybeth Simms? Yes, Mrs. Simms. I'm here with your husband, Jesse. He is under arrest after he took me and several of my friends hostage. No, ma'am, I'm not joking. Yes, ma'am. Ma'am? Mrs. Simms? Calm down please, Mrs. Simms. Listen, please. Jesse asked me to call you because he wanted you to know that he's safe. Ma'am? Ma'am? Did you understand me? Jesse is under arrest for terrorism but he's safe. Ma'am? Mrs. Simms? I'm going to hang up now, Mrs. Simms. Goodbye, Mrs. Simms."

She pocketed her screen, then met Jesse's wounded stare. "She knows you're safe now." She glared at the militiamen. "Anyone else's wife need calling?"

They were silent at first, and then Kenneth said, "Ma'am, you have every right to be angry at us, but that wasn't called for. Marybeth Simms didn't hurt you."

Everyone stared at Ana Lucía as she chewed this over: the Magas, the cops, me. Her jaw jumped, then she opened and closed her mouth. Finally, she pointed at Kenneth, her arm straight out in front of him, and began to speak. It was low and dangerous at first, but it got louder.

"No, mister, Marybeth Simms didn't hurt me. I didn't hurt her either. All that happened was that she got a few hours' head start on her new life as a terrorist's wife. That's something all your families are going to go through in a few hours, and it's nothing I did to them. It's what you did to them. You did it.

"Jesus fucking *Christ,* you gutless, mindless *fucks.* Are you fucking *kidding me*? You're all poster children—and I *do* mean children—for 'personal responsibility' right up until someone asks you to take responsibility for your own actions. Remember, no one pointed a gun at you and asked you to commit an act of terror. You, on the other hand, you *cowards,* you pointed guns at *us.*

"I see you there, looking sad and worried because you're going to be in court for years, maybe go to prison if your plute buddies can't bail you out. You think you're having a hard time? Right now, at this very instant, there are people on the road, walking down the road, with nothing but a mask between them and the toxic plume that's headed our way.

"Those are my friends. I *walked* with them. For *weeks.* Carrying everything they owned. The law entitled them to housing, and so they took their children and everything they owned and walked, and walked, and walked, for weeks. When they got here, you and your friends found a way to take away their legal right to a home and so they're out there *right now. Right now.* In the poisoned air. They are out there with their children right now in the poison air and *you* did that. You were terrorists before you showed up here today, gentlemen."

She was shaking. I tentatively put out a hand to comfort her or stop her or something, but she slapped it away and gestured with her screen.

"The fucking joke is on you, boys. Oh, this is *such* a good joke. That dioxin plume out there, the reason we're all hiding in here with tape over the windows? It is salting the Earth. The particulate that settles over this town will poison it for years. There is no dose of dioxin that is considered safe for human health.

"Burbank is a superfund site, my dudes. And you are all refugees now."

When the plume had passed, the city's emergency warning system came over every screen, explaining that we should minimize our outdoor visits, that pets and children should be kept indoors. We were advised to keep a set of outdoor clothing and to designate a changing room that we would only visit while masked, and leave all outdoor clothing within it, and to shower immediately after every outdoor trip.

The video also explained that FEMA would be here within a week, and that interim emergency services would deliver food and other essentials while we waited.

I was numb. How could this be? How could my home, my town, and everything I fought for be killed? Wiped away, in an instant? How had that happened?

Phuong knew what to do. She was already coordinating with Valley and LA DSA chapters and the Blue Helmet veterans' groups to figure out the game plan for mutual aid.

That's how I managed my first Blue Helmet deployment without leaving my hometown.

blue helmets

That deployment only lasted two weeks: one week of frontline services, at first in improvised safety gear, and then as the supply chains caught up with the crisis, another week with good bunny suits and a headquarters—that had once been Gramps's house—outfitted with decontam showers and scrounged beds and storerooms with the supplies we delivered all day to people waiting for FEMA to arrive.

FEMA was stretched thin. The plume had scoured the Valley, and Burbank wasn't the worst-hit place. They had a lot of customers, so we stayed on for another week.

But by the third week, it was time to go. There were still going to be Blue Helmets in Burbank for a long time, helping the evacuees pack their essentials and find new homes elsewhere, but I couldn't be one of them. I started having these middle-of-the-night crying fits. I couldn't say what I was crying about, but it wasn't good for me or for the other Blue Helmets in our HQ. I thought a lot about what Ana Lucía had said: *We didn't just leave Tehachapi, we buried it. It's dead. We can't go home. We don't have a home anymore. Going back? It'd be like digging up Grandma's bones and sitting her down at the end of the Thanksgiving table.*

Phuong and I discussed putting in for an overseas assignment—she still had friends in London working on Thames estuary retreats—but in the end, we decided we'd head for Santa Barbara.

Why Santa Barbara? Well, it was a town I'd visited several times and remembered as a beautiful place. It was facing the same dangers that lots of Southern California coastal towns were working through, only it had been a laggard, behind leaders like San Juan Capistrano.

And it was a place that said it would take in a lot of Burbankers. That made it weirdly perfect: Burbank may have been beyond saving, but I could still help my neighbors. I started by wrapping up a bag of gold krugerrands in construction-grade mylar, addressing it to the general relief fund, and leaving it on the receptionist's desk at the main resettlement office. I'm sure they had cameras and could have identified me, but they didn't. Sometimes I caught my fellow Blue Helmets looking at me in a weird way, especially Vikram, and I wondered if they knew. If so, everyone kept quiet about it.

Phuong and I woke late one morning. We had couples' housing, a converted shipping container with a kitchenette and a toilet, treated with insulating foam and air-conditioned with a combination of rooftop turbines and panels.

We'd worked late the night before: the heat pump in one of the new refugee high-rises we'd helped finish had died when everyone turned on their air conditioners, and the outside wet-bulb temp was up around 90°F, which was getting into lethal heatstroke territory.

I had just certified on heat pump repair and I dialed in a brain trust of senior techs around the world while Phuong, Wilmar, and Milena played dogsbody and we'd gotten it running again just after midnight. The system automatically redetailed our morning assignments to someone else and we remembered to turn off our alarms before collapsing into bed.

After breakfast, Phuong suggested we head to the beach and do some bodysurfing before the sun grew too hot, so we put on our UV-blocking bodysuits and flip-flops and grabbed our water bottles and walked through the midmorning town, first the new part we'd helped build, then the old part that had been heavily infilled, then the drowned part with its floating walkways, abandoned and soggy and sinking.

We threaded our way along the walkways until we came to a sandbar that the Blue Helmets had helped a bunch of surfers create. Some were bobbing out on the sea already, catching waves when they came but mostly content to just float in the cool water as the scorching sun rose overhead.

We joined them, and Phuong caught a couple of good waves and then I managed to catch one and nearly brained myself on some flotsam. It was scary at first, exhilarating in retrospect, and now the sun was getting high enough that we decided that we needed to go add another layer of zinc to our faces if we were going to stay out in it.

I was reapplying the orange and blue stripes across Phuong's cheeks and forehead when Armen and Dave found us, preceded by a bow wave of weed fumes.

Dave waved his hands in the air. "Holy shit you two, you *have* to see this." They were both in hi-viz and coveralls, with work gloves stuffed in the pockets. They'd proven to be surprisingly effective as a work crew . . . but only when paired with each other. When either one got paired with someone else, it was an unmitigated disaster all around.

Armen, a little more stoned perhaps, trailed him by a half step, but nodded vigorously. "Seriously."

So we scooped up our water and slid into our sandals and followed them around a bend in the coast, just in time to see three smartly turned-out Zodiacs with fuel-cell outboards tying up to half-submerged parking meters.

They were crewed by young men and women as smartly turned out as their boats in boat-shorts, formfitting, low-rise rock-hopper shoes, and pristine white sailing shirts. Each wore a ball cap embroidered with a cursive motto: THE MORAL HAZARD.

"Ahoy" was what the leader—an improbably good-looking Asian guy with a dazzling smile—actually said, as he leapt nimbly onto a floating pathway and headed for dry land . . . and us. "Permission to come ashore?"

Phuong narrowed her eyes at him. "You appear to be ashore, and the permission isn't ours to give. What can we help you with?"

The rest of the boaters were coming ashore now, scrubbed faces, white shirts, white, white smiles. "We're from the Flotilla!" he said. "It's about a mile offshore. We're doing an information tour down the coast and wanted to see about offering you and your neighbors a chance to come aboard and see what the future could be like!"

Armen and Dave found that very funny. I grabbed Phuong's hand and squeezed it, and she squeezed back.

acknowledgments

This book owes a debt to everyone who has struggled for climate justice. Yes, really, everyone. I wrote swathes of this book under a blood-red sky, in my backyard hammock, while ashes sifted out of the sky. I worked outside as much as I could, because it felt so important to be there while it was happening. But it was hard. It hurt. Not just my burning eyes and raw throat—it hurt my heart. Each climate rupture—every flood, every fire, every hurricane and tornado—hurts like that. I'm a father. I've got a fifteen-year-old daughter, Poesy, and when I think about her future, it *hurts*.

The only thing that stops the hurt is seeing the people who put their bodies between the forces of relentless, remorseless extraction and the preservation of the only planet in the known universe that can sustain human life. Greta Thunberg's fierce oratory, to be sure, as well as her rapier wit. But also, Extinction Rebellion, the Sunrise Movement, and especially the Water Protectors. They are the moral exemplars that refill my reservoirs of hope and keep me going.

So this book is for them. For you. For everyone who understands that sorting your recycling isn't going to cut it. For everyone who understands that the polycrisis isn't about individual changes, it's about systemic ones. For everyone who goes beyond shopping their way out of the emergency, and instead joins a group, a network, a *movement*.

Beyond all of you, I need to especially thank some of the usual suspects who are unusually good at their jobs and important to making this book and all my books happen.

My agents: Russell Galen, Heather Baror-Shapiro, and Danny Baror.

The folks at Tor: Patrick Nielsen Hayden (and his outboard spare brain lobe, Teresa Nielsen Hayden), Mal Frazier, Caro Perny, Laura Etzkorn, Sarah Reidy, and Lucille Rettino.

The folks at Head of Zeus: Nic Cheetham, Sophie Whitehead, and Polly Grice.

The folks from Wunderkind PR: Elena Stokes and Brianna Robinson.

And last, but actually first, and most important, my family: Alice Taylor, Poesy Taylor Doctorow, Roz Doctorow, Gordon Doctorow, and Neil Doctorow.